MARY GOLD OF CLINTON COUNTY, INDIANA

BONNIE L. SCHERMER

iUniverse

MARY GOLD OF CLINTON COUNTY, INDIANA

Copyright © 2019 Bonnie L. Schermer.

All rights reserved. No part of this book may be used or reproduced by any means, graphic, electronic, or mechanical, including photocopying, recording, taping or by any information storage retrieval system without the written permission of the author except in the case of brief quotations embodied in critical articles and reviews.

iUniverse books may be ordered through booksellers or by contacting:

iUniverse
1663 Liberty Drive
Bloomington, IN 47403
www.iuniverse.com
1-800-Authors (1-800-288-4677)

Because of the dynamic nature of the Internet, any web addresses or links contained in this book may have changed since publication and may no longer be valid. The views expressed in this work are solely those of the author and do not necessarily reflect the views of the publisher, and the publisher hereby disclaims any responsibility for them.

Any people depicted in stock imagery provided by Getty Images are models, and such images are being used for illustrative purposes only.
Certain stock imagery © Getty Images.

ISBN: 978-1-5320-7175-1 (sc)
ISBN: 978-1-5320-7176-8 (e)

Print information available on the last page.

iUniverse rev. date: 03/20/2019

Preface

Mary Gold's story has taken me a long time to complete. Part of the problem was that there is *too much* information about the American Civil War era. Even though the events mentioned in the Mexican-American and Civil Wars did not directly impact Mary Gold, the events DID affect society as a whole, including Mary Gold's relatives and acquaintances. And she surely heard the news discussed by people around her. News of the Catholic Church was not as available in Mary Gold's community, but some of it would have been told to her by various priests and other Catholics. Mary Gold is my ancestor, and I wanted to view her life against the background of her times. The result is, I think, worth adding to my other stories about my female ancestors...

Bonnie L Schermer
2019

1819

Monday night, September 6th

Mary Gold Hobbs knew many things. She knew love, having been cherished as a child. She knew loss, having been orphaned and led far from home, across the American wilderness, by strangers. She knew luxury, having been waited upon by slaves in her childhood home. She knew want, having suffered starvation and extreme weather conditions. She knew faith, having been catechized in the Roman Catholic Church. And she knew pain, having been beaten and raped. All in all, she knew far too many things for a fourteen year old.

Mary lay, wide awake, in the dark at Norris House, the young man who had served as her benefactor asleep in her arms. After his mother's funeral earlier that day, twenty year old Abraham "Bram" Norris had needed the sort of comfort that Mary knew how to provide. Late in the evening, she had led him to her bed, and held him until his sobs subsided. She stared into the darkness and thought about him. He seemed too good to be true: Tall and strong, handsome and kind, a gentleman by birth and in practice. Mary stirred beneath him, and Bram half wakened.

"Love me," she whispered. "Please."

She thought his answering kiss an affirmative response, but he disappointed her.

"No. It's not right. But some day it may be, if God wills..."

"God?" she thought. "Which one? And 'some day'...what if it never comes?"

She arched her spine and ran her hands over Bram's back, down below his hips.

"Stop that," he ordered. "Take your hands off me."

"Please. I want you."

"Sweet Mary, I want you, too. But just wanting is not enough. I'll go to my own bed, now, I think."

He left her, and she cried, remembering all the things she knew...

1805 - 1811

As a young child growing up in Caroline County, Maryland, on the Eastern Shore of Chesapeake Bay, Mary Gold Hobbs had been petted and spoiled by her grandmothers. The two old ladies contrasted greatly. Luckily, Mary never had to choose which of them she preferred; she loved them both.

Mary's maternal *Grand-mère* steadfastly ignored the fact that she had emigrated to the United States, remaining the consummate French aristocrat. The waists of her low cut, tight bodiced, silken gowns rose high under *Grand-mère's* bosom, and it seemed that every piece of fabric she owned had been edged in lace. Her satin slippers peeped from beneath full, ruffled skirts. When *Grand-mère* ventured into town, she carried a brocaded satin reticule (a draw string purse), while a huge, muslin hat (featuring eyelet trim at the brim and a bow around the base of the puffy crown) protected her head from the sun. At home, a frilly apron and matching mob cap, decorated with a satin cockade, covered *Grand-mère's* clothing and hair. No matter the time of day nor the occasion, *Grand-mère* always looked beautiful and smelled good, due to the judicious use of makeup and a delicate *parfum*.

Grand-mère possessed a fiery temper, easily awakened by any mention of current events in Europe. Because she had witnessed her parents' murder as they fled the onset of the French Revolution in 1789, *Grand-mère* remained unalterably opposed to the republic that had replaced the monarchy headed by her aunt and uncle, Louis XVI and Marie Antoinette. With streams of French invective, *Grand-mère* would lecture any luckless person who mentioned Napoleon Bonaparte in her presence, castigating the Emperor as a usurper sent by Satan to destroy France. *Grand-mère* seemed to understand, but refused to speak English, the language of her people's enemy across the Channel.

Some of Mary's earliest memories included *Grand-mère's* tales of the

French queen and her courage in the face of death. Mary even learned an anti-Revolution song:

> *Monarques, cherchez, cherchez des amis,*
> *Non sous les lauriers de la gloire,*
> *Mais sous les myrtes favoris*
> *Qu'offrent les filles de Mémoire.*
> *Un troubadour est tout amour,*
> *fidélité, constance,*
> *Et sans espoir de récompense.*

> [Monarchs search, search for friends,
> not under the laurels of glory
> But under the favored myrtle
> offered by the daughters of memory.
> A troubadour is interested in love,
> fidelity, and constancy!
> He is without hope of recompense.]

Grand-mère had very nearly been killed by the mob that slaughtered her parents, but Joseph Gold, an American sailor serving as a French naval captain at the time, had rescued her. Because *Grand-mère* married Joseph, she escaped the "Reign of Terror" in 1793 as war broke out between France and Britain. Joseph had captained a French frigate against the British, but resigned his commission before Napoleon seized power in 1799. With the help of the Marquis de Lafayette, Joseph removed his wife and their two children, *Jeanette* and James, from France, taking them to his home state of Maryland, in the United States.

During the early 1800s, Joseph used his family connections and his hard won experience with the American and French navies during their respective revolutionary struggles to good advantage at Baltimore. He became a marine merchant and later, captain of the *Cora*. (The *Cora* and her sister ship, the *Burrows*, were early examples of the Baltimore Clipper, a distinctive type of long, low, ocean going sailing vessel.)

The *Cora* and the *Burrows* were owned by a consortium of wealthy Baltimore and New York merchants. When one of the shareholders died suddenly, Joseph bought the man's interest in the company. Then, two things happened simultaneously that worked to the Golds' advantage: The economics of the times fluctuated wildly, frightening the other owners; and Joseph (with the tacit approval of the American government) found success as a privateer, or pirate. He seized British ships and cargoes wherever he found them, increasing his wealth vastly and enabling him to purchase the remaining shares of his ships.

Joseph built a career upon opposition to British restriction of American trade. He developed a reputation as a dangerous man, a wily sailor of outstanding courage and great physical strength. Although he registered his schooners out of Baltimore, even though his relatives lived to the South, on the Eastern Shore of Maryland, he maintained his family home high up the Choptank River at the tiny village of Denton, hidden from those who might be interested in reprisals for his questionable business practices. Concealing the location of his house, he thought, ensured that his wife would never again have to suffer the trauma of war nor of civic uprising as she had in France.

Grand-mère's son James at an early age joined his father, sailing far and wide aboard the light, fast ships. Her daughter *Jeanette* at age fifteen caused the family great distress by marrying a non-Catholic, shortly before Mary's birth in 1805. *Grand-mère* always called her only grandchild *Marie*, in memory of her cousin *Marie Antoinette*.

Grand-mère Gold's Medieval style house at Denton featured steeply pitched gavils (gables), vertical siding of weathered cedar boards, and leaded glass casement windows with diamond-shape panes. Because she had no American friends or family, and because her husband was rarely home, *Grand-mère* constructed a private world within the walls of the house. She decorated its interior lavishly, in the French manner. She used lace curtains, gold velvet drapes, and delicate carved furniture, much of it painted white and embellished in gold. The parlor wallpaper depicted Greek gods and goddesses in gold on an ivory background. Gold striped damask fabric covered the *chaise longue, canapé,* and other upholstered seating. Old paintings and mirrors (framed in carved wood painted gold to reflect the light) and tapestries hung from silken cords on the walls. At every meal, fine porcelain, antique silver, and cut crystal graced the linen and French lace dining cloths.

A true pirate's lair, Gold House contained hoarded treasure in the form of wondrous artifacts from many lands. Mary played with them all, except for the fragile items on the mantel and other high places. Available to her were sea shells, drift wood, brightly colored feathers, and decorated wooden boxes overflowing with polished semiprecious pebbles. A leather covered wooden chest held a collection of carved teak and ebony animals and ceremonial masks. A woven grass basket contained ivory pieces, either carved, or left in natural shapes and decorated with scratched and inked designs. A red and green *perroquet* screeched from a high perch in the plant filled sun room, occasionally uttering an intelligible word. For a short time a gentle, sweet faced but smelly monkey, or *guenon,* chattered in a cage in the back yard. An enormous white *chat* (cat) reigned over the place in a lordly manner.

Every few weeks, weather permitting, *Maman* took Mary to visit *Grand-mère* Gold. She would pack their clothing into canvas bags, and order one of the slaves to saddle a horse. Then she and Mary left the inland truck farm operated by Mary's father Robert Hobbs, riding West to the Gold's mansion at Denton. Not until many years later did Mary realize that these visits were timed to coincide with the periodic arrival of a peculiarly costumed old man.

This person's identity confused Mary. *Everyone* called him "Father," except *Grand-mère* who used the French term, *Père.* She could accept that perhaps he was her grandmother's father, but it turned out that her *maman,* uncle, and even her grandfather called him "Father," and that Mary, herself, was supposed to call him "Father." Until she received this instruction, Mary had been certain that "Father" was the tall, strong man at home who tossed her into the air and tucked her into bed at night. She loved her own father dearly, and the thought that he might be replaced by this wrinkled, bent individual worried her.

Mary had never seen any other man wearing a dress. *Jeanette* corrected her: The dress (black with red trimmings) was called a cassock. Over the cassock, "Father" wore a short cape, buttoned in front. Around his neck hung a large pectoral cross on a chain, and his head bore a round skull cap. On the third finger of his right hand reposed a golden ring, and whenever he stood up, (slowly, because of his advanced age), he grasped a crosier, or wooden staff carved and decorated with religious symbols.

Jeanette always greeted Archbishop John Carroll with respect, genuflecting before him and kissing the ring on his hand. In response, he regarded *Jeanette* and little Mary with a gentle smile, motioning oddly with his right hand and murmuring strange words over them. Once, when Mary reached toward his chest, in order to finger the shiny cross, *Jeanette* started to forbid her. But "Father" held out a restraining hand, and with surprising strength lifted Mary into his lap.

"Of such is the Kingdom of Heaven," he said.

Up close, his cavernous mouth and deeply wrinkled skin alarmed Mary. But "Father," wise in the ways of small children, turned her from him so that she could see *Jeanette*. He placed the cross in Mary's hands, and reached into a candy dish at his elbow. Mary received the treat from his fingers, and spent several minutes safe in the shelter of his arms before she lost interest and climbed down.

It often developed that Mary, entranced by the objects in *Grand-mère's* house, would lose track of the adults. They would quietly retire to a small, candle lit room, "*la chapelle.*" When Mary peeked in at the door, she beheld Father Carroll, attired in white alb, stole, and embroidered chasuble. He swung a fragrant, smoking censer, and recited litanies in that strange language of his. He placed bits of flat bread onto the tongues of the family members who knelt humbly before a cloth covered altar where seven candles burned, arranged around a large, gold cross.

"Father Carroll is a great man," *Maman* told Mary. "He is Archbishop over all the Catholics in the United States, and he influenced those who guaranteed our freedom of religion in the Bill of Rights. His cousin Charles, of Carrollton, was the only Catholic to sign the Declaration of Independence. Father John has been a friend to George Washington, Benjamin Franklin, and Thomas Jefferson. He visits this area in order to supervise the Jesuit missions. His mother was French, and I think your *Grand-mère* reminds him of her."

Mary had no idea what *Maman* was talking about. Great man or not, Father Carroll, his kindness, and the scenes of family worship at the Gold home were burned indelibly into Mary's consciousness.

Grandmother Hobbs' home differed altogether from *Grand-mère* Gold's. Descended from the founders of the colony of Maryland, her family had reaped the bounty of the American continent for over one hundred seventy years. Grandmother had married Solomon Hobbs, scion of another old Maryland family, owner of a sot weed (tobacco) plantation known as *Hobbs Chance*. Hard work, wise choices, and good luck combined to ensure that the plantation supported the Hobbs' extended family very well. Grandmother reared seven sons who gradually took over the day-to-day operations as well as the long term planning and the marketing of their produce. An army of slaves tended the fields. Each of the six married sons maintained his own home, but everyone lived close together and converged on the plantation house often.

The Hobbs' imposing, two story Georgian style mansion of whitewashed brick occupied an elevated "point" of land projecting into the broad, deep Choptank River. The house faced the plantation's own "landing," or wharf. A tree-lined avenue of white, crushed oyster shell connected the landing and the house. The long, wide front porch, with the house's main entrance at its center, was covered by a roof supported by round white columns. The flat porch roof, accessible from the second floor of the house, formed the floor of a vine-covered veranda with benches and potted plants, surrounded by a wrought iron railing. On both levels of the house, evenly spaced, tall, twelve-paned windows faced the river. The mahogany front door, installed before the American Revolution, featured an eight-by-five inch, rectangular, horizontally mounted brass lock imported at great expense from England.

Inside, a formal vestibule with crystal and brass chandelier, convex mirror, layered dental and crown mouldings, and winding, carved mahogany staircase were specifically calculated to impress the "factors" (merchant agents who traveled from farm to farm, purchasing tobacco). The spacious Hall, used for feeding large groups, could be converted for dancing by moving the dining furniture against the walls and into two alcoves that flanked the fireplace. These semicircular alcoves were topped by concave, fan-shaped seashell designs made of bent, carved and painted wood that curved upwards to the ceiling.

The ground floor also contained the plantation office, a traveler's lodging chamber, and a formal parlor. All these rooms, with their elegant furnishings and fifteen-foot-high ceilings, were intended for the comfort and entertainment of the family's business and social contacts. The pieces of furniture imported from England dated to the mid-1700s, but the newer ones had been locally manufactured by skilled slaves or indentured servants. Each object on display was of the highest quality available, from the gilded chandeliers and mirrored wall sconces, to the walnut tilt-top tables, chests, and damask-upholstered chairs and sofas, to the fire screens, "Turkey carpets," and painted floor-cloths. A lively mixture of bright colors delighted the eye.

The central vestibule continued beyond the open staircase to a separate wing added to the back of the mansion, causing the building to assume the shape of a "T." This rear wing, with much lower ceilings, incorporated the kitchen, which at one time had been a separate small building, or "dependency" of the main house. The other rooms in the rear wing, along with the upstairs chambers of the original structure, were designated for family use and therefore had been plainly furnished. Instead of expensive colored paint, whitewash was applied frequently to the walls and ceilings. The wide wooden floor-planks had been left bare, but in muddy weather were often strewn with protective straw and dry sand. The windows (South facing ones had a "noon mark" carved on the sill, to indicate time of day) either had been draped in unbleached linen cloth, or remained uncovered, to let in more light. These simpler window treatments contrasted greatly with the heavy damask and velvet drapes of the formal rooms.

Through these family rooms ran many children (Mary's cousins and her father's youngest sister, as well as black slaves), and dogs. The family furniture was distinctly American in design, of pine and maple, with straight, simple lines. The everyday tables were set with earthenware and pewter, rather than porcelain and silver, and the food was plain but plentiful, featuring cornbread and pork, wheat bread and beef, chicken and rice, plus wild game, seafood, dairy products, vegetables and fruits in season.

Symmetry had been given high priority in the design of the grounds of *Hobbs Chance*. Many small, whitewashed buildings balanced each other in a neat arrangement. These included a smokehouse, schoolhouse, tool shed, well house with buttery (for keeping dairy products cool), and separate necessary houses for whites and for black slaves. Extensive use had been made of boxwood hedges (the corners trimmed into urn like shapes) and white picket fences to divide the areas into rectangles. Flowers (crepe myrtle, hollyhocks, wisteria) bloomed luxuriantly during most of the year, and the kitchen garden (vegetables and herbs) was exactly matched by a flower cutting garden on the opposite side of a carefully maintained dirt walkway. Enormous shade trees in strategic locations, provided with benches, formed comforting retreats where cicadas, tree frogs, and birds sang overhead.

The barns (for tobacco, livestock, corn, and hay) as well as the slave row were located at a distance, in a direction calculated to be downwind of the plantation house most of the time. As an afterthought (because the river was the first and most important route for transportation), a gateway of stacked stone pillars and wrought iron had been constructed at the back of the property, facing the narrow dirt track to Denton. This "road" connected *Hobbs Chance* to land-locked neighbors.

Grandmother Hobbs, who put in long hours overseeing her household, as well as those of her slaves, dressed most often in comfortable, ruffled cotton gowns covered in front by aprons. Her soft leather moccasins were flat, and she could run when necessary, to rescue a child or a puppy from harm. Outdoors, her wide brimmed straw hat warded off the sun's glare. A cotton mob cap covered her hair when she remained indoors.

Mary's father, Robert, (whose marriage to the Catholic daughter of a pirate had precipitated dissension within the Hobbs family) operated the only piece of *Hobbs Chance* not contiguous with the others. Robert's farm had been received by the family in payment for a debt. (This meant, unfortunately, that Mary lived too far away to attend the plantation's school with her cousins.) As part of the huge agricultural operation, Robert needed to visit his family's home frequently, but *Jeanette* remained reticent to do so, never sure of her welcome in such informal and often chaotic surroundings.

Mary had no such compunctions. She saw *Hobbs Chance* as a place to run absolutely wild, becoming filthy while tagging after the other children (especially her Aunt Elizabeth, who was one year older than Mary).

When *Jeanette* scolded her, Grandmother Hobbs picked up Mary (who was always small for her age), and carried her toward the scullery for a wash, exclaiming, "For heaven's sake, *Jeanette*, children are *supposed* to get dirty! It's what they *do!*"

Mary adored Grandmother Hobbs. Besides protecting Mary from any form of parental discipline (keeping all the children up past bedtime to view the Great Comet that appeared in the fall of 1811), the woman gathered her grandchildren together frequently in order to sing with them and to tell stories. The older children were encouraged to share stories, and each one developed exceptional confidence as a result, girls as well as boys. Grandmother Hobbs' stories stayed with Mary forever.

"If we lived in Europe, each of you would be a count or a countess," began one tale, "and I will tell you why. Over two hundred years ago, in the days of Good Queen Bess, our ancestor Thomas of the noble house of Arundel attracted the royal favor. The Queen enjoyed the company of handsome, strong young noblemen, and kept a goodly number of them at court always. Thomas was one of these. Unfortunately for him, he was not shy about declaring his faith as a Roman Catholic. He did this once too often, and the Queen had him imprisoned. After he was released, Thomas sought to regain the Queen's grace. Toward this end, he subscribed one hundred pounds toward the defeat of the Spanish Armada. You may know that the Spanish in 1588 sent a host of warships to conquer England. Partly due to the contributions of people like Thomas, and partly due to bad weather and brave sailors, the English were able to defeat the Spanish.

The Queen was very grateful to Thomas. But because he was Roman Catholic, the Queen could not reward him without upsetting the Protestant majority in England. Instead, she recommended him to the Holy Roman Emperor, Rudolph II, who was at that time opposing the Turks in Hungary. Thomas joined the fighting, which culminated in a great battle at Gran. Our courageous ancestor led the charge, capturing the Turkish battle standard with his own hands, winning the day.

As a reward for valor, Emperor Rudolph created Thomas a Count of the Holy Roman Empire. And this is the important part: The Emperor made this honor 'descendible to all and each of the grantee's children, heirs, posterity and descendants *of either sex*, born or to be born, forever.'

Count Thomas returned to England and visited the Queen in order to pay his respects. When Elizabeth learned that he had received an honor from a monarch other than herself, she was furious! In a fit of jealous rage, she ordered Thomas cast into Fleet Prison for two months.

At last, the mercurial Queen relented. She released Thomas, knighted him, and bade him use the title *Sir* instead of *Count*. After Queen Elizabeth's death, Sir Thomas was created Baron of Wardour by Elizabeth's successor, King James.

The Holy Roman Empire is no more, but nevertheless, because of Thomas Arundel of Wardour, we know that noble blood flows in our veins!"

One of the more obnoxious grandsons sneered, "Because of a damnable Papist?"

Mary noted the flash behind her grandmother's eyes before the woman calmly responded, "Yes. We owe our present situation to him and to his daughter, the Lady Anne of Arundel, who married the second Baron of Baltimore, Cecilius Calvert. The Calverts founded the Colony of Maryland, more than one hundred seventy-five years ago, on the premise of religious toleration. It was designed as a place where both Protestants and Catholics could live in peace."

"But why," persisted Mary's cousin, "should we tolerate Catholics? They're all going to Hell anyway!"

"I think that you and I should have a little talk," replied his grandmother, "but first let me assure the rest of you that no one here is responsible for consigning anyone else to Hell. We'll leave that task to God."

From this conversation, and from others like it, Mary figured out that a religious schism existed within the Hobbs family. Even though Maryland had been founded by Catholics, Anglicans had settled there in great numbers during the Colonial Period. The English Anglican church had died out on Maryland's Eastern Shore after the American Revolution, and the religious affiliations of many Protestants had changed to Methodism at that time. Methodists remained strongly antagonistic toward Catholicism. Some of the Hobbs family who recalled their Catholic roots had become agnostic, while others had married Methodists and adopted their anti-Catholic views. These people had passed on their prejudices to Mary's cousins. Mary, whose mother descended from Catholic French kings, was perceptive enough to realize that none of the Hobbs grandchildren was aware of her Catholic heritage, and that it was better to preserve their ignorance of this point.

Although her grandmothers exerted a strong influence during Mary's early years, most of her time was spent in a small house on her father's truck farm. *Jeanette* Gold had been very young and very pregnant when she married Robert Hobbs, and it developed that she needed guidance from the black house slaves, who knew much more about child rearing than she did. Robert was older than *Jeanette*, as well as more emotionally stable, and he took to parenting far more easily than she. Many times it fell to baby Mary's father and to her mammy to figure out what to do for her.

As Mary grew, there were always puppies and kittens, sand, flowers, pretty rocks and shells to play with, as well as handmade dolls and wooden toys. Mary had been forbidden to leave the white picket fenced yard unless she was accompanied, and sometimes her mammy arranged short excursions to the pond, to the woods, and even to slave row to play with other children.

The slave children treated Mary as if she were an especially delicate and valuable doll, and Mary found the experience somewhat disconcerting.

As a result, during her early childhood, Mary never connected at an equal level with anyone else. She was either on a pedestal, at home or at Gold House, or left behind in a trail of dust at *Hobbs Chance*. This left Mary confused as to her place in the world, as well as tentative in her approach to other people. But she never forgot the kindness of the black slaves who had treated her with such tender care.

1812

At the dawn of this year, President James Madison and his infant nation teetered on the brink of unnecessary war against England. The primary causes of the conflict (economic problems brought on by various trade embargoes among France, Britain, and the United States, as well as boundary squabbles at the edges of the expanding frontier of the United States territories) had been worse in 1807, when Madison served as Thomas Jefferson's Secretary of State. Jefferson, a wiser and more patient President, adroitly avoided involvement in the Napoleonic Wars at that time. However, France and England continually used trade with the United States as a weapon against each other, with devastating effect on the American economy. The impressment of American sailors by the British Navy for use against the French added fuel to the flames of American wrath.

On April 30th, Louisiana entered the Union as the eighteenth American state. New Orleans, gate to the Mississippi River, formed a strategic keystone of commerce, and Congress wanted to establish it as part of their Union.

Throughout the spring, the rabid American "war hawk" Republicans screamed for blood. The strenuous objection of the minority Federalist party still ranks as the most vigorous opposition to any United States war with a foreign power.

On June 17th, the two houses of Congress narrowly acquiesced to Republican demands, each recording their closest votes on any declaration of war in American history. President Madison, under pressure from the war hawks, decided that he was "forced to choose between war and degradation." A slaveholder all his life, Madison yielded to the influence of greedy whites who wanted to subdue the North American continent by means of the slaughter and enslavement of Native Americans and black people. No one doubted that he would sign the war bill very soon.

Wednesday June 17th was also Mary Hobbs' seventh birthday. Although she remained unaware of Congressional activity, she had overheard references to war at *Hobbs Chance*, and resolved to ask her mother about it. She entered her parents' bedchamber, standing beside the mahogany dressing table with its damask skirt and matching upholstered bench. There, she watched *Jeanette*, who sat (wrapped in a rose colored, satin dressing gown that set off her ivory skin and enormous brown eyes), gazing into a looking glass and brushing her lustrous, black, curly long hair.

"*Maman*, what is war?" asked Mary.

"War happens when nations disagree so strongly that they send soldiers and sailors into battle. It is a very ugly, messy process, during which the fighting men wound and kill each other."

"Will the war happen *here*?"

"We must pray to God that it does not!"

"*Maman*, I don't know how to pray about that."

Mary had, of course, been taught bedtime prayers invoking her guardian angel:

> *Angele Dei, qui custos es mei,*
> *Me tibi commissum pietate superna;*
> *Hac nocte illumina, custodi, rege, et guberna.*
> *Amen.*

> [Angel of God, my guardian dear,
> To whom his love commits me here;
> Ever this night be at my side,
> To light and guard, to rule and guide.
> Amen.]

a before meal grace:

> *Benedic, Domine, nos et haec tua dona quae de tua largitate sumus sumpturi,*
> *per Christum Dominum nostrum. Amen.*

> [Bless us, O Lord, and these Thy gifts which
> we are to receive from Thy bounty,
> through Christ our Lord. Amen.]

as well as an after meal blessing:

> *Agimus tibi gratias, omnipotens Deus, pro universis beneficiis tuis, qui vivis et regnas in saecula saeculorum. Amen.*
>
> *Deus det nobis suam pacem. Et vitam aeternam. Amen.*
>
> [We give Thee thanks for all thy benefits, Almighty God, Who livest and reignest for ever and ever. Amen.
>
> May the Lord grant us his peace. And life everlasting. Amen.]

but these did not mention war specifically.

The dramatically beautiful *Jeanette* ceased brushing her hair for a moment, and regarded Mary soberly.

"You are of the right age now. Would you like to take instruction in the Catholic faith?"

"Oh, yes, *Maman*! Will you teach me?"

Jeanette frowned. Although she had been catechized in the Roman Catholic church, she possessed neither the depth of knowledge nor the patience for teaching. She could barely read and write, never having taken an interest in such things, even though her brother's tutor could have taught her. Her education had consisted primarily of preparing to attract a well to do husband, to entertain his growing collection of friends, neighbors, and business associates, as well as to direct the slaves who kept his house. Special areas of instruction had included French, ballroom dance, lace making, drawing, and music. Since her marriage, *Jeanette* had not discovered her education to be lacking in any way. Her husband and the slaves handled any task requiring practical knowledge or skills.

"I'll take you to *Grand-mère* Gold's. She will teach you, and if you work very hard, you may eventually make your Confirmation with Father Carroll, as did I."

Mary was too young to understand the complexities of her parents' attitudes toward her religious training. She had been baptized by Archbishop Carroll as an infant, but her parents probably would not have pushed her to continue as a Catholic had she not expressed interest.

Robert Hobbs regarded religion as an optional psychological comfort for women, children, and the weak. He did not permit it to directly impact his life. He viewed his wife's faith as a harmless emotional exercise. Having been trained in tolerance by his mother, Robert never would oppose his daughter's involvement with the church, although he might have taken exception to it had she been a son.

Mary's *maman*, even though devoutly Catholic, harbored ambivalence toward imposing its strictures on her daughter. *Jeanette*, especially since her wedding, had suffered the sting of Protestant scorn for Catholics, and was reluctant to pass that legacy along to her daughter. Nevertheless, sensing that her child needed something to occupy her mind, and knowing that *Grand-mère* would welcome the chance to inculcate Mary with her beliefs, *Jeanette* handed her over.

On the day after Mary's birthday, the president signed the following:

AN ACT Declaring War between the United Kingdom of Great Britain and Ireland and the dependencies thereof and the United States of America and their territories.

BE IT ENACTED by the Senate and House of Representatives of the United States of America in Congress assembled, That War be and the same is hereby declared to exist between the U. Kingdom of G. Britain and Ireland and the dependencies thereof and the United States of America and their territories, and that the President of the U. States be and he is hereby authorized to use the whole land and naval forces of the U. States to carry the same into effect and to issue to private armed vessels of the U. States commissions or letters of marque and general reprisal, in such form as he may think proper, and effects of the government of the said U. Kingdom of Great Britain and Ireland and of the subjects thereof, June 18, 1812.

Approved,

James Madison

Madison then sent out a call for 50,000 American fighting men, but received fewer than 5,000. With these and a meager Navy of ten vessels, he launched his totally unprepared forces against the best military machine in the world, into a struggle that could not, and would not be won by armed conflict. The disorganized, unrealistic and unsophisticated American military was led by aging relics of the American Revolution and by the untried sons of influential families. They faced British officers who were not only young and determined, but also tempered by their experience fighting Napoleon. Madison, the brilliant architect of the Constitution, proved willing to risk more than his nation stood to gain.

When news of the war reached New England, church bells tolled slowly in mourning, while shopkeepers closed their businesses in protest. The Republicans instigated riots at Baltimore against pro-peace Federalists. In July, a dozen Federalists were brutally beaten, one of whom died for his anti-war stand.

Americans inhabiting the Chesapeake Bay region, by and large, supported the war, even though they feared its effects. Plenty of them remembered the trials of the American Revolution, the loss of property and of life. With great bravado, they claimed mere annoyance at the war's interruption of their busy social calendars. But the economy of the Bay had suffered dramatic losses due to the recent trade embargoes, and therefore people scrambled to defend their property, protecting whatever they had left against probable British invasion.

Mary, on her way to *Grand-mére's* house in Denton, had no notion of the volume of religious information she would be required to memorize for her catechism, nor of the hours she would be expected to spend on her knees at Gold House. *Grand-mére* kept an ecclesiastical calendar (provided by Father Carroll), and observed the specified dates carefully. Seeking to please the old lady, Mary at first simply cooperated. Then, swept away by visions of the afterlife, she became insufferably holy for a time.

Repetition ensured that she remembered the following Latin prayers for the rest of her life:

In nomine Patri, et Filii, et Spiritu Sancti, Amen.

Pater noster, qui es in caelis, sanctificetur nomen tuum.
Adveniat regnum tuum. Fiat voluntas tua, sicut in caelo et in terra.
Panem nostrum quotidianum da nobis hodie,
et dimitte nobis debita nostra sicut et nos dimittimus debitoribus nostris.

Et ne nos inducas in tentationem, sed libera nos a malo. Amen.

*Ave Maria, gratia plena, Dominus tecum: benedicta tu in mulieribus
et benedictus fructus ventris tui Jesus.
Sancta Maria, Mater Dei,
ora pro nobis peccatoribus,
nunc et in hora mortis nostrae. Amen.*

*Gloria Patri, et Filio, et Spiritui Sancto.
Sicut erat in principio, et nunc, et semper, et in saecula saeculorum. Amen.*

*Salve Regina
Ora pro nobis, Sancta Dei Genetrix
Ut digni efficiamur promissionibus Christi.*

Oremus

Deus, cuius Unigenitus per vitam, mortem et resurrectionem suam nobis salutis aeternae praemia comparavit, concede, quaesumus: ut haec mysteria sacratissimo beatae Mariae Virginis Rosario recolentes, et imitemur quod continent, et quod promittunt assequamur. Per eundem Christum Dominum nostrum. Amen.

But she had no idea what most of these words meant. She seemed to be invoking magic spells each time she prayed.

Grand-mère Gold had not changed her concept of what a proper young lady should know, and therefore insisted that Mary learn ballroom dance, and to play the harpsichord, picking up a rudimentary ability to read music. But, because *Grand-mère* Gold refused to either read or write English, Mary, like *Jeanette,* never acquired these skills. She could not so much as sign her name.

Mary struggled to memorize a short version of the catechism in French. This body of theological information had been designed as a simple way to introduce young children to the mysteries of the Church. The actual lessons comprised a set of one hundred questions (incorporating the Apostles' Creed) posed orally in French by *Grand-mère,* to which Mary was required to respond in the same language with a set answer. The plan was that when Mary grew older, she would prepare for Confirmation and for First Communion by learning responses to an additional set of several hundred questions.

During August, *Grand-mére* and Mary celebrated the Transfiguration of the Lord and Assumption (Feast of Mary) with prayer, song, and meditation. In September they remembered the Birth of Virgin Mary and the Celebration of the Holy Cross. They were delighted that Father Carroll could be with them on Tuesday, September 29th, to celebrate the Mass of Archangels Michael, Gabriel and Raphael. Afterwards, Mary remembered for a long time his fervent appeal to God for peace among the nations. For the first time it struck her that prayer was supposed to have a direct effect upon human events, and she waited anxiously to learn the result.

Mary heard the news regularly while she lived with *Grand-mère* Gold. At her parents' home, mealtime conversations usually covered such topics as the weather, the condition of her father's crops, farm animals, and slaves. The activities of the neighbors occupied a share of the discussions, while a new baby on slave row commanded nearly as much interest as the birth of a new foal or calf. *Jeanette's* primary interests revolved around her own comfort, although the woman feigned interest in her husband's business matters.

At Gold House, current events and politics were chewed at dinner as thoroughly as the steamed clams and terrapin, crab cakes, oyster fritters, and other seafood that comprised a major portion of the family's diet. Because the depredations of the British Navy had sharply curtailed shipping, Grandfather Joseph and Uncle James remained at home. Mary, trained to listen to the adult conversation carefully until someone spoke to her, heard enough about preparations for war to impress upon her deeply the vulnerability of the Chesapeake Bay population to British attack.

Bright notes in the conversation often detailed the activities of privateers (pirates) who opposed the British in the Bay. Grandfather Gold knew most of these men, and he spoke especially enthusiastically about one of them, Commodore Joshua Barney. In July, Barney had sailed his ship, the *Rossie*, down the Bay. Within four months, he captured four British ships, eight brigs, three schooners, and three sloops, valued with their cargoes at more than one and a half million dollars. Seven of these prizes were burnt at sea, and two hundred seventeen British prisoners were sent to Newfoundland in one of the brigs.

During the summer and fall, the American and British forces clashed along the Canadian border. Things did not go well for the Americans, who attempted to throw out the British to conquer Canada. Instead, the British captured the forts at Michilmackinac and Detroit.

November brought All Saints and All Souls days to Gold House. Soon afterwards, James Madison struggled against DeWitt Clinton, the Federalist peace candidate, to win the Presidential election. Then Father Carroll visited, celebrating the Feast of Christ the King on Sunday the 22nd. Mary again heard the archbishop petitioning God for peace in the Americas, but it later seemed to her that God had not listened.

Mary became quite excited about Advent season. She helped *Grand-mère* to unpack the fragile *creche,* placing the painted, baked clay *santons* (little saints) carefully on a sideboard that had been especially cleared and covered with a purple cloth. Each member of the Holy Family wore a golden halo encrusted with seed pearls; the Magi sported crowns and carried gift boxes decorated with tiny, colored gemstones. *Petit Jesus* remained packed in his box, the rough wooden manger empty until December 25th; the Magi would not be placed near the manger until Epiphany on January 6th.

Mary helped *Grand-mère* to decorate the carved olive wood advent wreath base with sprigs of holly and ribbons of purple and rose. The flat bottomed wreath was designed to sit atop the dining table, and had evenly spaced holders for four candles. The four candles, lit on successive Sundays of Advent, represented not only the four weeks of Advent, but also the 4,000 years from Adam and Eve until the Birth of Christ. The purple ribbons symbolized prayer, penance, and sacrifice, while the rose colored ribbon, added on the third, or *Gaudette,* Sunday of Advent, symbolized rejoicing.

This year, for the first time, Mary would be permitted to light the candles of the Advent wreath. As the family prepared for dinner at midday on the first Sunday, November 29th, there was a knock at the front door. Peering into the vestibule, Mary watched as her grandparents and Uncle James greeted Commodore Joshua Barney. She remembered that Grandfather Gold had served under the Commodore in the American and

French navies. The two men had retired from military service, and taken up privateering for the American merchant marine, extending their careers of opposing the British. Unlike Grandfather, Joshua Barney continued to dress in his American naval uniform, which gave him a distinctive, antique look.

Commodore Barney's long hair had been neatly tied at the nape of his neck. He wore a wool coat of deep blue with buff colored turnbacks and facings, and buff breeches and vest. His gold epaulettes and brass buttons gleamed. His ascot, shirt, and knee length stockings glowed a snowy white. He had left his kid gloves, cocked hat, and small sword with the slave who answered the door, but Mary had caught a glimpse of these, and had been duly impressed, as she was by the bright, multicolored medals affixed to the breast of his coat.

Commodore Barney kissed *Grand-mère* Gold's hands, and murmured to her in French. *Grand-mère,* who apparently knew him very well, blushed like a girl. They led him to the dining parlor, where Grandfather repeated an Advent blessing. Mary lit the first candle, and dinner was served.

Joshua Barney and Mary's grandfather were of about the same age (in their early fifties), although their personalities and therefore their experiences had been quite different. Barney, ever impetuous and aggressive, had distinguished himself in naval service at a very young age (sixteen). While Mary's grandfather was still an ensign, Barney had become the youngest commander of an American navy frigate, holding his own in some thirty naval engagements against the British. He had suffered imprisonment three times, escaped twice, been shipwrecked twice, and had put down a mutiny. While serving with the French, he had risen to the rank of *chef d'escadre,* or commodore, commanding a squadron of ships. This rank put him below a rear admiral, but above a captain.

The man was a legend of the Chesapeake. Barney's larger than life presence filled the Gold dining room. *Grand-mère* Gold, usually outspoken and self assured, retreated into anxious silence. Because of her ability to fade into the background, never interrupting the adults, Mary was permitted to remain in her usual place at table.

Commodore Barney glanced around the room, taking in the elegant surroundings, mentally sifting the two pirates who sat across from him. Joseph's weathered face and deep tan betrayed his many years at sea. Gold chains encircled his neck. Gems sparkled on his finger rings, and a gold tooth gleamed in his mouth. But Barney did not need the glint of gold to confirm this man's ability to defend the Bay. Shoulder length black hair and flowing sleeves could not disguise the powerful set of Joseph's shoulders and arms. Nor could his friendly smile hide the iron will behind the piercing black eyes.

Neither was the Commodore fooled by James' sleepy look. Every move the youth made showed years of training, the grace and agility of an expert swordsman. Glossy black hair curled to the middle of James' back. He had permitted himself one gold chain and one ring set with an enormous emerald. But his ruffled shirt, like his father's, was of the finest silk. Everything he wore had either been imported at great risk and expense, or, like most of the goods in this house, stolen.

Barney commented, "You've done well for yourself here, Captain. It's amazing what a man can accomplish, given a few years of peace and prosperity. Where is that lovely daughter of yours? I trust that she is well."

Grandfather Joseph was lighting his after dinner pipe, and glanced at Barney sardonically. He had been patiently waiting for the Commodore to come to the point of his visit, and resolved out of pure stubbornness not to ask outright.

"My daughter is well. She married several years back, to a truck farmer, and Mary, here, is their daughter."

It struck Barney that Gold must be less than pleased with his son-in-law; otherwise, he would have spared him more than three words. He hoped that the husband was more than a mere truck farmer, and wondered how the match had come about. *Jeanette* as a child had displayed the beauty, fire, and pride of one born to the French court. Perhaps her impetuous nature had led her to grief... However, he kept these thoughts to himself, and addressed Mary in French, to discover whether she was being educated.

"*Bonjour, Marie, comment allez-vous?*"

"*Je vais bien, merci, Chef d'Escadre.*"

Barney leaned back in his chair.

At last he cast a level gaze at Captain Gold, and said, "I am formulating a plan for the defense of the Chesapeake, which must be sent to Congress very soon. I need someone with your experience and knowledge of the Bay to draw up the charts."

Grandfather let out the breath he had been holding.

"What makes you think the British'll invade? Perhaps Napoleon will keep them too busy in Europe."

He flicked a glance at his wife, half expecting her to explode into French, cursing the Emperor. In this case, remarkably, she deferred to Joshua Barney's knowledge of the international situation, permitting the Commodore to continue the conversation:

"Wishful thinking! Napoleon has headed for Russia with half a million men. Already the British are setting up blockades along our entire Atlantic coast. It's only a matter of time before the Bay is completely corked."

"They didn't invade here thirty-five years ago."

"The Bay wasn't the door to the nation's capital thirty-five years ago. They'll invade, all right, and we must be ready. Will you help?"

Joseph Gold puffed his pipe in silence for a time. Barney needed more than his assistance to draw up a few charts. He would not travel to this out of the way inlet to ask such a small thing.

He replied, "Of course! That shouldn't take long. Glad to help."

Grandfather Gold grinned broadly as if granting a great favor.

Barney continued to gaze at him.

"I need your ships," he continued, quietly. "I need your crews. And I need your influence to round up everything on the Eastern Shore that floats, to organize against the British."

It had been many years since Grandfather Gold had volunteered his services to a cause, and it was not something he could do lightly. Before his marriage, in his younger days, he had little besides his life to lose, and everything to gain from such endeavors. This was no longer the case. He glanced at his son, who was seated to his left, tightly gripping the edge of his chair.

"What do you think, James?" he asked, softly.

"Father," the young man replied as if the matter were a foregone conclusion, "Commodore Barney can't have just one of us. If he takes your services, he must take mine, too."

Grand-mère Gold, who had been pressing a lace edged kerchief to her mouth, abruptly left the table. Barney stared after her.

"She's not been well," said Grandfather to Barney, apologetically. "And she experienced too much of this sort of thing in France."

"I remember," said Joshua Barney. "War is not all that different from place to place, regardless of the cause. This one may cost some of us more than we are prepared to pay. Will you accompany me to the landing? We'll decide how to begin."

"*Pardon moi,*" said Mary, who stood, blew out the Advent candle, and started to follow *Grand-mère*. For the first time in her memory, dinner had ended without a final blessing.

Joshua Barney beckoned to her, and she paused long enough for him to take her hands, kiss them, and say, "*Au revoir, mademoiselle.*"

"*Bon traversée, Chef d'Escadre.*"

Advent continued. This year, the second Sunday, December 6th, coincided with St. Nicholas Eve. After lighting two candles at dinner, Mary spent the afternoon in prayer and meditation. She wanted *Pere Noel*, who reportedly traveled with his stern companion *Pere Fouettard*, to leave a gift for her that night. This would happen only if *Pere Fouettard* could find no fault in her behavior. Apparently, her performance was convincing; Mary found a bracelet of fine pearls on the table beside her bed on St. Nicholas morning.

Father Carroll visited on the third Sunday of Advent, December 13th, also known as *Gaudette* Sunday. He seemed pleased with Mary's progress, watched her light the three candles before dinner, and said a special blessing. Afterwards, he wore rose-colored vestments over his chasuble as he said a Mass of rejoicing for the family.

On the fourth Sunday, December 20th, Mary lit four candles at dinner, and returned to the routine of prayer and penance, waiting for Christmas at the end of the week. On Christmas Eve, the family stayed up until midnight, singing and repeating prayers in *la chapelle*. In the dining room, Mary placed *Petit Jesus* in the manger atop a few wisps of straw, and the family ate a late supper. A true Parisienne, *Grand-mère* served a traditional feast, including oysters and *pate de foie gras*, with a Yule Log shaped cake for dessert.

On Christmas morning, Mary found that *Petit Jesus* had left another gift: A necklace to match the lovely pearl bracelet.

On the following Sunday, the Gold Family celebrated the Solemnity of the Holy Family, unaware that the British had completed their naval blockade along the Atlantic coast, corking the Chesapeake and Delaware Bays.

1813

Grand-mère Gold showed Mary the Ecclesiastical calendar for the new year. The family began by celebrating the Solemnity of Mary on January 1st. Epiphany followed on Wednesday, January 6th, and the Baptism of the Lord was celebrated on Sunday, January 10th.

During the winter and early spring, Mary studied earnestly with *Grand-mère*. The two spoke nothing but French to each other, and before long Mary could carry on extended conversations with ease. She was an apt student of the harpsichord, and her ear for music and sense of timing were excellent. Mary became especially adept at sight reading music, and she memorized the French lyrics to some of the songs. Sometimes *Grand-mère* would play the music, and Uncle James would be drafted as a dancing partner so that Mary could practice her steps. Painting and drawing were more fun than the embroidery she had done at home. But alas, Mary had difficulty with her catechism. The hours spent in memorization and repetition seemed endless, and the notion of her sinful soul descending into Hell, or even into Purgatory terrified her.

To make things worse, *Grand-mère* seemed distracted at times, ill at others, and had trouble concentrating on the lessons. Mary figured out that the woman was worried about two wars: The nearby conflict that threatened the family's livelihood, and also the ongoing Napoleonic conflict in Europe. Partly as a result of her anxiety, *Grand-mère* developed a heart condition that drastically limited her activities.

The seriousness of the situation was made clear to Mary at Candlemas on February 2. Her grandfather and uncle had been away for several days, but returned during an overnight snowstorm. Mary was awakened when *Grand-mère* cried out at the news they brought. Hastily flinging on a gown over her shift, Mary ran down the stairs and saw *Grand-mère* collapsed on the *chaise longue*. Mary had never seen anyone look so ill. The woman's face was colorless and she gasped for breath. A housemaid hovered over her.

James perched on the edge of a damask covered *chaise*, hands clenched, his face a study in bottled fury. Grandfather Gold stood facing the fireplace, from time to time kicking one of the burning logs, and sipping from a tumbler of brandy. James, controlling his rage with an effort, regarded his niece.

"The British got the better of us this time," he said.

Uncertain of his meaning, Mary asked, "What happened?"

"We were probing British naval strength at the South end of the Bay, to determine whether we could access open ocean. Unfortunately, we were cut off by two frigates, and boarded. The *Cora* is lost. Father and I barely escaped with our lives."

"How terrible! Was anyone killed?"

A grim smile played over James' features, and an odd expression came into his eyes.

"I made them bleed a little. Before I've done they'll bleed a lot more!"

"James." Grandfather's voice sounded a warning, and the young man fell silent.

"What will you do now?" Mary asked him.

"We still have our flag ship, the *Burrows*, and your grandfather is more determined than ever to oppose the enemy. You must pray for us, and take special care of your *grand-mère*."

Ash Wednesday fell on March 3rd that year, and Mary with *Grand-mère* solemnly entered the Lenten season. Mary decided to give up her favorite substance, chocolate, for the duration. Father Carroll visited for *Mi Careme* (Laetare Sunday) on March 28th, the midpoint of Lent. He wore his rose colored vestments, and gave a homily in French about Christ's miracle of the loaves and fishes. (Mary wondered whether Christ could have multiplied the chocolate that sat, unused, in the kitchen.) Unfortunately, British activity in the Bay would prevent Father Carroll's visits to Gold House for a long time afterwards.

England's military strength remained divided as it fought wars on two fronts. Defeating Napoleon in Europe remained the priority. In the United States, the English engaged mostly in harassment, to "teach the Americans a lesson."

During the winter, the British navy had been content to blockade Chesapeake

Bay by maintaining an anchorage to the South, at Lynnhaven Bay (later called Virginia Beach), in the lee of Cape Henry, Virginia. But in early April, British ships were sighted moving slowly up the Chesapeake, and the Americans lacked any vessels with fire power to oppose them. The enemy raided island farms and coastal towns to secure fresh food. They seized packet boats, once stealing the mail intended for all of Caroline County, where the Hobbs and Golds resided. On April 12th, the British seized Sharp's Island (which has since been washed away), thereby corking the mouth of the Choptank River fifty miles below Denton. It is possible that they had figured out the location of the Golds' home anchorage.

During April, Napoleon, who had in December returned from his disastrous invasion of Russia and assembled a new army, arrived in Germany. He took the offensive against the Austrian, Russian, Prussian, Swedish and British armies allied against him. He won initial victories at Lutzen, Bautzen, and Dresden, but his forces remained vastly outnumbered.

Gold House celebrated Easter on April 18th, and it was easy for Mary to rejoice in the beautiful springtime. Fresh cream was readily available, and she indulged with gusto in dessert - chocolate mousse. But as spring progressed, it became clear that there was little else to celebrate.

United States troops continued their fruitless efforts to conquer Canada. On April 27th, they attacked and burned York (later called Toronto), capital of Upper Canada. During the following year, the British would use this as an excuse for retaliation against the American capital.

In Maryland, the British burned Frenchtown on April 29th. On May 3rd, they shelled and burned Havre de Grace (near the North tip of the Bay), destroying most of its sixty buildings. When the British turned a squadron of French renegades (former Spanish prisoners) loose on Little Hampstead, the renegades sacked the town, raping and murdering citizens in a manner so brutal that even the British officers were horrified. The British established a base at Kent Island, midway up the Bay, landing 3,000 men. It became obvious that they intended to stay.

Maryland, like the other states in the Union, maintained a citizen militia. The muster list consisted of every able bodied man (except conscientious objectors) between the ages of seventeen and forty-five. Annual musters were held in order to orient the troops. Nothing they did could accurately be called *military training. When needed, troops could be called up for active service, but the amount of time served was usually kept to an absolute minimum. Neither the counties nor the states had funds to pay the men, who in any case were needed at their regular jobs. Active service would often be limited to one or two days at a time, and those serving were rotated so frequently that there was no continuity nor group experience gained by the units.*

Members of the "regular" armed forces of soldiers, both American and British, regarded militia with scorn. One exception was the highly skilled riflemen from Kentucky. British troops in the Northwest Territories and Canada were learning respect for them. In Maryland, the British would eventually be taught another lesson by the citizen merchants and mariners of the Bay. But first, the quarrelsome Congress in Washington City had to recognize the danger to the capital, and to accept help from an old sailor, Joshua Barney.

Mary and *Grand-mère* celebrated Ascension on Thursday, May 27th, Pentecost on June 6th, and Trinity Sunday on June 13th. Despite the lack of supportive visits from Father Carroll, the two faithfully followed the calendar he had given them. Corpus Christi fell on Thursday, June 17th, and Sacred Heart of Jesus on Friday, June 25th, followed next day by Sacred Heart of Mary. Mary felt that she had mastered her catechism, and longed for the Archbishop's return.

Through the summer the British continued to harass, loot and burn the towns along Maryland's Eastern Shore. This brought trade and the normal movement of supplies to a complete halt. Grandfather Joseph and Uncle James Gold, by sailing at night with no lights, were able to sneak out the mouth of the Choptank (The *Burrows'* crew claimed that Captain Gold could "smell his way" past the British), but such journeys were too risky to be attempted on a regular basis. Because Father Carroll could not make the journey from Baltimore, as he had before the British blockade, he could not review Mary's mastery of her catechism. Waiting for his arrival gave Mary a longer time with *Grand-mère* Gold, and she enjoyed the additional practice with her beloved harpsichord.

In early August, the citizens of the Eastern Shore were put on alert. The British under Admiral George Cockburn (pronounced Co'burn) had embarked a force onto forty-five barges from their base at Kent Island (about forty miles West of the Gold's house in Denton). It was not known where they were headed. Eventually, fifteen hundred British soldiers attacked Queenstown (about thirty miles Northwest of Denton), while a like number approached St. Michael's, (thirty miles Southwest of Denton).

On Tuesday night, the 10th of August, Commodore Barney arrived unexpectedly at Gold House. It was a stormy night, and the family had retired early, having sent the servants to their quarters. Mary heard the pounding of a fist at the front entrance, which was located below her bedchamber. Afraid at first, she sat up in bed, straining to hear as her grandfather and uncle responded. Hearing their voices raised in friendly greeting, she dressed quickly. She slid a day gown over her night shift, donned a frilly mob cap, stockings and slippers, then tied a clean apron around her waist. As Mary ventured into the hall, she met *Grand-mère*, who was heading down the staircase.

In the dining parlor, Grandfather Gold was pouring carefully hoarded French brandy for his guest. Commodore Barney rose to greet *Grand-mère* with great formality, and then turned to Mary.

His eyes twinkled as he took her hand, bowed over it, and said, "Bonne nuit, Mademoiselle."

"Bonne nuit, Chef d'Escadre. Vous voulez prendre quelque aliment?"

Mary had been taught that every visitor was to be offered food as well as drink.

"Oui, Mademoiselle, Je voudrais aliment, s'il vous plaît."

"Do not waken the servants," warned Grandfather Gold, "this visit must be kept quiet."

"Yes, Grandfather."

Mary had never seen *Grand-mère* work in the kitchen, and was therefore surprised at the speed with which the woman put together a repast of bread, cheese, sliced ham, and cubed muskmelon sprinkled with fresh raspberries. Mary helped as much as she could, then began carrying the food into the dining room. When it was set before Joshua Barney, he ceased talking and ate hungrily for some minutes. At last, he sat back in his chair.

"*Délicieux!*" he declared with a sigh, looking at Mary and *Grand-mère*. "*Merci beaucoup.*"

Then he continued, apparently, what he had been about to say when the food had interrupted conversation.

"The British attacked St. Michaels last night."

The Gold family contained their shock well, although *Grand-mère* pressed her handkerchief to her mouth.

"Any casualties?" asked Grandfather.

"Not on our side," responded Barney. "But that reprobate Co'burn lost his favorite nephew, according to my sources."

"What happened?" asked Uncle James.

"As you know, the twelve gun brig, *Conflict*, has been moored at Kent Island. Last night, under cover of thunder squalls and heavy mist, the brig towed a flotilla of barges along the St. Michaels River [later called the Miles River] opposite the town, anchoring near Deepwater Point. Several hundred British marines rowed across the river and landed above Parrots Point, threatening the fort at the harbor mouth."

"Please tell me the fort made a brave stand," said Grandfather.

"I wish I could," responded Barney. "The garrison did not even see the British until they landed, and panicked when the British fired. All thirty of the Americans fled, losing every gun."

"Damnation! Devil take the honor of our glorious regular troops."

Mary had never heard her grandfather curse, and this had the effect of impressing her all the more with the import of the events being described.

"However," Barney continued, "the Talbot County Citizen Militia proved its value. As the *Conflict* positioned herself to shell the town, Brigadier General Perry Benson and his men organized a complete blackout of the town's regular lights. They quickly hoisted lighted lanterns to tree tops, as well as to the mastheads of docked ships. Of course, this caused the British gunners to aim high over the town, with most of the shot landing harmlessly in the woods and fields. Benson's men fired about fifteen rounds toward the British, forcing a retreat. Presumably, that's when the Co'burn whelp bought it."

Grandfather Gold growled, "I know that bloody Co'burn. He'll be after revenge."

Barney demurred, saying, "It's not as if this was a personal thing..."

"But he'll take it that way. Mark my words, he'll be back."

"Then we need to make sure Benson is aware, and that he prepares for that eventuality."

"How?"

"I'm glad you asked that. You can come with me to St. Michaels, and we'll figure it out!"

"What business is it of ours?"

Barney pulled a folded paper from his pocket and spread it on the table top.

"These are my orders from the Secretary of the Navy," he said. "I'm in charge of the marine defense of the Chesapeake and its tributaries. The boatyards at St. Michaels are building barges for us to use against the British. Therefore the defense of St. Michaels concerns the effort. With due respect, I'm ordering you to assist me."

James leaned forward to examine the document. The intense look on his face reminded Mary of his vow to spill more British blood.

"Tell us what to do, Commodore," James said. "We want to help."

Joshua Barney was gone before dawn. Grandfather Gold and Uncle James prepared to follow with the *Burrows*. As *Grand-mère* clung to her husband, weeping quietly, Mary found herself drawn aside by her uncle.

"Pray for our return," he said. "If we're successful in discouraging the British, I may be able to bring Father Carroll here. If I do, will you be ready for your first confession?"

"Oh, yes, Uncle! That would be splendid!"

"Then I want you to prepare. Be ready at any time, as we cannot send you advance warning."

"Yes, Uncle James."

Grand-mère and Mary settled in to wait, celebrating Assumption, the Feast of Mary, on Sunday, August 15th. Certain that God Almighty, or at least the Virgin Mary, was keeping track, the two of them said the Rosary together every night. Every day the slaves were sent through Denton to learn the news, but there were no reports. The uncertainty weighed heavily on *Grand-mère*. Her health suffered. Often the climb from the first floor to her bed chamber left her breathless and in pain.

Late on Thursday, August 26th, one of the servants told *Grand-mère* that there had been more trouble with the British at St. Michaels. It was unclear exactly what happened, but it seemed that both sides retreated before any actual encounter had occurred. However, Mary noticed that the servant seemed unusually agitated, and later learned that he had sent a message to her parents that they were needed at Gold House. They arrived on Friday, and *Grand-mère* with her daughter spent hours together in *la chapelle*, praying for Joseph and James' safe return. At dawn on Saturday morning, Mary accompanied her father into Denton, seeking more information.

Mary felt very grown up, walking with her handsome, well dressed father. Despite the red sun that warned of an oppressively humid, scorching August day interspersed with thunderstorms, both of them were covered by their clothing from head to toe, except for hands and faces, and Mary's neck. Over Robert's linen shirt and cravat, he wore a loose vest of yellow and white striped silk. This was topped by a matching cutaway suit coat with "claw hammer" tails and knee breeches, both of lightweight brown wool. The trousers were met by tall black boots over long stockings, and he wore a tall crowned, soft felt hat with a decorative yellow silk hat band.

Over Mary's calf-length cotton chemise, she wore an ankle-length, high-waisted, collarless, slim-cut gown of blue silk with long sleeves. Her best ivory satin pouffy bonnet, of which she was very proud, matched her reticule, and her feet were encased in black satin slippers.

Robert held his arm out for his daughter, and she grasped the inside of his elbow with one tiny hand. A natural teacher who seemed to Mary like a walking encyclopedia, Robert always told her far more than she wanted to know. As they strolled, he described the origins of the town.

During the 1700s, a bloomery (a furnace producing pig iron) had been established on a raised point of land projecting West into a bend in the Choptank River. The area was known as Mt. Andrew, and the point containing the bloomery was called "Pig Point." Melville's Warehouse, North of Pig Point, served as a storage and distribution area for goods brought up the Choptank River from its mouth on Chesapeake Bay, some fifty miles to the Southwest. The village that grew on this site was called Edentown, named for the British proprietary governor of Maryland, Sir Robert Eden. After 1776, the name had been shortened to Denton. The town became the Caroline County seat in 1790. Coincidentally, Caroline County had been named for Governor Eden's wife, Mary's distant cousin, Caroline Calvert Eden.

Construction of the Caroline County courthouse, a copy of Independence Hall in Philadelphia, started in 1791. Ten streets had been laid out in 1807, half at right angles to the other half, dividing the town into lots. A "causeway" had been constructed, extending Market Street West through what later became "West Denton," over a marsh toward a ferry line that crossed the Choptank. There was talk of someday building a bridge. North of the town lot containing the courthouse, prison, and school, across Gay Street, spread the "courthouse green." The green faced the river (which bent first to the West, then North around the town) and encompassed an open area near the landing often used as a market for slaves and produce. About fifty wooden and brick structures comprised the town at this time, and the courthouse dominated the landscape.

Mary and Robert Hobbs walked along dirt streets, first to the Brick Tavern, then to the ferry landing, then to the courthouse green. Everyone seemed slightly in awe of Mary's father, some whispering behind their hands and nodding in his direction. They all knew the story, how he had seduced, impregnated, then secretly married the beautiful daughter of Joseph Gold; how he had faced down the two pirates on a lonely road at midnight, convincing them to let him live. And here he was, in broad daylight, displaying the result of his adventures...

At last, Mary and Robert joined a knot of people gathered on the green. The mood of the people was one of excitement, and most were smiling.

In response to Robert's query, an old farmer replied, "Admiral Co'burn landed eighteen hundred men near St. Michaels at dawn on Thursday, leading 'em toward the town. Then, all v'a sudden, they stopped in their tracks, turned 'round, and got back on those boats without attackin'..."

Another man, who (from his nautical costume and his rough, red complexion) looked to be a mariner fresh off one of the barges tied at the landing, interrupted the farmer:

"It's American ships what scared 'em off. I'll wager Joe Gold an' the *Burrows* was right there—that man don't know the meanin' o' fear!"

The farmer glanced swiftly at Robert, then poked the mariner in the ribs with an elbow, growling, "Ya don't know any sich thang, but it still be good news. The British left Kent Island, and headed down the Bay. Long as they stay thar, we can git our produce to market. Halleluyer!"

Things went from bad to worse at Gold House. *Grand-mère*, her heart condition aggravated by anxiety, was carried to bed and died early on Sunday morning. One day later, Grandfather and Uncle James arrived on the *Burrows*, accompanied by Father Carroll. Uncertain of what to do, Mary watched as the men received the news about *Grand-mère*. *Jeanette* wept in Grandfather's arms as James sat, staring at the elegant wallpaper, Robert's hand resting firmly on his shoulder. Father Carroll seemed lost in thought, or perhaps in prayer. Presently, he retreated to *la chapelle*, where *Grand-mère* lay, and the family members followed him.

After the funeral mass, Father Carroll reviewed with Mary the religious instruction she had received from *Grand-mère*. Although quite distracted by *Grand-mère's* death and funeral, Mary was able to answer the archbishop's questions to his satisfaction, and to make confession. This first confession proved to be the easiest one Mary would ever make. She admitted to undisciplined thoughts and actions, to impatience and to sloth, and received absolution with a mild penance of a few Rosary repetitions. On the following morning, Father Carroll said a special mass, and Mary attended, even though she was not yet old enough to participate in the communion. *Maman* gave Mary *Grand-mère's* ivory crucifix as a memento of the day.

Grandfather Gold and Uncle James, grief stricken, yet determined to further the American cause, directed that their home, slaves, and furnishings should be sold. Eager to rejoin Commodore Barney, they asked Mary's father to handle the sale. The proceeds would be used to feed their mariners and to supply them with ammunition. On September 1st, they sailed down the Choptank River.

The August attacks on St. Michaels brought an end to active British operations in the Chesapeake for this year. It seemed as if Admiral Cockburn lacked the stomach for out and out war. He had been heard to say that the United States should be treated "like a naughty spaniel–if it snaps at you, hit it on the nose!" He had also been heard to exclaim that the lost life of his nephew was "worth [more than] the whole damned town" of St. Michaels. He feared the damage that a decisive defeat could do to his career, and preferred to wait for reinforcements and the orders he knew would come: Attack Washington City.

Mary returned to her parents' farm, bewildered and saddened by the loss of her *grand-mère*. *Maman* had gone into deep mourning for her mother, and seemed incapable of celebrating the fall and winter holy days.

The American situation improved. On September 10th, Captain Oliver Hazard Perry defeated and captured the British fleet on Lake Erie, forcing the British army to abandon Detroit. The British land forces retired to the East along the shores of Lake Erie, hotly pursued by American General William Henry Harrison. On October 5th, Harrison's forces defeated the British at the Battle of the Thames in Canada. The British Commander Proctor barely escaped capture. The Indian war chief Tecumseh was killed, and the Indians who had gathered in alliance with the British scattered.

Unfortunately, also in October, Napoleon was defeated by the European allies in the Battle of the Nations at Leipzig, and he retreated into France. A strong Napoleon would have helped the American cause by keeping the British attention.

Grand-mère's harpsichord was brought to Robert and *Jeanette's* farm, where Mary derived some solace by coaxing music from it. Not understanding the permanence of death, she imagined that *Grand-mère* listened from Heaven, wherever that might be, perhaps just above the rooftop. On Christmas Eve, she played especially loudly, praying that *Grand-mère* would hear and be glad. When *Jeanette* noticed Mary praying the Rosary every evening, she joined in, the recitation soon becoming a comforting nightly ritual for both of them. *Grand-mère's* ivory crucifix was installed over the head of Mary's bed.

1814

Mary began the year by celebrating the Solemnity of Mary on January 1st, Epiphany on Thursday, January 6th, and the Baptism of the Lord on the following Sunday. On these days she prayed, fasted, and sang religious tunes she remembered from her time with *Grand-mère*. After that, the Liturgical Year blurred for Mary into a scattered collection of seemingly random dates. Her mother did not keep track of the calendar as had *Grand-mère*, and Mary wondered forlornly whether God would notice their failure to keep His holy days. She tried hard to remember not to eat red meat on Fridays, but the cook had never been instructed to serve only fish on that day. *Maman* hardly ever ate red meat, while Robert expected it at every meal.

The British ships under Admiral Cockburn moved North from Lynnhaven Bay in early March to devastate and ravage seaport towns. The official **United States** *Navy was corked by a blockade of the Elizabeth River, but the British were not paying attention to the whereabouts of Joshua Barney. His flotilla was ready. He had spent the winter turning sloops and barges into twenty-six gunboats, manned by nine hundred seamen.*

During the spring, Mary became aware of tension between her parents. The adults avoided arguing in front of their daughter, but Mary noticed that they often broke off their conversations when she approached. *Jeanette*, still in deep mourning for her mother, seemed more melancholy and upset as time went on, rather than less. The reason was revealed to Mary during a trip to *Hobbs Chance*.

Mary had vaguely wondered whether she should be observing Lent, and was gratified to learn that there would be a Hobbs family Easter dinner on April 10th, attended by Grandfather Solomon, Grandmother Nancy, their six married sons (Emory, Robert, Solomon Jr., Nathan, Henry, and James) with their wives, as well as by their unmarried son Arthur. Mary had just run in to ask *Maman* for permission to go outside with the other children (who had been fed separately), when Grandfather rose to his feet.

"I have an announcement. My brother's widow has returned from Virginia, and will make the following deal: She will accept *Hobbs Chance* in exchange for her farm there, which has double the useable acreage we now own. If the British cooperate, we can schedule our move to Virginia for the fall."

The mood in the room changed to one of joy and excitement. Mary watched the adults (except for *Jeanette*) toasting Grandfather and exclaiming, "Hear, Hear!" in obvious approval. *Maman* pretended that Mary required her attention, bending over as she escorted the child from the room. In the passageway, *Jeanette* let go of Mary's arm, slumped against the wall, then crumpled onto the second riser of the staircase, her shoulders shaking with sobs inside her black crape dress.

"What's wrong, *Maman*, what's wrong?" asked Mary, greatly distressed.

Mary's father reached them in two long strides from the dining hall doorway. He encircled *Jeanette* in his arms and spoke softly into her ear.

"No!" she cried, twisting away from him. "I can't – I *won't* go to Virginia!"

Robert wrapped strong arms around his wife again, continuing to talk softly, urgently.

"This is our future," Mary heard him say.

"It will kill us all," *Jeanette* hissed. "Is that what you want?"

"Stay or go," Robert responded, "we all die somewhere. This is our big chance to get our own land, enough for our children."

"Please," she begged him, "let us stay. Virginia is not a safe place to die. There is no priest!"

"We're going," he said. "The decision is made. Perhaps Father Carroll will send priests."

Father turned to Mary.

"Stay with your grandmother," he told her. "We are going for a walk, and will return for you."

Much later, Mary's parents returned to the plantation house, and *Maman* appeared more calm, although it was obvious that she had been crying. Robert seemed self assured as always, confident that all was well.

In later years, Mary often wondered what promises, what words from her father had convinced *Maman* to disregard her own instincts and fears in order to follow him.

During the ride home, Robert described the home awaiting them in Russell County, Virginia. His tone of voice betrayed his eagerness for the move.

"The mountains are beautiful," he said. "My uncles and cousins have lived there for many years. All manner of good, edible things grow in the forests. We can feast off the land until our first tobacco crop is sold. It will be a kind of paradise. You'll see!"

Jeanette remained silent, and Mary continued to worry about her.

When they arrived at home, Uncle James Gold was waiting.

After greeting her brother, *Jeanette* retired for the evening. The men sat by the parlor fire, drinking rum, as Mary lingered near. Robert explained the move to Virginia to James, who had enquired about it, going into detail Mary had not heard before.

"My father is making this move for several reasons. The Hobbs family has increased in size. At the same time, the soil here is wearing out. Every year our production drops. *Hobbs Chance* simply cannot support everyone through the next generation. Another reason is that the operation of *Hobbs Chance* depends upon slave labor. You know that attitudes in this county are changing. The Quakers and Methodists are gaining in strength, demanding the manumission of slaves. As a result, the days of big plantations here are numbered.

"By moving to Virginia, my father is able to provide each son a larger farm with fresh soil, along with the opportunity to operate it according to conscience, with or without slaves.

"But enough of my family's business. Tell me, what brings you to the Eastern Shore?"

James answered, "I came to collect the barges being built at St. Michaels' boatyards. They weren't quite ready, so I thought I'd drop by here."

"How goes the war? We don't hear much unless some farmer has his chickens stolen by the British. Is it safe to bring our cows in from the marshes yet?"

James shrugged, drained his glass and refilled it. One of the slaves came in with a tray of bread, cheese, fruit, and ham, then left.

"It's a waiting game now. My guess is that the British are done with the Eastern Shore for now, but no one can tell how long it will be before the invasion of Washington City begins."

Robert asked him, "So, what is being done to defend Washington?"

James grimaced, and replied, "Not nearly enough. John Armstrong, Secretary of War, has refused to make any preparations at all. Little Jemmy Madison has created a new military district, with General William Winder in charge of defending the capital. But if Winder's a soldier, I'm Ambassador to Spain!"

"Surely it can't be that bad! The citizens will not stand idly by, watching the British take over."

"Rob, these are battle-hardened British regulars and marines we're talking about. Our citizens are no match for them, and our forces are completely unprepared."

"Why is that?"

"For one thing, there is no guarantee of the British intentions. Washington is a great symbolic prize for them, but taking Baltimore is by far more advantageous. That would be a drastic blow to our economy, and they know it. I heard that the *London Times* has referred to Baltimore as a 'nest of pirates' that should be cleared out."

Robert said, "Imagine that!" and grinned at James. Then he continued, "Perhaps they intend to attack both places at once..."

James broke in, "...or perhaps they'll feint at one, then thrust at the other. There's no way to be sure, and we cannot adequately defend both. But Winder has used the uncertainty as an excuse to do absolutely nothing. Joshua Barney is the only one with any idea what to do, and he is ignored because he is inexperienced in land battle tactics."

"How do you know all this?"

"Father and I serve directly under the Commodore. He has thoroughly familiarized us with the strategic importance of two locations. The first is St. Leonards Creek, the ideal place to defend the Patuxent River. The other is a small town called Bladensburg, on the East Branch of the Potomac, last position for a stand against a British land approach to Washington. Washington is only six miles West of the town."

"What about the Potomac itself? It seems an easy route from the Bay to Washington City."

"It's too well defended. Fort Warburton [also called Fort Washington] guards it, and the river is actually too shallow for the biggest ships. Co'burn has consistently taken the easier approaches, assuming our defenses to be much better than they actually are. It's one reason we expect him first at Washington. He's afraid of Fort McHenry at Baltimore."

"But the Patuxent...he can't get close enough to Washington that way!"

"We figure he must march his men at least twenty-five miles, dragging all supplies. If he tries that, our army and the militia could get him. That's where Winder comes in. He *must* be ready."

"Sounds as if the president should have put Barney in charge of the whole thing."

James agreed, saying, "It would make all of us sleep a lot better. The rest of this year could be very interesting indeed."

Their talk drifted to other things. Becoming sleepy, Mary went to bed. By the time she woke next morning, Uncle James had returned to his ship.

Once again, events in Europe had a direct effect on those in Chesapeake Bay. After the allies captured Paris in March, Napoleon abdicated on April 11th, and was exiled to the Isle of Elba by May 14th. Napoleon's wife and their son were sent to her father, the Emperor of Austria; Napoleon never saw his family again. The European allies restored the French Bourbon dynasty by placing Louis XVIII on the throne. This meant that the British (who mistakenly thought they were done with Napoleon) could and would turn their full attention to the Americans.

By April 25th, Commodore Joshua Barney had been commissioned by the president to attack the British. One month later he moved sixteen vessels down Chesapeake. His initial target: The British naval base on Tangier Island. However, by late May, Barney was seeing so much British activity in the Bay that he stationed his entire flotilla in the Patuxent River. He knew that his men represented a vital bastion of defense between the British and Washington City.

On June first, while exiting the mouth of Patuxent into the Bay near Cedar Point with thirteen barges and five hundred citizen mariners, Barney encountered HMS Lawrence and seven other British vessels. After a week of deadly hide and seek, Barney ordered his flotilla to retreat four miles up the Patuxent to St. Leonard's Creek. When the creek mouth was blockaded by two British frigates (HMS Loire and HMS Jasseur – fast, three-masted ships with forty-eight cannon), the Americans retreated two miles farther up the creek. Rather than sit quietly, Barney's men attacked, rowing barges toward the comparatively huge warships. In retaliation, the British Navy launched assaults against Barney, employing Congreve rockets.

These new weapons were particularly terrifying because they weighed up to sixty pounds each and could travel up to one and one-half miles, screaming and whistling the entire time. Luckily, no one had yet figured out how to aim these accurately.

Even though regiments of American regular infantry as well as militia were sent to assist Barney, these were of little effect. Barney's flotilla remained bottled inside Leonard's Creek until June 26th, when Colonel Wadsworth, of the American engineers, used artillery to drive the two British frigates from the mouth of the creek.

At this point, Barney's flotilla moved out of the creek and ascended the Patuxent, closer to Washington City. For about two months, Commodore Barney held the Patuxent against the British ships, defying their attempts to approach Washington City. On July 19th, the British (approaching from the Potomac River rather than the Patuxent) took Leonard's Town, the seat of St. Mary's County, where the 36th United States regiment had been stationed. The American regulars gave up the town without firing a shot.

In August, Uncle James Gold visited Mary's parents at their home. It was apparent that war suited him. He had grown in stature and musculature as well as in self confidence, and fairly glowed as he related his experiences. James was especially generous with praise for Commodore Barney's son, Major William B. Barney.

"You should have seen the Major in action against the British!" he exclaimed to Mary's parents as they sat listening to his tales. "An enemy rocket set one of our barges on fire, exploding barrels of our ammunition and injuring some of the men. The commander of the barge ordered his officers and crew to abandon her, but Will signaled his father, and received permission to attempt a rescue. Will boarded the barge and bailed water onto the flames, and rocked the barge from side to side to put out the fire. His action saved that vessel, as well as others nearby, from almost certain explosion. We spent three days altogether, rowing into battle, trying to get close enough to the big enemy ships to inflict damage on them. At last they were driven back. Several of their vessels were cut to pieces, and both schooners completely disabled. But now we're waiting for their next move."

"What does the Commodore suppose that will be?" asked Robert.

"Only one thing is sure. The British ships will not be able to ascend the Patuxent any higher than Benedict. We are prepared to fire the entire flotilla, blocking the river."

"So they'll be forced to walk?"

"If they go to Washington City, it will be on foot."

"And the Commodore is certain they will try?"

"He is. Yet, there are many who disagree with him."

Through the remainder of August, the Hobbs family waited for scraps of information indicating the progress of the war. The following facts reached them:

British forces in the Bay had been reinforced by Vice Admiral Sir Alexander Cochrane's fleet with Major General Robert Ross' army of 5,400 seasoned infantry aboard. Cochrane proved an implacable foe. Because his cousin had been killed in the American Revolution, he bore an obsessive personal vendetta against the Americans. He was heard to say that he wanted to give them a "complete drubbing before it's all over."

Barney's flotilla had been sacrificed (sixteen vessels blown up in a matter of minutes, blocking the river channel with debris) to prevent British ships from ascending the Patuxent. On August 24th, Barney's mariners had bravely faced the British on land at Bladensburg, suffering defeat because General Winder's American regulars and militia fled enemy fire "like sheep chased by dogs." (The British referred to this debacle, when the Americans ran away, as "the Bladensburg Races," and complained that trying to keep up with the fleeing Americans gave them heat stroke.)

Joshua Barney had been wounded and captured by the enemy.

Washington City had been occupied (albeit briefly), and torched by the enemy. The glow of the burning capital could be seen for fifty miles, but it was put out by torrential rains accompanying a hurricane on the night of August 25th. Strong enough to lift cannon, the punishing storm spawned a tornado that passed through the center of Washington. Battered and bewildered, the British withdrew to their ships, and the American government was able to return to the city by August 27th. Even so, Congress was forced to meet in a hotel, while the Cabinet met at the Post Office, the only surviving government building.

Secretary of War John Armstrong (who had refused to prepare for the invasion of Washington) had been asked to resign by the president, and was replaced by James Monroe (serving simultaneously as Secretary of State).

Fort Warburton had been blown up by the Americans, who retreated while the British shelled them. Alexandria, Virginia had surrendered without firing a shot. All of this reinforced the British view that the American army was an enemy unworthy of serious regard.

These news were especially hard for Mary's family to hear because there had been no message from the Gold men.

By early September, the American national situation was worse than it has ever been, before or since. Washington lay in ashes, the national treasury empty. The coasts were completely blockaded, commerce ruined. People in New England and some other states, disgusted with the president who had caused this hopeless situation, discussed ways to secure protection apart from the United States government. There was talk of secession from the Union.

The only good news for the American forces came from the Canadian border on Lake Champlain. The American Lieutenant Thomas MacDonough, with an inferior fleet of ships, outfought and outmaneuvered a British squadron under Sir George Prevost that had arrived to attack an American fort at Plattsburg. He thus prevented New York and all of New England from falling into British hands.

In Maryland, Baltimore's terrified populace mobilized to defend itself against certain attack. The city fathers had appointed a Revolutionary War veteran, Samuel Smith, as Major General in command of the local militia. When General William Winder, of the Bladensburg debacle, tried to take over for him, Smith scornfully told Winder to mind his own business.

September 11th that year fell on a Sunday, and it took people a little while to realize that the tolling bells of Baltimore signaled a warning rather than a call to worship. Major General Robert Ross' British army arrived in ships that day off North Point, about twelve miles Southeast of Baltimore, at the mouth of the

Patapsco River. Ross planned to attack the city from the East, bypassing Fort McHenry on the West, where Cockburn's warships would launch an assault of their own.

At the Light Street Methodist Church, Rev. Jacob Gruber was heard to pray that "The Lord would bless King George, convert him, and take him to Heaven, as we want no more of him." Of course, King George III of England stood in need of blessing, since he had been declared insane in 1811, and replaced by his son, the Prince Regent. His soul was not "taken to Heaven," or wherever it wound up, until 1820, when his son succeeded as George IV.

On Monday morning, all Ross' ships lowered their boats at 3 A.M. By 7 A.M. the army of 4,000 disembarked, and advanced inland for one hour. The general, ever scornful of enemy troops, especially militia, is recorded as boasting he would take Baltimore even "if it rains militia." Before the morning was over, Ross had been shot and killed by two teenage Maryland militia recruits. Determined to avenge their commander, the British attacked all day, but the Baltimore City Brigade of militia, under General John Stricker held them off, first by charging, then by forming successive battle lines and falling back slowly.

The British infantry, punished by the heat and humidity, discouraged by the loss of their commander, waited before Hampstead Hill outside Baltimore on Tuesday to hear news of Cockburn's attack on Fort McHenry. Once again, the British had reckoned without considering Joshua Barney and his citizen mariners.

Twenty days earlier, when Barney was put out of action at Bladensburg by a bullet to his thigh, he had commanded his men to abandon him. Knowing that the capital was lost, he sent them instead to defend Baltimore. Those who still had ships in the Bay (including Joseph Gold) brought sixty artillery pieces to Fort McHenry and unloaded them. Then they ran their vessels up the creeks and rivers to safety, some of them sacrificing boats to block the mouth of the Patapsco River. At the approach to the fort, on land at each side, they prepared a deadly reception for the British fleet. Directed by Major George Armistead, who had been sent by the new Secretary of War, James Monroe, to command the fort, they constructed two tiers of earthen shore batteries. It was largely because of these efforts that the fifty British ships could not get closer than two miles – too far to effect significant damage on the fort. Both the fort and the city of Baltimore, however, were shaken to their foundations by the bombardment. The American five point star shaped fort remained under attack for twenty-five hours, absorbing more than 1500 rounds of shot, shells and rockets.

Seeking to divert American attention from the infantry at Hampstead Hill, Cockburn made a nighttime flotilla attack on the Western flank of Fort McHenry, but the artillery batteries staffed by the American merchant marine held him off.

Cockburn gave up his naval assault of Fort McHenry at dawn on September 14th. The last cannon ceased firing by 7:30 A.M. As a signal of the fort's survival to both British and American observers, Major Armistead ordered the battered "storm flag" lowered, and the 30 by 42 foot, new American "garrison flag" (the "Star Spangled Banner") hoisted. When the citizens of Baltimore saw this sight, there was great rejoicing.

On land, meanwhile, the British infantry, carrying the corpse of their General, retreated to North Point. Once embarked on their transports, they preserved General Ross' body in a barrel of Jamaica rum, so that he could be buried on British soil. The American troops gleefully sang about Ross being "sent home in a pickle barrel."

In late September, Uncle James and Grandfather Joseph showed up at Mary's parents' house. In the past, Grandfather Gold had never been demonstrative of affection, but he then wanted Mary and *Jeanette* near him most of the time. He clung to their hands, and kept patting their arms, as if to reassure himself that they were actually there. It was obvious that he missed *Grand-mère* badly, although he did not mention her at all.

"Were you at the war?" Mary asked him.

He regarded her sadly, then seemed to gaze at something far away as he answered, "I was, indeed, at the war, along with your Uncle James."

"What happened there?"

"Many things happened, most of them so horrible that I hope you cannot imagine them. Thousands of men spent days on end shooting and killing each other, burning and blowing up ships and forts. No matter how many poems and songs you hear about the glory of war, there is always too much death, too much blood spilled."

"Is the war over now?"

"There are men gathered, at a place called Ghent, far across the sea.

They are trying to reach an agreement so that the war can end. Until then, we must continue to oppose the British in Chesapeake Bay."

"And Commodore Barney? Where is he?"

Grandfather allowed himself a smile as he thought of his old friend.

"The Commodore was paroled by the British for his bravery. Now he is refitting a flotilla, preparing to resume his efforts to protect Americans in the Bay. I shall join him soon."

Mary's father broke into the conversation, saying, "My family needs your advice, Father Gold. You know that we have been preparing to move to Southwestern Virginia, but our route across the Bay has been blocked by enemy activity..."

Joseph Gold frowned. Anticipating the loss of his daughter and granddaughter disturbed him deeply, but pride prevented him from expressing this. If only he had killed this damned truck farmer years before! Now there was no choice: His daughter and granddaughter legally belonged to Robert Hobbs. Solomon Hobbs ruled his sons absolutely, and there would be no change of plan.

Controlling himself with an effort, instead of arguing, he asked, "Where are you trying to go, exactly?"

"We want to head West up the James and Appomattox Rivers through Petersburg to Farmville. But getting *to* the James has been problematic."

"Yes. You want to cross the Bay. To go around by land would take you hundreds of miles out of the way. There is, of course, the Fall Line Trail from Washington City to Petersburg, but, again, you'd be walking an extra hundred miles. The water route won't really be safe until the British are no longer a factor." He added, "If you want to get everyone across, alive, I advise you to wait."

"I was afraid you'd say that. My father has reached the same conclusion. Our hope is that a peace accord is reached this winter, and that we can travel before planting season next spring. When peace breaks out, are you willing to help us with transport to Petersburg?"

The pirate's hand itched to grab his dagger, to thrust it into this man's heart. He turned away, so that Robert would not see the murder in his eyes, and said, "Much as I hate the thought of you leaving, I cannot refuse. Your family, James, and my ship are all I have left in this world."

The Peace Treaty of Ghent concluded the War of 1812 on December 24th. Little Jemmy Madison's representatives (including Albert Gallatin, Henry Clay, and John Quincy Adams) had maneuvered out of a difficult situation. The Americans could easily have lost their cherished independence from Britain. Instead, the negotiators reiterated that the United States would remain independent, and established the position of the Canadian-American border. The (temporary) capture of Napoleon had indirectly eased American conflict with the British at sea; trade could resume. The relationship of the two nations remained essentially the same as it had been before the war.

Native Americans, on the other hand, had lost the war. Since they had no voice nor representation at Ghent, they received no consideration. The British abandoned their Indian allies in exchange for Canada. Never again would Indians be able to effectively resist white American Westward expansion; their unity had died with Tecumseh.

American war deaths numbered nearly 5,000 people out of a total population of eight million.

The war quickened the growth of the United States' national identity. Its citizens afterwards assumed a god-given right to claim and then subdue a major portion of their continent. In the process, its citizens proceeded to construct economic, political, and social systems built on cruelty and greed.

In Maryland, the British continued to harass the Chesapeake Bay population in minor ways until news of the Peace Treaty reached them in early 1815.

At that point, the Hobbs clan headed West.

1815

Maryland

The logistics of moving the seven Hobbs families in some ways resembled a military campaign. Grandfather Solomon commented that he felt like Moses leading the children of Israel from Egypt. Involved were fifteen adults, seventeen children, a herd of livestock, many slaves, plus the household and farm implements and textiles necessary to sustain all these. Luckily, Solomon Hobbs and his sons were used to teamwork, advance planning, and the involvement of many resources to accomplish a goal.

Early in February, Grandfather Hobbs, his youngest son (Arthur), and a dozen slaves left for Russell County, Virginia, resolved to travel as rapidly as possible. The Hobbs family had negotiated with a childless widow (Solomon's sister-in-law) who had returned from Virginia to Maryland. She wanted badly to be rid of a large, partially cleared plantation with existing house, slave row, and barns.

Upon arrival in Russell County, Grandfather would finalize the land transfer and direct the slaves to plant a seed bed of tobacco, and to prepare the fields to receive the seedlings. The cash generated by the tobacco crop was essential to the families' survival, and this step received top priority. After the tobacco was in the ground, attention would be paid to growing corn and other food crops.

In France, Napoleon escaped from his first island prison during February, landing at Cannes March 1st. By the time he reached Paris on March 20th, Louis XVIII had fled, leaving Napoleon to conduct his final "Hundred Days" as ruler of France. The allied powers of Europe declared Napoleon an "enemy and disturber of the peace of the world."

Once their vanguard had departed, those family members remaining at *Hobbs Chance* concentrated all their energies into packing for the move. In early March, barges loaded with livestock, furniture, and tools headed down the Choptank, escorted by two more of the Hobbs sons, along with another complement of slaves. One of Mary's uncles, Nathan Hobbs, waited at Farmville, Virginia with wagons and the families' saddle horses, in order that the adults might ride rather than walk through the mountains.

In late March, just after Easter, the last three Hobbs men (Mary's father Robert was one of these), seven Hobbs wives with their seventeen children, as well as all the house slaves crowded onto the *Burrows* for the first leg of their journey. It was necessary to send a separate barge with all their belongings. Nearly everyone (never having moved more than a few miles in their entire lives) had trouble reducing the items they considered "necessary" to a small enough volume. Because they were traveling by water for the first two legs of the journey, it was difficult to see the importance of packing lightly for the more than two hundred mile trek they would make from Farmville across the Blue Ridge and into the Appalachian Mountains. Each family's belongings eventually had to fit inside a wooden wagon, although some things would be packed onto saddle horses. And since the wagons would not be acquired until they reached Farmville, the women could not easily visualize how much was feasible to take. The men, however, kept reminding and warning them, which resulted in some heated arguments.

Mary's mother was, in this respect, fortunate. Because she had only one child, she did not feel constrained to pack as many items as the women who had larger families. In addition, because *Jeanette* did not know how to cook, she had no requirements as far as numbers of pots and pans and other cooking implements. She had never felt that anything from Robert's house belonged to her. She had little interest in packing anything beyond textiles (clothing and bedding, mostly, including her prized duck down featherbeds and pillows), and a few religious keepsakes from her childhood home. It fell to the house slaves to decide what other items were absolutely necessary. Everything else, including all the furniture, had been sold.

Mary had been informed that the harpsichord was *not* making the trip, and this saddened her a great deal. Eventually, she secured her father's promise that she could have another one, some day, and ceased worrying about it. She worried more about another fact that her mother had shared:

There were *no* Catholic churches nor priests in the area where they were going. How could they conduct their lives, and especially their deaths, without the assistance of a priest?

The *Burrows*

The weather had warmed considerably by the time the families started the fifty mile (about twelve hour) voyage from *Hobbs Chance* down the Choptank River. Mary, aboard the *Burrows,* excitedly spent the entire day watching as, around each bend, another magnificent plantation house came into view. Ever so often, she saw a village, but the families were too well supplied at this point to consider stopping. They moved steadily down river toward the Bay.

Watching her father's family interact with Grandfather Gold and Uncle James amused Mary. None of the Hobbs could relate to the all-or-nothing attitude of the pirates. None of them was used to facing the threat of violent death on a daily basis. And none of them dressed with anything approaching the flamboyance displayed by the Golds.

The Golds' main pieces of clothing (tight, buttoned black breeches, white shirts with flowing sleeves, black boots, and long black coats) attracted little attention. But their huge plumed hats, colorful silk sashes, twinkling gold jewelry, and ubiquitous weaponry screamed warnings at sensible people to beware.

The Hobbs men and women, therefore, hid behind a formal correctness when speaking to the Golds. The children at first were frightened by the notion of traveling with pirates. Eventually, after observing James and Joseph's gentleness with Mary, they forgot their fears, distracted by the constantly changing scenery.

Mary was used to the smells and sounds of the water. She was familiar with the multitudes of birds (over two hundred forty species at various times of year), the edible aquatic animals (including fish, mollusks and crustaceans), and the plants of the Chesapeake. But because she had never traveled before, she knew little about boats. Standing next to Uncle James, she received instruction about the various types of vessels that appeared everywhere.

In general, any conveyance afloat could be called a boat (although the crews of large ships were apt to take offense if anyone so denigrated their vessels). Barges or bateaux were little more than flat bottomed, floating boxes designed to carry cargo. These were propelled by oars or poles, or towed by means of ropes attached to sailing vessels or to animals walking along the shore. A ketch or yacht was a one masted small boat rigged with sail fore and aft, while a yawl was a small boat with one mast far aft carrying a mainsail and one or more jibs (triangular sails). A sloop was a small one-masted vessel, rigged fore and aft with a jib mainsail, often with top sails and stay sails (fore and aft sails fastened on stays). Many Chesapeake Bay sloops, due to their maneuverability, had become sloops of war when equipped with artillery.

To be considered a ship, a boat needed not only masts and sails, but also to be of sufficient size to navigate deep water. A brig was a two masted ship with square sails. A schooner had two or more masts rigged with sail fore and aft. The *Burrows* was a long, low built schooner (of the type called Baltimore Clipper) that had sailed as a Letter of Marque ship. This meant that she had been licensed by the United States government to attack British ships, seizing cargoes and crew whenever practicable. Uncle James proudly showed Mary the six cannon that he had worked to recover after the Battle of Baltimore, and had reinstalled on the sides of the ship.

As long as the *Burrows* remained between the river banks, Mary and the other sixteen children felt energetic and excited. The nine older ones ran across the deck, exploring the hold and the topmost reaches of the rigging. There was no stopping them. But when, after dark, the boat entered the open expanse of the Chesapeake estuary, it rocked earnestly in response to wind and waves. Everyone quickly learned to be more careful when moving about the boat, and Mary herself felt quite ill. She sat quietly upon a coil of rope, waiting for the motion sickness to pass. It did not.

During the trip down the Bay, Mary could neither eat nor drink anything. She leaned over the ship's puke rail, and was joined by other members of the family when they were likewise affected. Once they reached the mouth of the James River, sailing upriver toward the Appomattox River, their motion sickness eased. Mary spotted tobacco plantations similar to the ones in Maryland. Each plantation house seemed grander than the previous one. Wooden landings at the riverbank led up wide, tree lined avenues toward tall brick mansions fronted by verandas, porches, columns, and many windows.

Spring flowers (magnolia, tulips, narcissus) bloomed, and, as one historian commented, "it seemed as if God himself smiled on a particularly wonderful time and place."

Mary noticed that something was happening to the light. She tried, several times, to ask the adults about this, but they did not understand what she was saying. The Eastern Shore of Maryland is completely surrounded by water, and the reflected light sheds a bright glare even on cloudy days. Colors in the out of doors, therefore, appear less intense and fade into each other. As the family faced West while ascending the Appomattox River, more and more sunlight was absorbed by the surrounding land surface. The intensifying green and black of deciduous trees coming into leaf, the red of Piedmont clay, and the startling blue of skies overhead slowly and inexorably enveloped Mary.

At about this same time, April 5th-10th, unbeknownst to anyone in the United States, the volcano Tambora erupted in Indonesia, killing at least 120,000 people. Tambora spewed ash high into the earth's atmosphere, an event that combined with other climatic influences to lower global temperatures by one to three degrees centigrade. All of this set up the agriculturally disastrous "year without a summer," of 1816. The impact on Mary's life would be significant.

At the wharf in Petersburg, Mary felt that a wrenching change was about to occur in her life. Immediately upon arrival, the Hobbs men departed for a local boatyard, seeking the bateau that their brothers had reserved for the families' trip upriver. They returned within an hour. As the unloading from the *Burrows* onto the bateau commenced, Grandfather and James (whose appearance had frightened the local people away) bade farewell to Mary and *Jeanette*.

"Try to remember me," Grandfather told Mary as he hugged her. "I will always love you, no matter where you are."

Mary approached Uncle James, who seemed very concerned about his sister. The woman had sunk into a kind of trance, her responses automatic and detached, as if given from a great distance.

"Uncle, what will become of us, in the mountains, with no priest?"

James hugged Mary and replied, trying unsuccessfully to keep his tone of voice light, "Sooner or later, a priest will come to the mountains. Until then, say your prayers, and take care of your *maman*."

Mary fought against panic. Once again, as with her *grand-mère,* she had been charged with the care of an older person, and once again she had no idea what to do. Was it her fault that *Grand-mère* had died? If something went dreadfully wrong with *Maman,* would it be her fault?

Uncle James clasped her hand in his, and when he let go, Mary found her palm full of small, golden coins. Because she could not read the letters of any language, she did not realize that these were African coins with Arabic script: *Pirates' gold.* She bound these tightly in a handkerchief, and placed them in her satin reticule, where they remained, dangling on a silken cord from her arm, unnoticed, for a long time.

Joseph and James did their best to set up a system of communication with *Jeanette.* They had learned from Robert that there was a post office at Russell Courthouse (later called Dickensonville), seat of the Hobbs' new home county in Virginia. They advised *Jeanette* that letters could be sent that would find them in Baltimore. However, since *Jeanette* would have to depend on someone else to read and to write messages for her, and since the Gold men intended to spend most of their lives at sea, these arrangements seemed tenuous at best. The pirates departed in great sorrow; it seemed likely that they would never see *Jeanette* and Mary again.

Virginia

Mary had never seen a large city such as Petersburg before. Since the cessation of hostilities with Britain, Petersburg had quickly resumed its role as an international port. The local economy was largely driven by tobacco, but other local products (wood, corn, pork, beef) were also exchanged there for goods from many lands. Hundreds of wooden and brick buildings crowded together: Boatyard sheds, warehouses, custom houses, banks and law offices, churches (none of them Catholic), taverns, general stores, the shops of skilled craftsmen, markets full of produce, bakeries (where the families purchased bread), as well as private residences, government buildings, and schools. Petersburg had experimented with paving some of its streets, and anyone who used these was grateful for the respite from the ubiquitous ruts and mud. Mary noticed that all the Hobbs men had availed themselves of the chance to sample the local whiskey, and to stock up on jugs for the journey.

Before she climbed from the wharf (between Commerce and Upper Appomattox Streets) onto the bateau that would become her home during the next days, Mary gazed at it curiously. The canal boat was lightly built, compared to the vessels of the Chesapeake. Made of wooden planks, it measured seven feet wide by sixty feet long. In the center, a covered shelter protected passengers from inclement weather. There was no difference between the two ends; that is, the boat did not have to be turned around to begin a trip in the opposite direction. Each end was pointed and had been equipped with a long oar, where a steersman would be stationed. The forward steersman, holding a pointed iron pole, took charge of navigation, calling out directions to the steersman in the stern. Since the families would be traveling one hundred miles of winding river upstream while ascending more than two hundred eighty feet above the elevation of Petersburg, teams of mules along the shore, managed by slaves, would provide the power necessary to move the boats.

The rate of progress would of necessity be slow; the families would be lucky to make fifteen miles per day. The advantage to this method of travel over the alternative use of wagons and horses was its comparative ease, safety, and comfort.

Beginning in 1745, engineering crews (with slaves doing the manual labor) had made substantial changes to the Appomattox River, deepening and straightening the channels leading to its wharves. However, two miles above Petersburg, a falls had prohibited navigation between the upper and lower reaches of the river. 1795 saw the creation of the Upper Appomattox Canal. This canal around the falls stretched some five and one-half miles, sixteen feet wide, and contained a series of four locks with "wing" or V shaped dams that raised or lowered boats a total of thirty-three feet. The canal bottoms and banks had been "puddled," or lined with a clay based cement to prevent water leakage and collapse.

Mary was quite impressed by the process of ascending the locks. Once their steersman had, by means of a shouted discussion with the lock operator, determined that no boat was waiting to descend, he directed that their bateau be poled and hauled into the first lock. The downstream dam was closed, the upstream dam opened, and the lock slowly filled with water, raising the bateau to the next level, where they exited the first lock, proceeding toward the next three. The entire process took a long time, and the families did not make much forward progress that day.

The journey along the upper Appomattox might have been dull, had not Mary's lively cousins constantly employed games and hair raising stunts to amuse themselves. Mary learned to play Nine Man's Morris, a board game similar to Tic Tac Toe. Her cousins scratched the outline of the board on the wooden deck of the bateau, and used beans filched from their mammies' food bags as markers. Very quiet and observant, Mary soon figured out how to win most of the time. The other children developed several favorite pastimes; they dropped objects into the water and tried to knock each other overboard. But Mary preferred to stare into the forest along the canal banks, often catching glimpses of the local fauna (mostly deer, birds, raccoons, and squirrels). Spring wildflowers bloomed; Mary admired crab apple, wild cherry, violets, dogwood, and redbud.

Finally, the families arrived at Farmville, where everyone disembarked. The town, established in 1798, was significantly smaller than Petersburg. It contained tobacco warehouses, mercantile houses, two taverns, two churches (one Methodist, one Presbyterian), and Hampden-Sydney College. Its shops were run by craftsmen including tailors, saddlers, wheelwrights, milliners, mantua (gown) makers, and confectioners. Mary heard one of her uncles scoff at the idea of actually purchasing a jug of the local mineral water; then one of her aunts did so, and everyone had a taste. Of course, the last tasters got mostly backwash. The mineral in the water was lithium, a lightweight metal that was supposed to be good for the digestion. The health benefits of backwash are still under investigation.

Mary's Uncle Nathan was waiting at Farmville with ten saddle horses, as well as seven Conestoga style covered wagons with teams of six horses and experienced drivers, hired for the trip into the mountains. It suddenly dawned on everyone how important it had been to pack wisely, especially since any attempt to sell extra goods to the citizens of Farmville failed. The wily people there knew that they had only to wait; items deemed too heavy for the wagons would be abandoned by the roadside, free for the taking.

In a magnanimous mood, Robert purchased a gentle white and brown pony for Mary. It came with a padded cloth saddle and leather bridle, and Mary could hardly wait for the trip to begin so that she could ride it. She induced one of her father's slave boys to teach her how to brush it, clean its hooves, and to comb out its mane and tail. She named her pony "Happy."

On the first night ashore in Virginia, the families began what was to become a routine. They camped in a cow pasture under canvas stretched between trees; everyone huddled together near campfires, wrapped in blankets to keep warm. Fortunately, the slaves knew very well how to set up camp and to cook outdoors in this fashion. Compared to the other Hobbs women who struggled to control their children, *Jeanette* had little to do with her one quiet, well behaved little girl. Mary watched the cooking process carefully until she figured out that it differed little from the open hearth cooking she had watched on the Eastern Shore. The main difference was that there were no ovens for baking. Baking was only made possible by the use of heavy, covered iron kettles buried in hot coals.

At first, Mary was reticent about leaving *Maman's* side; what if her mother needed something? Eventually, Mary gave in to the other children's invitations to accompany them as they explored the area surrounding their campground.

It developed that the Hobbs families were not alone on the road West. Many other groups had camped nearby, and the older children found others like themselves with whom to play and fight. The adults were too weary, busy settling themselves and the younger children for the night to pay much attention.

Mary was usually awakened at dawn by *Maman*. After washing faces and hands, the family ate a hasty breakfast of cold leftovers from the previous night's cooking. Ham and cornbread became the usual fare for much longer than Mary could ever have imagined. On Fridays, she and *Maman* refused the ham, although sometimes one of the slaves caught a fish for them to share. Each morning except for Sundays, the families loaded their belongings into the wagons, and started the day's journey, which usually totaled no more than fifteen miles.

Road conditions had deteriorated with the onset of spring. Deeply rutted, the hard packed red clay surface softened in the April rains, often stalling the wagons' forward progress. Riding on Happy's back gave Mary a much more comfortable trip than she would have had in the jolting wagon, or walking.

Crossing any stream or river became a major production. Ferries spanned the deepest waterways, operated under licenses granted by the local courts. Most ferries could handle only one wagon at a time, necessitating a considerable wait at each one. Often, the horses were tied to the ferry and forced to swim across, and Mary was deeply concerned each time until Happy had safely reached dry ground. At the smaller streams, the family used poorly maintained fords, where they struggled against the deep, muddy ruts and sharp rocks that lurked beneath the cold water.

The air had changed. Mary was used to the smell of open water, to air so thick with moisture that sea creatures could be tasted with every breath. This inland air was drier; unless enhanced by rain, the odor of soil, plants and animals could be discerned only with difficulty.

The families climbed. For three days, the narrow, winding road demanded an ascent of more than one hundred fifty feet per day; then they descended about one hundred feet for each of two days. The descents were no easier nor more gradual than the ascents; great care was required to keep the wagons under control.

Whenever she reached a vantage point, staring into the West, Mary discerned a wavering blue gray line above the horizon, extending from Northeast to Southwest. At times, its top was obscured by low clouds. But in general, day by day, the line (the Blue Ridge Mountains) appeared taller and clearer. Several times, individual mountains popped up, at first only a couple of hundred feet higher than the road, and at a distance (Bald and Piney Mountains). Later, Long Mountain, Jack Mountain and Candler's Mountain appeared, quite close by. These soared six to seven hundred feet above the road, and blocked the view of anything else. Candler's Mountain was especially picturesque; it was broken at the top into nine nearly uniform knobs.

The trip to Lynchburg from Farmville seemed interminable. The effort of constant motion and of setting up and striking camp daily exhausted everyone. The men announced a rest at Lynchburg as an enticement to keep the cavalcade moving.

On the first evening at their camp near Lynchburg, Mary noticed her aunts and grandmother suddenly erupting in a flurry of excitement. Grandmother Hobbs approached *Jeanette* who, as usual, was sitting quietly with Mary hovering nearby.

"There's going to be a celebration," said Grandmother. "General Andrew

Jackson, the hero of New Orleans, as well as former President Thomas Jefferson, will be feted tomorrow night. A parade and a formal ball are planned. Everyone is invited!"

There were few things that stirred *Maman* out of her long silences these days, but this time, she raised her head to hiss, with some animosity, "Jackson. He's a murderer."

Jeanette was referring to the fact that Charles Dickenson, a lawyer from Caroline County, Maryland had died in a duel with Jackson in 1806. Andrew Jackson's popularity on the Eastern Shore had been damaged as a result.

"Pooh!" responded Grandmother. "He soundly trounced the British in January, and we are going to celebrate. Besides, you should be interested to see the president. Didn't your mother know him, in France?"

Jeanette nodded, and sighed.

This was news to Mary. *Grand-mère* had avoided speaking of her days at the French court.

"And I know you love to dance. Why don't you unpack one of those lovely gowns, and I'll help you press the creases out of it, and arrange your hair?"

Jeanette didn't move, but said, "All right," in a listless tone.

"Good! In the morning we'll all fix ourselves up. No one will outshine the Hobbs family!"

Next morning, the children were corralled by their mammies, who spent great effort washing them in a nearby stream. They were all dressed in their "good" clothing, and threatened with violent punishment if they got dirty. Cloth caps, jackets, and long shirts tucked into trousers encased the boys. The girls donned long cotton shifts, topped by ruffled cotton gowns and wide brimmed bonnets.

Mary, as usual around her cousins, felt out of place. This time it was because her gown had been made from pale blue silk, unlike their cotton ones. It mimicked *Maman's* gown; both looked very French. These gowns were high waisted (*Maman's* neckline was daringly low), cap sleeved, banded in contrasting dark blue satin ribbon appliqué. *Maman* and Mary draped long scarfs of paisley patterned cloth (the print incorporating the blue of their dresses) around themselves, supporting the fabric with their elbows. A wide band of the same paisley fabric circled their gowns, sewn along the edge above the hems. Mary's mammy spent a long time arranging Mary's black curls around the edges of an elegant turban like *Maman's,* although *Maman's* was decorated with a tall feather cockade that would have looked out of place on her daughter. *Jeanette* wore a rope of her mother's pearls with drop earrings to match, quite valuable, while Mary wore her own dainty, smaller pieces made of the same materials. Satin slippers provided a final touch.

The other Hobbs women, including Grandmother Hobbs, wore colorful gowns of machine woven, store bought cotton print fabric. They had imitated the latest French styles (high waistlines with slim cut skirts), but, being farm women of a practical nature, had not invested in the most expensive fabrics. They looked very fine for back country Virginia (where homespun linsey-woolsey fabric – either gray or home-dyed with berry juice – was most common), but *Jeanette* appeared to have stepped directly out of the French court. She couldn't help it; this was the way she had been taught to dress up, and she could feel but not understand the others' resentment.

The five Hobbs men, including Robert, had dressed in linen shirts that tied at the neck under their over-the-chin ruffled cravats. They sported striped satin vests of various colors (Robert's incorporated the blue silk of his wife's gown), knee breeches, tall black riding boots, cutaway coats with tails, and flared top hats.

At noon, several hundred men and older boys formed a cavalcade that rode out of Lynchburg West on the Forest Road. They headed toward Poplar Forest, some ten miles distant, where Thomas Jefferson had designed and constructed his octagonal, domed getaway home. The cavalcade met the president and the general, escorting them into Lynchburg. At the edge of town, the women, children, and older men gathered as a citizen band tuned up, practicing a few sprightly marches. The mammies of the Hobbs children had been given strict instructions, and each of them held onto two squirming youngsters.

Before long, the band struck up in earnest, and marched toward the town center, followed closely by an elaborately carved and decorated wooden coach pulled by white horses. The men who had ridden out paraded behind the coach, and over five hundred of the citizenry followed to the court house, where the president and the general waved to them as they climbed to the portico above. Mary's mammy maneuvered until they stood quite close to the great men, and Mary clung tightly to her hand.

Mary stared at seventy-two year old President Jefferson. His thinning hair had gone completely gray, and his brown eyes and other features seemed unremarkable. He dressed much as the Hobbs men had, as if he were a simple farmer. On this occasion, he did not address the crowd, but by every gesture sought to acknowledge the importance of the tall, thin soldier at his side.

General Jackson, in his late forties, was an impressive man. His blue eyed, hawk nosed face seemed frozen in the stern expression required when ordering men to their deaths. Mary asked herself where she had encountered that austerity before, and concluded that both Commodore Barney and Father Carroll had shared it to some degree. Mary had, of course, overheard descriptions of the Battle of New Orleans; the man before her had, only a few months previously, overseen in a few hours the slaughter of two thousand British with their commander while losing "only" seventy-one of his own men. Mary wondered what it felt like to be responsible for such a thing. Surely, depending on who was killed, even a victory could be devastating...

Jackson had removed his black bicorn hat, revealing a thick, curling shock of red hair touched with white at the temples. His uniform was trimmed with brass buttons, epaulettes, and gold ribbon. White knee breeches were topped by a short, tight, dark blue coat with standup collar. A white, ruffled cravat bulged at his neckline, and a broad ribbon sash ringed his waist, tied in a large bow at his right side. Seeking to quiet the cheering crowd, Jackson leaned over the balustrade and motioned with his hat. The crowd cheered louder.

Jefferson, far more experienced in civilian crowd control, leaned close to Jackson and spoke into the man's ear. Jackson stepped back, crossed his arms over his chest, and nodded to John Lynch, founder of the town, who launched into a flowery oration of welcome. The crowd quietened, listening to the speech, often erupting in approval. Official after official added his two cents worth, until Mary wearied of ever hearing anything from either of the great men.

Finally, Jackson began to speak. His charisma and ability to inspire patriotic fervor quickly became obvious. In December and January, he had used this personal charm to coalesce a motley collection of about 4,000 people (the diverse population of New Orleans plus volunteer troops from all over the Southern states) against the British. Having been captured by the British during the American Revolution, Jackson at New Orleans used his position as Commander of the Seventh United States Military District to enact a personal vendetta. Luckily for the United States, Jackson's personal agenda exactly matched the young nation's needs. Had New Orleans fallen to the British, control of the entire Mississippi would have been up for grabs, despite the Louisiana Purchase. The British could then have exerted control on the Americans from the West as well as from Canada. Even though the peace had already been signed at Ghent, this final American victory left the young nation in a far more advantageous position than might have been.

Mary soon became lost in the stilted phrases and lofty terminology used by Jackson, but he *was* speaking English, and she came away with an impression. Freedom in the land she called home had been at risk. It had been defended, at great cost, by many men whose names she would never know. It was now up to Mary, and to the people round about her to take full possession of the continent, to continue the Westward expansion, to claim the land as their birthright. Jackson seemed very sure about all this, and Jefferson looked on, nodding his head.

Jackson's speech was applauded long and loud, as the mayor came forward unrolling a scroll. When the crowd quietened again, he read a proclamation creating Andrew Jackson Day, to be celebrated throughout the community. People cheered as the mayor handed the scroll to Jackson, who seemed to be thanking him as he re-rolled the parchment. There was an announcement that festivities would continue at the Bell tavern, and the crowd dispersed, heading in that general direction.

Mary's mammy had brought food for the two of them, and they shared a picnic while sitting on a log in the tavern yard. Mary's father checked to make sure his daughter was all right, then hurried back to the crowd, where men clustered around his stunningly beautiful, silent wife. Mammy had filled a flask from a public spring, and Mary enjoyed the cold, fresh water. Nearby, musicians tuned their instruments.

The first set, played during late afternoon, consisted of "country dances." The participants needed no special expertise; anyone able to stand in a circle, hold hands with a partner, and follow the general pattern of the dance could join in. During this time, the wealthier, educated people (who waited for the more complicated dances) queued to meet the president and the general.

Mary, peeking into the tavern, saw *Maman* approaching the great men, led by Robert. Curious, Mary watched *Jeanette* curtsey and demurely respond as the president took her hand. Mary could tell that they were speaking French to each other, but could not overhear exactly what was said. As *Maman* continued down the line, meeting Jackson, the mayor, and the other officials, Mary saw Jefferson staring after her. Then the president broke away from the receiving line, followed *Jeanette* to the side of the room, and questioned her at length. Seemingly satisfied, he nodded, returned to his place in line, and greeted other people. But, distracted, he kept looking for *Jeanette*, as if to assure himself that he had not imagined the encounter.

Lynchburg Mayor James Stewart presided over a public dinner that had been set up at Martin's warehouse during the country dancing. The musicians rested, some of the personnel traded places; then much more sophisticated music signaled the onset of evening. By the light of pine knot torches and bonfires, the more accomplished dancers (including Mary's parents) came together at the middle of the clearing. To Mary's surprise, she recognized the hand and arm motions, foot positions, and steps being performed. *This* was the purpose of the training she had received from *Grand-mère*! She glimpsed her parents among the dancers. What a handsome couple they were! How gracefully they moved!

All the Hobbs children had been gathered together in an effort to keep track of them. Mary's feet twitched in time to the familiar tunes, wishing that Uncle James Gold was there to be her partner. She could not help it – she began to dance. As Mary twirled and postured to the music, several of the children, especially the girls, circled around her in admiration. They copied her, and she paused to demonstrate, slowly, some of the foot and arm positions for them.

At a break in the dancing, a lone fiddler broke into a lively tune not intended for the entire group. It was a *gigue*, or jig, Mary's favorite dance. Mary moved with the music, losing herself in it completely. She slowed as the dance ended; the fiddle music ceased. Then she noticed that the children surrounding her had gone suddenly quiet. She looked in the direction their heads indicated, and beheld President Jefferson, backlit by torches. He strode toward her and took her hand, while she sank automatically into a curtsey.

"You learned to dance from your *Grand-mère*? Well done! I thought all the beauty of that society died in the French Revolution. Now I see that it is not dead, merely changed. What delight to see it here, in the Virginia countryside. Bless you, my child!"

Jefferson kissed the top of Mary's head, dropped her hand, and continued toward his carriage.

The families, as the men had promised, spent an additional day resting at Lynchburg. Mary rode her pony into town with her father, seeking fresh wheat bread. On the way, after commenting on the Masonic Lodge, the three year old courthouse, and the Methodist church, he fell into his teaching mode, and pointed out the surrounding scenery.

"To the North is Tobacco Row Mountain; the high peak reaches nearly three thousand feet. West of it is Miner's Mountain, less than half as tall. Farther West are the Peaks of Otter; we'll become better acquainted with them next week because we're riding that way. They approach four thousand feet. The North Peak has a flat top; the South Peak looks sharp from here, but actually consists of three irregular granite boulders. The largest is sixty feet tall with a ten foot, egg shaped rock on top."

Losing interest in the geography lesson, Mary asked the question that had been often in her mind.

"Papa, what can we do for *Maman*? She seems so sad all of the time. Uncle James told me to take care of her, but I don't know how."

Robert sighed. He had been trying very hard *not* to worry about his wife, convinced that her spirits would improve after settlement in Russell County.

"I'll tell you a secret, Mary. Your *maman* is expecting a baby. In the fall, you will have a new brother, or perhaps a sister. After that, when we are in our new house, we will all be much happier."

Mary smiled. For the first time since the onset of the journey, she had hope that everything would truly be as she wished: Happy.

Next morning, the families resumed their journey West along the Wilderness Road. During each of the first four days, as they approached the Blue Ridge, they climbed an average of two hundred feet. The trail took them through the seat of Bedford County, Liberty (later called Bedford), a tiny village compared to the town of Lynchburg. They continued, past nearby mountains such as Cobbs (the shortest at 1,380 feet) and Taylor's (the tallest at 2,550). But none equaled the spectacular Peaks of Otter that rose nearly three thousand feet above the trail, five miles to the North.

Mary felt totally engulfed by the grey green, flower sprinkled springtime. The sky, which covered Maryland as a vast dome of light, here had been reduced to a narrow, insignificant overhead strip. Often this strip was patrolled by turkey vultures, and Mary fancied they were waiting to feast on any unfortunate who lagged behind. Even when the weather was clear, the sun, moon and stars usually hid behind ever changing horizons of rocky, tree covered hills. Yet the road West continued, longer and farther than Mary ever could have imagined before beginning the journey.

It had become Mary's father Robert's habit, in an attempt to comfort his wife, to enquire at every stop, in every group of people, whether any Catholics were present. He was especially searching for a priest, but of course wanted anyone who could pray with *Jeanette*. Near Blue Ridge (at 1,300 feet, the highest point yet attained by the families) he met a family by the name of Davis that turned out to have Eastern Shore, Maryland, connections. Silas Davis, his son Silas, Jr., and his two stepdaughters, Lydia and Margaret, who used the name Davis, were en route to the Indiana Territory.

Silas Davis, Sr. was an attractive man. Of medium height and wiry build, he had sea blue eyes and long, light brown hair tied at the nape of his neck. His easy strength came from a lifetime of hard work; first in Maryland where he was born and first married, then in Kentucky where he, a widower, had married again. He had joined the Kentucky militia, fighting in Canada during the recent war. His second wife having died, he with his son and her two daughters had returned to visit family in Maryland. On this trip, they were following Silas' brother John to the Old Northwest Territory, where opportunities for unclaimed land abounded. A divergent thinker, Silas often saw unusual and practical solutions to problems. This, along with the skills, knowledge, and experience he had acquired, made him a valuable addition to any group of travelers.

Silas said, loudly enough for Mary and *Jeanette* to hear, that there definitely *were* Catholics in Indiana (unlike Virginia), and also in many of the towns of Kentucky between Virginia and Indiana.

Because the Davises were traveling alone, Robert invited them to accompany his family, and Silas responded eagerly to the opportunity for his family to pray the Rosary with others of similar beliefs. Evening prayer with the Davises became part of Mary and *Jeanette's* routine, causing the rest of the Hobbs family, especially the Methodists, to distance themselves even more than before. Silas Davis also kept track of the Ecclesiastical Calendar, and informed Mary and *Jeanette* whenever a special day required celebration.

After cresting the Blue Ridge, the families descended into the Great

Valley, a drop of some four hundred feet over the ten miles into Big Lick (later Roanoke City).

Roanoke straddles a natural crossroads, ringed by mountains with passable gaps on each side. The Great Road came through it from North to South, intersecting with the East to West Wilderness Road used by the Hobbs families. Because the spring of this year brought more Westering pioneers than ever before seen on the American continent, hamlets such as Big Lick experienced severe crowding.

After a day's rest, the families continued along the Wilderness Road. The trip suddenly became exceedingly arduous; during the twenty miles to Hans Meadows, or Christiansburg, they climbed nearly two thousand feet. There, they reached a wide open plateau that seemed a completely new world. The plants and birds had changed. Even familiar varieties of plants lagged in development behind those encountered at lower elevations, and therefore appeared strange. Surrounding the plateau, heavily forested mountain peaks rose in every direction, some reaching over four thousand feet in height.

As they traveled, Mary admired the handsome, younger Silas Davis. At fifteen years old, he had chin length blond hair, laughing blue eyes like his father's, and lean, rock hard muscles. Young Silas loved to tell stories, always striving to impress his stepsisters and Mary. Mary received but did not understand the impression that Lydia and Margaret were competing with her and with each other for young Silas' attention. Never having spent much time with boys, Mary was shocked by his physical energy. He was forever running, climbing, shouting, even wrestling with and tickling his stepsisters. It was patently obvious that the Davis family had little money; their clothing was homespun. Instead of a wagon, all their possessions were loaded onto two mules. Mary decided that she must be in love with Silas, Jr. She could think of no other explanation for the strong attraction she felt for him; in her eyes, he could do no wrong. If only he would love her, in return! Because Mary had her own pony, she was able to keep up with Silas, Jr. on his mule during each day's march, while the other girls, barefoot, were forced to walk.

And walk they did, as the entire group proceeded about eight miles along The Gap Turnpike towards Blacksburg. This turnpike represented early efforts to charge travelers for road maintenance, an effort that was at that time only sporadically effective. Silas Davis, for example, found a way to lead his family around the toll booth.

At Blacksburg the families rested. The men did not elaborate on the fact that they were approaching the most rugged and arduous portion of the entire trip, but Mary sensed their concern; the jokes and teasing among the adults had nearly ceased. Mary watched the married couples draw closer, showing more physical dependence on each other than ever would have seemed appropriate in Maryland.

One evening, Mary stood near the campfire while the elder Silas Davis drew a map on the ground, explaining the coming difficulties to his son. First indicating the top of his "map" as North, Silas swept his outspread fingers across it from the upper right hand corner (Northeast) to the lower left hand corner (Southwest). Mary saw that he had made furrows in the soil, but that he had gradually squeezed his fingers together, beginning about halfway across the map.

"Each furrow is a valley," Silas explained. "And the ridges between them are mountain ranges that we must avoid by means of mountain passes called 'gaps.' The valleys and the gaps always have water at the bottom, a river or stream that shows the way."

Silas paused to create a "gap" by drawing a finger across a ridge between furrows on his map, and continued, saying, "In this part of Virginia, the ridges crowd very close together, and the gaps are few and far between. This means that we will often be traveling many miles out of our way."

"We have our mules," said the younger Silas. "Why can't we just take off across country with them?"

"We could try that," responded his father. "But we might never be heard from again. There are strange people in the mountains, and we are better off staying with a large group for protection."

Alarmed, Mary could not refrain from asking, "What strange people?"

Silas shot her a piercing look, as if to gauge the impact his words would have on this beautiful child who scarcely looked old enough to participate in a serious conversation. It turned out that the man was one of the few who could speak directly to Mary without patting her on the head and calling her "sugar," or some such epithet. Silas operated on a much more basic level than Mary's father or any of the other men she had met. He understood and loved the earth, its plants and its animals, and he treated people as the most advanced animals, with tenderness and respect.

"The woods and mountains provide a place to hide," he explained. "And there are plenty of people who have reason to do so. Besides the criminals, runaway slaves, and other detritus from the East coast societies, there are Indians and Ramps."

"What are Ramps?"

"They are a dark skinned people who have inhabited these mountains for hundreds of years. They have their own, distinctive culture, and refer to themselves as Portugese, or Melungeons. We will be passing close to one of their settlements in the next few days."

"Are they dangerous?"

"They seem very peaceable, but no one knows much about them or their customs. It is best for all of us to keep together and stay on the path."

On the first day out of Blacksburg, the group descended from the plateau, following the twisting turnpike through a gap in Brush Mountain. Once again the sky shrank to a narrow strip overhead, and Mary was surrounded by greenery. The alarm calls of rare birds echoed off exposed, dripping rocks on either side of the trail, and flowers for which the travelers had no names provided occasional bright accents.

Between Clover Hollow Mountain (3180 feet) and Spruce Run Mountain (3175 feet), they entered a wide valley. At a bend in the trail on Sinking Creek, a semi-permanent market came into view, staffed by oddly dressed, olive skinned men. A few of their children played nearby, but none of their women appeared. Mary realized that these must be the Melungeons mentioned by Silas Davis. They had constructed booths in locations where the travelers could not avoid viewing their merchandise.

The travelers had been advised at Blacksburg to purchase goods such as steel pins and needles, flour, sugar, and cotton cloth. Those who had followed this advice found themselves in a position to barter with the Melungeons; cash money was of no value to these mountain people. Fresh produce (greens, spring onions, radishes, asparagus, rhubarb, herbs, even ginseng) had been carefully arranged on rude plank tables; live fish and crawdads from mountain streams splashed in leather buckets; live young chickens, sheep and pigs had been secured nearby. Also available were articles of clothing made from animal skins or woven from wool and flax, as well as hand carved jewelry of wood, polished stone, and bone.

Mary watched her father talking with one of the men, who softly, speaking in an odd accent, gave his name as Collins. Mary had never beheld a more exotic looking man; neither had she ever seen a man wearing so much jewelry. Multicolored beads, bear claws, feathers, and shiny metal pieces hung on leather sinews from his neck and wrists. Collins was short and wiry, his skin golden olive brown, his almond shaped eyes bright green. With every motion he displayed a feline grace and delicacy. Mary stared at his hands. Each of the man's thumbs grew from an extra-wide base, then divided like a twig, ending in two tips. His wiry, long bronze colored hair spiraled in a multitude of curled tubular locks that swayed as he moved. In addition to deerskin moccasins, leggings, and wide brim leather hat with a decorative band, he wore the remains of a uniform, which Mary vaguely associated with some of the military gear from the recent war. In response to a question from Robert, Burgess Collins responded that yes, he had served in the 4th Regiment Virginia Militia. Reluctant to discuss particulars of this experience, he instead asked for news. Robert spoke of the doings at Lynchburg involving Thomas Jefferson and Andrew Jackson, and Collins seemed satisfied. He concluded the conversation with a flowing hand gesture, bestowing a blessing on Robert and Mary, along with a verbal wish for peace.

The families followed the road as it descended steeply several hundred more feet over eight miles to the New River. From its headwaters in North Carolina, this stream flowed some two hundred fifty miles North through Virginia into what later became West Virginia, eventually contributing to the Kanawha and thus to the Ohio River. Over the previous millions of years, the fast flowing New River had cut deeply into the rising mountains, forming breathtakingly beautiful gorges with exposed rocky cliffs on each side. After crossing New River by means of a ferry, the families completed the few miles into Pearisburg (seat of Giles County) with little difficulty.

Although Pearisburg had struggled to develop the essentials of civilization, including a two story log courthouse with jail, general store, blacksmith shop and other public buildings, its look remained very crude. Nothing had been painted, and no one had gone to the trouble to obtain nor to install glass windows. The few window holes were either left wide open or closed by means of heavy wooden shutters, while the doors had been constructed of rude planks and attached with leather hinges. The people likewise appeared very uncivilized. Their clothing consisted of leather and homespun; the costumes bore little resemblance to those common on the East coast.

For the ten miles or so beyond Pearisburg, the road was extremely rough and difficult to follow, perhaps worse than at any other place in the journey. The problem was that no natural gap existed between East River Mountain and Peters Mountain. The New River had carved its way through, but the path along its banks was so steep and rocky as to be unusable. Travelers, therefore, had developed a road that skirted the edge of the cliffs, hundreds of feet above the river. This would have worked well, had the road surface not continually eroded, crumbling into the abyss. At last, about five miles past a point called "The Narrows" of the New River, an old Indian trail led to the Southwest, away from the river. Mary noticed immediately the improved mood of the adults around her.

The road led upward again, about eight hundred feet, before leveling off at a place called Princeton (in present-day West Virginia). Another day brought the families across Stony Ridge to Bluefield, where they entered a long, narrow valley along the Bluestone River. For several days, they followed this river, passing many farms where the growing season had begun. Tobacco plants were being set into the soil; corn was being planted. Cherry, apple, and other fruit blossoms promised good things to come from roadside orchards.

Mary's father expressed great excitement.

"This is why we're here," he said. "Just look at that rich mountain soil! As soon as we're settled, we can prosper on our own farm, in a way we never could in Maryland."

Mary's mother remained unimpressed.

"The fields are so small! How do they ever plant enough to make a living? And how do they get goods to market?" Mary heard her ask Robert.

"It's a lot of work to make a farm productive. Every South or East facing slope will be cleared, then planted in tobacco. The tobacco is cured, dried, then packed out on trains of mules. It is responsible for the economy of all the towns we have passed; the accumulation of wealth from tobacco increases as it reaches the East coast. But it all starts here, on the farms, and we will be part of it. And where we are going, the valleys are wider, the fields bigger."

Despite all difficulties, Mary's father expressed only optimism and hope. Mary concentrated so hard on believing him that she was totally unprepared for the reality of the following traumatic days.

Perhaps because it was a weekend, many travelers had gathered at the town of Tazewell (seat of Tazewell county). As usual, Robert Hobbs had enquired whether their were any Catholics, hoping to locate a priest, oblivious to the ill will that this caused among many Protestants.

Later, while Mary, *Jeanette,* and the Davises knelt in prayer at the crowded campground, a drunken, knife wielding man from a nearby group came staggering toward them.

"Damned Papists!" he yelled. "They'll ruin our country, just like they ruined France. Look at 'em, sayin' their mumbo jumbo. Let's throw 'em out, send 'em back where they belong..."

The man lunged toward *Jeanette,* but Silas was too fast for him. He grabbed the man's foot, yanked it, and the man fell heavily, seeming to pass out. Robert came running, began to lift his wife to her feet, but it was the last thing he ever did. The drunk sprang up, grabbed Robert's hair from behind, slitting his throat. The murderer then staggered off through the trees.

During the next few minutes, Robert's life pulsed from his body, leaking into the thirsty Virginia soil. So intent was Mary, watching him, that her mother's screams reached her as if from a great distance. And then she felt death for the first time. Even though what she saw differed little from someone collapsing into sleep, Mary's brain clearly registered a unique sensation. She felt her father's spirit detach from his body, rise up and diffuse into the air above her head. Many emotions overwhelmed her: Shock, fear, loneliness, and a worshipful awe. For several days thereafter, Mary felt her father's spirit around her, but this proved transient.

When it became clear that Robert had died, Silas carried *Jeanette* to the Hobbs' canvas shelter. He held her there for a long time, until the woman slept. Then he covered her with a blanket and instructed the slaves to keep watch.

Meanwhile, Mary followed as her uncles lifted their brother, carrying his body toward the Hobbs campsite. She saw Grandmother Hobbs collapse in grief over her son, then recover to direct that his body receive proper care from the family slaves. Robert's corpse was washed, then dressed in clean clothing, then placed in a hastily constructed wooden box (its planks pulled from the sides of the wagons), all while his stricken daughter watched. No one paid any attention to Mary; no one noticed her at all.

In the following chilly, foggy dawn, Robert's family gathered to commit his remains to the soil of a Tazewell churchyard. *Jeanette* had been dressed in black by her maid, but could neither walk on her own nor respond to questions. Mary found it difficult to realize that she would never see her father again, but remained coherent. Someone had located a Methodist deacon, who recited mangled King James scripture and prayed in backwoods English over Robert's coffin. Mary was shocked by this, never having attended a Protestant funeral before. How could prayers be efficacious if not said in Latin? At the end of the service, two women, perhaps thinking to ease the family's grief, sang a song while strumming small guitars. The refrain proclaimed, "I'll wait for you darlin' in my grave." This sent shivers up Mary's spine, and made her long desperately to escape the scene. She had determined, however, that she would remain after the others had left to pray the Rosary over her father. After she had accomplished this, she felt slightly better. Nevertheless, all her religious training led inexorably to the belief that her father's soul had gone straight into Hell.

Sitting with her mother later in the morning, Mary noticed Silas Davis at the center of the group of Hobbs men. Their discussion was animated, and they seemed in agreement at the end. Before long, all the men saddled their horses and followed Silas, who apparently had a plan.

It turned out that Silas, due to his time with the Kentucky militia as a scout, was an expert tracker. He identified Robert's murderer's footprints, and convinced Mary's uncles that they could and should bring the man to justice. The men directed the women, children, and slaves to travel five miles farther along the main trail, to Witten's Fort, where they would all reunite. This would remove the families from the scene of the tragedy, and avoid wasting more time at the overcrowded Tazewell campground.

Silas quickly found Robert's killer. The man had been so drunk that he did not remember what he had done, and therefore had not tried to leave the Tazewell area. Silas and the Hobbs men captured him, took him to Tazewell Courthouse, and made sure that the witnesses to the murder who lived nearby were willing to testify against him. Then they headed for Witten's Fort.

Grandmother Hobbs was furious.

"You didn't string him up, yourselves?" she screamed at her sons and at Silas. "That's not justice! He's a local, and they'll probably let him off, on the excuse that he was drunk."

The men let her rant until she was exhausted, in tears, before Silas said, "It's my fault, truly. I didn't think you'd want your sons arrested because of that scum. I stopped them. If the locals release him, they'll get what they deserve: A killer in their community. But we...we have a long road ahead."

Silas slapped on his wide brimmed, floppy hat and returned to his mule, leading it to pasture with the other animals.

It was true that Silas faced a long road. He was going to Indiana Territory. But the Hobbs families were in fact only a few days away from their destination in Russell County, Virginia. Overwhelmed by sorrow, they followed the Clinch River twelve miles from Witten's Fort to Claypool Hill, then six more miles into Russell County. Russell Courthouse, the county seat, lay a further twenty-five miles inside the county, and took an additional two days.

Mary looked around her. The steep, rocky cliffs and peaks had been left behind at the Narrows of the New River. As they crossed the second half of Tazewell County, the grieving families scarcely noticed the awe inspiring scenery. They progressed between majestic green mountain ridges, down narrow avenues of bottomland along the rivers. The trails gradually widened into green valleys more suitable for farming. Their general direction always tended Southwest, but the valleys were hardly ever straight or even, continually twisting and winding. In Russell County, these valleys widened even farther, in some places measuring several miles across. The sky had returned to view, and Russell County spread out before the travelers, one vast garden. There *were* high hills (House and Barn Mountain) studded with rocky outcrops, and two mountain ridges of moderate height (Moccasin and Copper Ridges) passed through the county. Dominating the landscape, along the entire Southern county border from Northeast to Southwest, stretched a formidable wall, Clinch Mountain, blue green in color. Although the county seat measured 1,951 feet above sea level, the long ridge of Clinch Mountain stretched high above, one of its peaks reaching 4,220 feet.

Since Robert's murder, Mary had felt cut off from the rest of her father's family. None of the Hobbs, including her grandmother, had considered Mary's, or even *Jeanette's* grief to be their concern. It became obvious that they blamed *Jeanette* (because of the practice of her religion) for the attack, and by extension, Mary.

Silas Davis continued to pray the Rosary nightly with Mary and *Jeanette*, and to offer emotional support. But after reaching Russell Courthouse, Silas and his family would continue "down Clinch," following the valleys to the Southwest, toward Cumberland Gap. Mary despaired, feeling incapable of caring for her mother, especially in the face of the relatives' hostility. And she had been so sure that she was in love with Silas, Jr.! What if she never saw him again?

Obtaining directions to the Hobbs property at Russell Courthouse, the families turned off the main road and ventured along Moccasin Creek, up one of the "hollows" or narrow valleys. It took the families half a day to move everyone with the wagons six miles from Russell Courthouse to the Hobbs property.

Mary never forgot watching Grandfather Solomon's face as he heard what had befallen his son Robert. Many emotions passed through his eyes, but the last one was a deadly anger. He called to a nearby slave to begin packing food onto his horse.

"I'm going to Tazewell," he announced. "There shall be justice done for my son, and I'll see to it. Who's going with me?"

Solomon's remaining sons all stepped forward. Tired as they were, even those who had just arrived were ready to follow their father. It struck Mary that if Solomon directed them all to leap off a cliff, the sons might have done so. Solomon Hobbs' iron will ruled their world. Then Mary noticed that *Jeanette* had stepped forward as well.

"*Allons*" (Let's go), she said, not loudly, but clearly enough to be heard.

Solomon glanced at his daughter-in-law, and responded curtly, "No. You'll be staying here."

"*J'absolument ne resterai ici pour aucune raison.*" (I absolutely will not stay here for any reason.)

Not waiting for anyone else to interfere, the woman climbed onto her horse and headed in the direction from which they had come. Mary watched to see whether the others would do anything, but heard one of her aunts saying, dismissively, "Let her go. Stupid Papist! If not for her, Rob'd still be with us."

Grandmother Nancy, who had remained in the background until this moment, glared at Mary's aunt and said, "We can't just let her go! She's with child, and she's not been well..."

Solomon passed a long arm around his wife.

"Let her go for now," he said. "We'll take her maid along; When we overtake her on the trail, we'll send them both back here."

Grandmother Hobbs nodded, wearily, as if that settled the matter, and headed inside to examine her new house.

Mary considered. She didn't think it likely that *Jeanette* would return to the Hobbs farm, nor did she want to be separated, even briefly, from her only remaining parent. She waited until the families were called inside for dinner, then slipped away to find her pony. Riding fast, she eventually overtook *Jeanette*, who had nearly reached Russell Courthouse.

"*Maman!*"

Jeanette slowed her horse, and reached out to clasp Mary's hand.

"*Nous ne retournons pas là.*" (We are not going back there), she whispered, indicating the trail behind. "*Nous n'appartenons pas avec eux.*" (We don't belong with them.)

"*Où irons-nous ?*" (Where will we go?) asked Mary, alarmed.

Shrugging her shoulders, *Jeanette* kicked her horse into a canter, toward the town. But Mary noticed that, rather than turning toward Tazewell, to the East, *Jeanette* followed the trail West, out of town. Without the heavy wagons to slow them, Mary and her mother covered a lot of ground that afternoon. At nightfall, they approached a campground where *Jeanette* found that which she sought: Silas Davis. Mary silently rejoiced. Now she could continue adoring Silas, Jr. until he noticed and returned her affection.

Mary watched, astonished, as Silas lifted *Maman* from her horse, and as he proceeded to care for her during the remainder of the evening. Understanding the depths of this woman's emotional and spiritual needs better than anyone, Silas held her all evening, feeding her with his own hands. The family recited the Rosary together, as usual. Then, after making sure that Mary had a place to sleep with his stepdaughters, Silas took *Jeanette* to his own blankets, and held her tenderly all night.

In the morning, the Davis family packed all their belongings onto the mules. Mary was glad to return to the trail. With the horror of her father's death still resonating in her soul, she felt as though leaving these mountains behind would somehow deliver herself and her mother from evil. Perhaps, if they ever reached civilization, there would be a way to contact Grandfather Gold, or a priest...perhaps a priest could write a letter...

On the first day, the Davis girls and Silas, Jr. chattered happily as they traveled, even singing sometimes. But later they fell silent, and Mary gazed about her in nearly total silence, straining to hear the calls of birds, the crashes in the undergrowth caused by startled denizens of the forest. The wagon road led downward, between steep hills cloaked in green. The sky again receded to a narrow strip overhead as the open space of the settlement was left behind.

Traveling with the Davis family proved to be much more fun than Mary's experiences with the Hobbs. During each day, there were jokes and laughter along the trail. All of the Davises accepted *Jeanette* and Mary from the first, ignoring any differences between them. Silas, Sr. was helping Margaret to study for her Confirmation in the Catholic Church, and included Mary in the daily question and answer sessions. The plan was that Margaret would be confirmed at Bardstown, Kentucky, by Bishop Flaget. Mary was not yet considered old enough to be confirmed.

Receiving religious instruction in English rather than French was an adjustment for Mary, as was the expanded form of the Catechism used for older pupils, comprising over four hundred questions and answers. Mary was old enough by this time to apply the principles of the Catechism to actual life, and the English words gave many of these principles an immediacy that Mary found troubling:

Q. What evil befell us on account of the disobedience of our first parents?
A. On account of the disobedience of our first parents, we all share in their sin and punishment, as we should have shared in their happiness if they had remained faithful.
Q. What other effects followed from the sin of our first parents?
A. Our nature was corrupted by the sin of our first parents, which darkened our understanding, weakened our will, and left in us a strong inclination to evil.
Q. Does this corruption of our nature remain in us after original sin is forgiven?

A. *This corruption of our nature and other punishments remain in us after original sin is forgiven.*

Q. Which are the chief sources of sin?
A. *The chief sources of sin are seven: Pride, Covetousness, Lust, Anger, Gluttony, Envy, and Sloth; and they are commonly called capital sins.*

Q. What is Hell?
A. *Hell is a state to which the wicked are condemned, and in which they are deprived of the sight of God for all eternity, and are in dreadful torments.*

Q. What is Purgatory?
A. *Purgatory is a state in which those suffer for a time who die guilty of venial sins, or without having satisfied for the punishment due to their sins.*

Q. What lessons do we learn from the sufferings and death of Christ?
A. *From the sufferings and death of Christ we learn the great evil of sin, the hatred God bears to it, and the necessity of satisfying for it.*

Q. Will our bodies share in the reward or punishment of our souls?
A. *Our bodies will share in the reward or punishment of our souls, because through the resurrection they will again be united to them.*

Each time the recitation reached this point, Mary would think of her father's soul, then his body, burning in torment for ever, and tears burned behind her eyes.

Q. What is a Sacrament?
A. *A Sacrament is an outward sign instituted by Christ to give grace.*

Q. How many Sacraments are there?
A. *There are seven Sacraments: Baptism, Confirmation, Holy Eucharist, Penance, Extreme Unction, Holy Orders, and Matrimony.*

Q. What is Baptism?
A. *Baptism is a Sacrament which cleanses us from original sin, makes us Christians, children of God, and heirs of heaven.*

Q. What is Confirmation?
A. *Confirmation is a Sacrament through which we receive the Holy Ghost to make us strong and perfect Christians and soldiers of Jesus Christ.*

Q. Is it a sin to neglect Confirmation?
A. *It is a sin to neglect Confirmation, especially in these evil days when faith and morals are exposed to so many and such violent temptations.*

Q. Does the Church forbid the marriage of Catholics with persons who have a different religion or no religion at all?
A. *The Church does forbid the marriage of Catholics with persons who have a different religion or no religion at all.*

Mary thought about her parents, and the heated animosity that had resulted from their marriage. Curiously, the fierce Catholic Gold pirates had accepted the situation with more equanimity than the Methodist Hobbs farm wives. She later attributed this to the frequency with which the Golds faced harsh realities; the Hobbs women led relatively sheltered lives.

Q. Who is the visible Head of the Church?
A. *Our Holy Father the Pope, the Bishop of Rome, is the Vicar of Christ on earth and the visible Head of the Church.*

Mary had, of course, heard of the Pope before, but learned from Silas Davis that the current Pope was called Pius VII. In addition, Silas described how the Pope had been dishonored and incarcerated by Napoleon. Mary realized that this information further explained the intensity of her *Grandmére's* antipathy for the Emperor.

Every night during Mary's journey with the Davises, there were music and stories around the campfire, with other travelers joining in. Some of the stories were particularly disquieting, detailing Indian raids, kidnapings, and massacres that had commonly occurred in Southwest Virginia as recently as 1794. Mary quickly caught on to the fact that many Indians had retreated to the West, the same direction that Silas Davis was headed.

Day by day, *Jeanette* remained oblivious to the threat of Indians, or of anything else, for that matter. She grew happier; soon she was smiling and speaking English again. Mary quietly rejoiced, although she did not understand the implications of her mother's and Silas' sleeping arrangements. They continued to share his blankets, and Mary often saw them kissing and embracing during the daylight hours as well.

Silas somehow acquired an additional horse, and his stepdaughters rode upon it. With this help, the Davises made the trip along the Wilderness Trail from Russell Courthouse to Cumberland Gap in about a week. On every Friday the family eschewed red meat; on every Sunday they rested.

The first night had been spent near Nickelsville; on the next day they arrived in Gate City Courthouse, where they rested for one day; on the next they reached Speers Ferry, where they were able to cross the mouth of Troublesome Creek. Next came nights camping near Stickleyville, Jonesville, Beech Spring, Rose Hill, and finally Cumberland Gap, where they rested for another day.

As the Davis family approached the town, they entered a clearing where Mary could glimpse the mountain heights soaring above either side of the trail. Silas Davis came to a halt. Ahead, Mary saw a small wooden house beside a long, narrow toll gate. Travelers were lined up at the gate, where an old man collected shillings from those desiring to pass through.

After studying the scene briefly, Silas turned his mule, motioning his family to follow him in the direction from which they had come. He led them around a bend to a wide place in the trail.

"We'll rest here," he said. "They'll likely not collect tolls at night."

Jeanette rummaged in her reticule, coming up with more than enough shillings to pay the entire family's passage through the Gap.

"No, no, my dear," Mary heard Silas murmur. "Save your money. You'll need it, later on..."

Mary had never before noticed adults showing concern over the cost of anything, and she watched Silas anxiously. He directed the children to make a "cold" camp in the clearing, and, although still anxious, Mary fell asleep after a meager supper of leftover ham and cornbread.

Hours later, *Jeanette* awakened her daughter. It was difficult to see anything in the dark, but Silas lifted Mary and placed her on Happy's back. All four females rode, while Silas Sr. and Jr. walked, leading all five animals. Cautiously, they approached the toll gate, barely visible in the moonlight.

The toll collector had tried to prevent anyone passing through by placing a log across the path. Fortunately, it was a small log (although sufficient to stop a wagon), and the Davis men simply led their mules and horses over it. At the gate itself, Silas Sr. lifted one end and silently swung it out of the way. Mary wondered where the toll collector spent his nights.

The family had passed the gate and were nearly out of sight when the toll collector appeared, running after them, yelling, and waving his arms. Silas simply kicked his mule, leading everyone swiftly away.

"Sorry, old man," Mary heard him mutter. "This was a trail long before you put up your gate…"

The town of Cumberland Gap was growing rapidly. Due to the huge influx of Westering pioneers at war's end, new businesses opened continually, supplying more goods and services. Many folk came down from the mountains for the first time in years in order to take advantage of new opportunities for trade. Long lines of horses, cattle, and hogs clogged the road, as young men drove them from farms in Kentucky to markets in the East.

Mary had never seen a stage coach before. On Sunday, walking through the town with the Davises, she paused with them outside the station house where the empty vehicle was parked. She overheard travelers, recent arrivals from Lexington, Kentucky, describing their ordeal. They spoke of "coach sickness" from the constant swaying, and of the coach "oversetting" onto its side at a rough ford.

As they talked, Mary, curious, approached the vehicle on tiptoe, trying to see inside. She froze at the sound of a low growl. A large, very ugly brown dog guarded the coach. The driver, (a cheerful, sweaty man dressed in layers of colorful flannel shirts and corduroy breeches) who stood nearby yelled, "Here, Rex! Stop that!"

"Go ahead, young Miss," he added in a kindly tone. "You can look inside."

Seeing that the dog had retreated to his master's side, Mary climbed several portable steps in order to peer into the coach. The vehicle consisted of a lightweight (pine), wooden box on wheels, containing three backless benches sufficient to seat six people. The benches were arranged so that passengers entered at the front of the wagon, climbing over the seats to reach the rear. All baggage (limited to ten pounds per person; more weight cost extra) had to be stowed under the benches. A makeshift roof of leather had been tacked across the top of the box. When completely unrolled, the leather covered the sides, protecting the passengers slightly from inclement weather but shutting out most of the light and increasing the discomfort of those prone to motion sickness.

Mary remained mystified that these conveyances were considered the height of luxury. Passengers could be transported reliably by coach from Cumberland Gap to Lexington, Kentucky in three days, stopping for the nights at inns along the way. Personally, Mary preferred to ride her pony.

Kentucky

On Monday morning, as the Davises with Mary and *Jeanette* headed North from the Gap, they scrambled to the side of the trail as the stage passed them on its way to Lexington. The driver blew his horn and cracked his whip as the horses lengthened their strides into a gallop, the coach swaying and creaking from side to side. The passengers clutched their hats, baggage, and each other in order to avoid calamity; the ugly brown dog raced frantically behind, trying to catch up.

The spring weather and scenery intensified. Flowers bloomed, birds sang, and crops formed green lines in farmers' fields. The warmth and beauty made Mary feel better than she had for a long time.

"You're in Kentucky now," Silas, Sr. told her, "home of the most beautiful women and the finest horses in the world."

Mary's mother gave Silas a look, and he amended his speech, saying, "EXCEPT for a very few women of outstanding beauty from France by way of Maryland!"

Jeanette smiled at Silas, adoration shining from her eyes.

Fifteen miles North and West of Cumberland Gap, toward the end of a long day's ride, Mary, *Jeanette,* and the Davises descended into the Narrows of the Cumberland River gorge, through a gap in Pine Mountain. The village there, Cumberland Ford (later Pineville) formed a second gateway to the West. The keeper of its tollgate proved less vigilant than the one at Cumberland Gap, and the Davis group was able to pass through during the night without rousting him.

To save money, they swam their horses across the ford, rather than spending money at Kentucky Governor Isaac Shelby's ferry. The notion of parting with money for any reason seemed to cause Silas, Sr. physical pain.

Mary was astounded at her mother's blossoming self confidence. At previous water crossings, in Virginia, her mother had exhibited anxiety, bordering on hysterics. Robert had been forced to lead *Jeanette's* horse each time. But now she seemed eager to swim her own horse across.

Drying her wet, muddy skirts by each evening's campfire, *Jeanette* further amazed her daughter with an easy acceptance of her disheveled state. In the past, Mary's father had protected *Jeanette* against this sort of inconvenience. There had always been a maid nearby to dress the woman's hair and clean her clothing, restoring a sense of civilized propriety. The Davises, who had never owned slaves, had the resourcefulness and resiliency required to carry on, day after day, independent of any help. *Jeanette* admired this quality of theirs, but never fully developed it, herself. Mary, through hard experience, did.

Neither Mary nor her mother, of course, had ever lived outdoors for such an extended period of time. Mary cast longing glances at the taverns they passed, especially when the weather turned damp. These taverns, built of logs or sometimes of natural stone wrested from the hillsides, typically housed travelers in one or two rooms on dirt or puncheon (split log) floors before an open hearth.

The tavern keepers were influential and well known members of their local communities. They dressed well, in white ruffled shirts with stocks at the necks, topped by broadcloth suits of long coats, and knee breeches met by long woolen stockings. They sported sturdy leather shoes, unless riding horseback, which called for tall leather boots.

Many of the taverns served as centers for gambling. Even the locals (some of whom had intended to move farther West, but due to some mishap had stopped along the way) gathered at these places in an attempt to lighten the purses of wayfarers. Wagers could and would be made at the slightest pretext: a fly on the wall's next move or the afternoon's weather, or on slightly more meaningful events such as a horse race or a game of cards.

Every man in Kentucky, it seemed, chewed tobacco, and spit the resulting brown saliva at irregular intervals. Wooden boxes of sand stood in the corners of every building, as well as beside the entrances, for use as spittoons. However, Mary heard someone complaining that the famed Kentucky skill with a long rifle did *not* carry over into spitting accuracy. Every tavern, therefore, was infested by a multiplicity of sticky brown gobs to be avoided while walking.

Travelers brought their own blankets or bear skins for sleeping at the taverns. They paid hefty prices for mediocre meals of wild game, pork, potatoes, and cornbread, augmented by seasonal vegetables and fruits, washed down with corn whiskey.

It wasn't the food that Mary coveted. The victuals provided by Silas Davis (he was of the "shoot something and pick greens to go with it" school of cuisine) were better than tavern food. But to sleep off the ground, away from mosquitoes, under a real roof...Would Mary ever fall asleep again, sure that she would awaken dry, sheltered from the dew and the rain? And a priest. Silas had *promised* that they would find a priest in Kentucky...

Mary needn't have concerned herself with staying at a tavern; the portion of the trail before them had no such conveniences, and few other marks of civilization. Onward through rugged country they traveled, to Barbourville Courthouse (a rude, muddy collection of log shanties surrounding one government building of brick and timber, enclosed by a split rail fence), seat of Knox County.

Wednesday evening, the family crossed the Laurel River before making camp along its banks. Silas, in an expansive mood, recounted Native American tales of the river spirits inhabiting this region, fifteen miles to the Southwest at the sacred, horseshoe shaped Cumberland Falls.

"The Indians believe that the sun, moon, earth, and all the cosmos were formed by the voice of the Great Spirit. They especially cherish the Moonbow Blessing of Cumberland Falls, as a sign that the Great Spirit reaches out to them. At certain times of year, and under special weather conditions, a Moonbow of many colors is visible at the falls, at night. At these times, the Indians believe that they can touch the fingers of Yahowah and receive a great blessing."

"Very few Indians have ever settled in Kentucky," he added, after noting Mary's nervous reaction to this information.

"This area was shared by multiple tribes, especially Cherokee and Shawnee, as a hunting ground, as well as a place for spiritual quests and enlightenment. Three and a half years ago, Tecumseh visited this place, undergoing a purification ceremony, washing his soul in the waters. He was trying to form a coalition of all Native Americans to drive out the whites. It didn't do him much good–we took care of Tecumseh."

"Then why," asked his stepdaughter Margaret, "is Kentucky called the 'dark and bloody ground'?"

"Because the Indians so vigorously opposed white settlement here. It makes sense, when you consider that the whites jeopardized their major food source, as well as their sacred places. But they're gone from Kentucky now," responded Silas.

Silas refrained from detailing his Kentucky militia service, including the Battle of the Thames, which had drastically decreased the horrific attacks, abductions, and slaughters perpetrated on each other by Indians and whites East of the Mississippi during the not so distant past. The topic seemed at an end, when Silas, Jr., with a blood curdling war whoop, leaped from the shadows to grab Margaret. He gently dragged her a few feet back from the fire. Having produced the desired effect, the youth dropped the screaming girl in a heap. The whole family, including Margaret, collapsed in laughter.

They continued through mountains, celebrating Trinity Sunday on May 21st. Mary remembered that only a short time ago, mountains had seemed a delightful novelty, scenic, inhabited by an amazing array of endemic flora and fauna. After the past weeks of ceaseless travel, she found herself jaded, dreading even the thought of climbing yet another steep, rocky path. Silas, Sr. told her that this section of trail, from Cumberland Gap to Crab Orchard Springs, was responsible for the descriptive name, "Wilderness Road." It would take this area far longer than the rest of Kentucky to become more than an uncharted, hostile land dotted by tiny, isolated communities.

The family celebrated Corpus Christi on Thursday, May 25th. By next evening, they had reached Hazel Patch, a village called by some the "crossroads of the wilderness." At this place, site of the earliest permanent (brick) buildings in the region, the Wilderness Road forked. The Northern trail became Boone's Trace to Big Hill and Boonesborough. The Northwestern one, Skagg's Trace, led toward Crab Orchard and Danville. Without hesitation, Silas led his family Northwest.

Skagg's Trace descended several hundred feet downward so that, near Livingston, Mary gazed upward at towering rock formations along the Rockcastle River. Narrow valleys, huge boulders, steep hillsides and swift, winding streams combined to ensure some of the roughest travel of the entire trip. The trail rose before them, and they climbed nearly three hundred feet in an effort to reach Rockcastle County's seat, Mt. Vernon, before nightfall on Saturday, May 27th. Passing through town, Mary dully focused on the log courthouse and jail, along with a general store, a blacksmith's, and other buildings.

As usual, Silas rested his family on Sunday, then headed out on Monday morning, this time toward Crab Orchard Springs. Two miles before reaching the springs, they passed Whitley's Station, location of a remarkable brick home built by William Whitley after the American Revolution. The bricks had been baked on site, glazed, and laid in a Flemish diamond pattern with the initials W.W. over the front door. The windows were located over six feet above the ground to prevent Indians from seeing in. William Whitley had been killed in 1813, at the Battle of the Thames, in Canada. Silas had known him, but not well enough to stop at this place.

At Crab Orchard Springs, the resourceful Silas, Sr. found a spot where his family could drink and bathe in the mineral water for free. Already the locals were finding ways to charge travelers for these privileges, and later on would build a spa.

By midday on Tuesday, Mary decided that she had *not* been imagining that the trail was becoming less arduous. They continued into Stanford, Lincoln County's seat. This was the second oldest permanent settlement in Kentucky, centered around a T-shaped log courthouse.

At that evening's campfire, along St. Asaph's Creek, a friendly crowd of pioneers gathered. Jugs of whiskey were passed while everyone wagered on wrestling matches, argued politics, and finally gathered for songs and stories around a roaring bonfire. A local farmer, drawn to the camp for entertainment, rose to his feet.

"Thish yere town is known as Stanford," he explained, "but 'tain't always been called that. A Welshman, Colonel Benjamin Logan, come out 'ere in '75 with Dan'l Boone. When Boone went North toward the *Cain*tucky River, Logan come West. He built a fort, an' called it St. Asaph's because construction commenced on that Saint's day [May 1st].

Seems that folks found it easier to call it Logan's Fort or Logan's Station. On the 20th May in the year of the bloody sevens [1777] the Injuns begun a siege 'ere that went nigh onto fifty-three days. The fort ne'er fell, and the Injuns give up. Ever after, this place become known as the 'Standing Fort,' or Stanford."

This speech spawned a series of Indian tales from various individuals, some quite lurid. Mary had some trouble settling herself for sleep that night.

Next morning, Silas, Sr. announced with great satisfaction, "We can say goodbye to the mountains. From now on, we shall encounter only rolling hills. And tomorrow night, we reach Danville, where there is a priest."

"Praise God!" sighed *Jeanette*. "Civilization!"

As they left Stanford, out Knob Lick Road, they passed the home of Kentucky's first Governor, Isaac Shelby, "Traveler's Rest." Hearing the name, Mary wondered why they, as travelers, had not stayed there. It was not until many years later that she realized the role that social class played in the extension of such hospitality. She and *Jeanette* would have been made welcome; the Davises would not.

Wednesday night found them at Danville. *Jeanette* refused to even consider locating a campsite before stopping on Fifth Street at St. Patrick's Catholic Church, a brick building. It proved empty, but the old woman who answered the door at the priest's house assured them that "Father" would return, and be available after supper.

"Please." *Jeanette* addressed the woman with great intensity. "We must make confession, and hear Mass. We can make a donation."

The woman instructed them to return after supper, assuring them all that "Father" would see to their spiritual needs.

While gathering sticks for the evening's campfire, Mary became aware that her mother was ailing. The woman had slumped beside a tree, and was gasping in pain.

"*Maman!* What is wrong?" Mary asked.

"It is nothing. I'll be all right."

But *Jeanette's* face would not support this lie for long. She remained uncomfortable for over an hour, then gradually improved. Unable to eat, she drank a little of Silas' whiskey, and felt stronger.

Together, the family returned to the church.

One by one, the Davises, Mary, and *Jeanette* met with the priest to make confession. Because Margaret expected to be confirmed by the Bishop when the family arrived at Bardstown, she was especially careful to follow the priest's instructions exactly. Margaret and Mary, who were not yet eligible to receive Holy Communion, waited at the rear of the building, softly reciting the prayers of the Rosary assigned as their penance, watching other parishioners arriving for evening Mass. At the conclusion of the service, they waited again, while *Jeanette* and Silas consulted with the priest. The man was excited, not only because *Jeanette* mentioned that she knew Father John Carroll, but also because the woman had given him a generous donation. Mary heard him agreeing to marry Silas and *Jeanette* next day at dawn.

During the night, two things happened to prevent the wedding. "Father" was called away to console a dying parishioner, and Jeanette's illness returned. In later years, however, Mary preferred to think of her mother as married to Silas Davis, and of Silas as her stepfather.

In the morning, Mary heard *Jeanette* say, "I'm bleeding," and saw her frightened look. Mary could see no blood, but became more worried about her mother than ever.

The Davises began Wednesday's journey late as a result, and Mary heard Silas promising *Jeanette,* who shed tears of disappointment, that they could be married at Bardstown, only two days away.

Thursday night, at Springfield, *Jeanette* was too weak and sick to eat. She lay beneath the tarp, moaning, yet refusing to let Silas search for a physician. Desperate, the family trudged on toward Bardstown, sure that the strong Catholic community there would offer them aid.

On the way out of Springfield, Mary noticed a brick church. "St. Rose Priory," Silas Jr. read from a sign. But Silas, Sr. told them that the priory had closed six years before, and that Mass was said at the church only on holy days.

Late Friday, the family entered Bardstown from the East on Market Street, proceeding to Courthouse Square at its very center. As the other travelers turned North on Third Street, heading for a campground on the outskirts of town, Silas continued straight West through town, then turned South. The Davis family proceeded three miles, then one-half mile East toward St. Thomas Farm, at Poplar Neck, where the Sisters of Charity of Nazareth had their compound.

Deeply fearful for *Jeannette's* health, Silas, Sr. nevertheless struggled to maintain a calm demeanor. As they traveled, he babbled information about the Catholic community at this place, and Mary tried to pay attention.

"After the American Revolution, the persecution of Catholics along the Eastern seaboard increased, partly due to the rise of Methodism. In 1785, a league of sixty Catholic families formed in St. Mary's County, Maryland, each pledging to emigrate to Kentucky within a specified time, as their circumstances permitted. Since then, the total number of Catholics West of the Allegheny Mountains has increased to about 10,000. More of them are concentrated in the Bardstown area than anywhere else," he said. "Because of all this, Archbishop Carroll requested that the Pope name Bardstown a See, with its own bishop, the Reverend Father Benedict Joseph Flaget. A seminary and then a convent were established here several years ago."

Upon their arrival at St. Thomas Farm, the place appeared deserted. The community was celebrating Sacred Heart of Jesus with a special Mass in the chapel, and Silas had to interrupt in order to gain the attention of a nun. He begged her to help *Jeanette*.

The sisters at St. Thomas were all novices under the direction of the Reverend B.J.M. David and Mother Catherine Spalding, not yet having taken their final vows. They were daughters of local pioneers - devout, strong, and practical.

Unfortunately, *Jeanette's* condition had progressed too far, and within an hour of their arrival, she miscarried.

The sisters had difficulty expressing this plainly to Silas and Mary, who had remained in the convent courtyard, frantic with worry. Finally, Sister Theresa blurted, "She is no longer with child," and Silas began to cry. Mary understood that the baby her father had promised for the fall was not to be. Sister Theresa, thinking Silas was the father, and patting his shoulder, began the usual comforting line, "You can always have more child-," but stopped in mid-sentence when Mother Catherine frowned and shook her head.

Calmly, Sister Harriet led the Davises to the convent dining hall, a separate building. Supper was over, and the place was empty, but several nuns appeared with food for the family. Seeing that Silas and Mary were too upset to eat, unlike the hungry Davis children, Sister Harriet suggested, "If you're not going to eat, you'd better pray."

When the two produced rosaries, she smiled, grimly, and led them to a small chapel. They had nearly completed the Rosary when Sister Theresa, agitated, interrupted them.

"Come," she said.

Swiftly, she led the way across the muddy yard to the convent infirmary, where *Jeanette* lay motionless, nearly as pale as the bleached linen sheets. Father David was murmuring softly in Latin, in a way that instantly took Mary back to Maryland, to Father Carroll, to *Grand-mère's* death.

Silas knelt beside the bed and wept brokenly while Mary clung to her mother's cold hand.

"Stay," she beseeched *Jeanette*. "Please stay..."

But *Maman* had gone. As at her father's death, Mary could feel the departing spirit hovering overhead, quite beyond reach or hope of return. She wondered whether the two spirits of her parents had any way of finding each other, of comforting each other.

Silas kept vigil at *Jeanette's* side all night. At some point, Mary fell asleep, and one of the nuns carried her to a pallet in a room where the Davis stepsisters slept. Being moved wakened Mary; after so many nights sleeping out of doors, she felt stifled, unable to breathe or return to sleep. She lay wide awake in the darkness, thinking, for a long time.

Mary was not worried about what would become of her. Between sobs, Silas had hugged her, saying, "I'll take care of you." He was a good man, and she did not doubt his intentions. But Mary had been watching and listening carefully. What disturbed her was that nothing indicated that God was paying attention to anything her family did. Her father had been cut down while defending his Catholic wife. Her mother obeyed her husband, then sought to rejoin those of her own religious beliefs, and now was dead to no purpose. If God was in charge, and could hear their continual prayers, what was the point of all this? In the years ahead, Mary asked this question of many people in many different ways, but never received a satisfactory answer.

Jeanette's death led the Sisters of Charity to devote a plot of land on a nearby knob as a cemetery. Eventually, many people were buried there, but *Jeanette's* grave was never marked.

After the early Saturday morning funeral and Mass, the Davis family with Mary sat on the ground under a big tree.

"I don't want to go on," said Silas, Sr. The overwhelming passion that previously drove the man Westward had dissipated.

His son, sympathetic after watching his father lose and grieve for three women, said, "We can rest here for awhile. Just rest, Papa."

Silas, Sr. did not respond, but they did rest that day, attending a special Mass on Saturday evening for Immaculate Heart of Mary. While there, Margaret made her Confirmation, confession, and First Communion with Bishop Flaget, while Silas Davis, Sr. wept tears of joy and sorrow. Mary wondered whether she ever would have the opportunity to receive these sacraments.

The family rested all of Sunday, but on Monday morning continued their journey, from the Western edge of Bardstown to its center on Market Street, then North and out of town on Third Street. Silas Sr., even though tears flowed whenever he thought of *Jeanette,* could still walk and ride his mule. He mumbled that they needed to reach Louisville as soon as possible.

Most of the towns Mary had passed during this trip gave the impression that they had just *happened;* usually buildings sprang up haphazardly around a water source or other geographic feature. Bardstown was different in this respect; it had been carefully planned and laid out. The Georgian style, two story stone courthouse with cupola, built in the 1790s, was finer than any building she had seen since Lynchburg. The shutters covering its windows served as a signal, opened whenever court sessions were being held. In the space surrounding the courthouse, carefully arranged, appeared a large stone slave sale block, two gaols (one for debtors, one for criminals), county office buildings, Lawyers' Row, and a post office. Farther along, other edifices with gable end chimneys, tall twelve paned, wood shuttered windows, and plank, brick, and stone walls called to mind buildings Mary had seen in Denton. Richard Head's Tavern was one of these. Bardstown boasted a horse drawn fire engine (a hand lever powered piston water pumper), one of the first in Kentucky. Mary noticed a Catholic Church, St. Joseph's, according to Silas, Jr. who read the sign. The nuns had explained that it was too small to hold the numerous local parishioners, and that Mass was said at private homes around the area. All businesses, market stalls, and shops, overseen by a Market Master, clustered in orderly fashion on the North side of Bardstown.

Mary noticed that the people of Bardstown displayed in their dress, speech, and manner more of the benefits of civilization than did the people she had encountered in the mountains. The clothing, even of farmers and laborers, was better made, the cloth of a finer weave, with buttons and finished seams that gave shape to the garments. In the mountains, Mary had seen many people wearing little else beside animal skins with holes cut in appropriate places, belted with rope. Any fabric the mountain people owned tended to be coarse linsey-woolsey, tacked together with homespun thread. Here, the more well to do women wore calico and other mechanically woven cotton fabric. The dresses were copied from styles brought down the Ohio River from the East. Even the ubiquitous slaves, who wore rags, had obviously obtained those ragged garments from owners who had access to well made cloth.

The speech patterns and topics of conversation had changed. People of the mountains excelled in knowledge of their environment and in coaxing a living from it. But when strangers passed by, they gave the impression of being mentally slow. They craved news, and often their unsophisticated comments indicated wonder ("Well, I swan!") and incredulity at the goings on in the rest of the world. At Bardstown, those people most interested in the travelers seemed quite sharp, anticipating separating wayfarers from their money. Other people, concentrating on maintaining their self images and social positions, postured as they discussed politics, the weather, and local court cases. The only ones who seemed genuine to Mary, at ease with themselves and self contained, were the slaves who either labored at their jobs or sat in the sunshine, awaiting their masters' next orders. Having spent her entire life around black slaves, Mary felt that she understood these people and could relate to them better than to anyone else in the town.

Apparently, times were good at Bardstown. People, horses, even the ragged slaves appeared sleek and well fed. Buildings were maintained in good repair. Mary wondered why Silas did not settle here, and asked him.

Silas came out of his reverie long enough for a laconic reply: "Kentucky is a cursed land; I've lost two women here."

Later, feeling better, he explained to Mary that land regulation in Kentucky was so primitive that the pioneers there frequently lost their homesteads in court. Clear, indisputable titles to "Congress Lands" (government surveyed land) in Indiana were by far more advantageous. In addition, Indiana land cost considerably less per acre, although most of those acres required clearing to make them usable.

Monday night was spent at "the Crossroads" (later called Mt. Washington) on the "Old Cumberland Trail" that led from Louisville through Bardstown to Nashville, Tennessee. It was obvious to the young members of the family that Silas, Sr. wished to be alone with his grief. The weather had become unbearably hot, so in the evening they wandered along the banks of Floyd's Fork, the stream where they had camped.

Silas, Lydia, and Margaret, having witnessed the deaths of their own mothers, had experienced extreme grief. Not having bonded with *Jeanette,* however, they remained immune to any emotion beyond regret at her passing. Mary's own feelings vacillated between a paralyzing sense of loss and an urgent desire to escape the painful thoughts that cycled endlessly inside her skull. She sat on the stream bank, knowing that the other three would provide a diversion. They did not disappoint her.

Silas, Jr. used a low hanging branch to swing over a pool at a bend in the river, dropping into the water. He dared Lydia and Margaret to copy him and, when they did, he rewarded each with a wet kiss. Mary had observed the three of them behaving thus more and more often, always out of view of any supervising adults. Most of their activities could be described as "games": Hide and Seek, Snap and Catch 'em, Tag, etc. All of these frequently involved full body contact as well as intense displays of affection. Mary did not possess the experience nor the vocabulary to identify this as courtship behavior, but on some level she recognized it as a copy of the actions she had witnessed between adult couples. The fact that Lydia had warned Mary not to say anything to Silas, Sr. made Mary wonder whether she should do so. She felt very jealous of the other girls, but just when she couldn't stand being with them another moment, Silas, Jr. would smile at her, or even touch her hand, deepening her infatuation.

Next day the Davises completed their journey along the Wilderness Road. Several miles before entering Louisville, they crossed Beargrass Creek, then continued Northwest in Louisville to the Ohio River, where the trail they had followed so far ended above the Falls.

The Falls of the Ohio at that time comprised a two and one-half mile long stretch of rapids formed by an irregular ledge of rocks that extended in most places across the entire width of the river. There was, depending on the vacillating water level, about a twenty-five foot descent from the Eastern end of the Falls to the Western end. These Falls had proven so deadly to river traffic that every Ohio River traveler found it necessary to stop at Louisville, where a thriving business of transporting goods by land around the falls had developed. After the advent of the steamboat in 1811, multitudes of manufacturing, transportation, and distribution businesses had sprung up. For this reason, Louisville, founded 1778 by George Rogers Clark, was poised to become a key location for nineteenth century American commerce. It also would become a major hub of the Western expansion.

The influx of traffic on the river created news that continually evoked astonished comment. As an example, during the week before the Davis family arrived, the steamboat Enterprise had completed the upriver trip from New Orleans in record time, just twenty-five days.

"Ah, it's so beautiful," sighed Silas, gazing at the water. "The French call it 'La Belle Riviere.'"

Mary blinked in the bright light, then deeply inhaled the scent of the river. The broad Ohio, with its fish, water birds, and boat traffic, seemed more homelike than any place she had been since Farmville. She smiled for the first time in days, then turned her pony to follow Silas West on Main Street for thirteen blocks. To Mary's eyes, Louisville rivaled Petersburg for bustling busyness and prosperity, although the buildings themselves seemed new, crude, and raw by comparison. Mary saw a bank, City Hall, and many structures made of logs, of wood frame and planks, and of brick.

At last, they reached the Northwest corner of 10th and Main Streets, where Father Stephen Theodore Badin had, supported by a core group of Catholics, built St. Louis Church four years previously. According to Silas, Bishop Flaget at Bardstown was angry with Badin, who, having purchased with his own funds the land where the Louisville church stood, refused to sign ownership over to the diocese.

The Davis family made confession, then bought bread and cheese from a nearby market while waiting for Mass to begin. After Mass, Mary, having planned what she would say, made an opportunity to speak with the priest.

"Are you able to send a message to Archbishop Carroll in Maryland?" she asked him.

"Yes. Do you know Father Carroll?" he asked, in a surprised tone.

"I do know him. And he knows my family in Maryland, which is why I want a message sent. You see, my father and *maman* have died," here Mary choked, near tears, then continued, "and I want to let my grandfather know..."

Father Badin patted her, kindly, on the shoulder.

"I understand that Father Carrroll is in poor health," he said. Seeing Mary's anxious look, he hastily added, "But I will send the message at once. What names shall I write for your parents?"

"Robert and *Jeanette* Hobbs," Mary responded. "And Grandfather is Captain Joseph Gold of the *Burrows*."

"And what shall I say has become of you?"

"I am going to Indiana with Silas Davis; beyond that, I do not know..."

At that moment, more than anything else, Mary wished that Uncle James was at her side, assuring her that everything would be all right. She could almost see him, feel his strong hand on her shoulder.

Silas had come up behind Mary quietly, and added, "We'll be settling in Warrick County, high up Little Pigeon Creek. A letter to Darlington, the county seat, will find us."

Father Badin found a pen, ink, and parchment, and in a few minutes wrote a short letter.

"Is this right?" he asked Silas, handing him the paper.

"This will do. Are you satisfied, Mary?"

"Does it say for Father Carroll to let Grandfather know?" she asked, anxiously.

"Yes. It is the best we can do for now," Silas assured her.

Mary thought for a moment. It would cost *money* to send the message to Father Carroll. She opened the reticule at her wrist, selected a golden coin, and offered it to the priest. He stared at it, as if afraid it would bite him.

"It's all right, little lady," he said. "I'll just send the letter with Brother Brody next week. It won't cost anything."

"An offering, Father?" Mary suggested. "I'll give it as an offering."

"No, my child. You may need your money later on."

Silas stared at the priest, amazed. He had *never* seen a priest refuse money before. Then he glanced at the coin, and understood. It was *pirate's gold*, undoubtedly obtained through murder and violent robbery.

"Come, Mary," he said. "We must go."

The family traveled toward the Western outskirts of town, seeking a camping area. Local tavern keepers, trying to generate more business, had limited the places for camping. But the resourceful Silas, having been here before, knew where the boatmen camped along the wharfs, and headed there. He did, however, caution the girls to stay close and not wander off alone.

"Not all these men are fine, upstanding citizens," he warned.

At daybreak, Silas wandered the wharfs, seeking transport down river toward the family's destination in Indiana Territory. At noon he returned, bringing more bread, ham and cheese. While they were eating, he explained his mission.

"We need to travel four days down river. It wouldn't pay to *purchase* a flatboat; we just aren't going far enough. We *could* go down by land, then ferry across the river, or ferry across here, to Clarksville, and go down by land on the Indiana side, but that could take weeks. We could go by steamboat, but the animals...we need them on the farm. Travel by river will be faster and easier, and I intend to find a way..." He found nothing that day, however, and the family rode into Louisville for evening Mass.

Silas, because of *Jeanette's* death, had her money and also money from her jewelry that he sold in Louisville. It apparently never occurred to him that these comprised Mary's inheritance, and should have been preserved for her. However, he *had* taken responsibility for her welfare, and doubtless felt that he was managing the money in Mary's best interest. Mary never found out how much he had received from her mother, nor did she collect any of it. In any case, Silas by nature was averse to spending much money at Louisville. He intended to use it to purchase land, once he reached Indiana.

Silas, Sr. and Jr. spent the rest of the day, until time for Mass, scouting the local boatyards, the river bank, and lumber yards, locating materials. After Mass, the Davis men moved the family's campsite to a spot down river, well screened by trees and shrubbery. They waited there until full dark, then disappeared, taking the mules, and were gone most of the night. The morning light revealed, neatly stacked, squared off logs, rope, metal spikes, and expensive looking tools.

"Borrowed," was the only explanation either Davis would give. Mary formed the opinion that the two Davis men would have made outstanding pirates; all they lacked were the costumes and the desire for true wealth.

They apparently felt it important to incorporate all the materials into their project as rapidly as possible, and set to work immediately after breakfast. Under their efficient hands, the base for a small Kentucky flatboat, or "broadhorn" took shape.

Friday morning revealed more materials beside the river: Planks, chain, wooden pegs, and long wooden poles. Although tired from their exertions and from lack of sleep, the men set to work at dawn, and took breaks only for meals and for evening Mass. On Saturday, they worked all day and into the evening past full dark, knowing they could rest all of Sunday.

The flatboat quickly took its final form, and Mary looked at it closely. This craft resembled a raft more than a boat. Its base was made of the squared off logs, roped together. Wood planks topped the logs, providing a platform with upright supports attached. The canvas tarps that had served the family as shelter across two states were fastened to these. (As Mary watched them stretch the canvas, she realized that Silas had very likely filched it from a sailing vessel somewhere along the Chesapeake. Mary had of course been carefully taught never to take anything without paying for it; Silas seemed never to have heard about this rule.) Posts attached to the sides, front and back of the raft would support the "sweeps" or oars necessary for steering. Mary had never seen a craft quite like it; it was altogether different from any of the Chesapeake Bay boats and from the Virginia canal bateaux.

"The Ohio is treacherous," Silas, Sr. explained to Mary, when she asked him about the difference. "It winds and twists for a thousand miles, from Pittsburgh to Cairo, and in no season is it ever the same; hardly ever is it the same from month to month. For three months of the year it's frozen; for the other nine it's either flooding or too dry. Deep bottomed boats and unmaneuverable bateaux would run aground in a minute here. Experience has shown this design to be the best method of travel in shallow, swift water, where rocks, submerged trees and other debris pose a constant threat."

While the men worked on the raft, Mary, Lydia, and Margaret strolled along the river front, noting the variety of goods being loaded and unloaded. Imports included bales of cotton and wool; kegs of salt fish; cases of wine and preserves; barrels of indigo, fish oil, rice, and molasses; bags of allspice, pepper, tea, and coffee; ceroons of cochineal; demijohns of lime juice; boxes of crockery, steel and pig copper; hogsheads of sugar; as well as bolts of cloth including nankeens, calimancoes, dimities, tamboured and jaconet muslin, Bertha lace; and ready made clothing such as paisley shawls and French heeled slippers. Exports included hemp (for rope making, although Silas Davis was fond of smoking it in a pipe), tobacco, bearskins, pork, cornmeal, corn whiskey, and barrels of salt.

Later, Mary accompanied the Davis girls into Louisville itself. Seeking to please them, she used one of the golden coins from her reticule to purchase peppermint candy, which she shared. The proprietor stared after Mary; what she had given him was *pirates' gold*, worth far more than the small sack of candy she had purchased. He bit the coin to test it, then shrugged. He couldn't help it if someone wanted to overpay him – he worked hard; he *deserved* a break.

At that time, the bustling city included twenty-four mercantile stores where one could purchase the imports visible at the wharves, plus the local products. In one section clustered the shops of skilled workers such as the silversmith, coppersmith, two printers, a chair and furniture maker, sign and house painter, tailor, blacksmith, coach maker, and baker. A newspaper was published every Monday evening, and there was a theater where traveling troups of actors and musicians performed on an irregular schedule. In addition to the Catholic church, there was a Methodist meeting house.

Educational institutions included Mr. Hill's Lancastrian Academy and Mr. Elliott's Female Academy. Piano lessons were available. A sign over a door proclaimed, "T.W. Ruble, Physician and Surgeon." On the outskirts of town lay the industrial establishments, including a brewery, six brickyards, a tan yard, two tobacco manufactories, a carding and spinning mill, a soap maker, nail and tinware makers, as well as a steam sawmill.

The Ohio River

By Monday noon the flatboat was nearing completion. After evening Mass, the men used the mules to launch it, making it fast to trees at the water's edge. That night the Davis men slept aboard the boat in order to guard it, and before dawn everyone and everything (including the two mules and three horses) were loaded. By the time the sun crested the horizon on Tuesday, the Davises and Mary had begun floating down river. Silas, Sr. took the rear sweep, keeping them on course, but he required his son as well as the girls to keep watch and to help avoid water hazards by working the other oars.

Mary at first was nervous about riding so close to water level. As long as she did not stare directly at the water, she felt none of the motion sickness that had plagued her aboard the *Burrows*. However, the other boats she had been in were built much higher, with sides to prevent accidental dunkings, and the speed of travel therefore had seemed much slower. Even though the flatboat only averaged three to four miles per hour, she felt as if they were speeding so rapidly down river that there was no hope of avoiding disaster. There was so much debris in the water! During her passage through Maryland and Virginia, the waterways had been clear. After awhile, though, she relaxed enough so that she could look across the water to the river banks. Compared to the friendly, long civilized banks of the Choptank, the rough banks of the wild Ohio threatened unexpected dangers. Only occasionally could evidence of people be seen, usually high atop a bluff, far above water level. Silas explained that flooding along the Ohio was a recurring problem, and that buildings along the water's edge were often swept away. Mary had never heard of such a thing on the Choptank.

Silas put out lines for fish, and at the end of each day the family kindled a fire on shore and enjoyed a feast, usually baked catfish or sturgeon. Some of these creatures were so large that they could not possibly eat all the meat.

The first night, they stopped near the future site of Mauckport, Indiana. Wednesday night found them at what became Derby, Indiana, and Thursday night they stayed at the village of Troy, near the mouth of Anderson River.

Troy, precariously clinging to a shelf of land under a protective sandstone hill, at least had buildings, and people. One of the first Ohio River villages established in Indiana below the Falls of the Ohio at Louisville, Troy had been surveyed and laid out three months before, with ninety-six lots and a public square. Not much was available at Troy in the way of provisions, but Silas seemed not to care; he was so close to his ultimate goal that he could, as he put it, "smell Little Pigeon Creek."

Indiana

The Indiana Territory had been carved from the Northwest Territory in 1800, an irregular rectangle enclosing an area of 36,291 square miles. At that time it contained 5,641 white people, hundreds of black slaves, and uncounted thousands of Indians. A very few white settlements, most designated as "forts" and garrisoned by United States Troops, dotted the maps at strategic locations.

By 1810 the white population of Indiana had reached 24,520, and the death of Tecumseh at the 1813 Battle of the Thames opened an opportunity for more whites to flood the area.

Most white farmers had, because of the Indian presence, entered the territory cautiously, settling along the Ohio River. As their numbers and confidence grew, they moved inland, at first confining their homesteads to an irregular U shaped Southern third of the territory. (The upward sides of the U were formed by Northern settlements along the Wabash River on the West, along the Whitewater River on the East.) This Southern portion had been taken from the Indians by William Henry Harrison and others by means of vigorous military campaigns followed by various treaties.

At this juncture Mary and the Davises arrived on their raft. Like other pioneer farmers, Silas had responded to what seemed an unlimited opportunity. Teeming with a wide variety of wildlife, the rich soil of Indiana's rolling hills and flatlands shouted a promise of endless bountiful harvests.

Late on a Friday afternoon, the Davises poled their raft into the mouth of Little Pigeon Creek, where Silas made his boat fast to a tree for the night. Saturday was spent poling the raft far upstream (everyone, including Mary, worked very hard at this), where the animals were used to haul it onto land.

Looking up the hill toward the woods where he had blazed trees, marking his claim the year before, Silas said to the children, "You're home. We'll tear apart the boat, then build our cabin up there, because of this." He knelt, grasping a handful of dirt, and showed them, proudly, "This is the richest bottom land in the world. The creek floods in spring, replenishing the soil."

The family spent the evening clearing a space at the top of the bluff, where they constructed a three sided enclosure of dead branches and brush, covered by canvas. Silas kindled a bonfire on the open side, which, he claimed, would "discourage" the bears and wolves. They ate their first meal in the new homestead, more leaf wrapped, unseasoned baked fish (of which Mary was growing weary) with dandelion and burdock greens. The animals grazed until full dark. Then, for protection, they were secured inside the enclosure with the family. Late that night, lying within her bedroll, wishing away wild animals, Mary remembered that it was her birthday, June 17th.

A few miles South of Brussels, Belgium, near the small town of Waterloo, Napoleon Boneparte waited out that night before his defeat in one of the most famous battles of all time. His fate was to be decided in a muddy field of clover and rye, one mile long and three miles wide. Four days later, after retreating to Grandmére's native Paris, the former emperor abdicated for the second time, plotting to escape to the United States. Once again, in an attempt by the European allies to stabilize France, Mary's relatives of the Bourbon dynasty were restored to power.

Next day, Sunday, the Davises and Mary ate a hasty, cold breakfast at dawn. Then they rode the horses and mules, following the creek (sometimes riding *in* the creek) back to the Ohio River. There, they came to a partially cleared trace that led along the river for a mile to the Warrick County seat, Darlington. Mary, having recently toured many small, new towns, was unimpressed by this one; no stores nor businesses had yet made their appearance. According to Silas, individuals provided merchandise and services from private homes on an irregular basis. The lack of a post office worried her; how would a message from the Golds make its way to the Davis homestead?

During the previous year, the General Assembly of Indiana Territory had divided Warrick County into thirds, organizing Posey County from the Western portion and Perry County from the Eastern third. The Assembly at that time appointed a commission to establish a new county seat for Warrick. Located on the Ohio four miles above the future site of Newburgh, Darlington included three hundred acres of partially cleared land. This space had been divided into town lots by the County Agent, and auctioned during the fall of 1814, four of the lots being reserved as the town square.

The first public building commissioned had been the two story jail, which occupied its own town lot. It featured double log walls (containing six inches of rock and gravel fill), three inch thick plank doors doubled and riveted together so as to be six inches thick, and iron barred, nine inch square windows. To Mary, the jail appeared strong enough to hold the fiercest criminals imaginable. Construction of a courthouse was planned for the coming November (the best time in the agrarian calendar for such projects), with the contract to be let to the lowest bidder.

Half a dozen private residences were scattered around the town on strategically chosen lots. Silas led the way to one of these, occupied by his brother, John Davis. Mary immediately took a strong dislike to the man. He was nothing like Silas; it turned out that the two were step-brothers. John was well educated, a barrister, but he was nasty of temperament, careless of his personal hygiene, and, Mary thought, ugly. His yellowish gray hair was receding so that the top of his head was nearly bald, although on the back of his head it grew long, tangled, lice infested, and greasy. His face, dominated by a large, bulbous red nose, seemed frozen in a snarl even when he was attempting to be pleasant. His teeth had rotted. His watery pale eyes boded no good for anyone or anything.

The best part about the visit, from Mary's perspective, was the abundance of good food available at "Uncle" John's house. Black slaves ran the place, keeping a large garden, a barn full of chickens, sheep, hogs, and a cow. John also owned land outside the town, where the beginnings of an orchard and fields of wheat, flax, tobacco, hay, hemp, and knee high corn promised a bountiful harvest for the fall.

When Phoebe Elvira, the cook, saw Silas and his family arriving, she flew into activity. Within an hour, the table was spread with more food than Mary had seen at one time since leaving the convent at Bardstown. Within another half hour, Mary had eaten so much that she thought she would burst. Later, she had trouble recalling everything she had ingested, but she definitely remembered the mulberry cobbler, because she had scarcely tasted anything so sweet since leaving Maryland. Phoebe Elvira seemed unused to compliments about her cooking; she reacted with embarrassment when Silas praised the food. Uncle John directed a scowl at her, and she fled the room.

Margaret remarked, "I didn't know slaves were permitted within the Indiana Territory."

This topic had been discussed thoroughly by other travelers around the evening campfires in Kentucky during the family's journey.

John sneered, "They're not. But how are they to know it's illegal? Old William Henry Harrison favors slavery, along with most people in the western part of this territory. Ten years ago, slavery *was* legal here; perhaps it will be again." He leered at Mary, inquiring of Silas, "Where'd you pick up this pretty little miss?"

Silas summarized the demise of Mary's parents, adding, "And, strange to say, you know her great-uncle."

"Who's that?"

"Remember your old buddy James Hobbs?"

"Yes, yes, I do. Is he anywhere about?" John seemed worried by that possibility.

"No. But the way things are in Maryland, he's hard put to make ends meet. I saw him six months ago, and he was planning to move East of here, up the Whitewater Valley."

Mary looked up, surprised. Then she recalled that her father's brothers, those whose Methodist wives opposed slavery, had also expressed interest in moving farther West than Virginia. They had reasoned that flat Ohio River Valley bottom land would be much easier to farm than the rocky hills of the Clinch Valley.

John responded, "Well, as long as the Hobbs stay on the Whitewater, we'll get along just fine. However, I can always take this one off your hands. She'd brighten things around the house." He stretched a long arm toward Mary, who backed up.

Silas said, "You just keep your distance. Mary, here, is very precious to me."

John cackled and winked, saying, "I'll just bet."

The conversation had made Mary nervous, but Silas' assurance that she belonged to him calmed her somewhat. She wanted nothing to do with John Davis. And there was always the possibility that Uncle James Gold would come to get her, or if the other Hobbs families moved to Indiana…maybe she could return home! She did not fully comprehend the impossibility of this, even though she knew that all the places she remembered as "home" now contained strangers, and that the closest surviving members of her family now lived elsewhere.

After dinner, Phoebe Elvira found clothing for Lydia, Margaret, and Mary from a trunk full of garments left by John's previous wives. She also let them know where in the town they could purchase cloth, either ready made, or homespun. But even as the girls thanked the slave woman, they realized that Silas, Sr. would never let them spend the money on such luxuries. Phoebe folded the garments tightly, and stuffed them into the girls' saddlebags so that John would not see what she had given them.

It was characteristic of Silas and of his brother that, even though they lived only about six miles apart, there was little contact between the two during the following months; Silas would never have asked for help; John would never have offered it. Therefore, Silas' family proceeded as if there were no relative living nearby. It was also characteristic of the two that John expected all work to be done for him by others; Silas liked being self sufficient. Mary learned later that Silas opposed slavery, while she, like her mother, assumed that slaves comprised a necessary feature of a civilized household. She sometimes wondered how *Jeanette* would have coped with farm life on the frontier.

Silas proved as efficient and hardworking at organizing a new homestead as he was at everything else. Within a month, the family had cleared nearly two acres. The acre along the creek had been covered in brush and was comparatively easy to clear, despite the presence of snakes; it was intended for the following year's crops. The other acre, containing dead trees that Silas had girdled during the previous year's visit, surrounded the space designated for the cabin. Felling these dead trees improved safety and made construction possible. Silas had brought the necessary tools for this work from Louisville, and encouraged everyone to use them. Clearing additional acres would have to continue for years before this farm could support the family and turn a profit, but Silas declared that they had made a fine start.

Working dawn to dusk during the long, steamy days of summer, the family tore apart the flatboat and put together from its pieces a log dwelling with attached lean-to for the animals. The cabin measured twenty feet square, and had a dirt floor. A rear exit gave onto a plank roofed outdoor kitchen and laundry. There was no furniture apart from upturned logs used as chairs and a few warped planks balanced on taller, though uneven, upturned logs that served as a precarious table.

Clay dug from the creek bank served as mortar that held together the cabin's rude hearth and chimney of field stone. All jobs relating to this clay fell to Mary, including stuffing it, mixed with plant fibers, between the logs of the cabin walls as "chinking." After weeks of this project, Mary's hands were so discolored that she despaired of ever cleaning them. In Maryland, she had never been permitted, much less encouraged, to tackle such a messy task, and would have been barred from the dinner table until her hands were spotless.

Desperate for variety in the diet, the family members combed the local woods and the stream banks for edible plants (berries, nuts, roots, and greens) and for anything they could kill. The wild mammals tasted terrible in the summer heat, so, until fall, they avoided those and stuck with wild birds, crawdads, frogs, snakes, and fish. Passenger pigeons at times were plentiful and easily obtained, but the enormous flocks did not stay in the same locations for long. The family's diet lacked milk, grains or flour, and salt or any other flavoring. All of them lost weight; even the clothing from Phoebe Elvira was wearing out, and there was no time nor would Silas spend money to replace it. Soon they resembled the people Mary had seen in the mountains who wore little besides belted animal skins. It was a good thing there was no mirror available; Mary would have been ashamed of her tangled hair and ragged appearance.

Silas did keep up with the ecclesiastical calendar, however, and the family solemnly celebrated the Transfiguration of the Lord on August 6th, as well as Assumption (Feast of Mary) on Tuesday the 15th.

Also in August, the former Emperor Napoleon was sent by the British to the South Atlantic island of St. Helena, where he spent the remaining five years of his life. It turned out that Admiral George Cockburn, who had during the War of 1812 invaded Chesapeake Bay, became Napoleon's gaoler. Cockburn served as governor of that island prison for a year.

After the downfall of his persecutor Napoleon, Pope Pius VII magnanimously offered a refuge in the Vatican to the members of the Bonaparte family. Princess Letitia, the deposed emperor's mother, lived there; likewise did Napoleon's brothers Lucien and Louis and his uncle, Cardinal Fesch. So forgiving was Pius that upon hearing of the severe captivity in which the imperial prisoner was held at St. Helena, he requested Cardinal Consalvi to plead for leniency with the Prince-Regent of England. When he was informed of Napoleon's desire for the ministrations of a Catholic priest, the Pope sent him a chaplain.

For the Davis family, the late Indiana summer and fall rushed past in feverish preparation for the winter months. More of the trees Silas had girdled during the previous year had to be felled, cut into usable lengths, and hauled near to the cabin for use as winter fuel. They all put in many hours pulling the long grasses that grew along the creek bank, drying them, and storing the resulting animal fodder in the loft of the cabin. Fish was easily obtained, so Silas constructed a smoke house in which to preserve a quantity of it. He also "found" several hogs in the woods, escapees from another farm. Ignoring the earmarks that identified them, Silas quickly slaughtered these and hid the meat amongst the fish in his smokehouse.

He led the family in remembering the Birth of Virgin Mary on September 8th, as well as Celebration of the Holy Cross and Mass of the Archangels on the 14th and 29th.

"Next year we'll make garden," Silas promised. "We'll manure an area for it during the winter, dig it in next spring, and plant whatever seed I can get my hands on. We'll have corn, melon, pumpkin, several kinds of squash and beans, peas, onion, potatoes, beets, turnips…" The thought of familiar, domesticated foods made all their mouths water, as he continued, "Also in the spring we'll plant fruit trees, so that we don't have to scour the forests for wild persimmon, pawpaw, and crab apple."

Mary noticed that he completely ignored the need for herbs, which both her grandmothers had insisted were necessary to decent cooking, and which even Phoebe Elvira used as a matter of course. Spices were out of the question, but what about honey…?

As if he had read her mind, Silas added, "There are bees in the woods that we can rob for honey. But it's best if we wait, build a hive, and start our own colony when they swarm in the spring. And we'll get a cow, for milk and butter next year."

Everything seemed to be next year, next year, and Mary began to realize that the agricultural calendar would rule her life in this place. All things began in Spring, and they had missed it, for this year.

The family celebrated All Saints' and All Souls' Days on Wednesday and Thursday, November 1st and 2nd. It seemed that fall would go on forever, but wintry weather arrived with a sudden rush at the Feast of Christ the King on November 26th.

The Davises found a grove of persimmon trees, where the freeze-dried fruits tasted like raisins dipped in honey. Whenever Silas brought in a freshly killed deer, the family would spit the ribs on sharp sticks and roast them for a quick and delicious meal. However, heavy snowfalls soon put an end to the easy gathering of wild foods. Silas, the eternal optimist, promised that things could only get better, if they held out for spring.

Despite the unremitting hard labor required for the family's survival, Silas saw to it that they all remained cheerful and cooperative. At the time, Mary found this unremarkable, but in later years she thought deeply about Silas Davis and his ability to keep the family working together under such difficult circumstances. Each family member recognized that he or she was vital to the effort to establish themselves in this wilderness. Each night, no matter how weary they were, no matter how terrible the weather nor how discouraging the day's events, they recited the Rosary together, and Sundays had been reserved for rest. If not for these routines, and for Silas' loving care, the Davises surely would have given in to despair during the following disastrous year.

At Darlington, the new $200 log courthouse neared completion, and the first court was held there early in December. The building measured twenty feet square, by eighteen feet (one and one-half stories) high. It had three windows downstairs, two above; court furniture including a bar, jury box and judges' bench; two plank doors, and a shingle roof.

At Corydon, the Indiana capital, the impetus for Indiana statehood was growing in the General Assembly. Indiana had originally petitioned Congress for statehood in 1811, but the population proved too small, and the War of 1812 had interfered with the process.

Indiana Territorial Governor Thomas Posey, appointed in 1813 by James Madison, was born in 1750 in Fairfax County, Virginia on a farm adjacent to Mt. Vernon.

Posey, among others from Knox and Gibson counties, voiced opposition to Indiana statehood. They claimed that Indiana lacked the financial resources to function as an independent state, that it should continue to draw two-thirds of its support from the United States government. But what they meant was that they preferred for personal wealth to determine policy; for example, many of them still favored slavery. They favored the centralized system of politics (established by William Henry Harrison) that would allow the status quo to maintain its power. But Posey lacked the charisma and the political clout to carry this point of view. The best he and his followers could do was to cast aspersions on those who favored statehood, calling them "empty babblers, democratic to madness, having incessantly the people in their mouths and their dear selves in their eyes..."

The General Assembly refused to listen to their objections. Jonathan Jennings, a passionate, well liked "man of the people" had been taking political choices directly to the voters since 1809. He strongly opposed the system of wealth as political influence initiated by William Henry Harrison. At this time, the notion of campaigning by visiting the voters and relating to them on a face to face basis was new, but it worked. Those General Assembly delegates elected from the Eastern portion of the territory supported Jennings' views, and the move for statehood prevailed.

In late November, Archbishop John Carroll died, and his large funeral procession at Baltimore included people from all walks of life. The funeral Mass was offered in St. Peter's Cathedral and the body was laid temporarily in the chapel of St. Mary's Seminary until 1824, when the cathedral crypt was ready.

Advent Season began on Sunday December 3rd, and Silas surprised his family by trading venison for tallow candles that he set into a makeshift Advent Wreath chopped from pine boughs. They celebrated the Feast of the Immaculate Conception on December 8th, then the second Sunday of Advent on December 10th.

In Washington, Congress on December 11th received a petition for statehood from Indiana's General Assembly. Because the thirteen counties of Indiana's population had passed the magic number - 60,000 - specified by the Northwest Ordinance for territories seeking statehood, it qualified for admittance to the Union as an equal member.

Gaudette Sunday was December 17th. Instead of the rejoicing required by the calendar, Mary secretly cried, remembering Father Carroll's lovely rose colored vestments and the beauty of the celebration at *Grand-mère's* house. But she managed to rejoice with the others on the fourth Sunday of Advent, December 24th. Together they sang, prayed, and at midnight ate a small ham that Silas had smoked and kept hidden until that time. On Christmas morning each of Silas' children found a present beside his or her sleeping pallet: The girls got wooden bead jewelry strung onto rawhide thongs, while Silas, Jr. received a new leather sheath for his hunting knife. Mary put on as cheerful a face as possible as she sadly recalled her pearl jewelry that, stored with *Maman's,* had been sold in Louisville.

On December 28th, Jonathan Jennings, Indiana Territorial Representative to Congress, laid a memorial for Indiana statehood before Congress. This matter was referred to a committee, of which Jennings was named chairman.

On Little Pigeon Creek, Mary celebrated the Solemnity of the Holy Family while watching the year draw to a close. Thus began the longest winter she would ever know.

1816

The Indiana weather seemed unreasonably harsh as the Davises celebrated the Solemnity of Mary on January 1st.

On January 5th, in Washington, the Congressional committee for Indiana statehood sent a bill to the House of Representatives requesting permission for the citizens of Indiana Territory to form a constitution. Five other states had already completed this procedure; Indiana would follow the same legal steps, borrowing freely from their examples.

By Epiphany, on Saturday January 6th, and the Baptism of the Lord on the following day, Mary could not remember the last time she felt warm. Although she had experienced extreme weather in Maryland, the cold West winds there had been ameliorated by warm air currents from the South. The Eastern Shore houses where Mary had lived were better constructed and better insulated than the Davis cabin. In Maryland warm clothing had been easily available, and slaves had kept the hearths blazing as a matter of course.

Candlemas on Friday, February 2nd, came and went. Silas Davis, Sr., kept encouraging Mary, along with the others, to warm up by chopping wood outdoors, to eat more of the greasy bear he had shot (it tasted *horrible*), and to pray for spring. Ash Wednesday fell on February 28th, and the family had trouble finding anything to give up for Lent. The children tried to choose things they did not have, such as dairy products. Silas sternly informed them that this defeated the purpose of Lent. Finally, they decided, collectively, to give up their evening game and story time in favor of Rosary repetitions and other prayer. Silas assured them that God would reward this sacrifice by sending the springtime early.

Solemnity of Joseph, husband of Mary, on March 19th saw slightly warmer weather. By Laetare Sunday on March 24th, and the Annunciation next day, it seemed that God heard their prayers. The weather warmed, and the Davises planted seeds for which Silas had bartered wolf scalps. Not every vegetable would germinate in cool weather, so they planted only lettuce, cabbage, radish, turnip, peas, and, in the field by the creek, hay seed harvested the previous fall. Silas tapped maple trees for the sweet sap, but the family lacked the equipment required to boil the liquid to syrup. Grateful that they had not given up sweets for Lent, the family drank it as it was. Palm Sunday fell on April 7th.

Four days later, Congress passed an Enabling Act permitting Indiana Territory to hold a constitutional convention.

The Davises celebrated Easter by picking spring greens and roasting a suckling fawn that Silas found in the woods. Mary thought that she had never tasted anything so good. They all stayed up late playing games, enjoying each others' company with an intensity that stayed with Mary forever. *This was how families should feel about each other.*

On the following Friday, President James Madison signed the Enabling Act. Jonathan Jennings returned to Indiana, eager to begin work toward the new state's constitution.

By this time the plants in the Davis garden (on a South facing slope) had pushed hopefully through the soil, and the growing hay measured a few inches in height. Trees budded and blossomed; insects, plants, animals and birds began their spring rituals of life. Suddenly, temperatures plummeted and ice fell from the sky, coating everything. Green plants turned black; snow covered the ground for seventeen days during May.

On May 13th, in Darlington, the sheriff held an election at the new courthouse to choose Warrick County's delegate to the Indiana Constitutional Convention. Only taxpayers who had resided in Indiana for at least one year were eligible to vote, which eliminated Silas but included John Davis. Later, they heard that Daniel Grass, a farmer, lawyer, and justice of Ohio Township had been selected. Daniel, one of the first white men to enter the Warrick County area, had been orphaned, his parents killed by Indians. He had served in the Indian wars, as well as in several different positions in the government of Warrick County; he would travel to the convention at Corydon, Indiana, in June.

Because of the discussion surrounding the election, Mary became aware that Silas had not yet purchased the land where they lived. Technically, the family was "squatting" on their farm. Silas said that he was waiting for the price ($2 per acre) and the minimum number of acres (160) to go down. Jonathan Jennings was known to favor squatters' rights, and Silas hoped that legislation would be passed to help them acquire their land more easily. He had buried all the family's money in a box under his bed, and seemed to have forgotten its existence.

Ascension was celebrated on Thursday, May 23rd, but the Davises did not feel like celebrating. The frosts and cold continued. The family members appeared gaunt and wasted. Silas' cherished mules grudgingly ate chopped, dried fish; Happy and the other horses died when the fodder gave out. (Poor Happy had been boiled and eaten, his hide tanned for leather, despite Mary's tears). Garden seeds would not germinate; woodland plants thrust skyward, some trying to blossom, only to be repeatedly frostbitten into dormancy. Mary longed for the easy, rich life she had known in Maryland, but dared not say so; the others likewise struggled to restrain their complaints. Each night, the family prayed the Rosary; sometimes this ritual seemed the only thing holding them together.

This "year without a summer" presented an unexpected trial for pioneers across the Ohio River Valley. Not knowing about the eruption of the volcano Tambora in the Dutch East Indies the previous year, and its sun blocking effect, no one understood the weather. Even if they had understood the cause, nothing could have saved their agriculture based economy. Thousands of families in their first year on the frontier were driven to extreme measures to stay alive. If not for the abundance of edible wild animals, many surely would have perished.

Pentecost was celebrated on Sunday, June 2nd, followed by Trinity Sunday on June 9th.

By June 10th, the weather was still quite cold; snow fell as forty-three Indiana Constitutional Delegates gathered at Corydon. Thirteen existing Indiana counties were represented: Clark, Dearborn, Franklin, Gibson, Harrison, Jefferson, Knox, Perry, Posey, Switzerland, Warrick, Washington, and Wayne. Because the capitol building was still under construction, the men met in the "courthouse on the hill." This wooden structure at the Northwest corner of Capitol and High streets had been converted from a partially finished house into a courthouse used both by Harrison County and by Indiana Territorial officials.

Corpus Christi fell on Thursday, June 13th, and the Davises dedicated the entire day to prayer for warm weather.

The Indiana Constitutional Convention elected officers: Jonathan Jennings, President, William Hendricks, Secretary, Henry Batman, Doorkeeper, and five Assistant Secretaries. They divided the elected delegates into twelve committees to form Articles of Constitution. Then the men set to work, taking the United States Constitution as well as the constitutions of other states as their models. Within days, at about mid-month, the weather returned briefly to what was considered normal, then abruptly rose above normal; temperatures at Corydon reached 90° Fahrenheit. Unused to the heat, the sweating delegates gathered out of doors in the shade of a large elm tree on Big Indian Creek. Daniel Grass fell ill, was excused from the Convention on June 19th, and returned to Warrick County. Because many of the delegates were farmers, they became distracted, longing to return home in order to plant crops.

The Davises, like other farm families, rejoiced at the warm temperatures, which proved to be a cruel hoax. They celebrated Sacred Heart of Jesus on Friday, June 21st, and Immaculate Heart of Mary next day, with wild abandon. But no sooner had they planted their last seeds (corn, pumpkins, beans, melons) than the temperatures fell once more.

At last, on June 29th, the work of the Indiana Constitutional Convention was finished. The constitution was sent to a printer at Louisville. Copies were ordered for the United States President, and for Congressional leaders.

Independence Day, usually a time of celebration, turned bitterly cold. Mary watched Silas standing over his drooping seedlings, tears of frustration staining his face. Luckily, the Davises had put off obtaining livestock; across the region farm animals starved or froze to death. Wild animals and birds suffered the same fates; many became unnaturally tame, seeking shelter and food inside peoples' homes and barns.

August 5th had been chosen by the Constitutional Convention as Indiana's first state and county election day. Jonathan Jennings defeated Thomas Posey, and was elected first Governor; Christopher Harrison became Lieutenant Governor. A lone Congressman, William Hendricks, was selected to represent Indiana in Washington, D.C. Each county elected its own sheriff, coroner, and representative to the Indiana General Assembly; Warrick County selected Ratliff Boon, a former gunsmith, as its representative.

By Tuesday, August 6th, the Transfiguration of the Lord, Silas Davis was finding it necessary to daily assure himself and his children that God had not abandoned them. This was a test; God would reward their faithfulness. They celebrated Assumption on Thursday, August 15th, in a kind of desperation.

The weather did not improve during this time. Sleet one-half inch thick on the ground was reported over widespread areas in August, as well as heavy frosts during the four months after that. It became clear that there would be no harvest; people made contingency plans for winter; many sought the solace of religious faith; others returned to the East from whence they had come.

On September 14th, for Celebration of the Holy Cross, the Davises traveled to Darlington to visit Uncle John. After one of Phoebe Elvira's enormous meals (delicious even though fresh ingredients were severely limited), Silas accepted his brother's offer of premium hemp for his pipe, and sat back to talk. Stung by what he took from John as insults to his ability to care for his family, knowing that his brother was not likely to be pleased by the content of the new Indiana Constitution, Silas asked about it.

John rummaged through a box of fire kindling materials in the corner, coming up with the document. "I got a copy of the damned thing from Vincennes. It cost me a quarter, and I'm sorry I spent the money," he growled.

Silas began to read silently. After some minutes, he laid the booklet on the table, and Silas, Jr. asked, "What does it say?"

His father tossed the document to him, but summarized aloud what he had read for the benefit of the girls as well as to irritate his brother: "It has a Preamble and Bill of Rights reminiscent of the United States Constitution. It separates governmental power into three branches, but prohibits the current practice of letting the same person serve simultaneously in more than one branch. It quotes Jefferson: 'All power is inherent in the people,' and seems to make the General Assembly the most powerful branch. The governor has a three year term; the same man can only serve as governor for six of every nine years. He can veto legislation, but the Assembly can override his veto. The people of each county will elect their own sheriff and coroner every two years; the counties also choose their own judges and clerks. Of course, militia service is required from every able bodied white male between the ages of 18 and 45; that lets you off the hook, John, and you for a couple years, son! They say the state will support a system of education from township schools to university, but it doesn't explain how they will fund that plan." Looking around to make sure Phoebe Elvira was absent from the room, Silas added, softly, "And it prohibits slavery."

John's lips curled into a snarl, "It'll be a cold day in Hell before they can enforce that one! It doesn't say a word about previously obtained slaves, nor about their children, who are still under contract to their masters to the age of thirty-two under the old law." He leaned across the table toward Silas and hissed, "If I freed that lazy bunch of niggers this minute, they'd crawl back here in a week, starving and begging me to take them in!"

Mary doubted this, but dared not say so.

Silas responded mildly, "Nevertheless, it looks like slavery will never again be legal in this state. You might want to consider that…"

John shrugged, and in fact kept slaves for the remainder of his horrible life.

The Davises celebrated All Saints' Day and All Souls' Day on November 1st and 2nd, Friday and Saturday.

Indiana's Constitution was implemented upon passage, before Indiana formally became a state. Indiana's first General Assembly under its new constitution convened November 4th. Twenty-nine representatives and ten senators met at Corydon, where the new statehouse was ready to receive them. The forty feet square, two story blue limestone building served as the State Capitol for the next nine years. Its walls were two feet thick, and its ceilings measured fifteen feet from the floor. Each wall contained tall, evenly spaced, twenty-four paned windows; a cupola topped the roof. Two United States Senators, James Noble and Walter Taylor, were chosen by the Indiana General Assembly. The State of Indiana had begun with the following counties: Clark, Dearborn, Franklin, Gibson, Harrison, Jefferson, Knox, Perry, Posey, Switzerland, Washington, and Wayne. As white pioneers flooded the region, the legislature quickly approved the formation of three new Indiana counties: Jackson, Orange, and Ripley.

Most white people had come to Indiana for one reason: They wanted easy access to cheap, rich farmland. Virtually all whites in the Southern third of the state crouched there greedily, ready to pounce onto the rich Indian lands to the North. Very few among them (the Quakers and Catholic priests being notable exceptions) had any moral compunctions about swindling native populations, or about driving them from their ancestral lands. Most whites subscribed to the view that anything written into a legal treaty became morally justifiable. And whites referred to themselves as "the civilized population" of Indiana, their version of civilization being the only one recognized.

To please their constituency, Governor Jennings and other state officials pushed the federal government to force native peoples into new treaties. The most impetuous and downright stupid whites refused to wait for this process; they crossed the boundaries laid down by old treaties, squatting illegally on Indian lands. This put them into considerable danger from vengeful, bloodthirsty warriors who had not forgotten their glory days under Tecumseh. The government had no legal way to protect the squatters, although its judges had historically refused to use the law to protect Native Americans.

The other major problem facing the new state was that of transportation. Most farmers and merchants looked to water routes for moving their goods, but this was not practical everywhere in Indiana. Governor Jennings favored digging a canal on the Indiana side of the Falls of the Ohio opposite Louisville; he also pushed for federal funding of other canals in order to connect and deepen Indiana rivers.

During November the national elections were held; James Monroe, the highly qualified Democratic Republican candidate for President, defeated the Federalist nominee, Rufus King. Monroe's administration ushered in the "Era of Good Feeling" for a nation optimistic about its future.

The Feast of Christ the King fell on Sunday, November 24th; Advent began on Sunday, December 1st, and once again the Davises faithfully lit the first candle in their wreath.

On December 2nd, Congress opened in Washington D.C. with Indiana represented as a full and equal member; on December 11th, President Madison approved Indiana's admission into the union as the nineteenth state.

Ever since Thomas Jefferson had inserted the notion that "all men are created equal" into the national consciousness, Americans had struggled with the issue of slavery. Many notable Americans remained schizophrenic on the topic; even Jefferson retained his own slaves until his death.

Some people excused slavery and the mistreatment of black individuals and Indians on the basis that these were not actually people, but rather, high functioning animals. Others, even though they accepted the humanity of people different from themselves, remained completely incapable of visualizing a multiracial society. The concept of moving people of color (including Indians) away from white people, keeping them strictly separate, was widely advocated.

In Indiana, the new Constitution forbade black people to serve in the militia, vote, hold office, or testify in court except against other black people. One important legal right permitted in Indiana was that black people could own property. A number of black people, often as members of rural communities, acquired land and other property. Many became skilled workers such as blacksmiths, shoemakers, bricklayers, etc.

After the 1808 ban on importation of slaves to the United States, the fate of black people already living in North America (about two million, of which two hundred thousand were free persons) remained an issue. Two groups of whites with opposing views agreed upon a new idea: One group consisted of philanthropists, clergy and abolitionists who wanted to free black slaves and their descendants, providing them with the opportunity to return to Africa. The other group included slave owners who feared free black people and wanted to expel them from North America. The flaw in this effort was that most black people had little interest in leaving.

Representatives of both these groups came together, forming the American Colonization Society on December 21st. On that date, influential whites including James Monroe, Bushrod Washington, Andrew Jackson, Francis Scott Key, and Daniel Webster met at the Davis hotel in Washington D.C., with Henry

Clay presiding over the meeting. One week later, the Society members adopted a constitution. For the following three years, the Society relentlessly pressured Congress and the president for support. Ultimately, after thirty-one years, their efforts resulted in the creation of the West African nation, Liberia.

Sunday, December 22nd, saw the fourth Sunday of Advent. At the Davis farm, the family drew together, determined to survive another miserable winter. However, before they could celebrate Christmas, Silas Davis, Sr., weakened by poor diet and unrelenting cold, slipped while chopping a tree and seriously damaged his leg. By the time his son found him lying in the woods, the man had lost consciousness from blood loss and hypothermia, and he died in the cabin soon after being brought inside. Mary slumped in a corner, feeling Silas' spirit rise above her. Prayers for the dead crowded everything else from her brain:

Deus, qui nos patrem et matrem honorare praecepisti: Miserere clementer animabus patris et matris meae eorumque peccata dimitte: meque eos in aeternae claritatis gaudio fac videre. Per Christum Dominum nostrum, Amen.

O God, who hast commanded us to honor our father and mother: In Thy mercy have pity on the souls of my father and mother and forgive them their trespasses; and make me to see them again in the joy of everlasting brightness. Through Christ our Lord, Amen.

Silas, Jr. knew the importance of digging his father's grave six feet deep; this would prevent wolves from feeding on the corpse. It was necessary to build a bonfire in order to thaw the topsoil, after which the digging became easier. The young man would dig for awhile, then break down in tears until the girls led him inside, where he would stare into the flames of the hearth. The girls would dig for awhile, then everyone would gather inside to eat a little of the leathery, tasteless dried meat intended to last until spring. Then fear would overtake them all as night fell: Fear of the howling wilderness, fear of the long, cold winter ahead, fear of death and of the unknown. It seemed very natural and right that the young orphans should huddle together, comforting one another until dawn. No longer was there any authority directing the Davis girls to sleep separately from young Silas. By the time they got Silas, Sr. safely buried and said a makeshift service over him, Silas, Jr., Lydia, and Margaret were having sex every night while Mary lay by the fire a few feet away. Mary suffered; she realized that Silas, Jr. would never belong to her. Her prospects of living a good life seemed very dim.

1817

Because Silas, Sr. had always kept the calendar, his children quickly lost track of the date, as well as of the days of the week. The creek froze, eliminating fresh fish as food; then the contents of the smoke house were used up. Luckily, there was plenty of gunpowder and shot; Silas, Jr. became expert with the long rifle. The family's existence depended on his ability to shoot whatever wild animal or bird came in sight.

During that winter's legislative session, the Indiana General Assembly added four more counties: Daviess, Jennings, Pike, and Sullivan. Also, they appointed Warrick County's first board of commissioners to serve under the new state government.

In February, this first board of three men met at Darlington. They ordered an election to be held the first Monday in April. Each township would elect Justices of the Peace, and the county selected members for the state General Assembly at Corydon.

On March 4th, James Monroe was inaugurated President in Washington City. The president's House had not yet been reconstructed after the British burned it, so Monroe and his family were forced to set up housekeeping in a private residence on I Street.

With the onset of spring, the farmers of the Old Northwest Territory became anxious. Would there be a harvest this year? Young Silas Davis, following his father's example from the previous year, traded wolf scalps and other skins and furs for garden seeds. Unfortunately, the seeds cost three times as much as they had the year before, and they did not come with a guarantee of germination. The family obsessed over the garden plot, marking the location of every seed with a twig, guarding the planted seeds round the clock against birds, mice, and other critters. When the first green blades pushed through the soil, there was great celebration, followed by fear that the killing ice would return.

Sometime during the spring Lydia and Margaret realized that they were each expecting a baby, and there was hushed discussion of this whenever they thought Mary was not listening. Finally, they announced that visitors would be told that Margaret's husband had died, and that Lydia and Silas had married "back East." This explanation would have worked for all but one visitor to the farm, and he arrived in June.

John Davis, not having heard from his brother since the previous fall, had exerted himself to discover the reason. Upon being told that his brother was dead, John swung down from his horse, pulled up his sagging trousers, stalked inside the cabin, and seated himself on a log "chair."

"Exactly how do you plan to stay alive out here?" he asked his nephew.

"'Zactly the way we have been," answered Silas, Jr. "We ain't give up yet."

"It won't work," said Uncle John. "You are living like animals out here; it's impossible for you to support them all. Have you paid for this land yet?"

Silas shook his head, and Uncle John continued, "Why don't you give me your father's money, and I'll take care of it for you?"

This sounded like a very bad idea to Mary, and she saw Silas shake his head again.

John said, "You can't continue as you are. And unless I miss my guess, your problems will multiply in the fall." He tossed his head in the direction of Lydia and Margaret, and asked, his lips curling in disgust, "They're with child, aren't they?"

Silas, Jr. had inherited his father's stubbornness and self sufficient attitudes.

"That's none of your business, Uncle. We're doing just fine," he said, convinced that the worst of the family's trials had passed. "And we don't require your help."

His uncle leaned toward him and threatened, "What if I send the sheriff out here to check things out? He can kick you off this farm, throw you in jail for illegal congress with these young ladies."

Mary saw a shadow of fear cross Silas' eyes.

John went on, "We can't have this kind of behavior in our brand new state, and the sheriff doesn't have enough real criminal cases to keep him busy..."

"You can't take me away from them! They'd starve without me."

"You'll have time to think about that while you're in jail!" Then, a crafty look crossed John's face, and he changed his tone, as if offering a great opportunity, "Or, if you like, you could let me look out for the sweet little one over there, the pretty one. And I'd forget all about mentioning this to my friend the sheriff."

Silas said, "No, you wouldn't send the sheriff."

"Oh, yes I would. Give her to me, and she'll have food, and clothes, and a good life. Or don't, and I send the sheriff; all of them will starve."

Silas stood, silent, as Uncle John grabbed Mary and pulled her, kicking and screaming, onto his horse, heading for Darlington. Mary later reasoned that Silas could not have known how badly she would be treated by his uncle; he very probably believed that she would be better off. Her stamina eroded by malnutrition, Mary blacked out after struggling during most of the ride, coming to only briefly when they reached John Davis' house. It was probably best that she later had no memory of that evening; she later awoke in John's bed, very sore, bruised, and with sticky blood between her thighs. She didn't understand what had happened to her, but in the next few days recovered her strength.

Phoebe Elvira became an angel of mercy to Mary. She bathed the girl, trimmed and untangled her hair, found more clothing left from John's last wife, and cut it down to fit Mary. As usual, the food at John's house was wonderful, including milk, eggs, meat, and spring vegetables. In fact, life at Darlington would have been as good as John had promised, had not Mary been dragged into the man's bed every night. When she resisted him, John beat her with a leather strap, and Mary considered running away.

She mentioned this thought to Phoebe Elvira, who said, "If you go, don't tell anyone about it. Master has ways of making us tell...An' he'll follow you. You must *hide* as you run."

Mary had become aware of John's mistreatment of his slaves; sometimes she thought that she was providing them with a welcome break from his attentions.

"Why don't *you* run?" she asked Phoebe.

"There's no future in it," was the answer. "One look at my skin, and folks'd wonder where I ran from, and they'd find out. But you– you can hide anywhere there's white people."

"I'd be lost," mused Mary. "I don't know my way..."

Phoebe gently grasped Mary's shoulder, and looked earnestly into her eyes, saying, "My people talk of nothing but escaping, running, the best way to find our way," she said. "One thing I always hear is to follow water. Follow it down, it takes you to a larger place, to more people. Follow it up, it takes you to a smaller place, a place to hide. If you stay in the water for half a mile, they say, the houn' dogs will never smell your track. And, always run in summer, so you don't freeze."

But Mary did not run. Despite the constant abuse, she held one thought in mind: What if Uncle James Gold tried to find her? If she left Darlington, the message she had sent from Louisville would be of no use. If she just bided her time, surely a way to contact him would surface; perhaps a priest would come. The notion of her formidable Uncle James rescuing her from the disgusting John Davis remained her only hope, and she clung to it.

John Davis, although reared as a Catholic, had no interest in following the ecclesiastical calendar as did his brother. Alternating fasting and contrition with feasting and celebration held no fascination for him. He seemed amused by other pioneers who observed Sunday as a day of rest, and worked his slaves continually. As a matter of self preservation, his slaves worked slowly, deliberately. They conducted an undeclared, continuing war involving malingering and also stealing from Davis; he beat those caught stealing, and also beat the others out of pure meanness.

Life at Darlington settled into a predictable pattern, and Mary discovered hard labor as a practical way to shut out the unpleasantness of life with John. She joined Phoebe Elvira in the slave woman's round of unremitting work. In this way, she learned to milk the cow, kill and clean chickens, as well as to prepare the frontier style food (mostly corn and pork, in every style and variation imaginable) to which she was becoming accustomed. The shucking and hand grinding of corn in large wooden mortars occupied many hours; until a proper mill was established nearby, there would be no easy method of obtaining the cornmeal upon which the daily pioneer menu was based.

In addition, Mary learned to spin wool from John's sheep, to pick cotton from his field, and to weave cloth upon the enormous loom that occupied its own lean-to shed at the back of the house. Summer passed into fall, and the flax ripened, was pulled, and spread to dry until the following spring. Phoebe Elvira promised to teach Mary its uses then.

Day by day, Mary's strength increased; she gained weight and began to look quite pretty. Whenever she glimpsed her own reflection, she was reminded of her mother.

In late summer, Indiana Governor Jonathan Jennings spearheaded continued efforts (begun by George Rogers Clark, Mad Anthony Wayne, and William Henry Harrison) to force the opening of Indian lands within the Old Northwest Territory to white settlement. Nearly a century of opposing land-hungry Europeans had cost the Indians tribes of Ohio and Indiana most of their original populations, leaving the survivors widely scattered. Starting in 1795, treaty after treaty had been negotiated, each one less advantageous to the native peoples. After the death of Tecumseh in 1814, the Indians clearly understood the inevitable outcome of any future dealings with the United States government.

Jonathan Jennings, Lewis Cass, and Benjamin Parke were appointed commissioners for the United States, empowered to conduct meetings with representatives of various Ohio and Indiana tribes (Potawatomi, Wea, Miami, and Delaware) at St. Mary's, Ohio. The point of the meetings, of course, was that the Native Americans should GET OUT OF THE WAY, giving their ancestral lands to white people. Weakened by disease, substance abuse, and dissention within their own ranks, the Indians agreed to a set of new treaties, with differing provisions for each tribe. They ceded a major portion of their lands and many of them agreed to move West of the Mississippi. The actual removals would take place over a period of many years, and result in more Indian suffering and death.

The Indiana land gained by the whites included about eight million acres, from which afterwards were carved more than a score of counties. In exchange for the rich soil of central Indiana, the Indians received promises, many of which were never delivered. These promises comprised a (deliberately) confusing package of cash, annuities, grist mills, salt, and land (both tribal reservations and individual grants). Negotiation of the Treaty of St. Mary's (New Purchase) ended on September 29th, but the various documents were not signed for about a year.

On December 10th, Mississippi entered the Union as the 20th state.

During the same month, Andrew Jackson, who had been serving as Major-General of the Southern division of the United States Army, was called into action. Seminole Indians, some discontented Creek, and groups of escaped slaves and vagabonds had been raiding American settlements North of the Georgia-Spanish Florida border. Despite severe problems with food rations for his men, Jackson conducted a highly successful thirteen week campaign (Later known as the First Seminole War). He crossed the international border, driving the troublemakers into the Florida swamps, giving pause to the Spanish officials who thought they controlled the peninsula. During his campaign, Jackson also perpetrated horrific atrocities on entire villages of Native Americans, considering that to be the most efficacious method of dealing with them.

Advent remained a non-event at John Davis' home. Mary stayed at Darlington among John's slaves, hidden from the rest of pioneer society. Whenever alone, she would pray, her spirit aching with pain, yet glowing with anger and hope.

1818

On New Year's Day, in Washington, D.C., the president's House was opened for use by his family for the first time since 1814. During this year, thirteen stripes on the United States Flag were made constant by law, and it was decreed that a new star would be added to the blue field for each additional state.

During a mild spell of weather in January, Silas Davis visited his uncle's house. Silas looked very good; even though he had aged, he appeared well fed and contented. Unfortunately, John's presence during the entire visit prevented Mary from expressing her misery. Silas mentioned that Lydia's and Margaret's baby girls were growing "like weeds," and that Lydia was expecting another child during the summer. John told Silas, in essence, that he needed to keep it in his pants, using language that embarrassed Mary and would have caused most men to punch him in the face. Silas simply shrugged, accepting his uncle's castigation as a kind of compliment. He had brought Mary's reticule, tucked inside his deerskin shirt, and managed to pass it to her while John was not looking. Mary quickly hid the bag, opening it later. Inside, she found *Grand-mére's* rosary beads and crucifix, as well as the remaining *pirate's gold*, still wrapped within the handkerchief. Silas was a good man, she thought, but not perceptive like his father, nor strong enough to help her. Curiously, she now regarded herself as older and wiser than he; through suffering she had acquired a vision and maturity beyond her years.

During its 1817-1818 session, the Indiana General Assembly created Spencer and Vanderburgh Counties out of land formerly included in Warrick County. Because this changed the geographic center of Warrick County, the Assembly appointed a special commission to investigate the relocation of the county seat. Mary became aware of this toward the end of March, during a rare outing with John Davis to the local general store.

Davis lounged against the counter, shooting the breeze with the proprietor, while Mary fetched and carried various items. Mary was at the back of the room, struggling with a particularly heavy bolt of fine broadcloth, needed for John's new suit, when she heard his voice, raised in anger.

Ratliff Boon, the local gunsmith turned state representative had shown up and was receiving the brunt of John's dissatisfaction with the commission's decision: Darlington would be replaced by a new town, to be constructed ten miles to the North east, where Boon already owned land. To her embarrassment, John was loudly cursing the man.

"Your damned asshole commission served you very well, didn't it? Just who the hell did you think you would fool? Now you can sell your property for a pretty penny, and folks will pay to immortalize your name by calling the place Boonville."

Davis vented for several minutes, scarcely pausing to draw breath, but when he did, he received a surprisingly mild response from Boon, spoken in his soft, Georgia drawl.

"We have given special consideration to those who are already established here at Darlington, Mr. Davis. If you choose, you can trade your place here for a brand new lot..."

Davis broke in, rudely, "What a bargain! You'll recall there were redskins living there seven years ago. They probably poisoned or diseased all the water. I'd have to break new ground, build again, re-establish my farmstead... You can keep your damned new lot!"

"Your choice, Mr. Davis, your choice."

Eventually, Darlington would revert to farm fields, and cease to exist. Anticipating this, John Davis soon decided to move to the new town, Boonville.

Phoebe Elvira taught Mary to plant a kitchen garden, beginning on what turned out to be Good Friday, April 4th. Because Good Friday coincided with the first full moon after the vernal equinox (the beginning of spring), planting cool weather crops was done on that day. Mary learned the germination times and conditions required for lettuce, beets, radishes, peas, carrots, cabbage, and other common vegetables. Many of the herbs in the kitchen garden were perennials, and would be transplanted to the new garden at Boonville. The warm weather crops such as melons, beans, and corn would not have time to mature at Darlington, so Phoebe and Mary traveled to Boonville in early May, to begin the garden there.

"New soil!" said Phoebe with a smile. "We won't have to manure it for at least a year."

Mary agreed that this would be wonderful; she had never dreamed, as a child, that her lot in life would include spreading manure as she had during this past year.

Phoebe Elvira and Mary took the previous year's flax from storage, spreading it to "rot" in the spring rains. It was afterwards processed in order to make wearable cloth. The fibers went first to the "break," then to the "swingle-board," (for beating and scraping away the woody portions) and to the "hackle," or comb, where the tow was separated out, then to the spinning wheel, and last to the loom, where the linen was woven. Sometimes pure flax was woven into yards of pale, yellowish linen that could be bleached into whiteness; sometimes it was interwoven with wool threads to form the grayish, warmer and softer "linsey-woolsey." The woven cloth was rolled into bolts until pieces were cut for clothing or other needed articles, such as bed sheets. Mary developed a new appreciation for the cloth that had, in Maryland, come to her so effortlessly.

By April 25th, Andrew Jackson had completed his military campaign into Florida, and returned to American soil. His habit of taking matters into his own hands (invading Spanish territory, then court martialing and executing two foreign nationals for supplying and stirring up the Indians) despite any consequences caused great controversy throughout the country, especially in Congress. However, because his actions gave the United States added leverage in negotiations with Spain to acquire Florida, and also because of overwhelming popular support, Jackson ultimately won Congressional approval.

As spring gave way to summer, John Davis moved his household to Boonville, and Mary despaired of Uncle James Gold ever finding her. Her mood swung between depression and anger; ever once in awhile John would say something about marrying her, which made her want to slit his throat and then her own. The crisis that ultimately drove her away was the death of Phoebe Elvira.

The black woman had been very ill with malignant bilious fever (a name used for undiagnosed fevers including typhoid and yellow fevers). After four days, during which she suffered spasms and "fits" of the most distressing nature, John accused her of malingering and beat her to death. Mary figured that John's previous wives had shared a similar fate, and that it was only a matter of time before it was her turn. Even as she helped to wash and lay out Phoebe Elvira's body, preparing it for burial, she made plans.

Running to Silas, Lydia, and Margaret would simply not do; John's threat to have Silas arrested could still be carried out, and their farm would surely be the first place John would search for Mary.

The obvious direction to flee was *towards* the Ohio River, she thought. Most roads and all of the creeks led there; more cleared farms and little towns lay along the river banks. But John truly was a close friend of the sheriff, who would return Mary to her tormentor, no questions asked. Mary's best chance for escape, she thought, was to avoid the river at first, staying North of the more settled portions of Warrick county. She tried not to think about wild animals and stray Indians in these areas; whatever threat they represented paled beside the abuse she endured every day. But Mary had been considering Silas, Sr.'s comment concerning Mary's Great-Uncle James Hobbs and his plan to locate in Eastern Indiana. There was a river there – the Whitewater. She would get there somehow, and look for her relatives. And if she did not find them, she was prepared to walk – crawl if necessary – back to Maryland, where life was oh, so good! compared to this godforsaken place.

Mary waited for a hot, muggy, moonlit night when John had eaten a large meal and had drunk a quantity of whiskey. Once his heavy snores began, she washed his stink off herself for the last time. Then she grabbed her reticule, bonnet, a flask filled with spring water, some bread and jerked beef, and an oiled pigskin that she had saved, and fled.

Mary headed East. Only one six foot wide road (a pair of wagon wheel tracks in the dirt, with tall weeds growing between) led through the woods out of Boonville in that direction. About four miles down the road, she came to a creek that she mistakenly assumed to be Little Pigeon. Remembering what Phoebe Elvira had advised, she stumbled upstream in the water for what seemed an eternity. Soaking wet and mud splattered, she scrambled onto the bank and covered herself with the pigskin. Then she ate the soggy food, and whispered the Rosary before falling asleep.

The sky at dawn proved uniformly gray, indicating no direction at all. Undaunted, Mary continued at right angles to the flow of water. Before long, she encountered what turned out to be a continuation of the rough track that she had followed the night before. The road had cut sharply North from the ford, and from this point led Northeast. On either side grew deep woods of beech, poplar, ash, hickory, and walnut trees, with thick, scratchy undergrowth of wild raspberry and sassafras. Curiously, Mary did not feel alone; in the trees overhead, birds as well as insects conducted their noisy lives. She heard, then saw, flocks of red, yellow and green *perroquets*, the bane of farmers common to both Indiana and Maryland. A flight of passenger pigeons blotted out the sun for an hour or so, coming to rest in nearby trees; Mary wished for a gun with which to knock some down, and the means to make a fire to cook them. Occasionally, a hawk or a turkey vulture sailed silently far overhead or swooped suddenly to claim its meal. Mary was not yet hungry enough to fight them for the raw flesh of the carrion they feasted upon.

Mary walked about eight miles that day, having no idea where she was in relation to the settlements to the South, but trusting that the blazed, partly cleared track would lead *somewhere,* out of Warrick County. She sneaked past three homesteads and their lazy hound dogs without being seen. She even managed to refill her leather flask with spring water at mid-day (knowing better than to drink creek water), while the nearby pioneer family ate their dinner. She forded two shallow creeks, following the road, but scurried aside at the slightest unusual sound. Twice, riders passed by on horseback as she cowered in the underbrush. Luckily, they either were not looking for her or they were not competent trackers; her moccasin prints would have shouted her location to someone like Silas Davis, Sr.

At last, she unknowingly reached the real Little Pigeon Creek, full from recent rains and too deep to ford. Mary noted a cabin on the creek bank, and several canoes tied to trees. She waited in the brush, napping until full dark, then, scratched and mosquito bitten, slid inside a canoe. She released the vessel from its tree, then floated across the creek, headed downstream of the landing, using a paddle to push toward the Eastern shore. She hesitated there; it would be possible to take this canoe to the mouth of this creek, whatever its name, to the Ohio River. But she possessed no nautical skills; she fully expected that such an attempt would result in her drowning or capture. Abandoning the canoe, she followed the creek bank North, seeking, then finding a track that seemed to lead Eastward. If only this path would go where she needed it to!

The clouds of the daytime had cleared; bright moonlight guided Mary far into the night. It struck her that, as long as moonlight lasted, night travel might be advantageous. Then she heard a low growl from the woods to her left. Not knowing what sort of creature had uttered this sound, she sped up, moving fast and looking fearfully to the side for the animal. Whack! She fell, knocked nearly senseless, having struck the side of a building. Shaking her head to clear it, she strained to see her surroundings. The moon, already low in the sky, had suddenly hidden behind a heavy bank of clouds; soon it sank behind the horizon of thick woods. The growling had ceased, but Mary thought she heard the animal close by, snapping twigs as it rummaged through the brush. Mary decided to stay put, waiting for dawn, and began her Rosary, but soon fell asleep.

Mary was awakened, past dawn, by a gentle hand shaking her shoulder. "Miss, oh, Miss! Wake up!"

Startled, Mary looked up into the thin face and dark, soulful eyes of a nine year old boy. She saw that he was barefoot, dressed in a tow linen shirt tucked into outgrown homespun trousers, both many times patched and repaired, with a straw hat covering most of his unruly brown hair.

The boy sat back on his heels, cocked his head curiously, and asked, "Air you that girl what Sheriff Brady's a-lookin' fer?"

Mary's heart dropped into her moccasins. It had not occurred to her that sheriffs in different counties cooperated with each other. She stood up, and gasped in pain, her feet blistered, a knot throbbing on her forehead from hitting the log wall.

"Please," she begged, stretching trembling fingers toward the boy. "Don't tell anyone I'm here."

He stared at her as several questions came to mind, but settled on what he deemed the most pertinent one: "Air you hungry?"

He, himself, was nearly always hungry, and could not imagine that she wouldn't be.

She nodded, and the boy withdrew a leather-wrapped packet from inside his shirt, where he had carried it. As he unwrapped the ubiquitous frontier ham and corn dodgers, it occurred to Mary that this was his lunch, meant to last all day. Hungry as she was, she restrained herself until he urged her to eat it all.

"It's all right," he insisted. "I'll git more, later."

After watching her try, unsuccessfully, to drink from her empty water flask, he asked, "You want water? I'll fill that for you."

This boy exuded concern and strength; she decided to trust him. She handed him the flask, and presently he returned with fresh, cold spring water.

Mary felt much better after eating and drinking. Some of her energy returned, along with all of her caution.

"Where am I?" she asked the boy.

"You're behind Will Jones' barn, and this here's Jonesboro. I'm a-workin' today in the ginral store." Lest she think that she had entered a huge metropolis, he added, "There ain't but a few folks about."

Nevertheless, fearful that someone would see them, she quickly followed the boy when he offered to lead her around the buildings of Jonesboro, through the woods to the road leading East.

As they walked, the boy chattered, glad of the company, and soon Mary knew all about him and his family. He had an older sister, Sary, his mother and father were Nany and Tom. They had moved to the village of Troy, Indiana late in 1816 from a farm in Hardin County, Kentucky, located about twenty miles Southwest of Bardstown. At Troy, on the Ohio River, Tom had operated a ferry near to the steamboat landing for about a year. Late the previous fall, the family had moved Northwest to a homestead of eighty acres, building a cabin and clearing land over the winter, and planting their first crops this spring.

"My mother died in Kentucky, at Bardstown," she told the boy, seeking to relate to him in some way, as well as to gain his sympathy. "And I stopped at Troy overnight on the way down river...How would I get to Troy from here?"

"You jist follow this trail to Santa Fe [later Santa Claus], cross Crooked Crick at the ford, then follow the road South t' the Ohio. You'll have to cross Anderson Crick at Troy; most folks take the ferry there. It's a long way; it took us days to get here."

Mary thought about her trip from Maryland to Indiana; by comparison, a trip of "days" sounded quite reasonable. But she wondered how many more days of walking her feet could tolerate, wishing she had her pony for this trip. Then she had an idea: At Troy, perhaps she could pay for steamboat passage upriver! She still had the gold coins in her reticule...

After walking about three miles, they reached the boy's family homestead, where Mary waited behind the corn crib while he fetched more food. An old brown hound dog quickly found her, but she succeeded in keeping the animal quiet by stroking its chest and speaking softly to it. Mary heard the sounds of scolding as the boy backed out of the cabin, balancing several corn dodgers across a tin cup of milk. After making sure he was not observed, he brought these to Mary, then dashed to the smoke house to slice a slab of smoke cured ham.

The boy wrapped the food for Mary to take with her, then asked, "What will you do, now?"

She wanted to ensure that he really would not give her away.

"I'll go on hiding because if anyone catches me, they'll take me back... You see, I was kind of a slave..."

The boy's eyes grew very round. "Slaves is black!" he exclaimed. "You ain't black."

"Anybody who is taken by somebody not their family, and made to stay somewhere against their will, and made to do things they don't want to do is a slave. There is a very bad man chasing me, who I never want to see again. I pray that you'll keep my secret."

"Don't worry. I'll not tell," he promised, making with his finger the shape of a cross over his left breast, which Mary took as an indication of a solemn vow. "But my father has worked as a slave-catcher, and you had best not stay around here!"

Startled, Mary hugged the boy, then turned to go.

"What is your name?" she called back, having reached the edge of the clearing.

"It's Abe. Abe Lincoln," he said.

"I'll always remember you, Abe. Thank you."

In this way, Mary became the first slave helped by the Great Emancipator.

It took Mary three more days to follow the track through Spencer County, to the mouth of Anderson River opposite Troy. She hid from people and dogs as she passed the widely scattered homesteads. She soaked her blistered feet in the creeks, then (as she had learned from the Davis girls) urinated on the wounds to heal them and toughen the skin. She searched the woods for edible roots, berries and greens. The farther she traveled, the weaker and more vulnerable she became; sometimes her mind played tricks on her, scrambling her perceptions of reality. As she neared Troy, however, there was no more easy gathering of food, and her blood sugar, already low, plummeted drastically. She lurked along Anderson River opposite Troy in a kind of stupor, feeling dizzy and nauseated. Remembering that she needed transport to Louisville, Mary begged a rowboat ride from a farmer, then cautiously made her way to the river boat landing.

"You're in luck," the proprietor told her. "I expect the *Liberty Belle* this afternoon, and you can board her IF you have the money." Noting the fear in Mary's eyes, he questioned, "What are you doing here alone, and where are your folks?"

Mary was very near the end of her emotional and physical endurance, but this man did not seem the proper recipient of her confidences. Her instinct was to hide everything, trying to seem normal.

"My folks are at Louisville, and I need to get back there."

The man sniffed, "Unescorted females are not my usual clientele; I really shouldn't allow you aboard."

Desperate, Mary pleaded, "Please. I can pay. Just don't make me walk to Louisville."

"Show me your money."

Mary extended her grubby reticule, opened it, and poured all of her pirate's gold into the astonished man's huge palm. Suddenly, what had seemed a fortune dwindled before her eyes into a paltry sum. Would it be enough?

The man bit one of the pieces to determine that it was, indeed, gold, then gave most of the coins back to Mary.

"Where did you get these?" he began, but the pure terror in her face caused him to rethink this line of questioning. This child was not a local; if she *had* stolen the gold, it did not concern anyone in this town. Pity overcame his usual suspicion of strangers. "Don't show these around," he warned her. "Only take out one at a time. Folks in Louisville will take all of them, and give you next to nothing in return."

Mary sat in the shade behind the ticket booth, her head buzzing in the heat, waiting for her boat. The matter of the gold coins puzzled her. How could she ever spend them without knowing their value? She was nearly ready to ask the ticket man about it, hoping to buy some food, when the *Liberty Belle* chugged into Troy, its arrival announced by the blowing of a bugle.

This vessel measured one hundred feet keel, twenty feet beam, and its whitewashed plank sides and railings glistened in the sun. She was a sidewheeler with a black smokestack, powered by wood fueled boilers below her single deck. The deck, accessed by a steep staircase, contained a wheel house for the captain and two cabins–one for men, the other for women passengers.

The ticket man told Mary to fetch her baggage and go aboard. Having no baggage, she teetered across the narrow gangplank, clinging to a rope that served as a railing, onto the vessel and peered around, wondering where to go.

"This way, this way!"

Mary followed the porter's call, mounted the steep stairs to the deck, and slipped through the swinging door into the women's saloon. She swept the room with the gaze of a hunted animal, then dropped onto a leather covered seat. Three extravagantly dressed and heavily made up women lounged nearby, perspiring in the stifling heat. The epitome of bored self involvement, they apparently felt no need to speak to such a ragged little nobody as Mary. She gazed out the grimy window, and instantly a bolt of alarm shot up her digestive tract. At the dock, a red faced, angry man demanded to be allowed aboard, shouting that he must find that "little strumpet" who had run away from Boonville. The ticket man, fortunately, was much larger than the angry stranger (who seemed to lack the official capacity of a sheriff), and, offended by the stranger's manner, refused to allow him aboard unless he also purchased a ticket.

"Our passengers have paid for their privacy," he insisted. Mary had no doubt that he consciously protected her as he announced, "They're shoving off, now. Good day!"

Instantly, the ropes connecting the *Liberty Belle* to the Troy landing were cast off; the engines, which had been quietly growling, roared as they drove the great wheel. Mary felt the boat swing away from the dock, slowly drifting to mid-river where its engines kicked into high gear, rumbling as the boat fought against the current, forging and bumping its way upstream. Its speed increased until they were cruising at about ten miles per hour. Luckily, the *Liberty Belle* refrained from rolling side to side as had the *Burrows;* Mary's empty stomach was spared the torment of motion sickness.

Mary hadn't realized how tense she was until, as Troy passed from sight, she slumped against the cushioned back of her seat. Unclenching her hands, she noticed deep, red indentations where her fingernails had nearly pierced the skin of her palms. One of the women who had bothered to watch her commented, "You got away, this time."

Mary gazed at her dully, and decided that this did not require an answer. After awhile, she began to notice her surroundings, her chief impression being that everything in the saloon was coated by fine, gritty soot. The windows, seats, floors, walls, even the ceilings could have used a good wash; what she did not realize was that the area had been cleaned every day, but that cleaning did not solve the problem. The swinging door to the cabin failed to keep out the sooty wood ash from the boat's smokestack. The longer Mary sat in the saloon, the dirtier she felt, and her skin turned slightly gray. The other women made use of a water bucket to freshen up periodically, but Mary simply sat, waiting for the journey to end. When the ladies unwrapped the food they had brought along, Mary heard one of them express false sympathy that the "poor little girl" had nothing to eat. They did not offer to share.

Late that afternoon, as Mary descended the gangplank at Louisville, she felt a sense of awe that such an arduous journey could be eased by the simple application of a piece of gold. She wished she had more coins; vaguely, she realized that more gold could have solved more of her problems.

The other passengers had planned ahead for the trek into Louisville itself; they either paid for a ride in a coach waiting at dockside, or were met by slaves holding saddle horses. Having rested her feet during the boat ride, and not wishing to part with any more gold pieces just yet, Mary walked unsteadily along the rutted, muddy track into town. She had no question of where to go; Father Badin would surely advise her. But when she reached the church, she was greeted by a suspicious custodian. The man showed no interest in the grimy ragamuffin; he had seen plenty like her on the frontier and did not want to get involved.

Mary was told that the priest had gone to Bardstown for a conference, and might be away for a month. When she mentioned Archbishop Carroll's name, hoping for an offer of shelter, the man said that Father Carroll had died two and a half years previously, and shut the church door in her face.

Stunned by this news, Mary did not consider seeking another priest, nor help from the church. She instead wandered back into the street and began to walk. After an hour, she found herself at the point where Silas Davis had first shown her the Ohio River, above the Falls. She collapsed onto a rotting log, dangling her bare, battered feet in the cool water, and felt tears burn behind her eyes. Unable to stop them, she buried her face in her filthy skirt and poured the bottled anguish from her soul.

As if from far off, she heard a voice asking, "Little girl, can we help you?"

Mary looked up but, blinded by tears, could see nothing. She rubbed her eyes with the backs of her hands, leaving sooty streaks across her face. Before her stood two young men, one blond with intense, sapphire eyes, the other brunette with long-lashed hazel eyes. Although their coloring differed, their builds – tall and muscular, and their faces – extremely handsome, bore strong resemblance. It struck Mary that they must be brothers. Dressed in the ubiquitous homespun work clothes of the frontier (linen shirts and linsey-woolsey trousers), their clothing fit well, was clean and in impeccable repair. Their cloth caps were of professional manufacture; expensive, shiny leather boots covered their legs to the knees.

"Please," she choked, and they both crouched beside her in order to hear. "Please. Let me go home."

"Where is home?" asked the blond, the younger of the two. There was something wrong with his voice; it rasped, with a unique, whispery quality.

Mary closed her eyes. The answer to that question seemed far too complicated. She moaned, "Don't, *don't* hurt me."

The older brother reached a hand toward Mary, palm up. Kindly concern shown in his eyes. "We'd never hurt you," he promised. "We can get help for you, whatever you need."

"Oh, please, God, help," she said.

Both brothers stood up, deep concern creasing their foreheads. The Norris boys' father, Richard, a Lawrenceburg merchant, purchased raw produce from Indiana farmers. He made his profit from transporting these goods to various ports along the Ohio River. As his boys approached maturity, they went to work for their father, and had just sold a boatload of baled wool. With a successful journey behind them and money in their pockets, they were ready for a night on the town. But they had been brought up in a household where one ironclad rule prevailed: Children's needs were instantly met with tender loving care. So strong was the upbringing received from their Dutch *moeder* that it was impossible for them to ignore this bereft little girl.

Abraham said, "Let's take her to the boarding house."

Cornelius Van Der Hoof remonstrated, "What will Mrs. Mitchell say?"

Bram retorted, "Who cares?"

So it developed that the Norris brothers carried Mary to the boarding house where they kept a room on retainer for their frequent trips to Louisville. They induced a grumbling Mrs. Mitchell to fetch some meat broth, milk, and bread, and to watch over Mary while they enjoyed their night out. After all, they had earned it.

Mary was deeply asleep on a pallet beside Mrs. Mitchell's hearth when they returned, slightly tipsy, well past midnight. The woman, irritated by being rousted at such a late hour, would not hear of them disturbing Mary.

"Leave her be, 'til mornin'," she whispered to them.

So the Norris boys went to bed upstairs, arising at dawn. They found Mary propped in a chair, slightly stronger and much more self contained than she had been on the previous afternoon.

Cornelius Van Der Hoof approached slowly, remembering her fears of being harmed.

"We've not introduced ourselves," he began softly, in his whispery voice. "I'm Van Norris, and my brother is Bram. We hail from Hogan's Creek, on the Eastern edge of Indiana."

A light flickered behind Mary's eyes. *"Eastern Indiana,"* she thought. *"Good."* But she said nothing.

Van tried again. "We need to know a little about you. For example, what's your name?"

"Mary." Realizing he wanted a last name, she hesitated, then said, "Mary Gold."

"Ah. And where are your folks?"

"My folks are dead. It was horrible. I want to go back home."

"Back where?"

But Mary had said all she intended, and shut her eyes, leaning back in her chair.

Van stood up, signaled his brother, and the two left the room.

"Next time it's your turn." he told Bram. "We must figure out what to do; we're going home this morning."

"Let's take her with us. *Moeder* will know what to do."

"Nah. Just leave her with Mrs. Mitchell. Pay the old biddy extra, and she'll take care of it."

Bram argued, "Mary's not an 'it.' There's something special about her..."

"Come on, she's just a stray kitten of the frontier. Chances are she's run off from somewhere, and will run off again, no matter what."

"Maybe. Let me talk to her."

They returned to the landlady's parlor, and Bram said, breezily, "Well, Mary, it's been great meeting you, but we must be on our way. Our folks expect us to home."

Mary nearly flew from the chair, grabbing him around the waist.

"Don't leave me," she begged. "I have no one, nothing...please!"

"Mrs. Mitchell has agreed to look after you. When you're feeling better, you can help out around the place to earn your keep."

Mary looked deeply into Bram's eyes, and said, "Mrs. Mitchell does *not* want me here. Please, take me with you."

His heart melted then, and he said, "All right. We leave after breakfast."

Bram purchased tickets for the three of them aboard the *General Pike*, a steamboat that plied the waters between Cincinnati and Louisville. When the large vessel neared their destination, the three travelers simply lowered themselves into the canoe that Bram had tied alongside the steamboat, released the rope, and paddled for home. By late afternoon, they approached Norris House, located up South Hogan's Creek, West of Lawrenceburg.

Mary was carried back in memory to the elegant estates along Choptank River. Never having visited any of the more established Indiana towns, she had no idea that such mansions existed within the state. After staring at the place for some minutes, she decided that the outstanding difference was its newness, the lack of aged grandeur that characterized, for example, *Hobbs Chance*.

Norris House, built six years previously, measured fifty feet across by forty feet along each side. A limestone walk and steps led to the wooden porch, which featured tall, square, white columns and a carved oak door at the center. The chimneys at each end connected to walk-in fireplaces on the ground floor, and also opened to smaller hearths in the second floor rooms. The ground floor of the place, furnished with carpets and damask draperies, as well as fine wood tables and chairs, was divided into dining room, parlor, office/library, and central foyer that showcased a brass and crystal chandelier. The kitchen was located at the rear, and opened onto the back yard.

The second story, accessed from the foyer by a graceful, curving walnut staircase with carved banister, consisted of the master bedroom, a sitting room (that could double as a guest bedroom), and two bedrooms – one for the boys and one for the girls. A garret above the second floor stretched the entire length and width of the house. The impressive brass lock for the front door, as well as eight large windows (twenty panes of glass in each one) had been imported (along with the chandelier) from the East for the front of the house; the sides and back made do with smaller, square windows. The interior walls had been smoothly plastered and painted in shades of blue and green. The wide boards and elaborate, layered mouldings of the woodwork had been whitewashed, and provided a pleasing contrast. Behind the house lay the barns, servants' quarters, and outbuildings; beyond these stretched rolling acres of cleared fields and orchards that produced all the family's immediate needs.

The household was headed by Richard Norris, 43, youngest son of a family of merchants. Before Richard and his four siblings moved to Indiana in 1811, they had owned a fleet of ships that traded out of New Jersey, up and down the Atlantic coast. After moving to Indiana, they specialized in the exchange of goods between the Ohio River towns. Richard also dealt in real estate and was a leader in the Methodist congregation (mostly because he was able to read scripture fluently and well) on an irregular schedule (because he traveled frequently due to the nature of his business interests).

When at last a hewed log meeting house was constructed, a "Union Church" open to different congregations and named Mount Zion Church, the Norrises attended services there. This church was located about two miles to the Southwest of Aurora. As a result, many of the Norris family members were buried on the grounds of that church (which later became exclusively Methodist, and then was demolished). *The space containing their graves is now called the Trester Graveyard.*

Richard's wife *Aaltje*, 45, had been a Dutch servant girl in Richard's mother's household before her marriage. Her ideas about cooking, child rearing, and household decor had remained firmly Dutch; only because Richard resisted her impulses was most of the ground floor of Norris House decorated in the plain, English-American manner. The upstairs and the kitchen bore the bright colors and Dutch embellishments that *Aaltje* loved.

Richard and *Aaltje* had produced nine children. Besides Bram, 19, and Van, 17, there were *Antje*, 15, John, nearly 13, Mollie, nearly 11, Joseph, 9, Richard Hendrickson (called Hendricks), 3, and Mathias, four months. Another child, Eden, first to be born on the frontier after the move from New Jersey, had died before his third birthday.

Aaltje had embraced the life of hard work to which she was born; only in recent years had she begun allowing her servants and children to take over part of the load. In truth, childbearing and life on the frontier had completely worn her out, as it did a majority of women of that time. *Aaltje* had become fond of sitting outside with her *kindje*, Mathias, watching the garden plants grow. She was doing just that, when her *zoons* appeared, leading Mary by the hand.

"*Moeder*," Bram asked, "can you help us?"

As the Dutch woman stood up, Mary studied her warily. It was easy to see that *Aaltje* had once been very beautiful, and that beauty remained within her heart and mind. Enormous blue eyes very like Van's dominated a lovely, serene, careworn face; platinum blond hair streaked with gray had been carefully arranged atop her head.

Quickly, the brothers explained about finding the girl, and that she needed care.

Aaltje stood up, saying, "Bram, hold the *kindje*, and I will see to her."

She led Mary into the kitchen, and told a servant to prepare a warm bath in the end of the room reserved for washing and laundry. Then *Aaltje* gave Mary some bread and milk to eat while she searched for some of her *dochter* Mollie's clothing that would fit. She thought that things were going well until she attempted to remove Mary's filthy rags.

"No!"

Mary whirled away from *Aaltje,* and her hand closed upon a nearby rolling pin, raising it as a weapon to defend herself.

Aaltje instantly sat down, and directed her servant to do the same.

"We will never harm you," *Aaltje* assured her, speaking softly. "And you need to get clean. You will feel so much better. Come on, no one can see you in this alcove; why not take off your things and step into the water while it is still warm?"

After a good deal of coaxing, Mary consented to be stripped and bathed in the tin tub. It was necessary to shave her head because it was infested with lice. *Aaltje* quickly bundled the hair and all the dirty clothing to be burned outdoors.

Aaltje saw that Mary had entered puberty, but was so thin and malnourished that it was hard to guess her exact age. When asked, Mary appeared puzzled, and finally decided that she must be thirteen.

"And now," *Aaltje* said when Mary had been nicely dressed, her head covered by a muslin cap, "you must tell us a little of your history. Is there someone we may contact, a relative, or friends who will care for you?"

Mary looked frightened, and shook her head. "There's no one," she whispered. "My folks are all dead."

From the way she said this, *Aaltje* doubted that the entire story had come out. She had noted the stripes crisscrossing Mary's back from the beatings, and resolved not to ask more. Instead, she turned Mary over to her *dochters,* privately instructing them to make the visitor comfortable, and to report to her any information they learned.

Mary had never experienced the tender sort of care that *Aaltje* lavished on her children. Bedtimes and mornings were times when each child received special attention. Stories, songs, and Dutch prayers were all part of being tucked into bed; each child was wakened to a warm face wash and more songs.

Since the Norrises occupied essentially the same class and economic level as the Hobbs and Gold families in Maryland, Mary quickly felt very much at ease, more than she had with the Davises. At Norris House there was food constantly available, and Mary discovered that it was not necessary to store table scraps in her pocket to be sure of obtaining the next meal. *Aaltje* encouraged Mary to change her clothing on a regular basis, and the girl was delighted at the variations of color and texture in the fabrics afforded by the bounty of the Norris household. Her hair grew slowly, but it was gently washed and fluffed out by the other girls, until she began to look quite pretty as her face lost its pinched, hungry look.

Aaltje's dochter Antje became the best friend Mary had ever known, and, bit by bit Mary told her story, carefully eliminating the location and circumstances of her latest residence, in Warrick County. Neither did she mention that she intended eventually to search for Hobbs and Gold relatives; the whole notion of having living relatives had receded to the back of Mary's mind.

One day, *Aaltje* found Mary standing in the adult Norris bedchamber, holding a clouded old hand mirror of Dutch design. Tears coursed down Mary's cheeks.

Slipping an arm around Mary's shoulders, *Aaltje* gently inquired, "Who do you see?"

"*Maman*. How can she be in this mirror?"

"This is *een spiegel*. It shows us who we are. For many years, I searched for my *moeder's* eyes in it, but saw only my own. Are you sure you see your *maman*?"

Mary nodded, wiping away the tears.

"Then you keep *een spiegel* by you. Let me know if it helps."

Between September 17th and October 6th, Governor Jonathan Jennings, with many others, signed the Treaty of St. Mary's (New Purchase) written the previous year. Separate agreements were reached and signed with separate Native American tribes; very few Indians would be permitted to remain within the state. The treaty particularly punished the Miami for their lack of support during the War of 1812, and took away most of central Indiana from them. The value of everything the Indiana tribes received in these treaties, when divided by the number of acres they gave up, averages to an estimated ten cents per acre. The United States government quickly built new land offices, selling this land for $1.25 per acre; white pioneers flooded central Indiana. Most whites remained ignorant of the actual terms of the treaty; they had no concern for the native people who they summarily displaced. Indians were regarded as a "temporary evil," to be disposed of as rapidly as possible.

Mary made it her business to fit into the Norris household as if she had been born there. At first she followed *Aaltje* about, pitching in to help with whatever project presented itself. But soon she was able to see what needed to be done without cues; *Aaltje* was surprised to note that her burden of work had lightened because of this slip of a girl. Best of all for Mary, Norris House contained a piano, imported from England. While the other children attended school, Mary practiced on the piano, recalling the tunes she had learned from *Grand-mére*.

Even though comfortable at Norris House, Mary could not dismiss the fear that had dominated her life for such a long time. Neither could she escape the superstitious dread that bad luck followed wherever she went. This dread was cruelly brought into the open that fall.

It was common for girls to be courted at an early age on the frontier, and *Aaltje* in November had granted permission for her *dochter Antje* to have dinner at the home of a young man whose parents were interested in meeting her. This seemed harmless enough; full adult supervision would be provided at all times, and *Aaltje* was not particularly worried, even though she had observed the young man stealing kisses from *Antje* with increasing frequency.

During the night after *Antje* returned from the dinner at these people's home, she became desperately ill. *Aaltje* instantly recognized the symptoms of food poisoning, and immediately began to do everything possible to keep her *dochter* hydrated. Unfortunately, *Antje* was unable to retain oral fluids, and died of resulting heart failure.

The family mourned *Antje's* passing, and *Antje's* young man, (who along with his family had also taken ill but had recovered), cast himself upon her grave, sobbing brokenly. But most surprising to the Norrises was Mary's reaction. She was sure that the death was somehow her fault, and that she should go away, in order not to bring more calamity upon the family. Bram, despite his own emotional turmoil over his sister's death, had to physically restrain Mary from leaving. He caught up to her when she wandered down the creek, gently lifted her, and carried her back home. Over and over, he reassured her that nothing was her fault, and that she would always be cared for and loved. After repeating this several times, he felt that it was true; he did love Mary, and he would always care for and love her. Even though she was young, he resolved to wait until the time was right, and then to make her his own. Unfortunately, he failed to mention this to Mary.

During the fall, the doctor was called from Lawrenceburg to examine *Aaltje's* baby, Mathias. A lump had formed in his belly, and kept growing larger. The child tired easily, and never looked comfortable. But the doctor had no remedy. "Sometimes these things happen," was all he said, and his facial expression offered little hope.

As the holiday season began, little Mathias's abdomen became quite distended, the veins in it bulging; the rest of his body appeared to shrink, emaciated. He had nearly quit eating, and ran a fever from time to time. When his urine turned bloody, *Aaltje* abandoned hope, although Richard continued in prayer for the child's recovery.

During this year, the Indiana General Assembly created more counties: Crawford, Dubois, Lawrence, Monroe, Randolph, Spencer, Vanderburgh, Vigo. They also felt constrained to prohibit black people from testifying in court, and from marrying white people.

On December 3rd, Illinois entered the Union as the twenty-first state. Missouri petitioned for admittance to the Union. However, 2,000 slaves lived within its boundaries. The volatile issue of spreading slavery into new states temporarily blocked Congressional action on Missouri statehood.

Mary was included when the Norris family attended the Christmas and New Year's Eve dances at Lawrenceburg. Escorted by the handsome Norris brothers, Mary and the boys' sister Mollie enjoyed these opportunities to dress up and to dance in the streets.

For the first time in her life, Mary was approached by dozens of young men attracted by her remarkable beauty and by her graceful dancing. Alarmed by the unexpected attention, she kept her arm threaded through Bram or Van's in order to keep the others at bay.

Later, she gave much thought to the mysterious power that drew the sexes together; she had never felt it so strongly before. With dismay, Mary realized that her body missed the regular sexual activity to which she had become accustomed at John Davis' house. Even though sex with John had disgusted her sensibilities, she found that it had given focus to a desire that had begun with her infatuation with Silas Davis, Jr. As she regained the weight lost since her arrival in Indiana, puberty hit her full force. *Aaltje* explained the mechanics of the female body to her so that she understood her monthly cycles. But Mary had difficulty controlling her attraction to the two older Norris brothers; it was all she could do to stay away from them when they were at home.

1819

By mid-January, baby Mathias Norris had grown very weak, and he died on the nineteenth. Mary took over care of the other children during this time; *Aaltje* had collapsed into grief so deep that nothing seemed to help.

In February, New York Representative James Tallmadge proposed an amendment to ban slavery in Missouri. "How long will the desire for wealth render us blind to the sin of holding both the bodies and souls of our fellow men in chains?" asked Representative Livermore from New Hampshire. Missouri statehood was again delayed as a result.

This year brought a financial panic in the Western states, brought on by the collapse of credit on the purchase of Western lands. Richard and his Aurora Association for Internal Improvements used this opportunity to purchase land for their town. Aurora, Indiana would be located about twenty-five miles down river from Cincinnati, Ohio. The Association bought the land for nineteen thousand dollars, payable in ten yearly installments. Jesse Holman, an attorney and one of the original Supreme Court Justices of Indiana, began laying out two hundred six town lots and six public squares. Plans were made for the addition of an ox powered sawmill and gristmill, a warehouse, and a bridge across Hogan Creek, which ran through the center of the town.

At the end of April, all two hundred six town lots were sold at prices ranging from sixty to four hundred dollars apiece, depending on location of the lot. The lots were sold mostly on credit, and some lots were donated to persons who agreed to commence improvements at once, thereby making the town more attractive to others. A public square was laid out, and lots were set aside for a library, schools, the Masonic order, Methodist Episcopal and Presbyterian churches. Even so, the sales totaled $28,553.

Growth of Aurora would be sluggish; even the town of Lawrenceburg by this time had only seven hundred residents (including five lawyers and three doctors) in one hundred fifty dwellings, along with five taverns. However, Richard could afford to wait for his investment (as agent for the Aurora Association, he had to post a personal bond in the amount of $40,000) to bear income; it proved to be a more reliable long range source of wealth for his family than his usual mercantile ventures.

The Independent Order of Odd Fellows was founded on the North American Continent in Baltimore, Maryland, on April 26, 1819. This lodge received its charter from Manchester Unity of Odd Fellows in England. At that time, Baltimore was suffering both a yellow fever epidemic and mass unemployment, so they dedicated the organization to "Visit the sick, relieve the distress, bury the dead and educate the orphans."

Muster Day was held at Lawrenceburg as usual, as soon as the spring floods had receded. On this day, most of the local men between the ages of eighteen and forty-five dressed in whatever military finery they possessed to practice their marching and battle formations. Bram had been in the militia for two years at this point, but this was Van's first muster. Mary had helped prepare his uniform, and was eager to see whether he managed to stay in step with the other men. She, *Aaltje*, and Mollie rode horseback the few miles to the open field where the event was held. They munched gingerbread sold at a makeshift stand and avoided the whiskey that flowed like water down the throats of those around them.

After the marching ceased, as had happened at the holiday dances, swarms of young men gathered, seeking Mary's attention. Once again, Bram filled the role of Mary's chief protector and best friend; she hid behind him. Since *Antje's* death, he assumed responsibility for Mary. However, he had never discussed future plans with her, and Mary had no idea what he was thinking. Marriage was not actually on her agenda; she longed to locate her family first.

Van, on the other hand, had absorbed the Norris men's willingness to allow women to entertain him whenever possible. His sexy, whispery voice and blond good looks drew them like a magnet. Mary thought about him often, but held herself back.

Because of her experiences, Mary did not regard marriage as prerequisite to sex. Surprisingly, neither did she consider sex to be bad or evil, nor did she associate it with the "lust" mentioned in her catechism with the other six capital or "deadly" sins. John Davis had been evil. But because of her current subservient position, she thought of sex, the essential bond between male and female, as a tool that, if used correctly, could secure her future. *Aaltje*, however, was no fool. She would protect her sons from any attempt to seduce them for personal gain. Mary feared, with good reason, that an affair with either of them would result in her expulsion from Norris House.

Instead, Mary accepted *Aaltje* as a *moeder*, and learned from her all there was to know about running the household. Mary learned some of the special Dutch recipes for treats loved by the family. She became a substitute older sister to *Aaltje's dochter* Mollie, who had been hit hard by the death of *Antje*.

Independence Day was celebrated at Lawrenceburg with feasting, long patriotic speeches, and the firing of cannon. Whiskey was readily available. When Van brought her some, Mary drank it, then wished she hadn't.

In mid-July, there was a funeral for Richard Norris' next older brother, William. Mary again heard the dreaded word, "cholera," given as the cause of death, and wondered about its causes. Most people thought it was contracted from breathing the mists or "bad air" from low lying lands and swamps; in fact, it was caused by a bacterium and was spread by food and water contaminated by the feces of infected people. However, the true cause would not be known for over sixty years, during which uncounted thousands succumbed to it, worldwide. The disease struck so suddenly that victims could progress from robust good health to death within one day.

The third of September fell on a Friday, and during the early morning, Mary realized that something was dreadfully wrong at Norris House. Everyone kept asking where *Aaltje* was, and the answer given by the frightened house maid was that "Missis" was ill. No, the children could *not* see her; they had best be off to school and get there on time. Bram and Van looked at each other, having noted the intensity of the housemaid's expression. They escorted the other children to school in record time, but returned immediately instead of attending class. (The older boys had been reading philosophy and law with the teacher, their Aunt Mary, Richard's older sister.) By then, Mary Hobbs had taken up a station outside *Aaltje's* bedchamber, running errands, fetching things, and generally trying to help.

In between such activities, she silently prayed the Rosary, not knowing what else to do.

Richard Norris had risen early in the morning, dressed, eaten breakfast, and ridden to town. When he returned at noon, he was surprised discover *Aaltje* in bed; he had never known her to lie down during the day except immediately after the births of their children. One look at her reminded him of his daughter, *Antje*; *Aaltje's* symptoms were similar.

Despite *Aaltje's* protests, Richard dispatched a servant to fetch a doctor from Lawrenceburg, and then retired to his study, his mind paralyzed by dread. An overwhelming, painful knot of fear was growing in his stomach, which he could not ameliorate. He tried prayer, but received no solace. He read scripture, and that helped a bit. He gathered the children when they returned from school, and brought them into the sickroom. Mary tagged along.

Aaltje gathered her strength. She sat up and tried to smile as they wished her a speedy recovery, but could not stifle her tears when they left.

After several hours, the doctor arrived from Lawrenceburg, accompanied by a visitor from Louisville, Dr. Hardin Weatherford. The men took one look at *Aaltje,* diagnosed her with cholera, and began treating her with medicines they had brought along. Through the afternoon and early evening, the doctors tended *Aaltje,* dosing her with opium and brandy to alleviate the pain of the muscle spasms that wracked her form. They worked to straighten her limbs after each painful episode of cramping.

Richard visited the sickroom several times, but could not bear to watch his beautiful wife made grotesque by the attacking disease. He remained in his study; trying to divert his mind by reading. When the children came in to ask after their *moeder*, he did his best to reassure them. Only Bram, Van, and Mary Hobbs could read the truth in his eyes, hearing the words he did not say to the younger ones. The three of them wandered out to the yard, where they sat together, quietly.

Then the housemaid came outside, crying.

By the time they reached the sickroom, Richard had collapsed in tears onto the bedside, clutching his wife's cold hand. His sons crossed the room in two strides to embrace him, their own tears mingling with their father's.

Mary remained in the doorway. As her mind struggled to absorb the loss of another parental figure from her life, her abdominal region registered a sickeningly familiar shock and panic. She glanced toward the ceiling of the little room, wondering why the Norrises did not notice *Aaltje's* spirit hovering there. Mary made the sign of the cross, sank to her knees, and mouthed the words of a prayer:

Quaesumus, Domine, pro tua pietate miserere animae famulae tuae Aaltje, et a contagiis mortalitatis exutam, in aeternae salvationis partem restitue. Per Christum Dominum nostrum. Amen.

[We beseech Thee, O Lord, according to Thy loving-kindness, have mercy upon the soul of Thy handmaiden *Aaltje*, and now that she is set free from the defilements of this mortal flesh, restore her to her heritage of everlasting salvation. Through Christ our Lord. Amen.]

Even though *Aaltje* had not been a Catholic, Mary hoped that God would at this moment notice what a good person the Dutch woman had been, and perhaps make an exception to consignment to the fires of Hell in her case. It was a matter for a priest, and the nearest priest was beyond reach. As soon as the family left the room, Mary hastily blessed some water and baptized *Aaltje*, "*In nomine Patri, et Filii, et Spiritu Sancti, Amen,*" hoping that would help. Before the family could return and notice what she was doing, Mary ran downstairs to make sure the servants would care for the body of their mistress.

Mary found herself well prepared to step into *Aaltje's* shoes, caring for the children during the next chaotic days. The place was overrun by relatives and neighbors, and a constant supply of food and drink was needed; cleanup crews of servants worked nonstop.

They buried *Aaltje* in the Methodist Mount Zion Church cemetery [later called Trester Cemetery in Aurora, Dearborn County, Indiana] on Monday, her grave defined by head and foot markers of plain field stone. Since the traveling Methodist minister was not available, *Aaltje's* cousin Moses Hendrickson's offer to serve as *voorlezer* was accepted; he recited the words of the burial service used by the Dutch Reformed Church. Abraham Hendrickson, *Aaltje's* nephew, recited the *"Onze Vader"* in Dutch, and Mary found herself reciting silently the Latin words for the dead.

Requiem aeternam donei, Domine, et lux perpetua luceat ei. Requiescat in pace. Amen.

[Eternal rest grant unto her, O Lord, and let perpetual light shine upon her. May she rest in peace. Amen.]

Domine Iesu Christe, Rex gloriae, libera animas omnium fidelium defunctorum de poenis inferni et de profundo lacu; libera eas de ore leonis, ne absorbeat eas tartarus, ne cadent in obscurum; sed signifer sanctus Michael repraesentet eas in lucem sanctam, quam olim Abrahae promisisti et semini eius. Amen.

[O Lord Jesus Christ, King of glory, deliver the souls of all the faithful departed from the pains of hell and from the bottomless pit; deliver them out of the lion's mouth, lest hell should swallow them up, lest they fall into the outer darkness; but let Thy standard-bearer, Saint Michael, bring them back into Thy holy light, which Thou didst promise of old to Abraham and to his seed. Amen.]

Richard had great difficulty leaving the burying ground that day. At length, he secured his children's promise that when it was his time, he would be put into the same grave with *Aaltje*, and a single stone used to mark them both.

"She is part of me now," he told them, "and I shall be part of her, forever."

At the time, Mary found this speech of his to be very romantic and wonderful.

After the funeral, at least one hundred people descended on Norris House, expecting to be fed. Fortunately, the servants had anticipated this; as soon as *Aaltje* was pronounced dead, they had swung into full production, preparing an enormous funeral feast. After the burial, people came to the house and remained until late in the evening.

Mary took the opportunity to thank Abraham Hendrickson for his participation in the funeral; he was doubly connected to the Norrises because he had married Mariah Norris, the daughter of Richard's brother Joseph Norris. The couple had a small baby girl, Deborah Ann, at this time.

"It's the least I could do – to say goodbye to her in Dutch," he told Mary.

"It's exactly what she would have wanted," she responded.

"I feel as if I've lost my second *moeder*," he said.

"I do, too."

Mary that night sought to console Bram Norris, whom she regarded as her rescuer, by offering him the comfort of her body. He, however, had been well schooled by his *moeder* concerning the advantages of self control and of saving sex for marriage. He proved incapable of violating *Aaltje's* rules on the night of her funeral. Not understanding any of this, Mary took his refusal as rejection. He still did not mention marriage.

Next morning, on Tuesday, Mary woke early as she usually did. The chickens were making a racket in the yard, and the odors of fresh baked biscuits mingled with that of sizzling bacon wafted upward from the kitchen directly beneath the girls' bedchamber. She noticed Mollie Norris (a night owl who habitually slept later than Mary), supine in her own bed across the room; the girl had probably stayed awake long after every visiting family member (aunts, uncles, and cousins) had left the house late last evening.

Mary, careful to make as little noise as possible, bathed herself before the small washstand, leaving half the clean water for Mollie's use. She changed her shift, then donned a fresh gown and apron; there would be plenty of work ahead.

The servants had completed their morning meal, and Lucy, the cook, was preparing additional food for the Norris family. Mary wandered through the downstairs rooms, straightening chairs, rugs, and benches that had been displaced by the after funeral crowd.

Collecting a few half empty cider cups and a plate of cake crumbs, she headed toward the scullery, but stopped when she noticed Richard Norris leaning in a doorway. The new widower looked very bad, having spent the night drinking heavily. His eyelids were puffy and red rimmed, his hair stood out at all angles, and his usually neat costume appeared disheveled.

Mary owed the roof over her head and the clothes on her back to the good grace of this man, but she had never found more than a few words to say to him. Nor had he spoken much to her, even though his attitude remained impeccably civil.

"Good morning, Mr. Norris," she said.

"Morning," he growled, with great effort.

"Coffee?" she asked him.

"Please."

When she returned with a steaming mug, he drank half of it quickly, then refilled the cup from an earthenware jug of whiskey.

His expression brightened then, and she told him, "Come sit down, and we'll feed you. You need to eat."

He shook his head, but nevertheless wandered forlornly toward the dining room, where he knew the children would gather.

"*The children!*" thought Mary. Their mother had always wakened them for breakfast, but now there was no one...

She filled a pitcher by dipping it into a kettle of hot water in the kitchen, and raced up the stairs to the boys' room. She poured the water into the boys' wash basin, soaked several clean rags therein, and proceeded to little Hendricks' bed. Pushing the hair back from his forehead, she softly bathed his face, exactly as his mother used to do.

"Wake up, wake up," she sang, "time to start the day..."

Four year old Hendricks sat up quickly, thinking that somehow his mother had returned. When he saw that she had not, his shoulders sagged. Mary hugged him gently, pulled him from the bed, and helped him into his trousers.

"Time for breakfast," she told him, swatting his rear lightly and sending him toward the stairs. "And then school."

She woke Joseph, ten years, and John, thirteen, in the same way, handing them their pants and turning away so that they could dress themselves. Van propped himself on one elbow, watching her.

Gravely, Mary tossed him a warm, damp cloth.

"Breakfast is ready," she told him.

"So am I," he whispered, his eyes challenging her to come closer.

Mary turned away, toward Bram, who remained sprawled across his bunk, his face to the wall. Remembering his deep need of comfort from the night before, she massaged his shoulder with one hand. As he turned toward her, Mary softly dabbed his face with the warm cloth, and he instantly awakened.

"Mary!"

He half sat up, then pulled her onto the bed with him, kissing her.

"Ahem," whispered Van. "I think I'll just go downstairs now. Come on, John, Jos..."

As they left, Mary sat up and pulled away from Bram.

"Don't go," he begged.

"It's breakfast time; I must waken your sister. Besides, you really don't want my help getting dressed, do you?"

She reached toward the blanket covering his legs.

"No, no. Stop that! Go wake Mollie. I'll be along directly."

At breakfast, the three younger children ate eagerly while Richard and the four older ones picked at their food. Richard set down his whiskey laced coffee and regarded them all, sadly.

"It's important that we all get back to normal," he said. "I'll send Bram and Van down river with a load of produce tomorrow; the rest of you must return to school."

"*Except for me,*" thought Mary, who had never been to school. "*I'll just stay here and earn my keep.*"

"What will you do, Papa?" asked Joseph.

"I have business in Cincinnati. I'll leave tomorrow, but don't expect me back for at least a week. If there are problems, go to Aunt Mary, or Uncle Joseph..."

Richard's daughter Mollie rose, and hugged her father tightly.

"Don't leave us, Papa, please..."

"I must. But if things go well, I'll not have to leave again for a long time..."

Mary wondered what he could mean, as did his older sons, who gazed askance at him.

"Business," Richard muttered. "Just business."

Three and a half weeks passed before Richard returned. During that time, Mary tried valiantly to keep the household on track. The servants knew all the routines and did the hardest work, but it fell to Mary to make sure that the three little boys (and their sister, to a lesser degree) washed, changed their clothing regularly, and ate something other than the sweets they loved so much. She enforced their usual bedtimes, and woke them in time to send them to school each weekday. She did not, however, escort them to church on Sundays; if their father wanted them to attend, he would have to return and supervise them himself.

Bram and Van were long gone. This latest trip, delivering their father's goods, would take them at least a month to complete.

Richard came home in early October. Mary had been hard at work in the kitchen all morning, baking bread. The children were at school; no formal dinner had been planned. Mary only noticed Richard's arrival because the servants suddenly scrambled to produce a meal.

Quickly washing her hands and face, then changing into a clean apron, Mary ventured into the parlor, where she was greeted by Richard, all smiles. He was accompanied by a rather imposing female personage. The woman was tall, dressed in deep blue silk, her large hat sprouting feathers. Pearls draped about her neck and dripped from her ear lobes; gems twinkled on her fingers and wrists. Even though she was only about four years older than Mary, her height, costume, and manner made her seem much older.

"Mary, this is my wife, Catherine," said Richard. "I'm sure the two of you will get along very well."

This last was not a request, but more like an order, and Mary heard all the implications thereof. Catherine peered at Mary, and a line of concentration appeared between her eyes.

"Are you daughter Mary, or..."

"Mary Gold, Ma'am," Mary responded. "They are just preparing dinner; would you care for some tea?"

"Coffee, I think," replied the personage.

This established a pattern with which Mary quickly grew familiar. No matter what was offered to Catherine, she always chose something else. Nothing ever seemed good enough; her food was frequently returned to the kitchen to be reheated or cooked for an additional period of time.

Mary noticed during the following days that the newlyweds seemed to know each other exceedingly well. They called each other, offhandedly, "Dicky" and "Caty," and shared many private jokes, the meaning of which escaped Mary. It did not surprise her that they spent much time locked within their bedchamber, but this upset the younger children, who were used to unlimited access to their parents. Mary forbade them to rattle the doorknob, urging them instead to seek assistance from herself.

The day after Catherine's arrival, fine English style bedroom furniture arrived from her former home in Cincinnati, and the heavy, Dutch style pieces treasured by *Aaltje* were stored in the barn. Shortly after the furniture exchange, Bram and Van returned home. Mary saw surprise in both their faces as they greeted their new stepmother, then saw Bram's eyes register shock as Catherine said to him,

"It's good to see you again."

Bram's smile froze as he managed to choke out the words, "And you as well."

He quickly turned to the children, hugged little Hendricks, then muttered his excuses, something about finding food. Mary followed him out.

Rather than stopping in the kitchen, Bram nearly ran through it and outdoors to the woodpile in the back yard. Locating the tools kept in the shed, he stripped off his jacket and shirt and flung them onto the ground. He chopped wood furiously, his face contorted by more anger than Mary would have thought possible. After a long time, Bram slowed his chopping and stopped, dropping the axe. He fished a large kerchief from a pocket, and mopped sweat from his face and chest, sinking onto a log beside Mary. He began to cry.

Mary slid an arm around his back, rocking him slightly as she stroked his damp hair.

"It's not that bad," she told him. "Catherine seems to make your father very happy."

"You don't understand." He gulped for air, then blurted, "That slut has been making Father happy for a long time. Bringing her here is a terrible insult to my mother…"

Mary was silent, considering what she knew of Richard's character. Like the other men of his family, he was highly intelligent, physically attractive, and, due to carefully nurtured wealth and influence, used to having his way. For him, wanting something was justification for taking it. His speech at *Aaltje's* grave now seemed to her like the worst hypocrisy.

Bram, however, because of his position as eldest child, combined with the influence of his mother, had developed the inclination to place other peoples' needs before his own. Mary had concluded that this accounted for Bram's reticence toward lovemaking, his unusual display of self-control. Well, she had grown weary of waiting for him to make love, but she could be his friend.

The afternoon was growing late; it would soon be supper time.

"I'm going to visit Aunt Mary," said Bram, donning his shirt and jacket. "Don't expect me back for a while."

Van, unlike his brother, cared little about the arrival of his new stepmother. Nothing the woman could do would take away his memories of his mother; if she proved difficult, he was more than willing to live elsewhere.

But his interest was captured by the dramatic change he noticed in Mary. The girl's appearance no longer evoked pity, but desire. Her figure had filled out, and could be described as voluptuous. Shiny black hair curled to her shoulders, and framed a gloriously beautiful face featuring rosy cheeks, full lips, and piercing black eyes. And there was something in those eyes that he had encountered before...

After the children were in bed that evening, he came to Mary, who was standing outside, enjoying the night air. Van didn't talk, but simply kissed Mary a few times, then led her by the hand to the hay loft in the barn.

Making love with Van was rather more pleasurably intense than anything Mary had yet experienced. She expected him to hurt her, as John Davis had done, but instead, she found the physical and emotional pain of the abuse she had suffered receding into the background. Lying in Van's arms, she felt safe for the first time since Silas Davis' death. And during her usual round of work, next day, she realized that she wanted more of Van, much more. That night, and each night thereafter, Van was more than willing to oblige.

Richard invited his relatives to a dinner, in order to welcome Catherine. Bram was brought along, under duress. Observing the group closely, Mary acquired the impression that Richard's brother, Joseph, had met the woman before; his sister Mary had not. Richard's siblings and Joseph's wife, Elizabeth (who remained totally clueless), greeted Catherine quite cordially, but Mary's husband, Moses Hendrickson, a cousin of *Aaltje's*, avoided speaking directly to the woman, and his eyes appeared troubled. John Norris, Richard's cousin, had traveled to the dinner from Brookville. He conducted himself with tight civility, but his French-Canadian-Indian wife, *Marie,* (who had been especially close to *Aaltje*) made little effort to conceal the scorn in her black, flashing eyes. Luckily, she declined on this day to speak English, and Catherine seemed not to understand *Marie's* dialect of Quebecois.

Mary understood her perfectly, however, and had a hard time keeping a straight face as the woman delivered horrific insults to the unwitting Catherine.

Autumn deepened toward winter, and the Norris boys were gone most of the time, transporting the products of harvest time (corn, beans, pork) up and down the Ohio River. Catherine made her influence felt at Norris

House, and Mary began to wonder how long she could tolerate the woman's domination.

Catherine had been shocked to discover that neither Mary nor Mollie Norris wore what she considered proper undergarments. The girls had previously copied *Aaltje's* style of dress; *Aaltje* had worn corsets only a few times in her life, for special occasions. *Aaltje* had used a chemise as both nightgown and underwear, donning her day gown over it. Henceforth, Catherine decreed that the girls were expected to appear below stairs only when properly encased in corsets between the chemises and their gowns. This change distressed Mary less than it did Mollie; Mary's *maman*, as well as her other female adult relatives, had all worn corsets, corselets, or some form thereof. Mollie, on the other hand, began to resent anything Catherine said or did.

What bothered Mary more than the corset issue was that Catherine had come up with a new system of management for the household. Servants, and Mary suddenly found herself included in this group, had to consult with Catherine twice daily. In the morning, they reviewed the plan for the day, detailing all chores. After supper, each of them was required to give account of his or her time, explaining why various tasks had taken so long, and why he or she had deviated from any portion of the morning's plan. Mary *hated* this method of housekeeping; Catherine made charts and lists that Mary could not read, and expected Mary to follow them. Besides that, when Van was home, there were hours for which Mary did not care to give accounting; she felt sure that Catherine would not approve.

Mary began to yearn for her own family; finally, she spoke to Van about it. With the arrival of cold weather, the two of them had relocated their trysts from the outbuildings to the garret. There, they snuggled against one of the warm chimneys, usually late at night. This, of course, required a certain amount of subterfuge, as well as the maintenance of nearly total silence. One night, as they lay together, Mary's arms around Van's neck, she spoke softly into his ear:

"Van, I'm thinking that I should leave Norris House."

"Oh? You don't like me anymore?"

She kissed him.

"It's not that. I think that I have relatives along the Whitewater River, and that I should look for them. But I don't know how to go about it."

"That's easy. We'll just ride over to Lawrenceburg. The postmaster there can contact the postmaster at Brookville, and ask after your people."

"Really? As easy as that?"

"Yep. But are you sure you want to do this? You've never explained how you got so messed up..."

"My relatives had nothing to do with it. Anyway, if I do have relatives along the Whitewater, they are not my very closest ones. The people I really need to reach are at Baltimore, on an irregular basis. I might *never* be able to contact them..."

Tears of frustration flowed from her eyes. Van wiped them away.

"Hey, hey, sweetheart. We can write to your folks at Baltimore. Please don't cry!"

She allowed him to comfort her, and next day at planning time she informed Catherine that she and Van would be riding to Lawrenceburg. Catherine's eyebrows shot up, and she began watching the two of them more carefully after that.

At Lawrenceburg, Mary was able to send two letters, penned by Van. She insisted on paying the postage herself, in pirates' gold, which shocked the postmaster (who had to come up with change in silver pieces), all of which vastly amused Van. One message went to the postmaster at Brookville, Indiana, enquiring whether any Hobbs families lived within the county. The other went to the Harbor Master at Baltimore, addressed to Joseph or James Gold. It repeated the information Mary had sent to Father Carroll before, concerning her parents' demise, but noted the change in Mary's location.

On the way back to Norris House, Van turned to Mary, and grinned.

"What's the deal with those gold coins? Did you steal them from a pirate? Is that who beat you?"

"No."

"You won't tell me?"

"No."

"But all this means you'll have to stay with us awhile longer, to see whether you get any response to your letters."

"Would it matter to you if I left?" she asked him.

He shrugged.

"I won't lie to you, Mary. I'd miss you, but I'd probably find someone else to be with. I'm just not the marrying kind, I guess." He saw deep pain in her eyes, and added, "I'm truly sorry."

"Don't be sorry, Van," she managed to say, nearly choking on the tears she held back. "Your family has saved my life, and I was foolish to expect any more. I must leave Norris House as soon as I can."

Two weeks later, a reply came for Mary from the postmaster at Brookville. She induced Mollie to read it to her. There were, indeed, several Hobbs families within Franklin County: The heads of households were Henry, James, James Jr., and Robert Hobbs. Mary resolved to visit the Whitewater Valley at the first opportunity.

During this year, the Indiana General Assembly formed the counties of Fayette, Floyd, and Owen.

Also, Secretary of State John Quincy Adams sent an ultimatum to Spain: Control the Seminole and other Indians, or cede Florida to the United States. As a result, Eastern Florida became **United States** *territory.*

On December 14th, Alabama entered the Union as the twenty-second state.

At the holiday celebrations, Mary danced with Van as if her life were at stake, and afterward the two of them made love in the garret. Bram seemed not to notice; his attention focused on his younger siblings who faced their first Christmas without *Aaltje*.

1820

During this year, Martin and Scott Counties were formed by the Indiana General Assembly.

The 1820 census showed that the population of Indiana had increased within four years from about 64,000 to 147,178; the General Assembly appointed a commission of ten men from different counties to select four sections of land for a permanent capital of the state, and the legislature decided that the new town would be "called and known by the name of Indianapolis."

The choice of this name resulted in the following editorial comments from a Vincennes, Indiana newspaper:

"One of the most ludicrous acts, however, of the sojourners at Corydon, was their naming the new seat of state government. Such a name, kind readers, you would never find by searching from Dan to Beersheba; nor in all the libraries, museums, and patent-offices in the world. It is like nothing in heaven nor on earth, nor in the waters under the earth. It is not a name for man, woman, or child; for empire, city, mountain or morass; for bird, beast, fish, nor creeping thing; and nothing mortal or immortal could have thought of it, except the wise men of the East who were congregated at Corydon. It is composed of the following letters: I-N-D-I-A-N-A-P-O-L-I-S!

Pronounce it as you please, gentle readers — you can do it as you wish — there is no danger of violating any system or rule, either in accent, cadence, or emphasis — suit your own convenience, and be thankful you are enabled to do it, by this rare effect of the scholastic genius of the age. For this title your future capital will be greatly indebted, either to some learned *Hebraist*, some venerable *Grecian*, some sage and sentimental *Brahmin*, or some profound and academic *Pauttowattimie*."

The American Colonization Society, founded for the resettling of free black people from the United States three years previously, had received $100,000 from Congress. In January the first ship, the Elizabeth, sailed from New York for West Africa with three white ACS agents and eighty-eight emigrants.

The ship arrived first at Freetown, Sierra Leone, then sailed South to what became the Northern coast of Liberia and made an effort to establish a settlement. All three whites and twenty-two of the emigrants died within three weeks from yellow fever. The remainder returned to Sierra Leone and waited for another ship. Despite this effort to solve the issue of slavery, it remained a volatile topic within the United States.

In February, Richard Norris' cousin, John Norris and his French-Canadian wife, *Marie*, visited. John Norris, an old Indian fighter and veteran of the Battle of Tippecanoe, as well as of Pigeon's Roost Massacre, exuded a forbidding presence. This was mostly for Catherine's benefit, as John had been particularly attached to *Aaltje*. But he intimidated Mary without even trying, and it took her several hours to work up courage to speak to him. Finally, she did.

"Mr. Norris, do you live in Franklin County?"

"Yes, we do."

"Do you know any Hobbs families?"

"Maybe. Why do you ask?"

"I think that some of my family may be living there. My parents have died, and I'd like to contact my relatives."

"You might want to think that over."

"Why?"

"You're Catholic, aren't you?"

Mary gasped. She had never uttered a word about her religious background to any of the Norrises. Her rosary beads had been carefully hidden from everyone but *Aaltje*, who had made her a new reticule to hold them.

"I saw you during the grace before dinner. You made the sign of the cross while you thought no one was looking."

Mary said nothing.

"Your Hobbs relatives, if that's what they are, in Franklin County, are rabid Methodists. One of them, Henry, tried to engage me in a discussion of predestination, hoping to save my immortal soul. I told him I was predestined for Hell, and that he should get the hell off my property. I love to make a grown man cry.

At any rate, if you expect any help from them, be prepared to pay the cost. You'll be dragged to church and to camp meetings until your brain turns to mush. Just my opinion, of course."

Mary instantly recalled her feelings when her faith had been blamed for her father's death, in Virginia. She wanted time to think, and she wanted out of this conversation.

"Thank you, Mr. Norris," was all she said, and she turned away.

"Just a minute," he said, and Mary stopped, looking at him. His usual, fierce expression had softened slightly into what passed for a friendly smile. "My wife is Catholic, and she would welcome the chance to pray with you."

"Thank you."

But Mary did not approach *Marie* at this time. Catherine was a Methodist who became more fervent as her sordid past receded in memory. Mary feared Catherine's reaction, had she discovered two Papists praying together. That would, she thought, spell the end of her welcome at Norris House.

On March 3rd, in Congress, Henry Clay, "the Great Pacificator," proposed a compromise on the issue of admitting Missouri to the Union. Maine had petitioned for statehood as a free state. If both states were admitted, a free Maine and a slave Missouri, the balance of power in Congress would be maintained. Thus, the widely hailed Missouri Compromise postponed the inevitable showdown concerning slavery in the United States for another generation. The Compromise further stipulated that all the remaining Louisiana Purchase territory North of the Southern boundary of Missouri would be free; the territory below that line would be slave.

Early during this spring, "The Prophet" Joseph Smith received his first vision in a grove of trees near his home in Palmyra/Manchester township, New York.

On May 17th, the commissioners appointed by the Indiana General Assembly to establish a new state capital set out from Corydon with Governor Jennings, traveling

North into the New Purchase. They had with them a black servant boy, a tent and "plenty of baken and coffy." By June 7th they had chosen the land on which Indianapolis now stands. Their report to the legislature reads, "The undersigned have endeavored to connect with an eligible site the advantages of a navigable stream and fertility of soil, while they have not been unmindful of the geographical situation of the various portions of the state; to its political center as regards both the present and future population, as well as the present and future interest of the citizens."

Mary continued her relationship with Van when he was home; his tenderness and affection were nearly the only bright spots in her life. But during this particular year, Richard had chosen to send his sons on repeated trips to Pittsburgh to fetch loads of goods (iron, glassware, fine furniture); Mary saw very little of either one. If she had found the time to brood on her situation, she might have become quite despondent. However, Catherine kept her so busy with housework that, when she collapsed onto her bed at day's end, she usually fell asleep before completing her Rosary.

By July, Catherine Norris realized that she was carrying Richard's child. The woman had been ill for more than a month, but from July onward she took to her bed, lamenting her delicate condition, insisting on extra care. The housemaid did her best to keep up with the woman's demands, but someone had to be within instant call at all times, and much of this fell on Mary, especially in autumn while the younger children were at school. Richard spent most of his time between Lawrenceburg and Cincinnati; he was rarely home. While he was gone, Catherine developed a penchant for demanding room service in the middle of the night; she was apt to order hot tea and toast at odd hours, which Mary was required to provide.

Even though the national presidential election held that November brought up serious national issues such as the economic depression of 1819 and the Missouri Compromise of March, 1820, the incumbents, President James Monroe and Vice-President Daniel D. Tompkins were re-elected with no serious opposition.

All during that winter, the three Norris men found work to occupy them at their warehouses in Cincinnati; Mary suspected that they were avoiding the unpleasant atmosphere at Norris House. Christmas passed by, almost unnoticed, and Mary mourned.

1821

During this year, the Indiana legislature created the counties of Bartholomew, Greene, Parke, and Union. In the spring, Elias P. Fordham and Alexander Ralston were hired to survey and plat the town of Indianapolis so that a land sale could be held. The advertisement of lot sales in Indianapolis began in June, with the first public sale held in October.

And Mexico won independence from Spain.

On an unusually cold, snowy night in February, Mary was awakened by Catherine's screams. The Norris men were gone, of course, so Mary quickly ran to Catherine's room, while the younger children peered after her, frightened. A first time mother, Catherine had failed to recognize the signs of early labor; she had blamed her discomfort on indigestion. Waiting for instructions, Mary realized that none would be forthcoming. Catherine was so intent on her own body, and so terrified that she was about to die, that she could do little else besides moan.

Mary wrapped herself in a buffalo robe that was kept on a peg by the back door, pulled on a pair of tall boots that someone had left there to dry, and trudged across the yard to the servants' quarters. She soon returned with two of the kitchen staff who were slightly acquainted with obstetrics, having themselves given birth more than once. The three of them agreed that sending for a midwife or physician was impractical; the snow was very deep, Hogan's creek frozen. Therefore, they kept vigil through the remaining night hours with the laboring mother-to-be. At midmorning, baby William L. Norris (named for Richard's brother) made his appearance, and they concluded that Catherine was likely to survive the ordeal.

The children were delighted; in the past, a new baby had always been presented to them as if it were a new pet that they could help to rear. As soon as Catherine regained her senses; she scotched this notion; the other children were not to so much as touch her baby.

When Richard arrived at home with his sons, Catherine berated him loudly for abandoning her during her travail. Richard did not take this sort of greeting well, especially in front of his children. He turned on his heel, departed hastily, and did not return home for another month.

On March 15th, Maine entered the Union as the twenty-third state.

On May 5th, Napoleon died in his island prison at the age of fifty-one.

The Nautilus sailed to what later became Liberia twice for The American Colonization Society during this year, establishing a settlement at Mesurado Bay on an island they named Perseverance. Life was difficult for these early settlers, mostly free-born black people from the United States. The native Africans resisted the expansion of the colony, causing many armed conflicts. Nevertheless, in the next decade 2,638 African-Americans migrated to the area. Also, the colony agreed with the United States to accept freed slaves from captured slave ships.

During this summer, an epidemic of ague (malaria) killed seventy-two, or one of every eight residents of Indianapolis. Ague was quite common during this time (Indiana contained many mosquito-infested swamps), and those infected who did not die were likely to exhibit intermittent symptoms such as lethargy, blue fingernails, chills, fever, and sweating. Because the symptoms were not constant, the common attitude was, "He ain't sick, he's only got the ager."

Since germ theory was unknown, educated people thought epidemics were the result of "miasmas," invisible substances rising from damp soil into the night air. Those people of a more religious bent believed disease to be signs of God's judgment upon sinful humanity. The list of common diseases included dysentery, scarlatina, phthisis (wasting), pneumonia, bronchitis, diphtheria, yellow and spotted fevers. Most children lost at least one parent before reaching adulthood, and every family was likely to be affected during an epidemic.

On August 10th, Missouri entered the Union as the twenty-fourth state.

In early November, James Monroe was re-elected as President, virtually unopposed.

After giving birth, Catherine Norris became even more difficult to live with. She took a deeper interest in Methodism, thinking that increased holiness would bind Richard to her more firmly. Apparently, she had forgotten what had attracted him to her in the first place: Her willingness to separate religion from daily life. When Richard was absent, which was most of the time, Catherine imposed her religious ideals on the rest of the household, even on the servants. Prayer times were established and enforced; Mary was running out of excuses to avoid revealing her Catholic roots.

One noon, Van returned home unexpectedly; he announced that Richard and Bram had stopped at Lawrenceburg and would arrive within the hour. Instead of expressing pleasure, Catherine launched into a diatribe against the irresponsible, ungodly ways of the Norris men. Van shrugged this off and went to find Mary.

Mary responded to Van's embrace of greeting with little enthusiasm.

"What's wrong?" he asked. "Didn't you miss me?"

"I need to get away from here," she answered. "When the warm weather returns, I think I'll leave."

He grinned at her. "I have a surprise. He should be arriving very soon. Why don't you get your cloak, and we'll walk to meet him?"

Curious, Mary quickly fetched her cloak and reticule, covering her head with a warm woolen hood. As the two of them walked toward Hogan's Creek, Mary heard a voice calling her name. The sound of it seemed to stop her heart; its tone and timbre recalled better days. Mary beheld a lithe, graceful male figure in full pirate's regalia: Uncle James Gold. Mary ran toward him, fast as she could, and James caught her into a fond embrace. Her tears had begun when she first saw him; now she sobbed in earnest.

"Mary, Mary, sweet girl," he crooned.

Meanwhile, Catherine and the children hurried into the yard, curious about the strange, black cloaked figure. Behind James stood Richard and Bram, who apparently had accompanied James and Van from Cincinnati.

Richard said to James, "Please come inside, out of this wind. Welcome to Norris House!"

Once the men were seated in the parlor of Norris House, with glasses of French brandy in their hands, Richard said, "I propose a toast. To Mary Gold Hobbs and her new life – as heiress and landowner!"

Mary looked confused as they drank, and Uncle James explained that Grandfather Gold had been lost at sea a year before. Joseph's only beneficiaries were James and *Jeanette*. Because *Jeanette* had died, her share would come to Mary. James had searched for his sister and niece, traveling through Virginia and Kentucky, even to Warrick County, Indiana, where he had conducted an unpleasant interview with John Davis. He had given up the search, heading up the Ohio River, but had encountered Richard Norris at Cincinnati. During their conversation, they discovered that Richard and his brothers (merchants operating out of New York) had met Joseph Gold before the war; before their move to Indiana, the Norrises had maintained an ongoing, mutually profitable business relationship with him. On the way from Cincinnati to Norris House, James and Richard had reached an accord.

"I could take you back to Maryland," James said to Mary. "But I must return to sea, and there is no one to look out for you there. I completely trust Mr. Norris to manage your finances; you could become a landowner here, with your own house, servants, and a guaranteed income. In addition, a certain young man has asked for your hand in marriage."

Mary still felt confused, but quickly realized from the look on Bram's face that *he,* not Van, was the young man in question.

Then she heard Uncle James asking, "What do you say?"

Mary looked at Van, and saw that he released her; she looked at Catherine and saw raw jealousy and hate. She looked at Bram and saw naked longing in his face; he had at last found a way to let her know his intentions.

Mary, overwhelmed, looked down at the reticule that dangled from her wrist, opened it, and asked, "Can anyone tell me what these golden coins are worth? Every time I try to spend one, I get such strange reactions…"

Then she began to cry.

Bram sat beside Mary, wiped her tears with his kerchief, and said, "Mary, please be my wife."

She nodded, and he slipped an arm around her shoulders, his expression one of great joy.

The holidays raced by. Uncle James stayed, in order to witness Mary's wedding as well as to assess whether the Norrises seemed likely to care for her properly. There were dances, bonfires, and feasting in the streets at Lawrenceburg both for Christmas and for New Year's Eve. Mary laughed at the reactions of local young women who had never before been asked to dance by a pirate. Mary joined Uncle James in some of the more formal dances, and their graceful steps and striking good looks caused much comment.

1822

Decatur, Henry, Marion, Morgan, Putnam, Rush, and Shelby Counties were formed in Indiana during this year.

Mary fell completely in love with Bram. She had always been attracted to him, but had never understood him very well, mostly because he had trouble expressing his deepest thoughts. At first, she simply could not believe that he wanted to marry her, and insisted that he discuss his reasons with her. Bram had a firm vision of the future, of how his life would proceed: Land plus sons equaled wealth. Therefore, he would work for his father, save money to buy property, and rear a large family. Mary discovered herself to be an integral part of his plan. She alluded to the abuse in her past, wanting to make sure that he knew she had been sexually assaulted. But he did not care to know the details. Over and over, he expressed his devotion to her strong, lovely spirit. Finally, she was able to believe what he said: The past did not matter to him, only their future together.

But something else bothered her. The one constant in Mary's tumultuous life had been her Catholic faith. She remained convinced that her failure to be confirmed in the church placed her soul in peril. Her betrothal to a non-Catholic made matters even worse. In addition, accumulated unconfessed daily sins made her total burden of guilt seem unbearable. After some thought, she persuaded Uncle James to escort her to Louisville, where she could consult a priest.

When they arrived at the church in late morning, confessions were being heard, and a queue of penitents waited to enter the confessional. Mary convinced Uncle James, who chose not to speak with the priest, to leave her there and to explore the town for an hour. Mary sat on a hard bench, waiting. An old woman, then an old man made confession, then proceeded through a door into the church to pray. A heavily veiled woman had been next in line before Mary, and entered the confessional. Immediately, strange noises began issuing from the closet like structure. It quickly became evident that the woman had come to the church for some other purpose besides making confession. When the unmistakable sounds of urgent lovemaking became too loud to ignore, Mary fled the church, never to return. In early afternoon, she and Uncle James boarded the steamboat, where they had ample time to talk. Seeing that Mary was upset, James asked her what the priest had said. Hesitantly, she told him about her experience.

James laughed aloud.

"Don't take that stuff so seriously," he advised. "Priests are human, just as we are. Can you imagine having to sit in a box all morning, listening to the paltry, imagined crimes of the faithful?"

"But, I needed to talk with him," mourned Mary. "My spirit is weighed down with sin… I have never been confirmed in the Church, and now I have agreed to marry a Methodist."

"Your spirit is weighed by *guilt*," said James. "And you overrate the magnitude of your sin. You are far from unique. Your mother, for example, went straight from Confirmation into marriage with an atheist! Yet, Father Carroll granted her absolution."

"Who will grant me absolution?" she asked.

James grimaced, then replied, "There is something Father Carroll told me, which I think applies to your case. He said that when there is no priest available, one can make a personal act of contrition, which absolves a person before God until a priest can be found. This is especially useful to sailors, who could drown at any moment. The priest at Louisville proved unworthy to hear your confession. Therefore, you should make confession directly to God, and your soul shall be cleansed."

Mary stared at Uncle James, wanting desperately to believe him.

"Who hurt you, Mary?" he asked, softly. "It's obvious that your spirit is in pain."

Many emotions passed over James' face as Mary told him about her experiences with the Davis family, including John Davis. It took him some minutes to regain his composure. Finally, he spoke, his tone grim.

"I'll be visiting John Davis again soon," he vowed. "And he won't be hurting *any* more women. He won't have the equipment."

Mary's eyes grew very round. "Don't, *don't* kill him!" she begged. "You could be hanged..."

"I suspect I *could* be hanged for what I will do to him," James mused softly, an intensity glowing in his dark eyes. "But no one will even know I have been in town, and leaving him alive, maimed, will be a worse punishment, I think."

Mary was silent. What had she done?

"I should have waited for a priest," she thought. *"No one should make confession to a pirate!"*

The two arrived at Norris House in late afternoon, where Uncle James made his excuses and disappeared, headed back to the landing. He returned, days later, from his trip to Warrick County looking very satisfied, but said nothing to anyone about what he had done.

Mary went into seclusion for twenty-four hours, fasted, and prayed repeatedly:

Deus meus, ex toto corde poenitet me omnium meorum peccatorum, eaque detestor, quia peccando, non solum poenas a Te iuste statutas promeritus sum, sed praesertim quia offendi Te, summum bonum, ac dignum qui super omnia diligaris. Ideo firmiter propono, adiuvante gratia Tua, de cetero me non peccaturum peccandique occasiones proximas fugiturum. Amen.

[O my God, I am heartily sorry for having offended Thee, and I detest all my sins because of Thy just punishments, but most of all because they offend Thee, my God, Who art all-good and deserving of all my love. I firmly resolve, with the help of Thy grace, to sin no more and to avoid the near occasions of sin. Amen.]

At the end of her fast, she felt weak and dizzy, but thought that any god listening must have taken pity on her. On reflection, she decided that any god who chose *not* to grant absolution after such an extreme effort, under such exceptional circumstances, did not deserve her worship. She continued faithful, but on bad days guilt continued to plague her; on good days she worshiped a god of her own making, a merciful, understanding Being who would bless her attempts to reconcile with Him.

Mary wanted to move out of Norris House immediately; she did not care to begin her marriage surrounded by Catherine, Van, and the others. She longed for a new start, and therefore urged Uncle James to purchase property for a house where she could construct a new life.

When James enquired about suitable locations for a house, Richard Norris escorted him to Aurora. At first, the pirate was less than impressed by the lethargic atmosphere of the place. To be sure, there were a few warehouses, distilleries, foundries, and cooperage shops, but there was only one residence. When Richard and James climbed the dirt track to the top of the hill overlooking the Ohio River, however, the potential for development became obvious. On Richard's advice, James purchased two adjoining lots high on the hill, as well as a farm along Hogan's Creek outside the town limits. To please Mary, Bram hired local laborers to quickly erect a log cabin on one town lot; a proper house would be constructed during the following months. The log cabin would serve as servants' quarters after the town house was built. For that reason, the couple furnished the cabin with cast-off, used furnishings, including some of the Dutch pieces of Aaltje's that had been stored in the Norris barn.

Mary basked in a warm glow. Never before had she experienced such a strong sense of security, of being wanted so much. Even though she could tell that Bram longed to be with her physically, he did not touch her except for hugs and gentle kisses. This had the effect of heightening her desire for him; she lived for their moments alone together. Mary wondered if Bram suspected her relationship with his brother, but, after discussion with Van, decided not to broach the subject. Van swore never to disclose their secret to anyone, and she believed him.

By January 10th, the wedding preparations were made, and the ceremony was held at Norris House. The Norris family had to swallow its religious preferences; James flatly refused to allow his niece to be married by a Methodist minister. A Justice of the Peace was called in. The Norris family gathered, as well as Richard's business contacts from Lawrenceburg and Aurora. To the Norrises, such events were all part of the crucial public posturing required to establish and maintain influence in the community. The marriage of an eldest son was a social statement; the family made sure that people heard about Mary's status as an heiress of French nobility.

Mary's dress (empire waist, long sleeves, V-shaped collarless neckline, skirt of layered ruffles) had been made of imported gray silk; a dressmaker from Cincinnati put it together, with a matching headpiece and satin slippers. The bodice was snugly tailored, showing off Mary's figure to perfection. Richard's sister Mary helped to arrange the bride's long, curling black hair; Bram gave her a freshwater pearl necklace that had belonged to his mother. Mary looked stunningly beautiful, and Uncle James whispered to her that she outshone *Jeanette*.

Bram wore a navy blue single breasted jacket over his shirt, and full length, gray wool trousers. The jacket's lapels were square cut, and decorated with buttons that gave a double breasted V-shaped effect. In the front, the jacket met his trousers at the waist, but at the rear it descended into full swallowtails, rounded at the hip, which then dropped to knee level. At his throat he wore a white ruffled frill; his feet were tucked into patent leather slippers. His father presented him with a gold watch on a chain, which Bram wore in the watch pocket of his trousers.

Only as she set up housekeeping in their own place did Mary feel as if she had awakened from a particularly pleasant dream. The reality of cooking, cleaning, and of being with Bram at night proved to be better than any daily routine she had ever experienced. But she realized how little she knew about this man; she studied him carefully in order to ensure that her happiness could continue. Whenever he looked at Mary, Bram's face betrayed pure worship; this expression rarely varied in the forty-one years they spent together.

After the wedding, Uncle James departed toward Baltimore. He promised to stay in touch, difficult as that would be. Bram continued working for his father, traveling up and down the Ohio River, and therefore was home on an irregular basis.

Construction of Mary's two story, Federal style mansion began. Because the Ohio River bent abruptly to the South above Aurora (the mouth of Hogan's Creek), the view of the water from the house would reveal an unusually wide angle, breathtakingly beautiful. The open sky, the smell of water, and the sounds of birds recalled Mary's childhood in Maryland; she was content.

After hacking space for the foundation into the rocky hill, the builders made a fieldstone lined cellar measuring fifty feet wide and forty feet long. Next, a sub-flooring and frame were constructed of sturdy oak. As the walls rose around her, Mary worked hard to visualize the completed structure, and drew pictures in order to show the workmen what she wanted.

Viewed from the front, the house appeared both solid and inviting. The red brick exterior was attractively set off by white trim and a shallow-pitched black roof. An impressive entryway occupied the South corner of the first floor and was offset by two separate black shuttered, tall, twelve paned windows to the North. A semicircular brick walkway and steps, complete with black wrought iron railings, led to the door and away again. The sturdy oak door panels were painted black in order to resist weather. White painted wood-framed, slender sidelights and a beautiful curved fanlight, each set with small panes of leaded glass, surrounded the door and by day illuminated the foyer that also served as the landing for the elegant, curved interior staircase. On the second floor, three evenly spaced twelve paned, black shuttered windows faced the river. Under the eaves, a broad band of white cornice topped the brick. The roof featured a tiny, open cupola with a circular bench where one could sit in fair weather, watching river traffic. (Mary had to fight for the cupola; the men all warned her that its construction would cause future problems with leakage from the roof. Mary did not care. She informed them that if they used enough tar as sealant, nothing would leak.)

The house would face Northeast; this meant that morning sun would flood Mary's house with light, but she would rarely view sunsets because the hill obscured them. Mary insisted that each of the front windows be built with an extra-deep casement to allow for padded window seats on the inside.

"What good is it to have a view, if no one can sit to admire it?" she asked. The sides and back of the house contained much smaller windows, and for that reason the rooms at the back of the house were darker than those at the front. Mary obsessed over the house's progress, touring the work site many times each day. She drew multiple floor plans, often insisting that changes be made. Bram felt constrained to pay the workmen more than first agreed upon because he thought that she interfered with their efforts.

When he mentioned this to her, she stared at him, then asked, "It's my money, isn't it?"

Bram had to agree. However, legally, it was *his* money, and he would have preferred to invest it in land. Houses grew old; they burned down and were damaged by acts of God. But land increased in value, year by year.

The first floor of Mary's house contained a large "best parlor" or reception room across the front, a small traveler's bedchamber under the stairs, a formal dining room in the center at the back, and a kitchen/laundry (that expanded into the small back yard in hot weather) at the rear North corner. On the second floor, a sitting room and a library/office faced the river. The master bedroom occupied one back corner, but adjoined both the sitting room and the bedroom under the stairs to the attic, which had been designed as a nursery. The attic would be used for storage, and for access to the cupola. Each room contained either a fire place or a stove that required connection to the brick chimneys.

The house neared completion. Mary selected from a narrow range of available paint colors. In the interest of speed, the upstairs rooms were whitewashed except for the master bedroom that was painted in the deepest green she could find. For the downstairs rooms, Mary chose shades of blue except for the kitchen. It would require frequent re-painting and therefore walls, ceiling and floor received a coat of buttermilk red. This paint obtained its distinctive brown-red color from a combination of ox blood and buttermilk. Around the fifteen foot high ceiling of the two formal rooms ran a border of white crown moulding. In the center of the two formal ceilings hung an elaborate crystal and brass chandelier with holders for many candles. Beneath the crown moulding in the best parlor and in the dining room, as well as the foyer, ran a wide band of color containing a delicate scalloped plaster and painted stencil design. Below this band ran another, narrow border of moulding. Each doorway and fireplace in the formal rooms was framed by fluted composite pilasters. These simulated Corinthian columns projected a short distance into the room, and lent a sophisticated classical look. The decor was saved from seeming completely Greek or Roman by the presence in prominent places of American eagles bearing shields of stars and stripes.

In a frenzy of nest-building, Mary continued living in the cabin while she furnished her house, beginning with the bed of the master chamber. Reflecting that she expected to bear children and to someday die in this bed, Mary determined that it must be comfortable and exactly to her liking. She chose carved, richly stained and varnished cherry wood for the bedstead and posts; the concealed parts of the frame were constructed of sturdy oak. The bottom of the frame was suspended high above the floor in order to accommodate a trundle bed for the couple's anticipated children. Rope stretched across the bottom of the bed frame supported the straw-filled tick. A feather bed rested upon the tick, then another mattress covered by snow white linen sheets, a woolen blanket, and a counterpane. To assist Mary in climbing into this billowing cloud of comfort, a small set of wooden steps was placed on one side. A bolster supported the two feather pillows, while a small muslin pocket suspended on Bram's side waited to hold his watch and chain at night. Enveloping the bed posts, voluminous bed curtains of floral print, heavy-weight cotton were suspended from rods concealed inside the bed frame. The matching cotton tester formed a ceiling for the bed, supported by the upper bed frame and posts. When the bed curtains were closed during cold weather, the bed became a cozy room of its own. In summer, the curtains and heavy bedding were removed to promote air circulation. At the foot of the bed, a cherry wood, cedar lined chest held extra bed linens and blankets. Because in times of illness people often spent days attending the sick, Mary added a matching pair of overstuffed wing-chairs upholstered in sturdy cotton print canvas. These usually flanked the hearth, but could be moved to the bedside when needed. A dressing table with padded bench held materials for arranging Mary's hair. On the wall above hung a large mirror placed to reflect light from a window. The wash stand contained soap, towels, a pitcher filled nightly with clean water, and basins for clean and for dirty water. A spacious, cedar lined armoire stood in a corner to receive their clothing, its space supplemented by the drawers of a chest nearby. Behind the armoire, in order to provide some privacy, stood a wooden toilet chair with a lid. Within the chair rested a removable ceramic chamber pot. Mary had furnished the entire room to be reminiscent of a garden: green walls, cherry wood, and floral designs in the fabrics. She found the result to be a soothing retreat.

 Anticipating visitors, Mary furnished the front parlor and adjoining dining room before she actually moved from the cabin into the house. Having fallen in love with the look of cherry wood as she decorated the bedchamber, Mary continued its use downstairs as well. She ordered twelve straight chairs to match a highly polished cherry wood dining table, two upholstered sofas, and six comfortable upholstered chairs. On the walls opposite the windows, she hung mirrored sconces with holders for candles. The dining room floor was left bare, to facilitate cleaning, but the best parlor floor was covered by a patterned, multicolored woolen carpet, stretched tight and tacked into place along the edges.

Mary transferred the cooking implements from the cabin into her new kitchen, and she began living in the house. Because she was at first doing the cooking herself, she tried her best to arrange the room efficiently. The focal point was the fireplace, which provided both heat and light. The foreman of the construction crew tried to interest Mary in one of the new box stoves for cooking, but she preferred the familiar open hearth, with ovens built into the stonework. The hearth was outfitted with a crane, from which kettles or pots could be suspended at varying heights, then swung over the fire to heat. The ceiling beams had been left exposed, in order to facilitate the hanging of herbs, fruits, and vegetables to dry. Even though they broke up the useable wall space, Mary had insisted on several windows to provide light. In warm weather the lower portion of these windows, which opened, had to be covered with screens to keep out flying insects, and sticky fly paper was hung from the ceilings to catch those bugs who managed to find a way in. A dark brown oilcloth protected the floor from spills and could be removed for cleaning.

Bram brought home items for the house, such as gold-framed paintings for the walls, after every journey he made. On one of these occasions, he returned with a piano for the parlor, which made Mary break into tears of happiness. By the end of summer, the place was completely furnished, and Mary was content.

Bram also brought home a few black slaves that he had taken as payment for debts from business acquaintances in Kentucky. Mary realized that Bram's father, Richard, had done the same thing, and that several of the servants she had worked with at Norris House were actually owned by Richard.

Because Indiana land was so inexpensive, it was difficult to hire servants within the state. Even the poorest immigrants could squat on land, raising cash crops in order to make a down payment on their own farms. Therefore, after transporting slaves to Indiana, Bram informed them that, legally, they were free. There would be no indenture to hold them in the Norris household. However, free black persons were not welcomed as landowners within the state, so it was much harder for them than for whites to strike out on their own. Bram treated his servants with respect. He paid them standard wages (about 75 cents per day) while helping the more likely ones to learn a trade. In this way, he earned their loyalty; many stayed with the family for years in gratitude for his kindness.

On Muster Day, in April, Richard and Catherine Norris visited Mary's nearly completed house while en route to Lawrenceburg. To her amusement, Mary realized that her elegant house in town was exactly what Catherine Norris had wanted for a long time. Being stuck at a farm along Hogan's creek had never been part of Catherine's plan. Despite the fact that Aurora did not yet qualify as a town, jealousy oozed from Catherine's soul.

On Independence Day, Mary hosted a dinner for her in-laws. She knew very well that Catherine considered corn and pork to be essentials for any meal, and deliberately chose to serve instead fish, rice, roasted vegetables, and sliced, fresh fruits. The meal ended with a high, light, and delicately sweet cake that Phoebe Elvira used to make. Mary's new cook had practiced all the recipes in the weeks preceding the dinner, and Mary was very pleased with the result. She made sure that everything used for this occasion surpassed the table service at Norris House. Keeping her tone sweet as the cake, Mary drove Catherine close to the edge of rage by offering her more of this and that.

Van, at the opposite side of the table, had trouble concealing his amusement at Mary's well-disguised attack. He was quite circumspect, never hinting at his former relationship with Mary, yet whenever he met her gaze, Mary shivered with remembered pleasure. By the end of the dinner, she knew that she was not completely done with Van.

Jonathan Jennings resigned as Indiana Governor on September 12th, in order to serve in Washington as the Indiana representative to Congress. Lieutenant Governor Ratliff Boon, of Warrick County, took Jennings' place until the new governor, William Hendricks, was sworn in on December 4th. Hendricks had served as representative to Congress for the previous six years; before that, he was secretary of Indiana's 1816 Constitutional Convention.

Bram surprised Mary by telling her that William Hendricks was actually a distant cousin on his mothers' side. Mary surprised Bram by confiding that she had met Ratliff Boon, but she declined to go into detail.

Richard Norris at that time had a business partner in Ohio, William

Raper, who specialized in the bulk purchase of farm crops. Richard provided funding and warehouse storage, while William evaluated crops, negotiated prices, and arranged for shipping of goods. By mid-September of this year, a full boatload of corn had accumulated at Richard's warehouse in Aurora. Richard and William each assigned their sons to accompany the produce to market.

Mary had met William's son, Richard Raper, a few times, but found him unremarkable. Although well built and strong, the youth had little to say on any topic. Because she had not accompanied Bram to the wharf before this journey, Mary scarcely recalled who exactly was making this trip to Louisville. It turned out that Bram had taken his brother John, 16, with him and Richard Raper.

Three days later, Bram, appearing unusually disheveled, arrived home in late afternoon, accompanied by Richard Raper. Mary sprang up, intending to fetch drinks for them, but turned back when Bram collapsed onto a chair with a groan.

"What is amiss?" she asked, but Bram buried his face in his hands without response.

"The steamboat boiler exploded," explained Richard in a soft voice. "It all happened very fast…there was a fire…we were in the water, and Bram was knocked senseless. I got him to shore, but we couldn't find John, not until too late."

"John's dead," said Bram, his tone flat. "However can I tell Father?"

Mary slipped her arms around her husband.

"This was never your fault," she said. "And I know Father Norris would rather hear about it from you than from strangers. You must go to him."

Mary turned to Richard.

"You saved my husband?"

He looked at the floor, embarrassed, but nodded.

Mary kissed his cheek, saying, "We are forever in your debt. Thank you!"

John Norris' corpse was brought home, and buried beside his mother and siblings in the family cemetery.

As Advent approached, Mary began to long for decorations similar to those at *Grand-mère's* house. She induced a local craftsman to carve a flat wooden wreath/candle holder for the table. On the first Sunday of Advent, Mary proposed lighting a candle at dinner, and Bram had no objection.

However, he balked at the notion of placing *santons* in a *creche* on the sideboard. These seemed like idolatry to him; he wanted no such things in his home. Reluctantly, Mary agreed. She wanted to re-create some of the magical Christmas displays she had enjoyed as a child, but did not want to upset Bram.

As usual, the Norrises all attended the Lawrenceburg holiday celebrations. There were dancing and music, bonfires, free food and drink, all provided by the town. While dancing, Mary found herself in Van's arms several times, and realized that these events were becoming, for her, the high point of the year.

During this year the Monroe Doctrine came into effect: The United States declared that it would not tolerate European interference in the Western Hemisphere.

1823

Hamilton, Johnson, Madison, Montgomery Countries were formed in Indiana during this year.

Shortly after Epiphany, Mary began to feel ill. Recalling that one of the servants had experience as a midwife, she discussed her symptoms with the woman. The two decided that Mary must be pregnant.

While waiting for Bram at the dock in Aurora on February 12th, Mary overheard a German Lutheran saying that it was Ash Wednesday. She rushed home, to the sitting room where she always prayed, and made what she intended as a personal act of contrition. Then she began keeping track, by means of hash marks on the back of a piece of leftover wallpaper, of the forty days of Lent. Mary intended to send a clear message to God that she deserved a happy end to her confinement: A healthy child.

During the previous summer, Bram's stepmother, Catherine, had become pregnant. Of course, she made a big production out of the whole thing. At that time it was considered coarse to mention the details of childbearing to people outside the family, so Mary was forced to listen to her mother-in-law far more than she wanted. She was glad NOT to be present when Richard and Catherine's son, George C. Norris, was born.

After the initial round of morning sickness, Mary regained her health, and felt good until the weather turned beastly hot and humid in late June. Bram made it a point to remain at home with her, and was there when Mary went into labor late on Friday, July 9th. It turned out that the servant woman that Bram had purchased in Kentucky was quite skilled in these matters. She applied hot and cold compresses to assist Mary, along with judicious amounts of whiskey to reduce her pain. Bram started to protest that his wife should NOT be consuming whiskey, but the servant stared him down, and he left the room. Early Saturday morning, Mary's efforts at expelling the child were rewarded with a strong son. Too exhausted to protest that the name was sure to cause trouble, she allowed Bram to name him after his rescuer of the previous year. The child was duly recorded in the family bible as Richard Raper Norris, but, following their custom of calling each other by middle names, the Norrises referred to the child as Raper.

Near Palmyra, New York, "The Prophet" Joseph Smith was visited by the angel Moroni in September. The angel directed Joseph to a set of golden plates containing a chronicle of indigenous American prophets. Smith subsequently translated the information on the plates and, in 1830, published it as The Book of Mormon.

More than anything, Mary was bothered by the fact that her child had not been baptized by a priest, even though a Methodist minister had been called in to pray over him. Mary simply could not believe that the coarse Methodist in his ill-fitting, badly designed suit could have any influence with God. It was nearly Advent (November 30th) when she heard that a traveling priest had stopped at the landing in Aurora. Bram was away, in Cincinnati, for which Mary blessed God. Frantic for the soul of her son, she bade a servant to watch the baby while she flung on a cloak and nearly flew down the hill toward the dock.

Easily identifying the priest by his cassock and stole, she approached him, knelt, and seized his hand.

"Father, please," she begged. "Honor my household by staying with us tonight. We have need of your blessing."

The priest smiled at Mary and asked, "What is your name, my daughter?"

"I am Mary Norris, and my father-in-law Richard is one of the founders of this place."

Signaling his slave to bring the baggage, the priest said, "I had heard that there were Catholics at Lawrenceburg, but did not expect any here; it is my mission to be of assistance to you."

"I have an infant in need of baptism, and I need to make confession."

"Very good."

The priest told Mary that the Pope, Pius VII, who had held that position since 1800, had died on August 20th. A new Pope had been elected, and would be known as Leo XII, but the Holy Father was in poor health and not expected to live very long. Mary resolved to pray for him.

During the priest's visit, Mary found it easy to let him believe that she had been confirmed in the Church, so hungry was she for the absolution he could give. After he left, it occurred to her that absolution given under false pretenses might not be efficacious, yet she prayed that God would understand, and bless her newly baptized son.

Mary began on November 30 to light the Advent candles at supper, and observed in private the holidays as best she could.

On December 2nd, James Monroe, in a message to Congress, warned Europe against future colonization in the Western Hemisphere. He also professed United States neutrality in future European conflicts. His words (actually penned by John Quincy Adams) seemed insignificant at the time, but would be recalled and used as a principle of United States foreign policy, the Monroe Doctrine.

Baby Raper grew quickly. Even as an infant, he was more active than anyone expected. By mid-December he had begun to crawl about the house. As Advent approached, Mary reflected that she felt happier than ever before. She began work on a new gown, anticipating the street dances at Lawrenceburg. During this year a road had been constructed from Madison, Indiana, along the Ohio River through the towns of Vevay, Rising Sun, and Aurora to Lawrenceburg. The New Year crowds promised to be larger as a result.

At the celebrations, she deliberately stayed away from Van, convincing herself that she could erase the attraction she still felt for him. Yet, watching him dance with the other women hurt just a little. Later, she learned that Van had become engaged to one of them, Mary Early, and the wedding was scheduled for the following May.

During this year, Mexico began offering cheap land in order to attract Americans and to build up its population in the territory which later became Texas.

1824

Allen, Hendricks, and Vermillion County, Indiana were organized by the Indiana Legislature during this winter's session.

1824 saw the beginning of a five-year economic depression that threatened the Norris investments. The development of Aurora seemed permanently on hold.

The priest from Cincinnati visited Mary near the end of February, and advised her that Ash Wednesday would be observed on the second day of March. Mary vowed to fast, pray, and repent of all sin during the Lenten season. At the time, it seemed a reasonable promise, easy to keep. But the priest's visit caused her to more closely examine her behavior.

Mary knew that pride was a capital sin. Previously, she had ignored that knowledge, allowing herself to become completely besotted with Baby Raper. He was obviously smarter, stronger, and more handsome than any baby had ever been. Mary spent every waking moment fussing over him. The priest's warnings of God's punishment caused Mary to worry that her pride would result in the loss of her child. Therefore, she repented, relinquishing the baby's care to a nurse she hired from a poor family in the town.

Mary was well aware of other available sins, but thought herself securely insulated from opportunities to commit most of them by her isolation from people. Because Aurora had no resident population to speak of, social life required travel to Lawrenceburg (four miles away). Bram traveled up and down the Ohio River most of the time, and seldom attended church. This protected Mary from the Methodists who might otherwise have intruded upon her life. Mary would never have attended a celebration without Bram. Mary's servants brought goods as needed; businesses at Lawrenceburg ran a tab for Bram, and he paid his creditors regularly. Yet, Bram's absence in itself proved problematic.

At mid morning on Laetare Sunday, March 28th, the Devil came to call. Mary heard the servant opening the front door. By the time she reached the vestibule, Van Norris had removed his hat and overcoat, and the servant was hanging them upon the wooden rack behind the door.

Van turned to Mary, and she murmured to the maid, "Make sure there is plenty for dinner."

The servant disappeared as Van took Mary into his arms with more than brotherly affection.

"I've missed you," he said in his whispery voice, as he kissed her neck, his hands hot upon her back.

"Van," she began, but stopped, feeling herself respond to his warmth. Arguments against being with him rose into her brain, then fell away. Mary had been alone, at this point, for more than a month. She recalled too well how good it felt to be held and caressed by this man. Resisting him seemed impossible.

"Mary."

His sapphire eyes bored holes into hers, and he drew Mary by the hand up the stairs and into her bed, where he continued caressing her, loosening and removing her clothing.

"You're so beautiful," Van murmured into her ear.

She knew this to be true. Oh, how she had missed being adored by a man!

The remainder of the morning passed on repeated waves of pleasure, a pleasure made more intense because Van used none of the precautions to prevent pregnancy that had limited their activities before.

By dinnertime, the two had replaced their clothing and resumed some semblance of dignified restraint. Van admired baby Raper, and Mary gave him back to his nurse to be fed.

During dinner, Van steered the conversation away from plans for his upcoming wedding. Instead, he discussed recent events at Fall Creek, in the new Madison County, Indiana. Nine Seneca and Miami Indians had recently been massacred by whites. Eager to think and talk about anything other than the morning's activities, Mary pressed Van for details.

"From what I hear, three Indian men, with three women, two young boys, and two young girls had set up camp between Fall Creek and Deer Lick Creek. They were harvesting sap from a sugar maple grove and doing some late season hunting. Six whites, out for a little Saturday entertainment, dropped into their camp, accepted a meal, and then started shooting. One of the Indian men got away, wounded. The other Indians were killed, mutilated, then dumped into a hole in a half-assed attempt to hide the bodies."

"That's horrible!"

"Yes. And what's worse is that it may incite the natives into retribution. All whites had better be on the alert for Indian attacks."

"Why would anyone start trouble with the Indians? We had all that settled, years ago."

"It's the old attitude that the only *good* Indian is a *dead* Indian. Too many whites absorbed that sentiment in their cradles, and will never change."

"Are we at risk, here in Aurora?"

"Probably not. If you hear anything to the contrary, take the baby and cross the river to Kentucky, fast as you can."

To Mary's relief, Van left after dinner. During the next days her feelings vacillated wildly, preventing rational thought. At times, she fasted and prayed, making personal acts of contrition, pleading with God to keep Van away. At other times, she told herself that, if there was a god, he had not demonstrated any particular interest in her life. As long as no one found out about her relationship with Van, what did it matter? She *liked* being with him. But then again, what if God was watching, keeping track of her sins?

One week later, Bram returned, having heard, on his way home, about the massacre at Fall Creek.

After greeting Mary affectionately, while holding baby Raper, he said, "I'm concerned about Indian attacks."

"But, surely, we are well protected here," Mary remonstrated.

"Never underestimate the ingenuity of people bent on revenge," he told her. "I expect that Father will send me to Pittsburgh, almost immediately. I'll ask Van if he can stay here while I'm gone, to protect you."

Mary turned away, as if upset by the idea, as indeed she was, for reasons Bram did not suspect.

Finally, she formulated what seemed to her a logical question: "What will people say?"

"Who cares? I trust Van to keep you and Raper safe, and that is an end to it!"

Mary nearly choked on her conflicting emotions, but allowed Bram to hold and soothe her. Later, they made love in their usual, mutually comforting way.

Van moved into Mary's house. In order to keep the traveler's bedroom open for guests, she placed a bed for Van in her sitting room on the second floor. Relegating baby Raper to the care of his nurse, Mary spent most nights and many afternoons there with Van while Bram was away. When the priest visited, she managed to make confession without scandalizing the poor man too badly; she left him with the impression that she imagined herself to be much more wicked than she actually was.

Van spent a great deal of time supervising the construction of his house near Mary's, farther North along the ridge overlooking Aurora. His bride-to-be, a mousy woman who obeyed his every whim, turned over all the planning of the place to him. Mary could not understand what he saw in her until he let it slip that she had inherited property from her parents.

After the May 17th wedding, Van's wife became pregnant right away, and was quite ill all summer and into the fall. Using this as an excuse, Van continued to spend afternoons with Mary.

Mary attended the Independence Day celebration at Aurora with Van. Public excitement was quite high because a new steamboat, the *Clinton*, was being launched at the mouth of Hogan Creek on that day. There was much drinking, dancing, and general merriment. Afterwards, Van spent the entire night in Mary's bed, and it seems not to have occurred to his wife to ask where he had been.

On October 7th, the sensational trial of James Hudson, accused in the massacre of the Indians at Fall Creek, began. Every pioneer on the frontier could recite horror stories of Indian kidnappings, tortures, and bloodshed. The notion that a white man could be held accountable for clearing the land of Native American "vermin" was shocking to them. Yet, a small minority of whites, including the Norrises and others of Quaker or Catholic background, respected the rights and needs of the Native Americans. Hundreds of persons of Indian blood gathered on the borders of white settlements in Indiana and Ohio, making their presence felt. A number of their chiefs attended the trial, bearing silent witness to the white man's justice. John Johnston, the United

States government's Indian agent, met with them continually, staving off potential retaliation for the murders. All of this ensured that the trial gained national attention.

After the conviction of James Hudson, Van read Judge William W. Wick's sentencing statement aloud to Mary from *The Western Censor,* an Indianapolis newspaper dated Tuesday, October 19th:

JAMES HUDSON, The constitutional accusing tribunal of the country for the county of Madison, a grand jury of your fellows and peers, have presented you for the murder of LOGAN, an Indian of a tribe at peace with the United States. You have been arraigned - have pled not guilty - and have put yourself upon your country for trial. A jury of your own selection have found you guilty of the accusation, after a patient and full investigation, in which much ability & ingenuity have been exerted by your legal advisors on your behalf. The court being, according to the benign maxim of the law, "of counsel for the prisoner," have anxiously sought for grounds for a rational doubt in your favor, but are constrained, by proof the most full, perfect & clear, to accord to the verdict of the jury their reluctant, but undoubting assent. As the organ of the bench, it has, for the first time in my life, become my duty to pronounce upon a fellow mortal the most awful sentence of the law. Believe me, my heart recoils from the discharge of this duty. I would that it were otherwise.

> **I feel as a dying man. As such permit me to address you and to call upon you to**
>
> **"Look down - On what? A fathomless abyss, A dread Eternity, How surely yours."**

The evidence in the cause clearly warrants the unhesitating and decided belief that you did, without any just provocation, in cold blood, and with malice aforethought, shoot Logan so as thereby instantly to deprive him of life. O my God! How could you do it? How could you deprive your brother man (for Indian

Logan was your brother) of that life that God gave him, and which was as dear to him as is yours to you? How could you do a deed at which NATURE stood aghast, and at the recital whereof the soul sickens? Did you do it in revenge for some fancied or real injury? Did you persuade yourself that because he was an Indian it would be less criminal to take away his life than that of a white man? Do you still persist in applying to your conscience any such balsam? Standing, as you do, on the verge of Eternity, I beseech you to believe that it is only out of a regard to your eternal interests that I solemnly warn you, and call upon you (as one who would minister to your weal in regard to those immortal destinies which await you) and conjure you in the name of that God, before whom you must shortly appear, to strip yourself of any such refuge of lies. We are not authorized to avenge our own wrongs. To give us redress for our injuries is the province of the constituted authorities of our government. To avenge us for our injuries is the prerogative of Heaven, expressly reserved in the character given us for our government here.

"Vengeance is mine, saith the Lord, I will repay."

O sir! This plea however it may be partly supported in the too partial forum of your own conscience, or by a bench of modern "bloods," "bullies," and "gentlemen of honour," who bend the law to suit their own cruel and bloody notions, will be overruled when you reluctantly "appear and plead" at the "bar" of the Judge of all the Earth.

But Logan was an Indian: He was an hereditary enemy of white men.

Stop, Sir! If any pretended friends have led you to this precipice, permit me to extend a friendly hand, and faithfully, though perhaps to appear harshly, arrest you ere your soul is engulfed in the deceitful abyss forever.

Logan, although an Indian, is a son of Adam, our common father. Then surely he was not the natural enemy of white men. He was bone of your bone & flesh of your flesh. Besides, by what authority do we vauntingly boast of our being white? What principle of philosophy or of religion establishes the doctrine that a white skin is preferable in nature or in the sight of God to a red or black one. Who has ordained that men of the white skin shall be at liberty to shoot and hunt down men of the red skin, or exercise rule and dominion over those of the black? The Indians of America have been more "sinned against than sinning." Our fore fathers came across the broad Atlantic, and taking advantage of their fears and their simplicity obtained a resting place among the Indians, then the "lords of the soil," and since that time by a series of aggressions, have taken from them their homes and firesides - have pressed them Westwardly until they are nearly extinct. We have introduced among them diseases and vice; we have done to them wrongs which cry to Heaven for vengeance, and which have, in many instances, brought down upon us a severe retribution. Our government has indeed always of late years treated them as an independent people, and have purchased their soil for valuable considerations, but those treaties and purchases have generally been made, either after some great victory while the Indians were humbled by recent defeat, or when our population was pressing upon them, and they were, as it were, beat back by the "tide of emigration." Certain it is, that, under the influence of the wily arts of the enemies to our government, they have made war upon us, and contrary to the rules of civilized warfare, have failed to exempt from the effects of their rage unoffending women and children, and even the unresisting prisoner has been sacrificed to their vengeance. Such is the manner in which all savage nations make war. They are not at least guilty of making invidious distinctions to our prejudice, for they make war in the same manner upon one another. If they are savage, as we affect to call them, what more could we expect from them? We, as a civilized and Christian people, ought not to retaliate even when smarting under the remembrance of a recent outrage. How much less should we make a savage and unprovoked warfare, in times of perfect tranquility, upon a friendly, unsuspecting Indian, who, by visiting our territory, had made himself as it were our guest.

I feel no wish unnecessarily to harrow up your feelings, but I must ask you why you could not permit Logan to revisit his former home, and to hunt in his native forests? How could you have the heart to make war upon, shoot, and destroy the venerable of chief, whose name ought to have been his passport and protection from Maine to Georgia and from the Mississippi to the Atlantic? The blood of a Logan has a second time gone up before Heaven crying aloud for vengeance. The blood of a Logan and a "friend of white men" rests upon your conscience, and has imprinted a stain too deep to be washed out but by the blood of a REDEEMER.

I entreat and charge you that, under a proper sense of your natural depravity, as well as of all your actual transgressions, you humble yourself before that God, whom you must shortly meet either as an angry Judge, or kindly Redeemer.

Listen to the sentence of the law - which is, that you be now taken to the place whence you came; that you be there detained in close custody of the sheriff of Madison county, until Wednesday the first day of December next, on which day, between the hours of ten o' clock in the forenoon and two o'clock in the afternoon, you be hanged by the neck until you are DEAD.

And a God of mercy have compassion on your soul.

In early November, John Quincy Adams was elected President in a bitterly fought, four-way presidential contest. So controversial was his selection by the House of Representatives over the popular choice, Andrew Jackson, that it became known as the "Corrupt Bargain." Seeking to reinforce the policies of his father's presidential administration, J.Q. began with lofty goals of encouraging education, internal improvements such as roads and canals, Western expansion and scientific experimentation. These won him the support of the Norris men, who enthusiastically celebrated Adams' ascent to power. But, because of bad administrative choices based on impractical political principles, he experienced a miserable, lonely, failed presidency.

On November 15th, James Hudson escaped from jail, but was recaptured after ten days, suffering from frostbite. He was undoubtedly lucky that the Indians did not capture and deliver justice to him, themselves. While Hudson was missing, his hanging was rescheduled from December 1st to January 12th.

With cold weather, Bram returned home, and remained there through the holidays. Advent began on November 28th, but the magic of it evaporated with the memory of Van's sardonic smile whenever Mary lit the candles.

However, at the Christmas celebration in Lawrenceburg, Mary met members of a Catholic family who invited her to their home for midnight Mass. This was celebrated by a priest she had not met before, a German, Father Joseph Ferneding. The man, only three years older than Mary, had a rather untamed aspect, wild hair and blazing stars for eyes. Mary, unsettled by the impression that he already knew her deepest secrets, made a carefully edited confession and was granted absolution.

Van and Bram escorted Mary to the New Year's Eve Celebration in the streets of Lawrenceburg. Van's wife, whose baby was due in mid-February, remained at her home. Mary was having a good time until she caught sight of Van dancing with their mother-in-law, Catherine. Mary had never felt jealousy so intense. Before this, she would have sworn that Van and Catherine could not have had a physical relationship, but now she was not so sure. After all, Van and Catherine were of about the same age, born in the same year...

1825

Next morning, desperate to obliterate Van from her mind, and to regain some vestige of her self respect, Mary fasted and prayed, observing the Solemnity of Mary.

Also on New Year's day, President Monroe honored Marie Jean Paul Joseph Roche Yves Gilbert du Motier, Marquis de Lafayette, at a reception in the White House at Washington City. Lafayette had been in the United States since the previous August, and would spend fourteen months touring the country he had helped to establish.

Clay County was formed by the Indiana Legislature during this year. At about this same time, increasing numbers of Indiana businessmen and politicians caught a serious case of internal improvement fever. Over the next decades, focused primarily on road, canal, and railroad construction as paths to Indiana's economic success, state leaders flirted with fiscal insolvency that nearly sank the fledgling ship of state.

As the scheduled hanging for James Hudson, perpetrator of the Fall Creek massacre approached, Native Americans gathered in Indiana. Many of them wanted to watch the sentence being carried out. Rumors circulated that two hundred fifty warriors had assembled at the headwaters of White River, prepared to avenge the deaths of their murdered relatives. This brought pressure to bear on the officials of Madison County; if any thing went wrong, a retaliatory massacre, or even an Indian war could result. On January 12th, Hudson's execution took place, the first recorded capital punishment of a white for the murder of an Indian.

Ice on the river melted in early February, and Bram with his father Richard prepared for their first business trip of the year. Bram packed clothing in a canvas satchel, explaining that they would take a steamboat to Pittsburgh for a shipment of glass. Van, knowing that Bram was leaving, showed up, presumably to eat breakfast with his brother and to say goodbye. Bram had no sooner gone down the front steps, however, than Van seized Mary, his lips caressing her neck.

Squirming away, Mary protested, "It's too dangerous! What if he comes back?"

Van's eyes blazed as he pulled her close, saying, "What if he does? I've waited too long to have you again. My wife is big as a house, and I need you."

Within minutes, despite all Mary's intentions to the contrary, their affair resumed as if the holidays had never interrupted. Through the rest of the cold, lonely winter, Van often brought heat to Mary's bed.

On February 12th, William Hendricks resigned as Governor of Indiana; James Brown Ray served as interim Governor, then won the permanent position in the fall, serving as Governor until 1831.

At about the same time, the state capital was moved to Indianapolis, and construction of official, public buildings began.

Ash Wednesday fell on February 16th, but Mary did not pretend that she would give up her sin for Lent. A few days afterward, she attended the birth of Van's first child, a boy named William. The new mother's expressions of gratitude loaded Mary's mind with guilt. Nor did she fool herself that Van would ever be hers alone. She did not have to ask whether he saw other women when he traveled to Cincinnati for his father; always truthful, Van often bragged to her about his exploits. In self defense, she pretended that these confessions of his did not tear at her heart. After a time, she convinced herself that she did not care what he did while he was away.

The Spring floods were notable in this year, and Mary realized the advantage of her hillside home site. Many of Aurora's warehouses and waterfront businesses were damaged.

On March 4th, John Quincy Adams was sworn in as President of the United States.

For Easter Sunday, April 3rd, Mary had asked the servants to prepare a special ham dinner with all the trimmings. As she and Van sat down at the table, she realized that her stomach was upset, and that she could not possibly eat anything.

During the following days, she continued to feel nauseated in the mornings, and came to the conclusion that she was pregnant, and not by Bram. When she told Van, he could not stop laughing, until she turned away from him, in tears.

"Stop it," he told her. "What difference does it make which of us is the father? The child will look like Bram, probably walk and talk like him, too. He'll rear it as his own, and never know. It's not as if he didn't *want* more children!"

Mary saw his point, yet could not help feeling bad about the whole thing. Perhaps the priest could help her... Then she remembered Father Ferneding's blazing eyes, and decided she'd better not confess this sin except in general terms.

By early May, Mary was feeling much better; pregnancy agreed with her. In the evening on Friday, May 6th, Van proposed a short horseback trip on the following day. Although Bram had remained at Pittsburgh, managing their warehouse, Richard had returned and would accompany Van and Mary.

"Where are we going?" she asked him.

"Perhaps you have heard of the great Revolutionary War hero, the Marquis de Lafayette."

"Of course! He helped to rescue my *grand-mère*, in France."

"Well, he is in the neighborhood, to visit Colonel Zebulon Pike, who was on his staff during the war."

"Not *the* Zebulon Pike? He died, didn't he?"

"Actually, the folks at the wharf were discussing this today. The more famous *General* Zebulon Pike was the son of this Zebulon Pike. General Pike led 'The Pike Expedition,' to explore the West in 1806. He was captured by the Spanish, escorted to their Eastern border, and kicked out. Then, he was killed during the War of 1812. He had led the attack on York, Ontario, and the British exploded their ammunition store as they retreated. Pike was killed by a chunk of flying rock."

"And because of his attack, the British burned Washington City."

"Yep. However, the Zeb Pike we will visit has had better luck than his son."

Next morning, Mary dressed in a frilly, low-cut, ruffled silk gown and arranged her hair with special care. She wore pearls at her throat and wrists, and carried a parasol that matched her dress. Luckily, the weather and temperature cooperated; she would not need to change clothing before meeting General Lafayette.

At dawn, Richard Norris arrived at her door with three horses, one a gentle mare for Mary to ride.

"Where's Catherine?" Van asked his father. "I thought she wanted to meet the general."

Richard replied, his tone a bit worried, "She's not feeling well, and says that she may be expecting."

Mary happened to be watching Van's face as Richard said this, and noted Van's expression of wicked mirth. She thought about Van's unexplained absences during the long winter afternoons while Richard was away, and her mind began a slow burn.

While Richard and Van ate breakfast, she nibbled at a crust of toast and thought about the Norrises. She realized that, for them, all of life was a game of exchange and purchase. They trusted their instincts, finding ways to acquire whatever seemed good at the moment. This opportunity to meet General Lafayette, for example, was for them a chance to gain social standing in the community. Her role would likely be to charm the French General, in order to impress the locals. The men would profit from reflected glory. Well, what did it matter? This would be, at the very least, interesting. And she owed her present comfortable position in life to these men. But this business with Catherine...she did not like it at all.

The trio rode into Lawrenceburg, then a short distance up a narrow track along Tanner's Creek to what became Greendale, Indiana. By using great care in guiding her horse, Mary managed to keep her gown from being splashed with mud.

Richard led the way into the Pike home, a log cabin glorified by the addition of plank siding. Van, who had lifted Mary from the horse, offered his arm to help her negotiate the uneven fieldstone step into the house. Richard had already met Lafayette, and turned, introducing Mary as she approached.

Mary had not been sure what to expect, but the man facing her seemed very ordinary. Instead of a grand uniform (to which he was certainly entitled), he wore the clothing of a prosperous farmer, much the same as Mary's father and grandfather had worn. Knee breeches, tall leather boots, a white ruffled shirt with over-the-chin collar, a striped silk vest, and cutaway double-breasted blue coat of light wool with brass buttons comprised his costume. His high, steeply slanted forehead emphasized his large Gallic nose. His white hair had been gathered into a queue at the nape.

Lafayette had been seated in the only armchair available, and rose to his feet. As if mesmerized, he stepped forward, grasping Mary's hand in both of his.

"Madame! What joy it is to behold your beauty!" he exclaimed, his eyes alight with pleasure.

"*C'est une honneur vous rencontrer, Monsieur de Lafayette,*" [It is an honor to meet you, Mr. Lafayette.] she responded, raising her eyes to his.

Because she had responded in French, Lafayette continued the conversation in that language, as did she.

"Pardon, Madame Norris, but you seem so familiar. Have we met?"

"Perhaps you are thinking of my *grand-mère*, the Princess Marie de Bourbon."

Lafayette's mouth opened in astonishment, then closed abruptly.

"Is this your husband?" he asked.

Mary blushed becomingly.

"This is my brother in law, Van Norris. He has insisted that we should meet."

Lafayette bowed formally to Van, then drew Mary by the hand to sit next to him on a low bench.

"Please tell me about your family. How did you arrive at this place?"

Briefly, Mary recounted her family history, expressing her gratitude for Lafayette's assistance to *Grand-mère*, then asked, "What is the current status of my family in France?"

A furrow of thoughtful concentration appeared between Lafayette's eyebrows as he replied, "Charles de Bourbon has been crowned King of France, but the future remains uncertain."

As more people crowded into the little house, waiting to meet Lafayette, he continued to gaze raptly into Mary's lovely face. At last, recollecting himself, he begged her pardon and rose to his feet. Mary's eyes signaled to Van, and he led her away, toward Richard. As the three passed the more prominent citizens of Lawrenceburg, Mary saw new respect for herself in all their eyes.

"Strange," she thought. *"It's good that they don't know my entire story."*

But Lafayette's response to Mary had bothered Van.

"I didn't believe it until today," he commented during the ride home.

"What?"

"All that about your noble relatives."

"Nevertheless," she replied, "it's true. You're dealing with a member of the French royal house."

The two Norris men dropped Mary at her doorstep. After supper, she congratulated herself on avoiding Van, and retired to her bed, but he found her there.

"How did you get in here?" she asked, annoyed.

"What's the matter?" he wanted to know when she pulled away from him.

"You and Catherine," she responded. "I just can't believe it."

He seemed surprised that she had guessed, but recovered quickly.

"Hey," he said. "I never promised you anything. I've made it clear that there are others..."

"But your mother in law! That's disgusting!"

"And you're what? My sister."

"Your sister in LAW," she snapped. "I'm not giving birth to your future brothers and sisters, as Catherine will."

He shrugged. "So what? She's my STEP-mother. I'm not related to either one of you, so far as I know. Catherine's fun in a limited way. But you, my French princess, you're special."

"If you're trying to win my affection, quit comparing me to Catherine. I despise that woman, and I don't see how you can STAND her."

Van proceeded to make love to Mary with intensity. She realized that she had gained value in his eyes, and suspected that, had they occurred before her marriage, the events of this day could have won Van as her husband. All of which left her wishing that she could keep Van for herself. He really was the best lover she'd ever known...

On Monday, May 9, the trials of the remaining three captured perpetrators of the Fall Creek massacre began, and Van read the accounts to Mary from the newspapers.

On Tuesday, Bram arrived home, breathless with news. General Lafayette had continued his journey down the Ohio aboard a steamboat. As the boat passed Perry County, it struck the jagged edge of Rock Island. While every article of baggage and clothing was lost, all passengers and crew were rescued. Another boat was sent out, and the general continued his tour of the country he had helped to found.

Mary told Bram of her pregnancy, and he rejoiced that he was to become the father of a new child. Mary could not bring herself to enlighten him regarding the child's true paternity, and ultimately convinced herself that he and the child need never know about it. But she did vow silently to keep Van out of her bed, a promise that lasted until Bram left on his next trip downriver.

Also on Tuesday, at the trial in Madison County, Andrew Sawyer was tried and found guilty of manslaughter in the deaths of one Indian woman and a small child. He was sentenced to two years hard labor in the state prison, and a fine of $100.

On Wednesday morning May 11th, the trial of John Bridge, Jr. concluded in a verdict of guilty for first degree murder. The young man was considered by the jury to have been under the influence of his father and uncle, and they recommended pardon; a petition was circulated, signed by many, and sent to the governor of Indiana..

On Thursday, John Bridge, Sr. was found guilty of murder and assisting to murder the women and children. Andrew Sawyer was tried and found guilty of a separate charge in the murder of Ludlow, a Seneca Indian.

All three men were sentenced to death by hanging.

On June 3rd, John Bridge, Sr., John Bridge, Jr., and Andrew Sawyer were led to the gallows constructed for this trial and previously used for James Hudson. A sermon was preached before a large crowd, and prayers were offered. The two older men were first allowed to speak, then executed. Everyone waited, expecting a last-minute pardon from Governor Ray for John Bridge, Jr. When no word arrived from Indianapolis, another sermon was preached. Finally, the youngest perpetrator was led onto the platform, the rope placed over his head. As the executioner waited for the signal, a cheer went up from the back of the crowd. People made way as a large horse cantered toward the gallows. Astride the horse sat a tall, well-dressed man with a broad, high forehead, and long hair tied at the nape of his neck. His features were pleasing, his attitude that of one used to command. He looked the condemned young man in the face.

"Do you know who I am?" he demanded.

John Bridge, Jr. shook his head.

"There are but two powers known to the law that can save you from hanging by the neck until you are dead, dead, dead. One is the great God of the Universe, the other is J. Brown Ray, Governor of the State of Indiana. The latter stands before you."

Governor Ray handed a paper to the sheriff.

"The prisoner is pardoned," he said.

The remaining perpetrator and probable instigator of the massacre at Fall Creek, Thomas Harper, had escaped capture and was never brought to justice, despite the posting of cash rewards.

Mary's pregnancy advanced with the heat of summer, and she grew quite miserable inside her swollen body. Her maid exerted herself, offering Mary frequent baths and cool fruit juice. According to Van, Catherine was complaining loudly to anyone who would listen. At last the weather moderated, in October, and Mary blessed God for the relief.

The Erie Canal was completed on October 26th from Albany to Buffalo, New York, a navigable water route from the Atlantic Ocean via the Hudson River to the Great Lakes.

Advent approached, and Mary prayed for a safe delivery. On Sunday, November 20th, she heard that, the previous night, Catherine had borne a daughter, Samantha. Two days later, Mary felt the well-remembered pangs of childbed, and retreated to her room with the maid. It seemed an eternity, but at last she was delivered of a baby girl. Bram was ecstatic.

Van, having been chastised by Catherine for causing her so much pain, approached Mary's bed hesitantly, to see his other new child. Mary just looked at him.

"What will you call her?" he wanted to know.

"I'll name her for the kindest woman I ever met, your mother. We'll call her Altha."

Van turned away, and it was one of the few times Mary ever saw him weep.

By the next Sunday, Mary was beginning to move around the house, and lit the first candle of Advent. Christmas and New Year were spent quietly by the fireside, the dances at Lawrenceburg foregone for this year.

Every day, Mary spent time in prayer, vowing to remain faithful to Bram.

1826

Clay County, Indiana was formed during that winter's legislative session; during this year, the Indiana State Legislature also formed Fountain and Tippecanoe Counties.

Individual whites continued their exploitation of the Miami and Potawatomi Indian tribes, giving them food, alcohol, and cheap gifts in exchange for tracts of land. Most Hoosiers wanted the Native Americans to exchange all of their Indiana land for equal acreage on the Missouri River, West of the Mississippi, leaving Indiana to the whites. Officials in Washington considered this to be the best option, due to the constant friction between Native Americans and early settlers. There was also what whites perceived as an urgent need for right-of-way for the construction of the Michigan Road and the Wabash and Erie Canal. The Michigan Road would eventually connect Lake Michigan to the Ohio River, while the canal would connect Lake Erie to the Ohio River. Both were attempts to establish routes for trade and for travel, improving the economic standing of the state.

However, some Hoosiers - the Indian traders - wanted Native Americans to stay in Indiana, and their motive was pure greed. Trade with Indians meant guaranteed profit, since the national government picked up the tab for bills run up by the Indians. Traders simply presented the bills, frequently inflated, to the Indian Agent for reimbursement. Coupled to this was the tradition of annual money-gifts called annuities which the federal government had pledged to each tribe in individual tribal treaties. The Indian traders counted on this "pocket money" as they peddled supplies to Native Americans. Agent (Captain) John Tipton's files were bulging with appeals from the traders and their friends to keep the tribes intact and living on their own land within the state, an idea Tipton himself found appealing.

During this spring, Congress made an appropriation for a treaty meeting to acquire additional land from the Indians. Governor James B. Ray of Indiana, Governor Lewis Cass of Michigan, and Captain John Tipton were appointed as commissioners to represent the **United States** *Government.*

Captain Tipton was assigned the task of locating a site for the meeting. He found a place convenient to members of both Miami and Pottawatomie tribe members, with a plentiful spring and enough open land to construct the treaty camp (a collection of small log shacks) during the spring and summer of 1826. The site of the Treaty Grounds, now called Paradise Springs Park, today is a city park at the East end of Market Street in Wabash, Indiana.

The treaty meeting was planned for October, and would last approximately two weeks.

During March of this year, the brick courthouse at Lawrenceburg burned, and all Dearborn County records located therein were destroyed.

Perhaps because she was looking for spirituality wherever she could find it during this spring, Mary was impressed by her son Raper's intensely emotional reaction to everyday life. Even as an infant, he had been quick to respond to light, shadow, color, and movement. Now that he was more mobile, he would rush eagerly to examine anything new, such as a flower or a dead bird. Mary carried him to the cupola atop her house, where he would gaze at the sky in any weather, exclaiming over the colors and the patterns of clouds. Mary especially enjoyed teaching him new words, helping him to express himself. He truly was a wonderful little boy.

Baby Altha, once she had overcome the colic that plagued her early in the year, became a happy baby with an especially sunny nature. Mary dressed her in beautifully embroidered, lace-edged gowns. The weather remained cold far into the spring, however, and Mary kept the child at home for fear of illness.

Bram had taken Van with him on his trips up and down the river, and Mary thought that God had at last heard her prayer, delivering her from the temptation of having Van nearby all of the time.

She reckoned without the Reverend Joseph Ferneding. Every time she attended Mass at Lawrenceburg, Mary noticed her own physical attraction to the priest, and strove to resist it. Unlike the tall Norris brothers, this man was close to her own height. His dark, curling locks fell to his shoulders, except for a comma of hair that swept from the right side of his head, ending just above his left eye. His eyes glowed pale blue in a swarthy, devilish face set with flashing white teeth. More than anything, his small body size attracted Mary. She imagined holding him, entwined around her, as an unparalleled pleasure.

Ash Wednesday fell on February 8th, and Mary planned to leave the children with their nurse, traveling the four miles to Lawrenceburg weekly during Lent. She wanted to make confession and to hear Mass at the home of the Catholic parishoners there. Mary always contributed food to the carry-in dinner after Mass, and she also gave a substantial offering to Father Joseph's expense fund. At the gatherings, the priest would circulate among all the members of his tiny flock, but he always made a point of standing or sitting near Mary. Often, his hand would brush hers, and his burning eyes sought contact that never failed to make her stomach contract.

Mary had attended Mass on Laetare Sunday, March 5th, and was disconcerted next morning to find Father Ferneding at her door in Aurora.

"May I come in, my child?"

"Of course, Father. What brings you out this way?"

"You *did* mention that your daughter needed baptism."

"Yes. Oh, yes! Thank you for coming."

Father Joseph stepped close, took Mary's hand, and turned it over, inspecting her palm. Her face flushed a deep red. Surely he could not guess her secret regarding this child's paternity! He continued holding her hand and stroking her arm as they talked. Presently, Mary pulled her hand away.

"I must prepare the baby for baptism; will you have tea?"

"Yes, but I must know the child's name."

"We're calling her Altha."

"I don't recall a Saint Altha; does she have a middle name?"

"No."

"Well, what about your own name? Mary is the holiest of all female names...Altha Mary is very nice."

He stroked her cheek, and again Mary flushed. Desperately concentrating on the business at hand, Mary explained that Altha's godfather, James Gold, would be unable to attend, but that he would be summoned if Mary died, and would assume spiritual responsibility for Altha. She did *not*, however, mention that this godfather happened to be a pirate, nor Uncle James' opinions about the moral values of priests.

"All right," Mary said, reclaiming her hand and shaking off her own powerful reaction to the man's touch. "Altha Mary it is."

The priest nodded, and Mary led him to the parlor, then directed her maid to fetch tea and sweet biscuits. She raced to the nursery, quickly washed the baby and, with the nurse's help dressed her in the white, embroidered gown that had been worn by her son Richard.

As Mary entered the parlor carrying baby Altha, Father Ferneding raised his hand in a signal for her to stop. Having been through this ritual with baby Raper, none of the following ceremony surprised Mary. However, the other priest lacked Father Joseph's intensity; he had neither frightened nor excited Mary nearly so much. Instead of reading the words of the baptismal ceremony, Ferneding recited them from memory while gazing raptly into Mary's eyes. At every moment when he could possibly touch Mary, he did so, such that the sacrament was punctuated by caresses that properly could only come from a lover.

"Mary Norris, are you willing to bring up this child as a Christian?"

"Yes."

Father Joseph said, *"Mary, Ego vindicatum vos pro Christos nostrum Saviour per Subcribo of Suus Crux Crucis."* [Mary, I claim you for Christ our Savior by the Sign of His Cross.]

He traced the sign of the cross on the baby's forehead, and took Mary's hand, making it do the same. He then led the way to a small table that he and the maid had cleared of bric-a-brac and moved away from the wall. He had covered it with a white, embroidered silken scarf, and placed upon it a basin, a lighted candle, and four blown-glass cruets. Two of these contained holy oil; another held blessed salt, the fourth held blessed water. Mary advanced to the make-shift altar, and tried to focus on the ceremony as the priest's eyes burned into her soul. He was reciting something in Latin, probably from the Bible, she thought. Then he prayed, and she copied him when he made the sign of the cross.

Then he looked at Mary. "What do you ask of the Church of God?"

"Faith."

"What does Faith offer you?"

"Everlasting life."

"If then, it is life that you wish to enter, keep the commandments. Love the Lord your God with your whole heart, and love your neighbor as you love yourself."

Raising his hand, he blew gently three times into the face of baby Altha, who wrinkled her nose and squirmed. He began the exorcism, endeavoring to erase inborn sin from this minute bit of humanity.

"Exi ab ea, immúnde spíritus, et da locum Spirítui Sancto Paráclito." [Depart from her, unclean spirit, and give place to the Holy Spirit, the Consoler.]

Using his thumb, he made the sign of the cross on the forehead and on the breast of the child, saying, *"Accipe signum Crucis tam in fron te, quam in cor de, sume fidem cæléstium præceptórum: et talis esto móribus, ut templum Dei jam esse possis."* [Receive the sign of the Cross on your forehead and in your heart. Have faith in the teachings of God, and live in such a way that from now on you may be enabled to be a temple of God.]

Saying, *"Oremus,"* [Let us pray] he then descended into prayer, and Mary did not try to follow, except to copy whenever he made the sign of the cross, and to respond at the end:

"Preces nostras, quæsumus, Dómine, cleménter exáudi; et hanc eléctam tuam Mary crucis Domínicæ impressióne signátam perpétua virtúte custódi: ut magnitúdinis glóriæ tuæ rudiménta servans, per custódiam mandatórum tuórum ad regeneratiónis glóriam pervenire mereántur. Per Christum Dóminum nostrum." [O Lord, we implore Thee, in Thy kindness hear our prayers, and guard with unfailing power this Thy chosen Mary, who has been stamped with the seal of the Lord's cross; so that, holding fast to the first truths she has learned of Thy great glory, she may, by keeping Thy commandments, attain to the glory of rebirth. Through Christ our Lord.]

"Amen."

Next, he placed his hand on the baby's head and said, *"Oremus. Omnípotens, sempitérne Deus, Pater Dómini nostri Jesu Christi, respícere dignáre super hunc fámulam tuam Mary quam ad rudiménta fídei vocáre dignátus es; omnem cæcitátem cordis ab ea expélle; disrúmpe omnes láqueos sátanæ, quibus fúerat colligáta; áperi ei, Dómine, jánuam pietátis tuæ, ut signo sapiéntiæ tuæ imbúta, ómnium cupiditátum fœtóribus cáreat, et ad suávem odórem præceptórum tuórum læta tibi in Ecclésia tua desérviat, et profíciat de die in diem. Per eúmdem Christum Dóminum nostrum."* [Let us pray. Almighty and everlasting God, Father of our Lord Jesus Christ, be pleased to look upon this Thy servant, Mary, whom in Thy goodness Thou hast called to be instructed in the Faith. Rid her of all blindness of heart; break all the nets of Satan in which she has been entangled. Open to her, Lord, the gate of Thy mercy so that, penetrated by the sign of Thy wisdom (salt), she may be rid of the stench of all evil desires and, moved by the pleasing fragrance of Thy teachings, may joyfully serve Thee in Thy Church and daily advance in perfection. Through Christ our Lord.]

He looked at Mary, who responded, "Amen."

He shook blessed salt from a cruet, placed a bit of it into Altha's mouth, and said, *"Mary, accipe sal sapiéntiæ: propitiátio sit tibi in vitam ætérnam."* [Mary, receive the salt of wisdom. May it win for you mercy and forgiveness, and life everlasting.]

Mary said, "Amen."

"Pax tecum." [Peace be with you].

This time, Mary knew the Latin, *"Et cum spíritu tuo."* [And with your spirit.]

"Oremus. Deus patrum nostrórum, Deus univérsæ cónditor veritátis, te súpplices exorámus, ut hanc fámulam tuam Mary respícere dignéris propítius, et hoc primum pábulum salis gustántem, non diútius esuríre permíttas, quo minus cibo expleátur cælésti, quátenus sit semper spíritu fervens, spe gaudens, tuo semper nómini sérviens. Perduc eam, Dómine, quæsumus, ad novæ regeneratiónis lavácrum, ut cum fidélibus tuis promissiónum tuárum ætérna præmia cónsequi mereátur. Per Christum Dóminum nostrum." [Let us pray. God of our fathers, God the Author of all truth, we humbly implore Thee to look with favor on this Thy servant, Mary, and grant that she who is now tasting this salt as her first nourishment may not hunger much longer before she is given her fill of heavenly food, so that she may always be ardent of soul, rejoicing in hope, and ever loyal to Thy name. Bring her, O Lord, we ask Thee, to the font of the new birth, so that in company with Thy faithful servants, she may gain the eternal rewards that Thou hast promised. Through Christ our Lord.]

Mary said, "Amen."

"Exorcízo te, immúnde spíritus, in nómine Patris, et Fílii, et Spíritus Sancti, ut éxeas, et recédas ab hoc fámula Dei Mary: Ipse enim tibi ímperat, maledícte damnáte, qui pédibus super mare ambulávit, et Petro mergénti déxteram

porréxit." [I exorcise you, unclean spirit, in the name of the Father and of the Son and of the Holy Spirit. Come forth, depart from this servant of God, Mary, for He commands you, spirit accursed and damned, He Who walked upon the sea and extended His right hand to Peter as he was sinking.]

"Ergo, maledícte diábole, recognósce senténtiam tuam, et da honórem Deo vivo et vero, da honórem Jesu Christo Fílio ejus, et Spirítui Sancto, et recéde ab hac fámula Dei Mary, quia istam sibi Deus, et Dóminus noster Jesus Christus ad suam sanctam grátiam, et benedictiónem, fontémque Baptísmatis vocáre dignátus est." [Therefore, accursed devil, acknowledge your condemnation and pay homage to the true and living God; pay homage to Jesus Christ, His Son, and to the Holy Spirit, and depart from this servant of God, Mary, for Jesus Christ, our Lord and God, has called her to His holy grace and blessing, and to the font of Baptism.]

Using his thumb, he signed baby Altha on her forehead, saying, *"Et hoc signum sanctæ Crucis, quod nos fronti ejus damus, tu, maledícte diábole, numquam áudeas violáre. Per eúmdem Christum Dóminum nostrum."* [Then never dare, accursed devil, to violate this sign of the holy Cross which we are making upon her forehead. Through Christ our Lord.]

Mary said, "Amen."

He placed his hand again on Altha's head, saying, *"Oremus. Aetérnam ac justíssimam pietátem tuam déprecor, Dómine sancte, Pater omnípotens, ætérne Deus, auctor lúminis et veritátis, super hanc fámulam tuam Mary ut dignéris eam illumináre lúmine intelligéntiæ tuæ: munda eam et sanctífica: da ei sciéntiam veram, ut digna grátia Baptísmi tui effécta, téneat firmam spem, consílium rectum, doctrínam sanctam. Per Christum Dóminum nostrum."* [Let us pray. O holy Lord, almighty Father, eternal God, Source of light and truth, I ask for this Thy servant Mary, Thy fatherly love, eternal and most just, so that Thou mayest be pleased to enlighten her with the light of Thy understanding. Cleanse and sanctify her; grant her true knowledge, so that she having been made fit for the grace of Thy Baptism, may retain unwavering hope, true judgment, and sacred teaching. Through Christ our Lord.]

Mary said, "Amen."

After this, the priest placed the end of the violet stole that hung from his left shoulder upon the infant, and said, *"Mary, ingrédere in templum Dei, ut hábeas partem cum Christo in vitam ætérnam."* [Mary, enter the temple of God, so that you may take part with Christ in everlasting life.]

Mary said, "Amen."

He then recited the Nicene Creed, as well as the Our Father, and Mary joined him: *"Credo in Deum, Patrem omnipoténtem, Creatórem Cæli et Terræ; et in Jesum Christum, Fílium Ejus únicum, Dóminum nostrum; Qui concéptus est de Spíritu Sancto, natus ex María Vírgine, passus sub Póntio Piláto, crucifíxus, mórtuus, et sepúltus. Descéndit ad Inferos; tértia die resurréxit a mórtuis; ascéndit ad Cælos; sedet ad déxteram Dei Patris omnipoténtis; inde ventúrus est judicáre vivos et mórtuos. Credo in Spíritum Sanctum, Sanctam Ecclésiam Cathólicam, sanctórum communiónem, remissiónem peccatórum, carnis resurrectiónem, et vitam ætérnam."* [I believe in God, the Father almighty, Creator of Heaven and Earth; and in Jesus Christ, His only Son, our Lord; Who was conceived by the Holy Ghost, born of the Virgin Mary, suffered under Pontius Pilate, was crucified, died, and was buried. He descended into Hell; the third day He arose again from the dead; He ascended into Heaven; and sits at the right hand of God, the Father almighty; thence He shall come to judge the living and the dead. I believe in the Holy Ghost, the Holy Catholic Church, the communion of saints, the forgiveness of sins, the resurrection of the body, and life everlasting.]

Mary said, "Amen."

"Pater noster, qui es in Cælis, sanctificétur nomen tuum. Advéniat regnum tuum. Fiat volúntas tua, sicut in Cælo, et in Terra. Panem nostrum quotidiánum da nobis hódie, et dimítte nobis débita nostra, sicut et nos dimíttimus debitóribus nostris, et ne nos indúcas in tentatiónem: sed líbera nos a malo." [Our Father, who art in Heaven, hallowed be Thy name. Thy kingdom come. Thy will be done on Earth as it is in Heaven. Give us this day our daily bread, and forgive us our trespasses, as we forgive those who trespass against us, and lead us not into temptation, but deliver us from evil.]

Mary said, "Amen."

The priest continued the exorcism, *"Exorcízo te, omnis spíritus immúnde, in nómine Dei Patris omnipoténtis, et in nómine Jesu Christi Fílii ejus, Dómini et Júdicis nostri, et in virtúte Spíritus Sancti, ut discédas ab hoc plásmate Dei Mary, quod Dóminus noster ad templum sanctum suum vocáre dignátus est, ut fiat templum Dei vivi, et Spíritus Sanctus hábitet in eo. Per eúmdem Christum Dóminum nostrum, Qui ventúrus est judicáre vivos et mórtuos, et sæculum per ignem."* [I exorcise you, every unclean spirit, in the name of God the Father almighty, and in the name of His Son, Jesus Christ, our Lord and Judge, and in the strength of the Holy Spirit, that you may depart from this creature of God, Mary, whom our Lord has called to His holy temple in order that she may become a temple of the living God and that the Holy Spirit may dwell in her. Through Christ our Lord, Who will come to judge the living and the dead and the world by fire.]

Mary said, "Amen."

After that, the priest took saliva from his mouth with his thumb, and he touched Altha's right, then left ear, while saying, *"Ephpheta."* [Be opened.]

He then touched her nostrils, saying, *"In odórem suavitátis. Tu autem effugáre, Diábole; appropinquábit enim judícium Dei."* [So that you may perceive the fragrance of God's sweetness. But you, O Devil, depart; for the judgment of God has come.]

Next he questioned Mary, who would speak for Altha: *"Mary, abrenúntias Sátanæ?"* [Mary, do you renounce Satan?]

Mary responded, *"Abrenúntio."* [I do renounce him.]

"Et ómnibus opéribus ejus?" [And all his works?]

"Abrenúntio." [I do renounce them.]

"Et ómnibus pompis ejus?" [And all his display?]

"Abrenúntio." [I do renounce it.]

Dipping his thumb in the oil of catechumens, the priest anointed the infant on the breast and between the shoulders, making the sign of the cross, saying, *"Ego te línio óleo salútis in Christo Jesu Dómino nostro, ut hábeas vitam ætérnam."* [I annoint you with the oil of salvation, in Christ Jesus our Lord, so that you may have everlasting life.]

Mary said, "Amen."

He wiped his thumb and the anointed places with a soft cloth. Then, he took off his violet stole and replaced it with a white one. He then asked Mary, *"Credis in Deum Patrem omnipoténtem, Creatórem Cæli et Terræ?"* [Do you believe in God, the Father almighty, Creator of Heaven and Earth?]

Mary said, *"Credo."* [I do believe.]

"Credis in Jesum Christum, Fílium ejus únicum, Dóminum nostrum, natum, et passum?" [Do you believe in Jesus Christ, His only Son, our Lord, who was born into this world and suffered for us?]

"Credo."

"Credis et in Spíritum Sanctum, sanctam Ecclésiam cathólicam, Sanctórum communiónem, remissiónem peccatórum, carnis resurrectiónem, et vitam

ætérnam?" [And do you believe in the Holy Ghost, the Holy Catholic Church, the communion of saints, the forgiveness of sins, the resurrection of the body, and life everlasting?"]

"Credo."

"Mary, vis baptizári?" [Mary, do you want to be baptized?]

"Volo." [I do.]

Mary removed the white embroidered cap from Altha's head. Three times, the priest slowly poured blessed water over the back of the child's skull. He moved the cruet in such a way that the water poured in the form of a cross, then dripped into the basin below. He said, *"Mary, Ego te baptízo in nómine Patris,"* and poured the first time. He continued, *"et Fílii,"* pouring the second time. *"Et Spíritus Sancti,"* he said, and poured the third time. [Mary, I baptize you in the name of the Father, and of the Son, and of the Holy Spirit.]

Then the priest dipped his thumb in the sacred chrism (oil), and anointed the infant on the crown of the head in the form of a cross, saying, *"Deus omnípotens, Pater Dómini nostri Jesu Christi, qui te regenerávit ex aqua et Spíritu Sancto, quique dedit tibi remissiónem ómnium peccatórum, ipse te líniat Chrísmate salútis in eódem Christo Jesu Dómino nostro in vitam ætérnam."* [May almighty God, the Father of our Lord Jesus Christ, Who has given you a new birth by means of water and the Holy Spirit and forgiven all your sins, anoint you with the Chrism of salvation in Christ Jesus our Lord, so that you may have everlasting life.]

Mary said, "Amen."

"Pax tibi." [Peace be with you.]

Mary said, *"Et cum spíritu tuo."* [And with your spirit.]

The priest then again wiped the oil from his thumb and from the baby's head, and placed upon her a piece of white linen, saying, *"Accipe vestem cándidam, quam pérferas immaculátam ante tribúnal Dómini nostri Jesu Christi, ut hábeas vitam ætérnam."* [Receive this white robe and carry it unstained to the judgment seat of our Lord Jesus Christ, so that you may have everlasting life.]

"Amen."

The priest then lifted the lighted white candle and handed it to Mary, saying, *"Accipe lámpadem ardéntem, et irreprehensíbilis custódi Baptísmum tuum: serva Dei mandáta, ut, cum Dóminus vénerit ad núptias, possis occúrrere ei una cum ómnibus Sanctis in aula cælésti, et vivas in sæcula sæculórum."* [Receive this lighted candle, and keep your Baptism above reproach. Keep the commandments of God, so that when the Lord comes to His marriage feast you may meet Him in the halls of heaven with all His saints, and may live with Him forever.]

"Amen."

In conclusion, he said, *"Mary, vade in pace, et Dóminus sit tecum."* [Mary, go in peace, and may the Lord be with you.]

"Amen."

Mary blew out the candle, set it down, and turned away, carrying baby Altha from the room, up the stairs, and into the nursery. Father Joseph followed her closely. She set the child down in her crib, and began removing the christening gown, but found that her own clothing was being removed, from behind. The hands that had baptized the child were caressing the mother in places that cried out to be touched.

Gasping, Mary pulled away.

"Father Joseph, this is sin!"

"Yes. It is, isn't it."

He gathered Mary close, covering her face with tiny kisses, ending with a long, slow exploration of her mouth with his.

"Oscular te osculo sancto sincere tuus in Domino frater [I, your brother in the Lord, kiss you with a holy kiss]," he whispered.

Mary remembered enough French and Latin to translate this, and to recognize it as sacrilege. Once again, she pulled back, and looked into his eyes.

"To whom can I confess, and who will grant me absolution for this?"

"My child, give yourself to me. Afterwards, you need never bear the burden of the sin, for I can grant you absolution."

To her credit, Mary did not believe him. And she did continue to resist for some minutes. But this only served to inflame his lust further, and hers even more. The recently intoned words about renouncing Satan's works echoed in Mary's mind, a mockery of the holiness she had sought. As she lay with the priest, she wondered if she could ever trust any man. Even more, she wondered if she ever would be worthy of a man's trust.

Afterwards, in Mary's bed, Father Ferneding heard Mary's complete confession. She told him, weeping, that she had never been confirmed in the church, that she had betrayed her husband by sleeping with his brother, and that baby Altha was not Bram's child.

"Is your husband a Catholic?" he asked.

"No."

"That being the case," he said, "you are not married in the eyes of God. Your sin is no worse than that of any harlot."

This notion seemed to please the priest.

She stared at him.

"Tell me what to do," she begged.

Father Joseph sighed.

"Your husband must convert, and become a Catholic. If he refuses, you must leave him. Perhaps he will grant you a divorce, and you can marry a good Catholic. If not, you can enter the convent in Kentucky. These are the only ways to become righteous in the eyes of God."

None of this sounded like good advice to Mary.

"I have confessed," she said. "Tell me my penance; grant me absolution."

"When you have done as I say, I'll consider it. In the mean time, let's have a little more pleasure, shall we?"

Mary slid out of the bed. She pulled on a dressing gown, then turned to face Father Joseph.

"Get out of my house," she hissed. "Don't ever come back here."

He laughed, but nevertheless got out of bed, slowly dressed, and left the house.

Mary ceased attending Mass at Lawrenceburg. She feared any slip of the tongue or unguarded glance that might reveal her guilt. When she miscarried in May, she considered the child she might have borne to be the product of pure evil.

Mary became incurably perplexed. The path toward righteousness seemed blocked by the Devil. Perhaps God did not intend for her to continue as a Catholic. Only with Bram at home did she feel protected from further iniquity.

The Mississinewa Treaty (also called the Wabash Treaty) of 1826 was actually two treaties in one, signed separately between the Pottawatomis on October 16th, then the Miamis on October 23rd. Between them, these treaties accomplished significant goals for transportation routes in the state, specifically the Michigan Road and the Wabash-Erie Canal.

Before this treaty, Native Americans of two tribes claimed nearly all of Indiana North of the Wabash River. At this meeting, the Pottawatomis gave up considerable acreage in Northern Indiana as well as a strip of land one hundred feet wide for the building of a road from the Wabash River to Lake Michigan. The Miamis relinquished their claim to a strip of land from the Ohio State Line along the Maumee River to Fort Wayne, across a portage to the Wabash River, to the Tippecanoe River on the West.

To get the signatures of Indian chiefs and head men on the treaty, each chief was given a wagon, a yoke of oxen, and a "Treaty House" worth $600. A total of nine Treaty Houses were built - notably the Richardville House near Ft. Wayne, Allen County, the only Treaty House still standing nearly 200 years later.

The Commissioners agreed to the payment of Indians' debts to white traders as well as to continue the annual annuity to each tribe, together with a distribution of trader goods to be given to the Indians over the next two years. There was also a donation of herds of cattle and hogs made, and a grist mill was built for the Pottawatomis as well as providing a miller, a blacksmith and eight laborers to work for the Indians.

These treaty provisions may not sound as if either the Miami or Pottawatomi were planning to leave Northern Indiana very soon, but there were likely fewer than 3,000 Indians within the Northern third of the state in 1826. The Indians had little hope of holding out against the increasing avalanche of settlers crowding into Indiana.

The Mississinewa Treaty was ratified in Congress the following January.

Within ten years, construction of the Wabash-Erie Canal between Toledo, Ohio, on Lake Erie and Lafayette, Indiana would be underway. Also, the Michigan Road began at Madison, Indiana on the Ohio River, continued through Indianapolis, and ended in a swamp on Lake Michigan that later became Michigan City, Indiana, a total of two hundred sixty miles.

These new transportation routes opened Upper Wabash markets, and settlers entered first as a trickle, then in floods, causing even greater pressures for Indian removal West of the Mississippi.

In Mid-November, Mary attended Molly Norris' wedding to Justus M. Cure at Norris House on Hogan's Creek. Bram had arranged to be home for his sister's big event, but neither he nor Mary was impressed by the preparations made by Richard's wife Catherine. Norris house had seen grander times, and it was clear that the servants deliberately undermined any plans that had been made by their despised mistress.

On Sunday, December 3rd, with great relief, Mary lit the first candle of Advent at a fine dinner she served to Bram, Van, and Van's wife Mary. The three attended the holiday celebrations and the wedding of Bram's brother Joseph (to Lydia Wilcox, held a few days after Christmas) together. Mary had lost interest in Van, to the degree that even the sight of him dancing with Catherine did not distress her at all.

1827

During this year's legislative session, Delaware, Hancock, Perry, and Warren Counties were formed in Indiana.

Mary used the holidays to take stock of her life. At twenty-two, she thought she had everything she could want: A good husband, a fine house, two healthy children, and every material good she could imagine. But the constant, uncontrolled ebb and flow of emotions plagued her; there seemed no relief in sight. She had no friends. Indeed, Aurora contained few people and almost no women. The town itself remained a morass of mud and pigs. Mary scarcely ventured past her own property, where a tiny yard had been dug into the hillside and planted in grass and flowers.

Mary had never been fascinated by children. But Raper and Altha were *her* children, and her maternal instincts blossomed. She automatically knew what to do for them at any given moment, and she became a rather good mother. However, the ongoing household chores such as spinning and weaving and sewing, the manufacture of soap and candles, and the preparation of food from scratch bored her to tears. She left such work to the servants and instead spent time in her cupola, gazing at the river. Staring at the Kentucky shore evoked sad memories, and she often thought about the past, wishing things had gone differently and better.

After such reflection, she would convince herself that she could never have behaved in any other way. The past was past. But she longed for more control over her own future, for wisdom and knowledge and strength...

By the time Bram left in mid-February for his trading trips on the river, Mary thought she had figured things out; she felt in control. She proceeded through the Lenten season, determined to banish sin and the resulting plague of guilt from her life.

Summer had nearly arrived, in mid-June, when Mary's father-in-law, Richard Norris arrived at her door, unannounced. His face was grim, and at first Mary feared that something had happened to Bram.

"It's Catherine," he said. "She's been ill all winter, and now is taken with the ague."

Mary was not surprised; nearly everyone in the region had symptoms of malaria from time to time.

"Is there any way I can help?" she asked, leading the way into the parlor. "I have some Peruvian bark…"

She politely hid her true feelings toward Catherine behind her real concern for her father-in-law. Mary knew very well that she owed her present comfortable lifestyle to this man and his economic acumen.

He waved away her offer of the anti-malarial drug.

"We've tried that; it's not helping. But I'd like to bring the children here. The doctor says that Catherine must be kept quiet."

Mary thought about them. "The children" included Catherine's horribly spoiled progeny: William L., called "Willie," age six; George C. or "Georgie," age four; and little Samantha, or "Manthy," seventeen months old. Because of them, Mary had developed a strong aversion to visiting Norris House on Hogan's Creek. She feared that they would negatively influence her own carefully trained offspring, if not physically damage them. Willy, Georgie and Manthy had been given a false view of their own importance in the world, and confused by the differing expectations of various adults in their lives. Richard and Aaltje's youngest living son, Hendricks Norris, twelve years old, avoided them like the plague, using any excuse to get away from the house. They would be a handful to manage, yet, perhaps, Mary thought, she could do them some good.

"Of course," she responded. "Send them over here right away."

Richard gave a tired half-smile, then his face crumbled. His hands came up to cover his face, and Mary moved to wrap her arms around him as he cried.

"The doctor says Catherine will not live," he mourned. "I don't know what I'll do without her…"

Afterwards, Mary could never figure out how comforting Richard turned into having sex with Richard. He was incredibly skilled at this activity, she found, and very quick. Before she could react to what transpired, and to what it might mean, Richard was straightening his clothing and heading for the door.

"I'll send the children over here in the morning," he promised. "And I'll be back to see you again soon." He gave a devilish smile with a wink, and left.

"Well," she thought, *"at least I cheered him up a bit. If he's going to lose Catherine, he'll need someone else, and he'll need her very soon."*

Then what she had just done hit her full force. Guilt descended like a lead weight, and she retreated to her bedroom, where she kept a vigil candle burning when Bram was not at home. For the rest of the day she fasted, and then made a personal act of contrition. By sundown, she was feeling much better, albeit weak and hungry.

Next morning, she broke her fast, and mentally prepared herself to deal with Catherine's children. Escorted by a servant who showed visible signs of stress, the boys were squabbling, and Manthy crying before Mary reached the front door.

Nodding to the servant, whom she had seen before at Norris house, she said, "Rest yourself in the kitchen, Lucy, and have some food."

Flashing a relieved smile, the girl said, "Thank you, Miz Norris."

"How is your mistress doing?"

"Oh, turrible. She has the shakes and the chills."

The boys were still squabbling. Mary seized each of them by a shoulder, shook them, and sent them upstairs to the nursery, while she followed, carrying Manthy. Handing the toddler to her own children's nurse for a diaper change, she again arrested the boys, who were flinging toys around the room, narrowly missing the windows, Mary's own astonished children, and each other.

Mary instantly grabbed the nearest boy, George, bent him over a chair, and spanked him soundly, with intent to cause pain. As he collapsed onto the floor, screaming, she chased down his brother, who was out the door and headed for the stairs. Even though Willie was larger and stronger than Georgie, she repeated the punishment, pushing him down beside his brother when she was through. Squatting in front of them, she grasped the two damp, grubby little chins, one in each of her hands, and said, forcefully, "You don't act like that here. Behave yourselves, and you won't get hurt."

Seeing their puzzled looks, she elucidated. "Don't throw things," she told them. "Stop fighting. And be *quiet!*"

The two had obviously never been threatened so effectively before. For the next few days, the boys walked as if on eggshells, wanting at all costs to avoid Mary's wrath. They had lapses, of course, where they forgot what she had said. But they found a variety of activities in this new place that helped them stay out of trouble. Mary sent them to the wharf with a servant, let them chase pigs through the empty, hard dirt streets, and induced them to help with some of the chores around the place.

She found it harder to deal with Richard, who showed up every night after the children had been put to bed, and left before daylight. He lacked, she decided, any notion that he should be faithful to his dying wife; he had no compunctions about bedding his son's wife, and Mary felt truly sorry for any woman, including Catherine, who fell in love with the man. Being with Richard felt good, even right at times. But try as she might, she could not shake the guilt that had been ingrained since childhood, and she spent as much time as she could in prayer.

On Wednesday, June 20th, Mary sat in her wooden tub, soaking away the ache of Richard's lovemaking with a hot herbal bath. Her servant appeared within the curtained alcove, looking worried.

"Lucy's here from Norris House. She says Miz Catherine died, and she's s'posed to take the children home."

Mary's first impulse was to leap from the tub and rush to Norris House, but she restrained herself.

"Take it easy," she thought. *"You don't want anyone to guess what's been going on."*

"Give Lucy the children," she said. "And find out when the funeral is."

But as the morning progressed, Mary could think of nothing else except the coming funeral. Richard *needed* her to prepare for the crowds of people sure to descend, as they had after *Aaltje's* death.

Finally, she could stand it no longer. Leaving her children in the care of their nanny and an old gardener, Mary directed her four other servants to bring a change of clothing and accompany her up Hogan's Creek.

Mary had underestimated the chaos at Norris House. The place had been micro-managed by Catherine. Her resentful servants had ceased cleaning and straightening as soon as their mistress became ill. Mary did not need to tell her own staff what to do; they pitched in, washing, cleaning, cooking. Catherine's servants, embarrassed by the outsiders' efforts, joined them.

Mary checked on the Norris children, and found that Lucy had them well in hand. When she proceeded to Richard's study, she found him deep into a bottle of whiskey, a local product.

"Mary," he moaned. "Help me."

Richard grasped Mary hard and pulled her close.

"Stop it," she hissed at him. "Stop it!"

When he backed off, Mary asked him, "Have you notified the family?"

He shook his head. Disgusted, she made him sit down at the desk.

"Make a list," she told him. "Then you'll write messages and send them."

It turned out that Catherine had few relatives; Richard had no idea how to contact any of them. He did know where the Methodist minister was likely to be, and his own family. Mary was relieved when Richard and *Aaltje's* daughter, Molly Cure, arrived in mid-afternoon.

Although two years younger than Mary, Molly had retained a firm idea of how things should proceed. Motioning to Mary, Molly asked, "Has anyone tended the body?"

After consulting the servants, the two women determined that Sam, one of the servants, had made a coffin from old boards he found in the barn.

"We'll lay her out in the parlor," Molly decided. "Let's find a dress for her to wear."

Mary and Molly discovered that they shared the same notion for vengeance on Catherine: They would take enough care so that outsiders could detect no impropriety, but they would arrange things to suit themselves, not as Catherine would have preferred. They selected an old dress for the corpse that looked good enough in front, but not one of the elegant gowns that Catherine had brought from Cincinnati. They lined and covered the open coffin with lengths of elegant, brocaded curtain fabric, but they made sure these would be removed before the interment. There was no sense, they thought, in burying anything with this despised woman that could be useful to the living.

Plans for the funeral proceeded in the same vein, and three days later Norris House hosted a funeral similar to that put on for *Aaltje*; there was plenty to eat and to drink, a more or less dignified Methodist minister, and a graveside service conducted in dripping rain. But Richard, other than drinking large quantities of alcohol throughout that week, did not seem as emotionally devastated as he had been at *Aaltje's* passing.

After the funeral, Molly and Mary chose a few keepsakes for Catherine's three children, boxed them, and placed them in the attic. Catherine's jewelry was sold; everything else in the house belonging to or selected by Catherine they gave to less fortunate members of the local community. Molly and her husband temporarily moved back into her father's house, taking on the burden of rearing Catherine's spoiled progeny. Richard seemed not to notice nor to care; it developed that he was already considering where to find his next wife.

Advent began on Sunday, December 2nd, and Mary celebrated as best she could, struggling at various events to *never* be alone with Richard or with Van.

1828

The United States Congress passed an act establishing the Wabash and Erie Canal.

Carroll County and Hancock County, Indiana were formed by the state legislature during this year.

Richard Norris disappeared over the holidays, and returned at the end of January with his new wife, Margaret Wilcox. A cultured woman from Virginia, Margaret's lovely accented speech and gentle manner won the admiration of the entire extended Norris family.

When Richard visited Mary shortly before Easter in April, expecting to take her to bed, she questioned him about his wife's view of such activities.

"She's too much of a lady to notice," he replied. "She makes an elegant addition to my household, I think. But she's not interested in producing children."

Looking back, Mary realized she had become pregnant by Richard that afternoon.

A new courthouse was built at Lawrenceburg during this year.

In October, Mary was less than impressed with Margaret's ability to cope with life on the frontier when Richard's daughter Samantha by his previous wife, Catherine, became severely ill. Margaret almost seemed grateful when the child, nearly three years old, succumbed to fever.

The United States' presidential campaign of 1828 has been called the "dirtiest campaign in American History." Andrew Jackson and the Democratic Party again opposed the incumbent John Quincy Adams of the National Republican Party, this time using the competition for the presidency as a personal vendetta against Adams for the "Corrupt Bargain" of 1824.

As the two candidates strove to gain support, issues concerning government were ignored, replaced by a smear campaign focusing on the candidates' personalities and "character." Jackson, the son of Scots-Irish emigrants to the Carolinas, a military hero, cast himself as a man of the common people, and Adams as a member of the elite.

Adams, a News England native, diplomat and former Secretary of State who helped formulate the Monroe Doctrine, allowed his National Republican supporters to descend into mud-slinging, calling Jackson a barbarian and making an issue of Jackson's premature wedding to Rachel Donelson Robards, whose divorce from her first husband was not yet final. Charles Hammond in his Cincinnati Gazette asked: "Ought a convicted adulteress and her paramour husband to be placed in the highest offices of this free and christian land?" Hammond continued the offensive against Jackson by publishing a series of pamphlets, the "Coffin Handbills," that described Jackson's peremptory courts martial and execution of deserting soldiers under his command, his inhuman massacres of Indian villagers, and his hot temper that led to numerous duels. Democrats countered that Adams, as Minister to Russia, had provided an American servant girl as a bed partner for the Czar. Adams was also accused of gambling and "Sabbath-breaking" in the White House. It turned out that he had purchased a chess set and a pool table, and was innocent of all the wildly exaggerated charges.

Jackson's opponents, in a play on his last name, dubbed him "Jackass" with a picture of a mule on their anti-Jackson posters. Jackson's party embraced the mule as a symbol of the hard-working common people, and Democrats permanently adopted the mule as their party mascot.

Mary, listening as the Norris men discussed the presidential race, in support of Adams, recalled the tall, inspiring General Jackson she had seen in 1815 at Lynchburg. She did not approve of the horrible things of which his opponents accused him, but did not see that Adams had accomplished much for the country during the previous few years. Wasn't it better to elect a strong, proven military leader as commander in chief of the country?

Jackson had shown repeatedly his ability to get things done. Silently, she wished the man well.

Jackson won the Presidency in a national "landslide" of popular votes. On November 3, Indiana electors pledged to Jackson won in a similar surge of popular opinion. When they met in December at Indianapolis, their five votes for Old Hickory were announced by five rounds from a "six-pounder" cannon. The national Electoral College met in December and finalized the decision in his favor. But on December 22nd, his wife Rachel, tormented by the negative campaign publicity, died of heart failure. Jackson's presidency stretched before him as he struggled to rise above bitterness and grief.

The "Age of Jackson" spawned churning waves of economic havoc that pushed white settlers Westward, desperate for the security of land ownership. Literally over the dead bodies of Native Americans, they swarmed into forcibly vacated Indian lands. During the thirty months from fall 1834 to spring 1837, the **United States** *Government conducted the largest volume of land office business in the history of the country. The areas affected by this land rush included central Indiana, and the Norris family was swept along by the tide.*

Advent began on Sunday, December 2nd, and Mary lit the candles, pretending a holiday joy that she did not feel. Whenever she looked at Bram, overwhelming guilt unsettled her stomach.

During the cold winter, Bram's brother Joseph lost his wife, Lydia, to the constant round of fever that plagued everyone. After the funeral, Mary heard that Lydia had been carrying a child, which died with her. Joseph seemed devastated by the loss, and never remarried.

1829

Cass County, Indiana, was organized during this year.

Brothers John, William and Nicholas Pence, previously of Warren County, Ohio, settled in 1829 at the location which became the city of Frankfort, Indiana. In 1830, the brothers donated 60 acres of their land to the county commissioners. This donation led to the establishment of the county seat at Frankfort rather than at Jefferson, a community which had also been vying for the honor. The new town was named Frankfort at the brothers' request and honors their German great-grandparents' home of Frankfurt am Main.

A House committee recommended that agricultural societies be formed in each Indiana county to award prizes for the best specimens of clothing from Indiana grown textiles. This was protectionism at its most personal, an attempt to decrease Indiana's dependence on imports from other places. Other items targeted for protection included iron, lead, and whiskey.

Finding themselves troubled by the notion of allowing free black people to live among them, whites during this year formed the Indiana Colonization Society. They became part of an existing national movement which had begun in 1821 to remove black people from the United States, sending them to Liberia in Africa. The native Africans resisted the black American settlers, instigating many armed conflicts. African Americans resisted being relocated. Nevertheless, by 1831, 2,638 African Americans had been shipped to Africa. The colony at Liberia entered an agreement with the **United States** *Government to accept freed slaves captured from slave ships.*

Bram was delighted to be at home for the birth of what he assumed to be his daughter Elizabeth Altha on January 12th. Mary concluded that his math skills were lacking; he seemed not to realize that her last two children could not have been his. But at least their surnames were correct; they would have been Norrises in any case. Mary's guilt was intensified by her belief that Bram had always been faithful to her. To ease her conscience, Mary decided that any man who wanted to be reasonably sure of the paternity of his wife's children should spend more time at home than Bram did. As usual, he left on a business trip as soon as the river ice melted in mid-February.

Mary visited her Catholic acquaintances in Lawrenceburg to determine the dates for the coming Holy Days. While there, she had the idea to invite them to her home for the baptism of her new daughter. That way, Mary would surely be protected from the priest's sexual overtures.

As a result, the tiny (about five families) Lawrenceburg congregation came to Norris house in Aurora for Mass on Sunday, March 1st. Mary's servants prepared and served a dinner for them, after which the baby's baptism was held.

Mary had hoped that Father Ferneding had moved on to other women after their encounter two years before. But his scorching hot glances and exceedingly warm hands had not changed; when he heard Mary's confession before Mass, he probed for details of her private life that she refused to reveal. Surprisingly, he granted her absolution, and she felt great relief when he left with the other parishioners after the baptism.

Ash Wednesday passed on March 4th (also President Andrew Jackson's inauguration day), followed by Laetare Sunday March 29th, Palm Sunday April 12th and Easter on the 19th. Mary observed them all with appropriate fasting and prayer, and felt more spiritually whole than she had for a long time.

Bram had no sooner left on his next trip, however, than Father Ferneding arrived, looking downcast. Mary's experience with Richard stood her in good stead here, and she resisted feeling too sympathetic as he talked. He had just received word that Pope Leo XII died on February 10th, and that Pope Pius VIII was elected on March 31st. But the new Pope's constitution was said to be delicate, and it was feared that he had not long to live.

Instead of remaining alone with the priest in the parlor, Mary retreated to the kitchen on the pretext of fetching refreshments. While there, she carefully instructed three of her servants to help serve food in the dining room and to remain close to her chair no matter what the visitor said or did. With their help, Mary fended off the priest's obvious intentions, and they all saw him on his way back to Lawrenceburg. He had mentioned that Immaculate Heart of Mary would be celebrated the next day, Saturday, June 27th, and Mary felt this to be appropriate to her situation. She fasted and offered prayers of thanks to the Virgin.

Mary had intended to use the same technique to avoid sex with Richard, but he took her by surprise early on Sunday morning, August 9th. Half-awake, she answered the front door because the servants were at a local worship service, and had taken the children with them. Richard, wiping tears from his eyes, explained that his wife Margaret had died the night before. He *needed* comfort. There was no one to hear Mary's protests, and she quickly gave in to his advances, seeing the futility of resistance. Afterwards, in Mary's bed, Richard began talking about the "bad air" believed to cause so much illness in the Ohio Valley. The true causes of typhoid, yellow fever, malaria, and cholera were unknown. It had been noticed, however, that settlers in higher, drier areas stayed healthier. Richard, after losing so many of his immediate family, was looking around for a better location.

"I've sunk my fortune into Aurora," he explained. "When enough of the lots have sold, I'll have the capital to move elsewhere."

"Where will you go?" Mary asked him.

"We'll all go together," he replied. "I have contacts among the land speculators. I'm looking at an area closer to Indianapolis, Northwest of the city. Already people are settling there, and have started a school."

"But..."

Richard waved his hand to silence her.

"You don't want to stay here, to risk losing your children, or even yourself to disease!"

As Richard dressed and headed for home, Mary felt a knot forming in her stomach. She did *not* want to leave the house at Aurora–not ever. It was *her* home, designed and arranged exactly as she wanted. Her children were not sick. She was not sick. It wasn't her fault if others succumbed to the "bad air," or whatever caused the others to have fevers. She began to think how to avoid the move. What arguments would convince Bram? He always went along with his father's plans, and he never asked Mary's opinion about them.

But it turned out that the move would require years of planning and economic machinations. Mary listened to the Norris men carefully to determine whether they had set a time frame – it seemed that nothing concrete had been decided. She also watched to see how long it would take Richard to find a new wife. She comforted herself with the notion that Richard would find a local woman who did *not* want to move North, and who would also keep a tighter leash on her husband.

One day in early September, Mary wandered down the steep hill to the riverbank market. Most of the time her servants took care of the shopping, but she was particularly interested in fresh apples, which were just becoming available. She had selected several bushels to be delivered to the house when her peripheral vision registered a shocking sight. She moved behind the farmer who had sold her the apples, and peered around him. John Davis, her old tormentor, had disembarked from a steamboat and was marching toward the center of town with a determined air.

Since there were many people about, Mary followed him at a distance and watched while he met another man who looked so familiar... After a few moments she realized that he was one of her Hobbs cousins. Not daring to go any closer to the men who might recognize her, Mary returned home, making sure that no one followed.

The first Sunday of Advent fell on November 29th that year, and Mary lit the first candle on her table wreath. Two days later, she and Bram attended the wedding of Richard Norris to his fourth wife, Clarinda Porter.

Mary had not met the woman before, but had received Richard's somewhat biased assessment of her character several months before, at their last tryst of the summer. Adjusting himself comfortably in Mary's bed, he had said, "I met Clarinda at church, actually at her parents' funeral – they and their other children all caught the usual intestinal diseases as soon as they arrived from the East... Now she claims she's pregnant with my child... And she's inherited a chunk of land from her folks."

Mary's sarcasm was lost on Richard when she asked, "Is she any good in bed?"

Absently, he had responded, "Does that matter?" and covered her face in kisses, preparing himself for another onslaught on his son's wife. Mary reflected that the man, despite his Methodist pretensions, actually had very few ethical or moral standards. But he *was* highly skilled at the matter at hand...

After Richard and Clarinda's wedding ceremony, as Mary passed through the receiving line, she encountered John Norris from Franklin County (to whom she had spoken, briefly, in the past), and his French/Indian wife, *Marie*. She was surprised when John addressed her in French, but soon realized that he did so in order to keep the conversation confidential from the Americans around them.

"*Connaissez-vous un homme du nom de John Davis*? (Do you know a man called John Davis?)" he asked her.

Mary's frightened expression, followed by her slight nod, told John all he needed to know. He led her to an alcove, apart from the other wedding guests.

"I was at the court in September," he continued, in French, in a low tone, "when your uncle James Hobbs applied for his war pension. Since he had lost his papers, his brother Robert and this John Davis gave depositions that they knew him well in Maryland and had seen him many times in uniform of the Maryland Continental Line.

While they were waiting to speak to the court, I heard an *unusual* story about an attack upon John by a pirate...you wouldn't know anything about that, would you?"

"You know that my uncle James is the pirate of whom they spoke," she responded, fearfully. "Do they know where to find me?"

"No. But they are searching for information about your pirate uncle. It could lead them to you. And they mentioned your name."

Certain that the Hobbs men would believe whatever John Davis told them, she asked, "What can I do? I cannot leave my children..."

John Norris reached into his boot and drew forth a leather sheath containing a razor-sharp steel knife with a six-inch blade and well worn wooden handle. It was of the type known as "Arkansas Toothpick," or Bowie knife, that was becoming ubiquitous on the frontier. This particular knife was smaller than most, intended to serve as a concealed weapon, a weapon of last resort.

"Do you know how to use this?" he asked her.

Mary's eyes went very wide, then she shook her head.

Urgently, he pressed her, "Haven't you butchered pigs? This man is a pig, nothing more."

Mary thought back to her days with Phoebe Elvira, preparing pork for the Davis table.

"Of course. I could butcher him like a pig. But he would have to die first."

"You must put aside fear," he told her. "Expect him to appear around every turn, and decide what you will do. Depend only on yourself. Because until you destroy this pig, you will always be afraid. Distract him, move quickly, and strike to kill."

"He's bigger than I am."

"But you are smarter and faster than he is. You can do this; women have been killing men for millennia."

Mary was rapidly becoming nauseated as a result of this conversation and the images it was forming in her mind. Her one desire was to get away from this man, even though he represented perhaps her only chance to leave her past completely behind.

"Excuse me, Mr. Norris, I must oversee the kitchen now..."

John Norris bowed slightly to Mary, then sauntered away as if nothing of import had been said. He noted with satisfaction, however, that she had concealed the knife in her own sleeve.

Mary went through the motions of preparing for the holidays, hoping that Bram would not notice her inner turmoil. Having believed John Norris' warning, she expected John Davis to appear around every corner, and her dread increased daily. Whenever she could arrange to be alone, which wasn't often, she practiced throwing her knife until she felt confident that she could hit a target, at least one that did not move.

At last she grew weary of constant fear and defiantly decided to attend the New Year festivities at Lawrenceburg with the rest of the Norris family. But she brought her knife along.

New Year's Eve fell on a Thursday that year, and the weather remained favorable for the outdoor party – crisply cool, but dry. Lawrenceburg then boasted a population of seven hundred people, one hundred fifty brick and frame houses, nine stores, five taverns, three doctors, and six lawyers. People from surrounding farms would be drawn to the celebration as a result. Huge heaps of wood for bonfires had been piled strategically to give light to the musicians and dancers, and pits had been dug for the roasting of meat. The streets had been scraped flat by teams of oxen dragging heavy logs.

Mary thoroughly enjoyed the music and dancing, especially when the tiny orchestra broke into music for the more formal dances. At first, she resigned herself to merely observe these, since none of the immediate Norris family had received classical training in dance. But when first Father Ferneding and later John Norris asked her to dance, she joyfully agreed.

At the end of the second set of dances, Mary looked for Bram where she had last seen him, near one of the riverside docks. She had just rounded the corner of a building when she felt the strong arms of John Davis seizing her from behind. She did not need to see his face; his stench had not changed over the years. Although she screamed, no one heard, and her frantic struggles accomplished nothing. Finally, she collapsed, requiring her captor to support her body weight. Swiftly, silently, he dragged her toward a small boat tied to a post.

Mary waited, her mind cold with hate, knowing her chance to strike would come. As Davis, expecting his captive to remain passive, relaxed his hold in order to maneuver her into the boat, Mary pulled the knife from her left sleeve, squirmed, and thrust the blade up, through his linen shirt and skin, into his heart. As he stumbled, she twisted the blade in order to do more damage.

No one heard or responded to the crack of Davis' head striking the edge of the boat, nor the following splash as his body hit the water. Horrified, Mary watched as it bobbed to the surface, face down. Nimbly, she stepped into the tiny vessel, seized an oar, and pushed the corpse away from the dock, but it floated back toward her. Forcing herself to remain calm, she considered her options. Should she try harder to dispose of the body? Or should she leave it here for others to find, while she rejoined the party as if nothing had happened?

Deciding on the latter, she straightened her clothing and hair and took some deep breaths. She knew that if her participation in Davis' death (she refused to admit to herself that she had killed him) should become known, her reputation would be permanently stained, and her comfortable future threatened.

With so much at risk, Mary circled around the buildings and approached the party from the direction opposite the docks. She found her father-in-law,

Richard, talking to a local magistrate, and slid her arm through his and smiled with what she prayed seemed to be daughterly affection. At a pause in the conversation, Richard excused himself to the judge and led Mary toward the dancers. The two joined the frontier-style dance, hopping and skipping about to the music, and Mary considered this alibi to be practically air-tight. Oddly, the physical activity of the dance dissipated the guilt and fear that threatened to take over Mary's consciousness.

At the conclusion of that musical number, Richard hugged Mary tightly and whispered, "Let's find a place to be alone... I want you!"

Mary patted his cheek. No longer afraid of John Davis, she nevertheless needed this man to defend her in case she should be accused of murder.

"Where's your wife?" she asked him.

"She's feeling poorly...this is her first baby, you know how it is... I need you!"

With surprise, Mary felt a new strength, a new control over this situation.

"Papa, I need to go find Bram. You know how it is."

She backed out of his arms, turned, and walked away.

Just then, midnight was declared, and the New Year arrived amid cannon fire, shots of whiskey, and cheers. Mary quickly found Bram, and felt herself to be starting a New Year and a new life.

1830

Boone, Clinton, Elkhart, and St. Joseph counties were formed in Indiana during this year.

Clinton County, named after DeWitt Clinton, is twenty-four miles in length from East to West, and seventeen in width. The population was 1,423 at this time. On May 3rd of that year, Jefferson was designated as the first county seat. When John Pence donated sixty acres located four miles to the East of Jefferson, along with $100, the Indiana State Commissioners ordered, on May 19th, that a new town be platted. Pence became the first proprietor of the town, with the right to name the place. He called it Frankfort because his great-grandparents came from Frankfurt-au-der-Main, Germany. The focus of Clinton county was agriculture, a focus that has continued into the twenty-first century.

Mary rose early on Friday morning, January 1st, completely exhausted. She had experienced the worst night terrors of her entire life, sure that she had dumped John Davis straight into Hell, and fearful that she might end up there with him some day. Yet she vowed to get through *this* day as if nothing were amiss. Luckily, after nearly eight years of marriage, Bram expected her to celebrate holy days frequently. He had ceased quizzing her when she fasted and prayed, and he had developed a deep respect for what he assumed to be Mary's intense spirituality. Mary's household staff took over for her on these occasions, caring for the children, and allowed her the privacy she craved.

At about noon, Mary heard the bustle caused by visitors arriving, and she cautiously peered downstairs. John Norris and his wife, *Marie*, had stopped on their way from her father's house in Lawrenceburg to their farm near Brookville. Mary heard Bram asking them whether they would stay for

New Year's dinner, which would be served within the hour. John started to decline, explaining that his wife was celebrating the Solemnity of Mary by fasting. At that, Mary descended the stairs, holding out her hand to *Marie*.

"*Allez-vous prier avec moi?* [Will you pray with me?]" she begged.

Marie nodded, handed her woolen cape to the servant, and followed Mary up the stairs.

Mary heard John's voice behind them, addressing Bram, "I guess I'll be staying to dinner, after all. Thank you!"

The two women spent little time in prayer, but after an hour's talk, Mary felt confident that John Davis' death would never be connected to herself. The corpse had been found floating at daybreak, and would be transported to Brookville for burial tomorrow. John Norris had thrown the local officials off track by claiming Davis had been arguing with an unknown man from Louisville, who surely was long gone by now.

When Richard Norris' name came up, Marie told Mary the details of Richard's infidelity to Aaltje. Years previously, Marie had provided sanctuary to Aaltje when she had become aware of Richard's philandering. Although this information did not surprise Mary, it gave her perspective on his behavior, and encouraged her to rise above the temptation to participate in it in the future.

Using John and *Marie* as her example of a mixed faith couple, after they departed, Mary made sure that Bram would allow her to train their own children in the Catholic faith.

"I have no objection," he said. "I know how important this is to you. But when they are adults, and marry, we must let them decide for themselves concerning religion."

During the rest of the winter into early spring, Mary stayed in close contact with the Catholic congregation at Lawrenceburg. She found a family with a son close to Raper's age, and arranged for the boys to study together for their first confessions. Epiphany, the Baptism of the Lord, Candlemas, Ash Wednesday, the Solemnity of Joseph, husband of Mary, and Laetare Sunday all came and went. Mary and Raper carefully observed the holy days, making confessions (Mary's were carefully edited) frequently and receiving absolution from Father Ferneding. With each passing day, Mary felt safer from the threat that her connection to John Davis had represented.

On Thursday March 25, while celebrating the Annunciation in Rome, Pope Pius VIII published the Brief, "Litteris altero abhinc," in which he declared that marriage could be blessed by the Church only when the proper promises were made regarding the Catholic education of the children; otherwise, (in cases of marriage to a non-Catholic) the parish priest should only assist passively at the ceremony.

Late on Holy Saturday night, April 10th, Mary went into the kitchen searching for a snack. She had fasted, and worked more strenuously than usual preparing food for the Easter feast she planned for the following day. Poking in a bin where dried fruits were kept, she heard a small sound behind her, and turned quickly. In the shadows crouched a black woman holding a baby, both dressed in rags.

When she had recovered from the surprise of finding a stranger in her kitchen, Mary asked, "Who are you, and what are you doing here?"

The woman's reply was nearly unintelligible, but sounded like, "Sorry, Mum, so sorry," as she crept toward the door.

"Wait! I'll not harm you. Where's Katy?"

"Doan' know, Mum."

Mary opened the door, and found her servant Katy coming across the yard with clothing and blankets she had brought from her cabin. Nearly dropping the bundle, Katy begged for Mary's forgiveness.

"Please doan' be angered, Miz Mary. Please! This'n just come acrost the river, Miz Mary. She been beaten, an' chased by dogs. I jes' wan' t'hep her..."

Mary recalled her reception by *Aaltje* at Norris House so long ago, and Phoebe Elvira's kindness before that. She gestured toward the kitchen.

"We'll *both* help. Let's settle her for the night," she said. "And tomorrow we must make plans to send her North. It's too easy for her to be found, here."

Mary had heard about other runaway slaves crossing from Kentucky to Indiana. Because of their high value as property, and as a lesson to other slaves, they were often pursued, caught, beaten, and returned to their owners.

During the next week, Mary by great good luck was able to place the runaway and her child with a Quaker family headed for Richmond, Indiana, where it was less likely they would be found. From that day on, Mary listened intently for news of runaway slaves and of the developing routes of what became the "Underground Railroad" to freedom.

On May 26, the Indian Removal Act of 1830 was passed by the Twenty-First Congress of the United States of America. After four months of strong debate, Andrew Jackson signed the bill into law. Within ten years, more than 70,000 Native Americans had moved across the Mississippi, many dying along the way; thus the name "Trail of Tears" or "Trail of Death" was applied. This removal eventually included Indians of the Miami and Potawatomi tribes from Indiana.

Early in July, Richard Norris' wife Clarinda gave birth to baby Lucretia. Mary sent a hand-knitted blanket, but kept her distance from the household with the excuse that her children needed her. This was true. Raper, Altha, and Elizabeth would be seven, five, and one years old this year, and she felt compelled to supervise them more directly all the time as their activity levels increased. She fervently hoped that Richard Norris had moved on to other women and would leave her alone.

In France, the Revolution of July broke out and King Charles X was obliged to flee, being succeeded on the throne by Louis Philippe of the younger Orleans branch. Pope Pius VIII hesitated to recognize the new regime.

Mary celebrated the Transfiguration of the Lord on Friday, August 6th, and Assumption (Feast of Mary) on Sunday, August 15th. Raper made his first confession at Lawrenceburg, and Mary cried tears of joy.

Toward the end of that week, Bram came home, in an expansive mood. Business was going very well, he said, and by way of celebration, he enticed Mary to accompany him on a short trip to Louisville. They stayed several nights in a hotel, went out dancing, and generally enjoyed themselves.

Snow began to fall in early autumn and continued at frequent intervals. Between the snowfalls were periods of sleet, which formed crusts of ice between the layers of snow. With an uneasy feeling, Mary recalled the long winter of 1816, and the drastic effects it had on her life.

By the Feast of Christ the King on Sunday, November 21st, Mary knew she was pregnant, and by her own husband. She rejoiced, and lit the first candle of Advent on Sunday, November 28th.

Pope Pius VIII's last months were troubled. The revolutionary movement in France, Belgium and Poland extended to Rome, where a lodge of Carbonari *(a secret revolutionary society) with twenty-six members was discovered. In the midst of anxiety and care, Pius VIII, whose constitution had always been delicate, passed away on December 1st. Before the coronation of his successor, revolution broke out in the Papal States.*

Mary, of course, knew nothing yet of this news from Rome, and continued with her fellow Catholics to celebrate the season. With each passing day, Mary felt stronger, more in control of her life than ever before.

1831

During this year, Boone and Grant counties were formed in Indiana. The Indiana Legislature passed a new requirement that black people moving into the state post a bond of $500 as security against becoming public charges.

Indiana Congressman Ratliff Boon, running for reelection, advocated reduced duties on "necessities" such as coffee, tea, salt, and sugar as a modification of the tariff of 1828. "The pockets of the people," he said, "are the safest repositories for their own money."

The Whig political party was formed during the early 1830s in opposition to President Andrew Jackson's policies. Whigs supported the supremacy of Congress over the presidency and favored a program of modernization and economic protectionism. The name was chosen to echo the American Whigs of 1776, who opposed tyranny. The Whig Party continued through the mid 1850s, and counted among its members such national political luminaries as Daniel Webster, William Henry Harrison, Henry Clay of Kentucky, Zachary Taylor, Winfield Scott, and Abraham Lincoln. The Norris family supported the Whigs, as can be seen by names chosen for several sons born to their family.

Mary wondered when the snow would melt. Usually, due to sun exposure and the elevation of her home, melting occurred rapidly after each snowfall, and, although muddy, the road leading to Lawrenceburg was clear. Even one month earlier, despite the snow and ice, she and Raper had been able to make their way to Mass.

But now that proved impossible. Descending the hill into Aurora had become a hazardous venture, requiring the use of poles and ropes to prevent uncontrolled sliding. Bram stayed at home, not attempting his usual trips to talk business with his father and brothers. The Ohio River froze, along with all its tributaries, and crossing it would have been easy if not for the deep snow cover.

In Rome, a conclave to elect a new Pope continued through the first week in February. On the Feast of the Purification, Cardinal Capiliaria was elected, and took the name of Gregory XVI. Hardly was he elected when the Revolution, which for some time had been smouldering throughout Italy, broke into flame. Within a fortnight nearly the whole of the Papal States had repudiated the sovereignty of the Pope. The papal forces being unable to cope with the situation, Gregory appealed to Austria for help. It was immediately forthcoming. On 25 February a strong Austrian force started for Bologna, and the "Provisional Government" soon fled to Ancona. On April 3rd the Pope asserted that order was re-established.

In the same month, the representatives of the five powers, Austria, Russia, France, Prussia and England, met in Rome to consider the question of the "Reform of the Papal States." On May 21st they issued a joint Memorandum urging papal government reforms.

Unaware of the turmoil in Europe, and unable to leave home due to the severe weather, Mary and Raper observed the religious calendar drawn up for them by Father Ferneding. Because Bram was there to read it for her, she was, for the first time in years, sure that she celebrated each holy date correctly. Ash Wednesday fell on February 16th, followed by Laetare Sunday and Palm Sunday in March. The first weekend in April brought Good Friday and Easter, and Bram did not protest when Mary served an elaborate feast that Sunday.

But still "the deep snow" persisted. Occasional reports reached Aurora of immense numbers of wildlife killed by the cold, and available for the taking, had not the pioneers near them been trapped inside their cabins. There was great suffering and near starvation for many.

As spring finally arrived, the enormous mass of snow and ice melted rapidly so that Hogan's Creek and the other tributaries of the Ohio overflowed their banks, causing devastating flooding of the entire Ohio Valley.

At about this same time, a band of Sauk Indians led by Black Hawk, or Makataimeshekiakiak, returned after winter hunting in what became the state of Iowa to their ancestral village in Western Illinois. Because the land in Illinois had been ceded by Indians to the United States in 1804 and again in 1830, Illinois Governor John Reynolds declared that his state had been invaded.

Responding to Governor Reynolds's call, General Edmund Pendleton Gaines brought his federal troops from St. Louis, Missouri to Saukenuk to insist upon Black Hawk's immediate departure. Black Hawk left temporarily, remaining West of the Mississippi.

By mid-May, Mary was larger and more uncomfortable with her pregnancy than she remembered from past experience. As Pentecost Sunday approached, her labor began late on Thursday, May 19th. The process was so difficult that several times she despaired of delivering the child at all. But early on Friday a strong baby boy made his appearance and was named John Burroughs Norris by his father. Bram explained that Burroughs (or Burrowes) was the surname of a family that had emigrated to New England in the 1600s and married into the Norris family in the early 1700s. Burrowes Norris, Bram's grand uncle, had served the Americans during the Revolutionary War. At this point, Mary was too exhausted to care about names. This son became known as "Burr" Norris, to differentiate him from other John Norrises.

As soon as the floods had abated sufficiently to allow river travel, Bram left on a business trip for his father. Mary sent word inviting Father Ferneding and the tiny Catholic congregation to the baby's baptism at Norris House on Trinity Sunday, May 29th.

When Mary attended the Independence Day celebrations at Lawrenceburg in July, she and Bram met Noah Noble, a Whig politician. A native of Virginia, Noble grew up in Kentucky and then settled in Brookville, Indiana where he served as Sheriff and then Representative to the Indiana Legislature. Tall and slim, with a winning smile, the man at thirty-seven years old appeared too delicate and gentle for the time and place. He asked Mary to dance, and she was surprised by his grace and agility as they joined the hopping, skipping throng in the street. After watching people gather around Noble that afternoon, Mary was not surprised when, in the fall elections, he won the governorship of Indiana, ending the tenure of James

Brown Ray. (Few if any pioneer governors completed a term so thoroughly discredited and so much a political has-been as James Brown Ray – he was ever verbose, pompous, contentious, and lacking in civility.)

In Italy, the Austrian troops were withdrawn on July 15th, but by December much of the Papal States was again in revolt.

On the second Sunday morning of Advent, December 4th, Mary had bundled up warmly and taken a foot stove with her into the high, enclosed cupola atop her house. The cold had discouraged her from attending Mass at Lawrenceburg, but she intended to spend the morning in prayer. Bram had gone to a Methodist church meeting in the village, taking Raper with him, and the other children were being watched by their nanny, the baby asleep. Mary sat on a padded bench, repeating prayers while watching the Ohio River. The water had frozen in places, severely limiting river traffic.

For that reason she was quite surprised to see a steamboat headed down river, probably bound for Marion, Indiana, and then Louisville. The boat was behaving strangely, zigzagging its way through floating ice. Then, its pilot apparently reached a decision and put in at Aurora. Mary watched as the passengers disembarked and stood uncertainly in the cold wind. As they turned for the only available shelter, a tavern and inn located along Judiciary Street, Mary assumed that nothing of further interest would happen. She headed downstairs to make sure that dinner would be served on time, and that the advent candles were ready to light.

From the dining room, Mary heard the front door open, but, expecting Bram, Van, and their father Richard, she did not respond. She soon heard her husband's voice calling, though, and saw that two additional men accompanied them. Signaling a maid to set extra places, she called to another servant who would take the men's greatcoats and hats. To her surprise, she could hear that the strangers were speaking in French.

Richard said, "Mary, these are Alexis de Toqueville and Gustave de Beaumont, who are touring the United States in order to report to the King of France about our prison system."

"Prison system?" Mary thought, wrinkling her brow. She recalled the rude, log gaols she had seen during her journey across Virginia and Kentucky, and the ones at Darlington, Boonville, and Lawrenceburg. Aurora had not yet constructed a facility of that type.

Van added, "They are also looking at the way our economy, educational status, and personal autonomy may have changed as a result of our break from Britain and the establishment of a republic. They will look for parallels in France as their government changes."

Mary thought, *"In other words, they are spies."* For the first time, she felt vaguely threatened by visitors to her house, and wished they had stayed away. She smiled at them, however, and murmured, *"Bonjour,"* as the Frenchmen kissed her hand.

Both seemed young, of about Mary's own age. The two were dressed similarly, in tight, expensive, dark suits, their shirts with over-the-chin collars. Their short-cut, dark, wavy hair had been tossed by the cold wind, and stood out from their heads. Stylish sideburns flared down their jaws, but the rest of their faces were clean-shaven. Alexis' face featured a charming cleft chin and wide set, dark eyes. She led the group toward the dining room, where the servants were setting out a feast. Mary lit the Advent candles, and the visitors appeared confused when Bram said an obviously Methodist grace in English. Mary surreptitiously crossed herself and then lifted her spoon to taste her soup, signaling the meal to begin.

The two visitors spoke some English, and the Norrises understood quite a bit of French, so that it was possible to communicate without Mary's assistance. For this she was grateful. Knowing Mary's interest in the Bourbon royal line in France, and seeing Mary's reticence to speak in the company of so many men, Van asked questions, and Mary listened intently to the replies.

In July of 1830, Mary's cousin Charles X had abdicated in favor of his ten-year-old grandson, Henri, Duke of Bordeaux. He left the boy in the care of Louis Phillipe, a descendant of another branch of the royal family whom he foolishly trusted to carry out his wishes. Louis Phillipe, as regent for the child, failed to mention Charles' intent concerning Henri to the popularly elected Chamber of Deputies. Instead, Louis Phillipe graciously allowed the Chamber to install himself as king. Mary felt sad that *Grand-mère's* immediate family had fallen from power, but said nothing.

Then Van let the cat out of the bag: "Our hostess is descended from the Bourbon family; her grandmother was the Princess Marie."

Mary saw astonishment in the faces of the visitors, and she sought to alleviate it by murmuring that *Grand-mère* had left France a very long time ago.

"*Il ne compte pas vraiment plus du tout,*" [It truly doesn't matter any more] she said.

The man called Alexis seemed perturbed by these comments, but let the subject drop. Mary, however, sensed that he wanted more information.

After dinner, the men enjoyed cigars and brandy in the sitting room, but Alexis made a point of following Mary into the foyer as she headed for the stairs. Their conversation, in French, took much longer than Mary wanted it to.

"Wait, please!" he entreated. "*Madame* Norris, could I speak with you?"

"I must see to my children…"

"I beg your pardon – I hoped to speak with you about your family."

"My family is doing very well, thank you!" She turned from him, placing a delicate hand on the stair rail.

"And what would your *grand-mère* say to me about life in America? I very much want to know."

Mary turned back toward him. His gentle, charming manner encouraged her to speak.

"*Grand-mère* always believed in the monarchy of her youth. She isolated herself; her behavior, her religion, her thoughts never changed."

"And what are your thoughts about democracy?"

"I think that if the president were instead a king that my life would not be much different. Perhaps we would be richer, perhaps poorer."

"And your religion? I see that your Catholicism is pushed to the background in this place."

"Indeed. But I do the best that I can."

"Please tell me about the black people here…are they slaves?"

"Certainly not. They are paid, and their personal lives are their own. But it is difficult for them to leave us, as they are not welcomed by whites in the surrounding area."

"And education. Will your daughters become literate?"

"Yes. Their father has insisted that it be so."

"But do you yourself think that education for women is important?"

"Monsieur, there are many kinds of education. No one can stop women from becoming educated in one way or another. And now, I must tend my babies."

Mary proceeded up the stairs, did not turn back, and did not return to bid the visitors farewell. She had had enough of de Toqueville's probing questions. Bram later told her that Alexis behaved much the same wherever he went, and that he planned to write a book about his observations of democracy in the Americas.

Mary with Bram and the children settled in for another winter at Aurora. The cold weather of that year froze the Ohio River, with resulting flooding as soon as the temperatures warmed.

1832

Huntington, LaGrange, LaPorte, Miami, and Wabash counties were formed by the Indiana State Legislature during this year.

The Legislature chartered eight railroad lines. However, none of these lines were built because state funds were committed mostly to the building of canals.

Indiana state law was amended this year to permit land sales as small as 40 acres for $50.

In Italy, the French and Austrians stopped the revolutionists but, against papal approval, continued to occupy cities inside the Papal States. Despite international protests, the foreign troops did not leave Italy until 1838.

Flooding during this spring in the town of Aurora broke all previous records for the town, and for many years it was thought that it could never be equaled.

By Easter, in late April, Mary heard rumors of an Indian uprising.

The economy and culture of the Sauk Indian tribe was based on their ability to move between land in present-day Illinois (where they raised corn in summer and buried their dead) and other lands across the Mississippi (where they hunted and trapped fur-bearing animals in winter).
The disgruntled Sauk war chief, Black Hawk, had on April 5th again crossed the Mississippi River from the West into North central Illinois. After observing white settlers plowing and planting the sacred burial grounds of his relatives,

Black Hawk claimed ignorance of the provisions of a land treaty he had signed in 1816.

One afternoon in early May, Mary was surprised to find Richard Norris' current wife, Clarinda, on her doorstep. The woman was heavily pregnant, and had brought with her all the Norris children who remained at home, along with several servants. Mary immediately ushered Clarinda inside, bidding her to sit in the parlor with her feet elevated on a hassock.

The children greeted Mary in their own ways. Hendricks Norris, *Aaltje's* son, at seventeen years had fond memories of Mary's love and care before and after his mother's death. He hugged his aunt and kissed her cheek. William, 11 years old, and George, 9, (Catherine's sons) regarded Mary with some amount of trepidation. They recalled her ability to dominate them when they had stayed at her home five years previously. Little Lucretia, at 1½, sucked her thumb and clung to her nurse's skirts. Mary removed the thumb and kissed the child's cheek.

When the four younger children had been sent to the kitchen for bread and milk, and cups of cool cider had been brought for Clarinda and Hendricks, Mary sat down to talk with them.

"It's the Indians," Clarinda explained in a distraught tone. "We're not as close as you to the river – could we stay here until things calm down? I'm in no condition to protect the little ones, and Richard...he's away on business."

Hendricks rolled his eyes and added, "There's been a stampede of settlers from up North. No tellin' what they'll do next, and they seem pretty desperate. I'm more worried about them than I am about the Indians four hundred miles from here."

Mary had avoided getting to know Clarinda because of her experiences with Richard and his previous wives; she did not trust his taste in women. But this one (four years Mary's junior) possessed a singular lack of spirit.

Mary combined the younger visitors with her own brood (Raper 8½, Altha 6½, Elizabeth 3, and Burr, 1), and hoped fervently that William and George would not hurt the little ones. She thought that preemptive threats might be counter-productive, but she warned the children's nurses to keep a close watch on the boys. Lucretia and Burr turned out to be ideal playmates, mostly because Lucretia was a shy and gentle child.

Mary put Clarinda in the upstairs sitting room, and Hendricks in the first-floor bedroom reserved for travelers. Then, she began to wonder how long she would have to endure these crowded conditions and the chaos that ensued. She began daily walks to the wharves in search of news concerning what was known as the "Black Hawk War."

Black Hawk had received promises of support from other tribes and from the British. He therefore returned on April 5th to Northwest Illinois from his winter home with about five hundred Sauk, Fox, and Kickapoo warriors and one thousand old men, women, and children. When the promised support from British and Indian allies did not materialize, Black Hawk found that over 9,000 United States volunteers and regular federal troops had gathered to oppose him.

On May 9th, a small Illinois militia battalion began the pursuit of Black Hawk from Dixon on the Rock River. On May 10th, the militia burned the Ho-Chunk prophet White Cloud's village. Upon hearing of this, Black Hawk decided to return with his band to Iowa. Events at Stillman's Run (about fifty-five miles from Dixon) prevented this, and further hostilities ensued.

Major Isaiah Stillman commanded the militiamen present at Stillman's Run. When the militia killed one of the three men sent to parley by Black Hawk, the Indians rallied forty mounted warriors and attacked the militia camp at dusk. Though Stillman's men numbered about two hundred seventy-five, cohesion quickly collapsed and they fled to Dixon's Ferry. During the encounter, eleven militiamen under John Giles Adams were killed. It was later said that, if not for the incompetence of the Illinois militia, the Black Hawk War could have ended May 14th.

On May 27th and 28th, their one month enlistment expired, the first of the militia were mustered out of service. The federal government then ordered General Winfield Scott into action. Scott assembled a force of about one thousand regular troops and three hundred mounted volunteers. They embarked on boats from Buffalo, New York, making their way towards Chicago. To wide-spread horror, cholera attacked the troops. Soldiers became ill, and many of them died. At each place the vessels landed, the sick were deposited and soldiers deserted. By the time the expedition landed at Chicago, fewer than two hundred effective troops remained.

At Aurora, Mary struggled to control the children and to keep Clarinda comfortable in the hot weather. She had begun preparing her daughter Mary to make first confession in the fall, and tried to keep the process secret from Clarinda and the younger children. She celebrated Ascension on Thursday, May 31st, Pentecost Sunday on June 10th, and Trinity Sunday on June 17th. All the while she concealed the practice of her Catholicism from Clarinda, sure that the woman would not approve.

Two days after Corpus Christi, on Saturday, June 23rd, Clarinda delivered a healthy son. But Clarinda herself lost a lot of blood, weakened, and in fact never fully recovered from the delivery. The child was called Thomas, and did well, partly because Mary found a wet nurse for him.

The Black Hawk War stretched through July as a number of battles, skirmishes and massacres took place. When the Illinois Militia and Michigan Territory Militia finally caught up with Black Hawk's "British Band" following the Battle of Wisconsin Heights, the decisive clash of the war occurred on August 1-2. Near the mouth of the Bad Axe River, hundreds of Indian men, women and children were killed by white soldiers, their Indian allies, and an attack from a **United States** *gunboat, the* <u>Warrior</u>.

The Black Hawk War resulted in the deaths of seventy settlers and soldiers, and hundreds of Black Hawk's band. In addition to the combat casualties of the war, General Winfield Scott's force lost hundreds due to desertion and disease. The residual atmosphere of fear seriously affected pioneers, including the Norrises, who anticipated moving North into central Indiana. Even Indians who previously had shown only friendship to settlers were viewed with suspicion by their white neighbors.

The Black Hawk War provided a boost to several political careers. Abraham Lincoln served in Reynolds' militia, but never saw action. Zachary Taylor commanded troops under General Atkinson. Jefferson Davis, on leave during most of the Black Hawk War, returned in time to escort Black Hawk to Jefferson Barracks, just South of St. Louis, Missouri in September 1832.

By early September, Clarinda finally felt strong enough to return with the children to Norris House on Hogan's Creek. Mary rejoiced, and looked forward to the fall Holy Days and Altha's first confession. Her plans were often interrupted because of the Norris men's need to gather at her dining table to discuss their business.

Articles of a treaty made and concluded on Tippecanoe River, in the State of Indiana, between Jonathan Jennings, John W. Davis and Marks Crume, Commissioners on the part of the United States, and the Chiefs, Headmen and Warriors, of the Pottawatimie Indians, this twenty-sixth day of October, in the year eighteen hundred and thirty-two.

Article I.
The Chiefs, Headmen and Warriors, aforesaid, agree to cede to the United States their title and interest to lands in the State of Indiana, (to wit:) beginning at a point on Lake Michigan, where the line dividing the States of Indiana and Illinois intersects the same; thence with the margin of said Lake, to the intersection of the Southern boundary of a cession made by the Pottawatimies, at the treaty of the Wabash, of eighteen hundred and twenty-six; thence East, to the Northwest corner of the cession made by the treaty of St. Joseph's, in eighteen hundred and twenty-eight; thence South ten miles; thence with the Indian boundary line to the Michigan road; thence South with said road to the Northern boundary line, as designated in the treaty of eighteen hundred and twenty-six, with the Pottawatimies; thence West with the Indian boundary line to the river Tippecanoe; thence with the Indian boundary line, as established by the treaty of eighteen hundred and eighteen, at St. Mary's to the line dividing the States of Indiana and Illinois; and thence North, with the line dividing the said States, to the place of beginning.

Article II.
From the cession aforesaid, the following reservations are made, (to wit:)

For the band of Aub-be-naub-bee, thirty-six sections, to include his village.

For the bands of Men-o-mi-nee, No-taw-kah, Muck-kah-tah-mo-way and Pee-pin-oh-waw, twenty-two sections.

For the bands of O-kaw-wause, Kee-waw-nay and Nee-bosh, eight sections.

For J.B. Shadernah, one section of land in the Door Prairie, where he now lives.

For the band of Com-o-za, two sections.

For the band of Mah-che-saw, two sections.

For the band of Mau-ke-kose, six sections.

For the bands of Nees-waugh-gee and Quash-qua, three sections.

Article III.
In consideration of the cession aforesaid, the United States agree to pay to the Pottawatimie Indians, an annuity for the term of twenty years, of twenty thousand dollars; and will deliver to them goods to the value of one hundred thousand dollars, so soon after the signing of this treaty as they can be procured; and a further sum of thirty thousand dollars, in goods, shall be paid to them in the year eighteen hundred and thirty-three, by the Indian agent at Eel river.

Article IV.
The United States agree to pay the debts due by the Pottawatimies, agreeably to a schedule hereunto annexed; amounting to sixty-two thousand four hundred and twelve dollars.

Article V.
The United States agree to provide for the Pottawatimies, if they shall at any time hereafter wish to change their residence, an amount, either in goods, farming utensils, and such other articles as shall be required and necessary, in good faith, and to an extent equal to what has been furnished any other Indian tribe or tribes emigrating, and in just proportion to their numbers.

Article VI.
The United States agree to erect a saw mill on their lands, under the direction of the President of the United States.

In testimony whereof, the said Jonathan Jennings, John W. Davis, and Marks Crume, commissioners as aforesaid, and the chiefs, head men, and warriors of the Pottawatimies, have hereunto set their hands at Tippecanoe river, on the twenty-sixth day of October, in the year eighteen hundred and thirty-two.

    Jonathan Jennings,
    John W. Davis,

Marks Crume.

Witness:

Geo. B. Walker.
Louison, his x mark,
Che-chaw-cose, his x mark,
Banack, his x mark,
Man-o-quett, his x mark,
Kin-kosh, his x mark,
Pee-shee-waw-no, his x mark,
Min-o-min-ee, his x mark,
Mis-sah-kaw-way, his x mark,
Kee-waw-nay, his x mark,
Sen-bo-go, his x mark,
Che-quaw-ma-caw-co, his x mark,
Muak-kose, his x mark,
Ah-you-way, his x mark,
Po-kah-kause, his x mark,
So-po-tie, his x mark,
Che-man, his x mark,
No-taw-kah, his x mark,
Nas-waw-kee, his x mark,
Pec-pin-a-waw, his x mark,
Ma-che-saw, his x mark,
O-kitch-chee, his x mark,
Pee-pish-kah, his x mark,
Com-mo-yo, his x mark,
Chick-kose, his x mark,
Mis-qua-buck, his x mark,
Mo-tie-ah, his x mark,
Muck-ka-tah-mo-way, his x mark,
Mah-quaw-shee, his x mark,
O-sheh-weh, his x mark,
Mah-zick, his x mark,
Queh-kah-pah, his x mark,

Quash-quaw, his x mark,
Louisor Perish, his x mark,
Pam-bo-go, his x mark,
Bee-yaw-yo, his x mark,
Pah-ciss, his x mark,
Mauck-co-paw-waw, his x mark,
Mis-sah-qua, his x mark,
Kawk, his x mark,
Miee-kiss, his x mark,
Shaw-bo, his x mark,
Aub-be-naub-bee, his x mark,
Mau-maut-wah, his x mark,
O-ka-mause, his x mark,
Pash-ee-po, his x mark,
We-wiss-lah, his x mark,
Ash-kum, his x mark,
Waw-zee-o-nes, his x mark.

Witnesses:

William Marshall, Indian agent,
Henry Hoover, secretary,
H. Lasselle, interpreter,
E.V. Cicott, Sint. interpreter,
J.B. Bourie, interpreter,
J.B. Jutra, Sint. interpreter,
Edward McCartney, interpreter,
Luther Rice, interpreter.

After the signing of this Treaty, and at the request of the Indians, five thousand one hundred and thirty-five dollars were applied to the purchase of horses, which were purchased and delivered to them, under our direction, leaving ninety-four thousand eight hundred and sixty-five dollars to be paid in merchandise.

Jonathan Jennings,
John W. Davis,

Marks Crume.

The United States presidential election of November, 1832 saw incumbent President Andrew Jackson, candidate of the Democratic Party, easily win reelection against Henry Clay of Kentucky. Jackson won 219 of the 286 electoral votes cast, defeating Clay, the candidate of the Whig party, and Anti-Masonic Party candidate William Wirt.

By the time Advent Season began on Sunday, December 2nd, Mary had nearly forgotten the inconvenience of housing so many Norrises at once; life returned to a peaceful serenity. At Lawrenceburg, Altha completed her first confession and became a member of the Catholic parish.

1833

Bram remained at home, as he did nearly every winter and early spring. By Palm Sunday on March 31, Mary noticed the familiar twinges of early pregnancy, and guessed that she would deliver in the Fall.

On April 1st, 1833 Antonio de Padua María Severino López de Santa Anna y Pérez de Lebrón (often known as Santa Anna) was elected president of Mexico for the first time. He was among the first military leaders of modern Mexico, sometimes called the "Napoleon of the West," and served as president during eight separate time periods.

In April, Black Hawk and a few of his warriors were taken East on the orders of President Andrew Jackson. They traveled by steamboat, carriage, and railroad, and were exhibited to large crowds wherever they went. Once in Washington, D.C., they met with Jackson and Secretary of War Lewis Cass, though their destination was the prison at Fortress Monroe, Virginia. They stayed only a few weeks at the prison, during which they posed for multiple portraits by different artists. On June 5th, the men were sent West by steamboat on a circuitous route that took them through many large cities, including New York, Baltimore, and Philadelphia. Again, they were a spectacle everywhere they went. In Detroit, a crowd burned and hanged effigies of the prisoners. Black Hawk died in 1838, in Southeastern Iowa.

Bram's step-mother, Clarinda, became ill from one of the area's ubiquitous fevers, and died on Wednesday, June 12th. Because the men were away, the closest family members gathered for a simple funeral, and buried the deceased beside Richard's other wives. Mary took Clarinda's young children (Lucretia, almost 3 years old, and Thomas C., 1) to her home in

Aurora, waiting for their father to return. Cynically, Mary wondered if he already had a new mother selected for them.

Bram's sister Mary/Molly (who had married Justus Cure) died in August, and the family grieved together. Her husband later remarried, and much later moved to Decatur County, Indiana.

On August 28th, in England, the Slavery Abolition Act was given Royal Assent, which paved the way to end legal slavery within the British Empire.

Before Advent, on November 7th, Mary and Bram's son Joseph Dailey was born. To differentiate him from the other Josephs in the Norris family, this child was always known as "Dailey." Mary had recovered from the delivery sufficiently by Sunday, November 24th, to preside over a big dinner, the Feast of Christ the King.

Also on November 7th, Mormon "saints" who lived in Jackson County, Missouri were forced by persecuting mobs to flee across the Missouri River.

Advent commenced on Sunday, December 1st, and the remainder of the Holy Season progressed in stately order, accompanied by occasional, melting snow.

1834

White County was formed during the 1833-1834 Indiana Legislative Session. Over the next two years, Indiana enjoyed peak economic prosperity.

The Catholic Diocese of Vincennes, including Indiana and about one-third of Illinois was created during this year, with the Reverend Simon G.W. Brute as its first bishop.

Mary had become accustomed to receiving a short letter from Uncle James Gold during each Christmas holiday season. By this time he was over forty years old, and had made a concerted effort to transfer his illegally obtained wealth into a legitimate shipping and trade business. In order to appear more respectable, he had in 1818 married a young woman in Maryland who had borne him two sons, then died. James then married Anne Neale, and relocated their home to Philadelphia, where fewer people were acquainted with his former life as a pirate. He adjusted his mannerisms and style of dress accordingly.

James had discovered, however, that because the economic climate fluctuated wildly, land purchase was the best way to preserve his wealth. His impatience with legalities of operating a legitimate business caused a deep frustration with life in established communities. In his most recent Christmas letter, he had indicated that a move to Indiana was in the works.

Therefore, when the Gold family - James and Anne, with sons James, 15 and William, 10, - arrived at Aurora in late March, Mary was thrilled but not overly surprised. The Golds remained at her home for nearly a week, celebrating Good Friday on March 28th and Easter two days later. On the Monday after Easter, they headed North to Franklin County, where James staked a claim to eighty acres.

Not intending to become a farmer, however, James located his claim close to a proposed canal route, and engaged in trade while pouring his profits into additional land, which he then rented out for a share of the produce. His skill as an intimidating negotiator and his experience with various weapons stood him in good stead on the frontier, and he prospered.

On August 1st, *all slaves in the British Empire were emancipated, but they were indentured to their former owners in a two-stage apprenticeship system; the first set of apprenticeships came to an end in August of 1838, while the final apprenticeships ended two years later on August 1st, 1840.*

Mary had prepared to celebrate the Transfiguration of the Lord in early August, but her plans for a day of prayer and fasting were interrupted by the unexpected return of the Norris men. Since her home had become their usual meeting place, she asked the servants to prepare a meal for them, then sat to hear their conversation.

Anti-Indian hysteria, resulting from the recent Black Hawk War, continued unabated among the settlers of Indiana. This strong public sentiment put pressure on both local and national government officials to remove the Native American population to lands West of the Mississippi River. The Norris families represented only a tiny fraction of the thousands planning to move into North Central Indiana as soon as the Indians left.

Mary heard about the richness of North Central Indiana soil (light clay topped with loam), in Clinton County. Clinton County lay just North and West of the geographical center of Indiana; the county seat was called Frankfort, and had a population of one hundred fifty people. Frankfort by that time was connected to several other frontier towns (Newcastle, Munceytown, Lafayette) by an improving system of roads, and the first grist mill was being built in the county during this year.

Late that night, Mary confronted Bram in their upstairs chamber.

"What's this about buying land up North? Don't we have enough acres here to meet our needs?"

He frowned, and reached for her hand, drawing her close.

"My Love, at this point we're just exploring options. I don't want us to miss what could be an exceptional opportunity."

"Your father definitely stated that the whole family will pack up and move North!"

"That doesn't mean we *must* go along with the plan. But to refuse even to consider a move is foolish."

"I may be a fool, but I don't want to leave this house! I love it here."

"Mary, listen to me. This house is just a box. Boxes like this one can be constructed *anywhere* the ground is level enough. And from what I hear, Clinton County has plenty of level ground. What's important is that we provide an opportunity for our children to lead a good life." She allowed him to pull her onto the bed and to kiss away her fears, at least temporarily.

Next day, the men left, traveling Northwest across Dearborn County to Napoleon in Ripley County, where they accessed the Michigan Road. They crossed Decatur County, passing through Greensburg to Shelby County and Shelbyville. Entering Marion County, they stayed with John Van Clift, the son of Richard's brother-in-law and husband of Richard's niece Catherine Norris. They also met with Joseph Wheatley, another of Richard's brothers-in-law, and spent time at the land office, consulting with the agents there. From Indianapolis, they continued on the Michigan Road, crucial to trade and agriculture, which led them North through Hamilton and Boone Counties and then into Clinton County.

When they returned to Aurora, Mary wondered exactly what sorts of social opportunities the men had sought in the State Capitol, because Richard brought back a new wife, a widow several years older than Mary, named Lavina. Lavina came from a large family, the Balls, that had moved from Virginia into Kentucky, then into Indiana. Lavina's mother was born a Harding, and that family had moved with the Balls, much as the Hendricksons had moved with the Norris family. The Hardings and the Balls had settled first in Henry County, then moved to the Indianapolis area in 1830.

Mary was instantly entranced by the woman. Not only was Lavina stunningly beautiful, with lustrous, waist length black hair and chocolate brown eyes, but she had *presence*. Tall, statuesque, with regal posture and demeanor, Lavina never doubted her own ability to handle any situation. She instructed Mary on any topic as if Mary were ten years old, and Mary lapped up the information and the attention as if she were Lavina's pet dog.

Mary began a campaign to win the woman's favor, bringing small presents frequently to Norris House on Hogan's Creek. When Lavina responded to these overtures, Mary assumed that Lavina was her friend. And Mary privately vowed *never* to be alone with Richard again. However, knowing Richard, Mary wondered how much Lavina knew about his wayward behavior, and what Lavina would try to do about it.

On August 11th & 12th, in Charlestown, near Boston, Massachusetts, a Protestant mob burned down a convent, home to Roman Catholic Ursuline nuns. The event was triggered by the reported abuse of a member of the order, and was fueled by the rebirth of extreme anti-Catholic sentiment in antebellum New England.

The Norris men came home in early fall, bringing another addition to the family. Richard and *Aaltje's* youngest surviving son, Hendricks Norris, had married Polly Lauderbaugh during their trip. After depositing her at Norris House on Hogan's Creek, the men took off again, anxious to further their business arrangements. Unlike Lavina, and more like Mary, Polly had no living family and had been nearly destitute when the Norris men found her in Indianapolis. Her parents and siblings had died shortly after arriving in that city.

Lavina, as Polly's new mother-in-law, tried to include Polly in daily life at Norris House, and Mary began to feel jealous of the attention she felt she was missing from Lavina. But it turned out that Polly was very young, painfully sad and shy, and apt to spend a great deal of time in her room with the door locked. She was dreadfully intimidated by Lavina.

Lavina came to Mary's house at Aurora to ask what she thought, and the two women agreed that Polly just needed time to settle in. But Polly had great difficulty breaking out of her shell, and it turned out that she could not speak without stammering. She continued to avoid conversations, but became more friendly out of sheer loneliness.

Articles of a treaty between the United States and the Miami tribe of Indians, concluded at the Forks of the Wabash, in the State of Indiana, on the 23rd day of October, 1834, by and between William Marshall, commissioner of the United States, and the chiefs and warriors of said tribe:

ARTICLE 1. The Miami tribe of Indians agree to cede to the United States the following described tracts of land within the State of Indiana, being a part of reservations made to said tribe from former cessions, now conveyed for and in consideration of the payments stipulated to be made to them in the 2d article of this treaty of cession. One tract of land, thirty-six sections, at Flat Belly's village, a reserve made by the treaty of Wabash of 1826.

Also, one tract of land, about twenty-three thousand acres more or less, a reserve made at Wabash treaty in 1826, of five miles in length on the Wabash river, extending back to Eel river. Also, one other tract of ten sections at Racoon village, and a tract of ten sections at Mudd creek on Eel river, reserves made at Wabash treaty of 1826. Also, one reserve of two miles square, on the Salamany river at the mouth of At-che-pong-quaw creek, reserve made at the treaty of St. Mary's of 1818.

Also, one other tract being a portion of the ten mile square reserve, made at the treaty of St. Mary's of 1818, opposite the mouth of the river Aboutte, commencing at the Northeast corner of said reserve, thence South with the Eastern boundary of the same ten miles to the Southeast corner of the reserve, thence West with the Southern boundary one mile, thence North nine miles, thence West nine miles, thence North one mile to the Northwest corner of said reserve, thence to the place of beginning.

The Miamies also agree to cede a portion of their big reserve, made at the treaty of St. Mary's of 1818, situated Southeast of the Wabash, extending along the Wabash river, from the mouth of Salamany river, to the mouth of Eel river. The part now ceded shall be embraced within the following bounds to wit: commencing on the Wabash river, opposite the mouth of Eel river, running up said Wabash river eight miles, thence South two miles, thence Westerly one mile, thence South to the Southern boundary of said reserve, thence along said boundary line seven miles to the Southwest corner, thence Northerly with the Western boundary line to the place of beginning.

ARTICLE 2. For and in consideration of the cession made in the first article of this treaty, the United States agree to pay the Miami tribe of Indians the sum of two hundred and eight thousand dollars; of this sum fifty-eight thousand dollars to be paid within six months from the ratification of this treaty, fifty thousand dollars to be applied to the payment of the debts of the tribe, and the remaining sum of one hundred thousand dollars in annual installments of ten thousand dollars per year.

ARTICLE 3. From the cession made in the first article of this treaty, there shall be granted to each of the persons named in the schedule hereunto annexed, and to their heirs and assigns, by patent from the President of the United States, the lands therein named.

ARTICLE 4. It is agreed, between the parties to this treaty, that a patent in fee simple shall be issued by the President of the United States to John B. Richardville, principal chief of the Miami tribe, for a reserve of ten sections at the Forks of the Wabash, made to said tribe by treaty of twenty-third October, 1826, he having an Indian title to the same, a copy of which, marked A, accompanies this treaty.

ARTICLE 5. The United States agree to furnish a skillful miller, to superintend a mill for the Miamies, in lieu of the gunsmith promised by the 5th article of the treaty of St. Mary's of 1818.

ARTICLE 6. The United States agree to have the buildings and improvements on the lands ceded by the first article of this treaty valued. To cause a similar amount in value, laid out in building, clearing and fencing ground, for the use of the Indians, on such place or places as their chiefs may select, and that the Indians have peaceable possession of their houses and improvements, on the lands ceded in the first article of this treaty, until the improvements are made as provided for in this article.

ARTICLE 7. The United States agree to pay the Miami Indians fifteen hundred dollars, for horses heretofore stolen from them by the whites.

In testimony whereof we have hereunto affixed our signatures this tenth day of November, A.D. 1834.

Me-shin-go-mask-a,
Wa-we-esse,
Wa-pa-pen-shaw,

Flat Belly,
Ne-con-saw,
Ne-con-sau,
Little Charley,
Ca-tah-ke-mun-quah,
Chen-qua-quah,
Ma-gure-ca,
Pe-wa-pe-ah,
Che-cho-wah,
O-san-dear,
Ne-con-saw,
Shappeen,
Ma-con-saw,
Keel-swa,
Little Maquri-ca,
Wa-pe-shin-wuah,
Shappen-do-ce-ah,
Ne-ah-lin-quah,
Ne-pa-wa,
Co-wy-sey,
Pin-daw-lin-shau,
To-pe-ah,
Men-na-tuo,
Ma-wuah-co-nah,
Poqua,
Me-ca-to-mun-quah,
Min-se-quah,
Wa-pe-mun-quah,

In presence of

A.C. Pepper, Indian agent.
Allen Hamilton.,
F. Comparet, interpreter.
Lucien P. Ferny.

In November, Governor Noah Noble was successful as the Whig candidate for re-election, defeating his competitor, James G. Reed, by 7,662 votes. The Norrises approved.

Mary invited Lavina and Polly to visit before the holidays, and the three women conspired to create Christmas gifts for the younger children in their care. Mary's brood by this time included Raper, 11 years, Altha who turned 9 just before Advent, Elizabeth, nearly 6, Burr, 3½, and Dailey who turned 1 in early November. Lavina and Polly bore responsibility for Catherine's child George, 11, as well as for Clarinda's Lucretia, 4, and Thomas, 2½.

Rag dolls were constructed for the girls, small wheeled wooden toys for the boys, and wooden board games were painted for the older children to share. Warm socks, mittens, scarves and hats were knitted for all of them. In addition, Mary showed Lavina and Polly how to make some of the sweet treats that *Aaltje* had served at the holidays.

All this was done in great secrecy, and the presents were left near each child late on Christmas Eve (a Wednesday night), with the result that there was great delight at both Norris homes on Christmas morning. So successful was the women's plan that they decided to continue this practice for years to come. What seemed odd to Mary was that Lavina let everyone know that this had all been Lavina's own idea, and that everyone should be grateful to her.

What seemed even more odd was a visit from Lavina late one evening in the week before New Year's Eve. The woman seemed quite upset when Mary greeted her. Lavina swept past Mary, headed for Mary's sitting room, and sat, tears welling from her eyes.

"Lavina, what--" Mary began, but Lavina waved her into silence.

After what seemed an eternity of silent tears, Lavina spoke. "I think that I am pregnant," she told Mary. "And the father is my husband, that lying, cheating philanderer."

"Ph-philanderer?" asked Mary. "How do you know?"

"I caught him, of course. He was in the back room with Polly, and had pulled nearly all her clothes off."

Mary gasped, covered her mouth with her hand, and hoped that she looked sufficiently shocked. "What will you do?" she asked.

"Nothing. There's nothing to be done. I've married this bastard, and I'm pregnant with his child. I'm trapped."

With that, Lavina rose, re-wrapped herself in the buffalo robe she had flung aside in the warm room, and strode through the doorway, down the stairs, outside to find her horse and ride home.

Not knowing what to do, or whether anything could help the situation, Mary did absolutely nothing. But her mind replayed the scene repeatedly, until even the thought of Richard seemed the most repugnant thing on earth.

1835

Adams, DeKalb, Fulton, Jasper, Jay, Kosciusko, Marshall, Newton, Noble, Porter, Pulaski, Starke, Steuben, Wells, and Whitley Counties were formed by the Indiana State Legislature from confiscated Indian lands during this year.

Continual violent incidents in Florida between white settlers, escaped slaves, and Native Americans escalated into what became the Second Seminole War, lasting until 1842. This was the most sustained and successful effort in United States history by slaves to win freedom through force of arms. Hundreds of black fugitives fought beside Native Americans who had given them a haven. The treaty at the end allowed most of the black people to accompany their Indian benefactors to the trans-Mississippi West.

During this year, a new Mexican constitution outlawed slavery in all of its territories. This outraged the American emigrants in Texas, who had moved there since 1823 when the Mexican government had enticed them with cheap land. Slaves were a major piece of the Texian economy, and the Texians began serious discussion of secession from Mexico.

The weather had warmed, and Mary rode her horse to Lawrenceburg for Ash Wednesday services on March 4th. Returning home at supper time, she found Bram waiting for her.

"We're going," he said, softly.

"What do you mean?"

"I mean that we, you and I, will sell this house and relocate to Clinton County next year."

Mary sat down, overcome with emotion. Did he not know, did he not care about her fears?

"You aren't the only one who had a difficult trip West to Indiana," he said. "My family traveled the Pennsylvania mountains by covered wagon, then the Ohio River by flatboat. Some of us didn't make it. It was the first time I watched men die, trying to live their dreams. This move to Clinton County will be nowhere near as difficult, nor as long."

"But I feel *safe* here," she said.

"And you'll feel safe in our new home. I promise you that."

Mary did not have to ask whether there was a priest at Frankfort, Indiana. Her fellow parishoners at Lawrenceburg had assured her that there was not. She had begun training daughter Elizabeth, preparing for the child's first confession, and now felt renewed urgency in this endeavor.

After Easter (April 19th), six men including Richard Norris, Mary's husband Bram, Richard's sons Joseph and Hendricks Norris, and Richard's nephews Stephen Norris and Abraham Hendrickson rode their horses to Clinton County, Indiana. Stephen and Abraham were brothers in law because Abraham Hendrickson had married Stephen's sister, Mariah. Mary had met but was not yet familiar with Mariah or with Stephen's wife, Esther.

With the men went three youths, thrilled to be part of such a great venture. This group consisted of Richard's sons William L. and George C. Norris, along with Abraham Hendrickson's son Joseph.

The first order of business would be selecting a "home place," for Richard, one for Bram, and one for Abraham Hendrickson, where log cabins would serve as the first outposts in their new neighborhood. They would get advice from other pioneer settlers, and study the land.

One of the portions of Clinton County most attractive to farmers was called the "Twelve Mile Prairie." This sector was an anomaly. The soil was rich and suited to crops, but no trees had grown there. To pioneers who had given years of their lives chopping wood to clear land, a Twelve Mile Prairie seemed like paradise.

The absence of trees was both a blessing and a curse. Prairie land was notoriously difficult to plow (due to deep layers of sod, or plant roots), and often needed extensive draining by means of laboriously dug ditches. Trees for building materials and for fuel had to be transported to the prairie. Forested soil, on the other hand, needed improvement with lime and manure after the trees were removed so that crops would grow well.

Capitalizing on this opportunity, Bram staked a claim to 40 acres on the Northeastern corner of the prairie. Part of his property had trees, and part did not. Using the same strategy, Richard chose three parcels close by, a total of 240 acres, along either side of a road that flanked the prairie's Northeast edge. This road ran diagonally from the Norris claim, about four miles Northwest to Frankfort, and about eight miles Southeast to the Michigan Road.

Abraham Hendrickson claimed 40 acres of forested land several miles to the Northeast of the Norrises, away from the prairie, along a stretch of wagon road connecting Frankfort and Boyleston. Boyleston was a minor stop on the Michigan Road, and the connector became known as the Boyleston Road.

Leaving the other men and young boys to begin cabin construction, Bram, Richard, and Abraham Hendrickson rode to the land office at Crawfordsville, Montgomery County. There they registered claims and made down payments on May 13th.

Mary was called on the last day of May to assist at the birth of Richard and Lavina's child. The new mother named the baby Mary Catherine, and Mary was given the impression that it was named for herself. But she also came away disappointed by the impression Lavina gave that nothing Mary had done was good enough.

While running (unsuccessfully) for President during this year, William Henry Harrison was received during May and June by Democrats at dinners and receptions in Indianapolis and Lafayette (near the site of the Battle of Tippecanoe).

During the summer, Richard claimed over 532 more acres in Clinton County. Because it was impossible to guess which towns and connecting roads would become important in the future, Richard hedged his bets by staking claims to separate parcels located in different parts of the county. In addition, Richard claimed 200 acres in Marion County near Lavina's family North of Indianapolis, 80 acres in Hamilton County and 80 acres in Boone County near to the Michigan Road (connecting the Ohio River at Marion to Indianapolis and to Lake Michigan at what became Michigan City, Indiana). He spent quite a bit of time securing his properties, arranging for local men to begin clearing the land, and renting out cleared fields to farmers for the following year.

When the Norris men returned to Aurora, in mid-November, Halley's Comet was putting on a show nightly in the sky.

Bram seemed completely consumed by plans for the move. Choosing and buying land was all he talked about. Whenever she questioned him about the necessity of leaving Aurora, Mary received essentially the same answer: He was deeply and totally committed to establishing a solid economic base for their growing family, and Clinton County was *the* best place to do that.

For this reason, Mary felt especially good about revealing, on Sunday December 27th (feast of the Solemnity of the Holy Family) that she was expecting a child in the summer. If only she did not have to leave her beautiful, perfect house, life would be much better, she thought. And if only there were a priest at Frankfort to baptize her baby...

1836

Adams, Brown, and Marshall Counties were formed in Indiana during this Legislative Session.

A record number of acres, more than 3 million, of Indiana land passed from public to private ownership during this year. It is reported that swarms of customers lined up outside the land offices hours before opening time every day, giving rise to the expression: "Doing a land office business."

Governor Noah Noble signed into effect "An Act to Provide for a General System of Internal Improvements," a plan doomed to end in failure four years later. The act authorized borrowing up to $10,500,000 for several projects, including the extension and completion of the Wabash & Erie Canal and also a new railroad line from Madison on the Ohio River to Lafayette on the Wabash via Indianapolis.

The completed Madison line provided an important lesson to inexperienced American railroad builders. The grades were too steep for standard locomotives, necessitating the use of 8-horse hitches to haul cars up the hills. Down-grade trips were worse, and a dangerous build up of speed often resulted in derailment, explosions, injury and death. As a result, trains were often called "bombs on wheels."

The first locomotive to run in Indiana was the four-wheeled Elkhorn, a British manufactured engine that could not meet the demands of the American landscape. Indiana's second and third locomotives, the Madison and the Indianapolis, were of an improved design called the 4-2-0, manufactured by the Baldwin Locomotive Company.

These early locomotives averaged between 10 and 15 miles per hour, taking up to 35 hours to cross Indiana. Even though this seems painfully slow by modern standards, at the time it seemed miraculously fast and easy compared to the alternative foot, wagon, and canal boat travel.

The town of Aurora saw steady and substantial growth, with a bridge constructed over the mouth of Hogan Creek and another bridge West of town. This meant that property values rose just as the Norrises prepared to sell and move out. However, Richard retained a few choice town lots, while Van decided to stay in Dearborn County with his family. Richard's brother Joseph delayed his family's move North, thinking that local prices were bound to increase even more.

During a break in the late winter weather, Mary took Elizabeth to Lawrenceburg to make first confession. Her joy was tinged with sorrow; this would likely be the last of her children to receive the sacrament, and Confirmation did not seem likely for any of them. Bram had been taking Raper to Methodist services when he was in town, and Mary feared that her other children would eventually go that direction.

Whenever the men were away and the weather was mild enough, Mary would ride her horse the short distance up Hogan's Creek to Norris House to visit Polly, Lavina and baby Mary. The three women became quite close. When the conversation steered toward the Norris men, however, Mary had to be careful not to say too much. Even though Richard had aged badly (he would soon be sixty-one, but looked much older, gray and careworn), Mary doubted that he had bothered to change his wayward sexual behavior when traveling. Mary did not want to hurt Lavina by revealing what she knew.

Lavina, on the other hand, had no compunctions about discussing Richard, comparing him to her previous husband, John Stephens. She had, at age twenty, married John in 1822. Soon afterward, the couple had purchased seventy-three acres of land along the White River, Southeast of Indianapolis. They had lived together there for about nine years before he was killed in a construction accident and buried in the Greenlawn city cemetery. They had no children, and Lavina seemed to be at a loss concerning baby Mary Catherine. Luckily, the servants had experience with children and were willing to help. What interested Mary was that Lavina often referred to Richard as being "undisciplined," with no elaboration of what she might mean, and no further specific mention of his philandering ways.

Mary did not expect to see Lavina on Ash Wednesday, February 17th.

She had gone to Mass at Lawrenceburg that morning with Raper, Altha, and Elizabeth, and they had been "ashed" as a sign of penitence. Mary had fasted during the day, and rested in her upstairs parlor, watching the younger children (Burr, and Dailey) who played on the floor.

Suddenly, the maid opened the door, showing Lavina into the room.

"Hell-o, my dear," Lavina began, then gasped, "What happened to your head? Are you hurt?"

"N-no," Mary responded. "I was at Mass this morning, that's all. All of us received ashes on our foreheads."

"You're *Catholic*? I had no idea! I thought all the Norrises were Methodists!"

"I try not to make a big deal of it–some Methodists can be very intolerant."

"Well, I'll tell you a secret. I was *christened* Catholic, back in Kentucky, but never confirmed in the church. My grandmother always kept the Catholic holy days, as best she could, God bless her."

"Does Richard know?"

"Yes, I told him, but I'm not sure he was listening. He was trying to get me into bed at the time."

Mary knew exactly what Lavina meant.

"Well, Bram knows I'm Catholic, but he tries to ignore it. It amounts to the same thing, I guess."

"Can you teach me? About the Catholic customs, I mean. I think it would help me feel closer to my grandma."

Mary was silent for a few moments.

"I can teach you, but this must stay between us. If the Norrises think I'm a bad influence..."

"I understand. I can say I learned these things long ago, from my grandmother."

After that, the two women prayed together, in Latin, whenever they could manage to be alone. Because Lavina could read and write, they were able to follow the ecclesiastical calendar more reliably than Mary could on her own. Mary also convinced Lavina to have baby Mary christened by the priest. Perhaps because of her ability with the calendar, and also because she questioned everything Mary said, Lavina made Mary feel as if Lavina was teaching Mary the proper way to be Catholic.

THE ALAMO'S MUSICAL DUEL - February 28, 1836 - Susannah Dickinson's eyewitness accounts of the Alamo siege are the most heavily relied upon source of information regarding the last days of the Alamo defenders. Although most of her stories were tragically somber, she did have a joyful tale to tell from Day 6 of the siege.

According to Dickinson, Davy Crockett took it upon himself to raise the morale of the men. He decided to that the best way to do that was by challenging John McGregor to a musical duel of instruments. McGregor, a Scotsman by birth, took up his bagpipes while Crockett took up his fiddle. They played back and forth, loudly enough for the Mexican soldiers to hear – and they created one of the most legendary moments in Texas history.

It is said that McGregor won the duel because he was able to play the loudest and the longest. Texas legend claims that the Mexican soldiers coined the term "gringo" after hearing the men singing "Green Grow the Rushes Oh." While these stories have undoubtedly grown and been embellished throughout the years, the heart of the tale is based in fact and it was undoubtedly one of the few happy moments for the beleaguered Alamo defenders during their ordeal.

On March 2nd, the Mexican state of Texas declared independence from Mexico. The Mexican government was violently opposed to losing this land, and an army had been assembled under Generalissimo de Santa Anna. On March 6th, the Texians (mostly pioneer emigrants from the United States) were over run by the Mexican army at The Alamo (now San Antonio, Texas). Up to 250 Texian defenders of the fort were killed on the day of the battle, and more than 342 Texian prisoners were executed by Mexicans at the Goliad Massacre on March 27th. On April 21st, at the battle of San Jacinto, the Texians led by General Sam Houston defeated Santa Anna, shouting, "Remember Goliad, Remember the Alamo!"

On April 3rd, Jesus Christ appeared to Joseph Smith and Oliver Powdery in the Mormon Temple at Kirtland, Ohio. Moses, Elias, and Elijah also made an appearance, handing over the priesthood keys to the men.

On April 22nd, a small band of Texians captured Mexican Generalissimo Santa Anna dressed as a private of the dragoons, hiding in a marsh. On May 14th, Santa Anna, in exchange for safe conduct out of Mexico via Veracruz, signed the Treaties of Velasco, intended to conclude hostilities between Mexico and the Republic of Texas. These treaties were soon declared null and void by a new government in Mexico City. Continued political divisions continued to weaken the Mexican position in North America, and this was exploited by the United States Government for decades to come.

Spring arrived, and final plans were made for the Norris trek North. Thirty people were involved, but the men decided that Abraham Hendrickson and Stephen Norris, with their wives and nine children, would leave first, traveling separately and more slowly. They would take farm breeding stock for all the families with them; each family would need a dairy cow, laying hens and a rooster, and several ewes with their spring lambs. The families would share a "starter" breeding herd of hogs, a ram, a bull, and a pair of goats. Mary insisted on the goats because goat milk was best for infants whose mothers lacked milk or whose mothers had died in childbed. At the last minute, she kept one of the cows, the best milker, to travel with her own wagon. She liked to drink milk, and thought that the children should have some every day.

Mary heard that the servants would be "let go," and realized that she, personally, would be taking a step back from the civilized existence she had so carefully built. She had watched other pioneer women, who worked from before dawn to well past dark while bearing children and fighting off constant rounds of illness. They typically lost their "bloom" of health and beauty in their teens, looked tired and run down before age thirty, and seemed old at forty. At thirty-one, she intended to keep going for a long time, and to enjoy whatever years she had left. To do this, she was prepared to make whatever accommodations necessary, once they reached Clinton County.

The finality of the men's decisions hit home to Mary one afternoon when Bram escorted a sleazy-looking steamboat operator through her house. His personal hygiene was definitely lacking, and he wore flashy, store-bought clothing along with too much jewelry. He bought the place, including some of the furnishings, and paid in cash. Bram's satisfied smile let Mary know that the house would soon be hers only in memory. She retired to her cupola, where she cried and tried to pray.

Mary, Polly and Lavina organized the packing and removal of household goods from their respective houses. Textiles, being the most difficult to replace, occupied the highest priority. The furniture, including Mary's piano, imported at great expense from the East, was deemed too heavy to make the trip, and would be left behind, stored in a warehouse on one of Richard's lots in Aurora.

Lavina, Mary, Raper, Altha, and Elizabeth attended the Catholic services on Laetare Sunday and Palm Sunday on March 20th and 27th at Lawrenceburg. After Palm Sunday dinner, the kitchens were dismantled by the servants. Everything was packed into three ox-drawn wagons, and the seventeen family members headed North early next morning over muddy roads.

The men of the group included Richard, Bram, Joseph, and Hendricks Norris. The women were Lavina, Mary, and Polly. The youths deemed old enough to help included William L., 15, George C., 13, and Raper, 12. Small children included Lucretia, 5, Thomas C., 3½, Mary, 10 months, Altha, 10, Elizabeth, 7, Burr, 4, and Dailey, 2.

Copying *Aaltje's* example from years before, Mary had carefully trained her older children to take care of the younger ones. Several times before the journey began, she sat them down (with tasty cookies in their hands) and explained her expectations. Altha would be in charge of Dailey; Elizabeth would manage Burr. There were many moments during the trek when she congratulated herself on this strategy.

Both Mary and Polly were pregnant, and discussed in advance the wisdom of riding horses during the trip versus bouncing along in the wagons. Each had insisted on her own gentle saddle horse for the journey, as did Lavina. Due to the strong likelihood of rain, they had brought large poncho style coverings made from oiled pigskin, and broad brimmed hats of the same material. This enabled them to keep riding through inclement weather in relative comfort instead of retreating to the canvas-covered wagons.

On the first day, the cavalcade covered about ten miles, following Hogan's Creek West through Dillsboro while climbing a hilly, rugged section of Dearborn County. The Norrises were headed for Napoleon, in Ripley County, where they would find the Michigan Road that led to Indianapolis. But the routes between Dillsboro and Napoleon were little more than horse trails, and the wagons bogged down so many times that the group nearly despaired of getting through. At twilight, they camped beside a fast-flowing stream known as Hayes Branch. The men unyoked the oxen and unsaddled the horses, staking them out to graze for the night. The young boys built and tended a fire.

For Monday's meals, the women had packed leftovers from Sunday's dinner. At noon, everyone except for baby Mary snacked on bread and cheese; those without Catholic dietary restriction ate cured ham. The first night's meal featured pre-baked potatoes to heat over the fire on sticks, a serving of fresh dandelion and dock greens picked beside the road and boiled in a large pot, and chunks of wheat bread with blackberry jam. Roast lamb was available for the Methodists. Lavina had brought half a dozen pies, which disappeared among the family as if by magic. Clean up from supper required an hour, and settling the youngsters for sleep took much longer than usual. Everyone slept beneath the wagons or under canvas tarps spread between available trees. By the time Mary lay down, exhausted, next to Bram, he was sound asleep, snoring softly as he often did.

At first, she could not sleep. Mary had not lived out of doors for many years, and her body struggled to adapt to fluctuating temperatures. She heard strange noises in the nearby underbrush. She felt overwhelmed by the stress of caring for the children in constantly changing surroundings.

After thinking for awhile, Mary realized that the other women were under a similar strain, and that they were all battling their emotions in order to retain a semblance of calm. The men and youths, on the other hand, were exuberant, eager to tackle any challenge that might present itself. The children, of course, for the most part lived in each moment, reacting to whatever happened. Mary remembered the long trip across Virginia, over the Blue Ridge mountains and through Kentucky. It had not seemed so emotionally draining as this, at least not before her parents died…

The fire had been banked for the night, and was quickly coaxed back to life next morning. Oatmeal was cooked in the pot and dished out, along with dried apples from the previous fall. Hot coffee was not Mary's usual drink – she much preferred tea – but on this morning the strong coffee helped her waken and get moving.

The group started earlier Tuesday than they had the previous day, moved as quickly as possible, and stopped later. As a result, they left Dearborn County and crossed part of Ripley, but halted on the banks of rain-swollen Laughery Creek. According to the men, Versailles, the county seat, lay just a few miles past the creek, but everyone was exhausted; no one wanted to attempt the crossing in the fading light.

The women sliced ham and bread, while the men and boys made camp. As the temperature dropped, Mary wrapped blankets around herself and the younger children, wondering how much more of this she could take.

On Wednesday morning, the men moved the oxen and wagons across the creek while the women cooked cornmeal mush in a big pot. As soon as everyone had eaten, the breakfast gear was hastily washed and they all forded the creek. The water was brown with mud; it was impossible to see the rocks and holes beneath. Bram carried Burr and Elizabeth on his horse. Mary fearfully grasped little Dailey, while Altha, riding on the saddle behind her mother, held on tightly as their horse made its way across.

Mary relaxed as they entered Versailles, the Ripley County seat. Established on one hundred acres in 1818, the town looked very organized. A courthouse occupied the center of the town square, and an additional building for county offices sat nearby. Various shops lined the main streets – a general store, a blacksmith, a tavern, and a bakery.

The women, delaying the inevitable descent into corn bread at every meal, hastily purchased a dozen loaves of wheat bread. Everyone else kept moving with the wagons, and the women caught up as the group left town, headed Northwest.

They reached the tiny (at this point, hardly more than a crossroads) village of Napoleon in late afternoon as a drenching rain began to fall. The women and youngest children took shelter as best they could, while the men set up camp. William Norris rode to a farmhouse in the distance to "borrow" a start for their campfire. It was Mary's idea to speed things up by building *three* fires and cooking the food in *three* kettles. By shielding the flames from the rain and by covering the kettles, they were able to heat water faster than usual. Once the water boiled, the women made a nourishing soup by throwing in some potatoes, dried peas, and carrots they had brought along; chunks of ham went into two of the kettles while the Catholics ate from the one without meat. This, with dried apples and the wheat bread, comprised their supper.

On Thursday morning, the men announced that the families *must* cover more ground each day in order to reach Indianapolis by Sunday, Easter.

Trying hard to comply, the women passed out dried fruits and bread, without the usual time-consuming cooking over the fire.

As she turned her horse into the Michigan Road, Mary was astonished at the sight. She had, of course heard about this route since 1828, when construction began. But by comparison to the rough paths the group had followed through the woods before reaching Versailles, this road seemed unbelievably smooth and open. A one hundred foot wide swath had been cleared through the forest; stumps had been grubbed from the middle thirty feet to facilitate wagon travel. In marshy areas, where horses could lose their footing and wagons become stuck, the road was corduroyed; logs laid across the muck had been covered with sand. Fords at the creeks had been improved by the addition of rocks, even though no permanent bridges were yet in place. Evidence of settlement appeared sporadically – farm houses and barns – connected to the Michigan Road by crude wagon tracks. At some points that could be called "crossroads," villages made their first attempts at establishment.

The ox wagons made much better time on this road, entering Decatur County, and the families did not stop long at noon to eat. Rather, the women grabbed food from the bags and distributed it among the group. As a result, they passed through the county seat, Greensburgh, while it was still light. Mary reflected upon the similarity of small towns. The public square with its old jail and two story, forty foot square brick court house looked much like those she had seen before. Several miles past Greensburgh, they made camp beside the road.

On Good Friday morning, Mary woke before daylight because Polly was urgently shaking her shoulder, whispering, "Help me!"

Not wanting to waken Bram, who still snored in his blankets, Mary hastily rose and, shivering, followed Polly out from under the canvas canopy where she had spent the night.

"I-I'm bleeding!" whimpered Polly.

Mary's stomach contracted, and she was carried back in memory to Kentucky, to the fear she had felt as *Maman's* pregnancy, and then her life, terminated.

"You must lie down," she told Polly.

"B-but we'll be moving in an hour – I'll lose the baby if I go along!"

"You go lie down, and I'll see what we can do."

Mary wakened Lavina, and the two made a heavily padded bed in one of the wagons for Polly to lie upon. In addition, they decided that Polly was to do absolutely no work until she was feeling better.

Mary rode her horse behind Polly's wagon all that morning. First, she made a personal act of contrition, then surreptitiously fingered her rosary beads as she spent the hours in prayer for Polly's recovery. Lavina had ruled against fasting while riding horses – it seemed a bad idea, but she and Mary had avoided red meat all week, saving that luxury until Sunday.

Shelby County appeared exceedingly flat compared to the hills near Aurora. Sluggish streams abounded, often widening into muddy sloughs. The land would have to be trenched and drained, Mary thought, if they hoped to use much of it for farms. At nightfall, they reached Shelbyville, where a brick courthouse occupied the town square. Passing through, they camped on the Northwest side of town.

Bram showed Mary a track of wooden rails on the ground, passing through the town from Southeast to Northwest, roughly parallel to the road they had been following.

"It's the railroad from Cincinnati to Indianapolis," he said. "If they ever get an actual locomotive, and passenger cars, we could ride here from Lawrenceburg."

Polly said that she felt much better that evening, but Lavina and Mary let her stand up only for necessary trips into the shrubbery to relieve herself.

On Holy Saturday, the families completed the trip across Shelby County and into Marion. Late in the day, they turned off the Michigan Road at New Bethel (later called Wanamaker), and headed West to the home of Richard's sister Alice and her husband, Joseph Wheatley.

Joseph was a veteran of the American Revolution, seventy-five years old at this point, but he seemed much younger. Alice, at sixty-one years, appeared as strong as when Mary had first met her, over sixteen years previously, at *Aaltje's* funeral. Their house was large and comfortable; no expense had been spared on the furnishings, all imported from the East.

The Wheatley's spinster daughter, Mary, lived with her parents at this time, and helped with the work. In addition, several hired men and girls ran the farm and house, respectively. Lavina quickly explained the concerns about Polly to the Wheatley women, and they made a pallet before the hearth in one of the bedrooms for her to lie on.

"Have you given her cramp bark?" Alice wanted to know.

Mary shook her head. Dried cramp bark, harvested from the twigs of a species of viburnum (often called highbush cranberry, among other names), was made into a tea and used to treat a variety of feminine ills including threatened miscarriage.

Alice quickly provided cramp bark tea for Polly to drink, as well as chicken soup, jam and bread for her to eat. Before long, Polly was feeling better than she had for several days.

Surprise visitors at supper were John Van Clift, Richard's step-nephew, with wife Catherine (Norris), Richard's niece. They lived about six miles South of the Wheatleys, and were also interested in moving Northwest. Mary listened to the men's discussion of land acquisition; Lavina apparently thought she knew as much as the men did, and joined in.

Selling the properties the Van Clifts and Wheatleys had already "improved" by clearing and tilling would yield higher prices than they had paid, enabling them to buy larger farms with more potential to increase in value. All of them wanted property close to the Michigan Road North of Indianapolis. Richard mentioned that his brother Joseph, Catherine's father, anticipated a move very soon. Even old Joseph Wheatley sounded determined to head Northwest, to Boone County, and Alice seemed slightly startled by this.

Mary, although ensconced in one of Alice's fine feather beds with Bram, slept poorly that night. Land fever was a terrible disease, she thought. Why couldn't these people be content with what they already had? None of them was hungry or impoverished.

Her thoughts drifted back to Aurora, where she had been so happy. She silently mourned her inability to confess to a priest and to attend Mass; this would be the first week she had missed for several years. And at Easter!

Next morning, the Wheatleys and their guests breakfasted at dawn. The plan was for everyone to attend Methodist services at the Wesley Chapel on the Circle at Meridian Street in Indianapolis. Mary immediately offered to stay at the Wheatley house with the smallest children and Polly. Lavina indicated that she would remain behind as well.

Alice Wheatley frowned. She had intended for the *entire* group to attend church, and for the servants to care for the children and Polly; exceptions bothered her. But her brother, Richard, convinced her that this plan was for the best. Mary could tell that she and Lavina had been removed from Alice's favored persons list; they apparently lacked the spirituality required of Norris family members. After some thought, Mary decided that she did not care. Lavina was the very best friend she had ever known, and she had never been impressed by Norris family values.

The churchgoers (six Norrises and three Wheatleys) left soon after, scrubbed, dressed in their best and mounted on their fastest horses. Luckily, the weather was good – they would be able to cover the ten miles into town in about two hours.

Mary, Altha, Elizabeth, and Lavina made personal acts of contrition, and spent the morning in prayer. After the past week's struggle, this rest seemed a wonderful blessing. Easter dinner was served at mid-afternoon, the churchgoers chattering incessantly about people they had met in town. Lavina and Mary indulged in large portions of red meat and grinned smugly at each other.

Next morning, the group ate another huge breakfast (food at the Wheatleys was amazingly abundant), hitched the oxen to their wagons, and headed Northwest for Indianapolis. Polly was feeling better after the rest and herbal treatments at the Wheatleys' house, but Mary and Lavina insisted that she ride lying down in a wagon, nevertheless. Throughout the morning, Lavina seemed increasingly agitated, but said nothing to Mary about it.

The site for Indianapolis, about fourteen miles Southeast of the state's geographic center, had been chosen largely because of the White River. The waterway was expected to carry passenger and freight traffic to and from the capital. Unfortunately, the river proved too sandy and shallow; even the attempted addition of canals never fulfilled the expectation.

The federal land office had originally set aside four square miles for the capital of Indiana, but its chief surveyor, Elias Pym Fordham, had plotted only one square mile, bounded by the appropriately named North, South, East, and West streets. No one thought there would ever be a need for more lots within city limits. But during 1836, largely due to the promise of improved transportation routes, the city expanded beyond its original boundaries.

Alexander Ralston, a former assistant to Pierre Charles L'Enfant, had been hired to design Indianapolis. Since he was so familiar with the layout of Washington, D.C., he had saved himself additional work by adapting that design.

Starting with a three acre central circle surrounded by an eighty foot wide street, he set broad streets that branched out diagonally to the Northwest, Southeast, Northeast and Southwest. These were named Indiana, Virginia, Massachusetts, and Kentucky Avenues, respectively. Meridian Street bisected the city from North to South; Market Street from East to West.

The National Road had come through town in 1831, following Washington Street all the way across, from East to West, one block South of the city's center. The Michigan Road approached from the Southeast and departed to the Northwest.

As the families entered the Southern edge of Indianapolis, Mary heard Lavina raise her voice to Richard in a tone Mary had never heard before.

"Don't try to stop me – I'm going!"

Lavina kicked her horse, and set off at a fast canter. The woman intended to visit her former husband's grave, in Greenlawn Cemetery, on the Southwest corner of the city, and Richard had forbidden her to leave the group. Richard quickly signaled to the others that he would catch up later, and followed his wife. They all stared after him, astounded by her outburst and his reaction.

Governor's Circle, at the center of Indianapolis, was first used as a market for more than six years. In 1827, an impressive Governor's Mansion had replaced the market.

Mary was surprised to hear that Governor Noble lived elsewhere, using the mansion only for public functions and for offices – the man apparently cherished his privacy. She saw the church the others had attended on the previous day, but did not ask to look inside.

The state government had moved to Indianapolis from Corydon, first convening in the Marion County Courthouse in January of 1825. In 1831, the Indiana General Assembly approved construction of a new statehouse. In response to a design contest, the architectural firm of Ithiel Town and Alexander Jackson Davis created a plan for a structure inspired by the Greek Parthenon, with a central dome. It had been finished in 1835.

Mary stared at the statehouse. It was built of blue limestone, wood, and brick, two stories high. Landscaping and walkways were not yet complete;

piles of brick and flagstone for that purpose stood in random places. Bram told her that rooms for the governor and the Supreme Court occupied the lower floor, and that the Legislature and Senate occupied the upper floor, each house with its own wing.

On their way out of town, the families approached the proposed Central Canal that would run through the Western downtown area. Planks had been laid across the ditch as a makeshift bridge – the canal had yet to be filled with water and in fact would never be used to ship goods because the project rapidly went bankrupt.

Luckily, the Michigan Road was well maintained North of Indianapolis, and the families continued travel past dark, by torch light. Exhausted, they finally reached the turnoff to Richard's Marion County property, about nine miles North of the city center, just South of Augusta, a tiny village.

For some reason, Mary had missed the fact that Lavina's mother, Mary Ball, and brother in law Elijah Harding, along with several of Lavina's other family members lived a quarter of a mile East of the Michigan Road, between that road and Richard's property. Richard and Lavina had already arrived at her mother's, their horses able to travel faster than the ox wagons.

A supper awaited the group, but it lacked the quality and quantity served at the Wheatleys'. Mary had to shush the children, who kept asking for more bread – it was all gone. She took them out to the wagons, where she distributed dried apples while instructing them to say nothing more about being hungry. To her credit, they listened.

Mary felt very tired. It had been a long day, and she had been in charge of all the children for most of it. For that reason, she thought later, she *might* have been less than tactful at supper when speaking to Lavina's mother and sister. Lavina found it necessary to hunt Mary down at the wagon, setting her straight.

"How could you say that?" demanded Lavina angrily.

"W-what do you mean?" Mary asked.

"Your comment to my sisters about Richard 'finding love at Indianapolis.' You made me sound like a whore."

"I assure you, I had no intention…"

"*I* have no intention of tolerating that kind of insult. Not even from you."

Mary fled, in tears. What had she said? Certainly it was nothing that anyone would find offensive. Except Lavina. Lavina was her only friend in all the world, she thought. And now she might lose her because of one careless remark.

Mary declined to join the family for the remainder of the evening, saying she was not feeling well, and spent time lying down in her wagon. Bram checked on her several times, but she did not confide in him, and lay there awake, crying off and on, all night. Near dawn, it occurred to her that the *reason* Lavina was so upset by the remark was that Lavina had given in to Richard's sexual overtures before the wedding had taken place. This was something Lavina did not want her mother and sisters to know or to guess. But still, Lavina's attack had hurt, more than Mary would have thought possible.

Next morning, Tuesday, Lavina behaved toward Mary as if nothing had happened between them, but Mary remained wounded by her mother-in-law's outburst. The families, after the frugal breakfast provided by the Ball family, returned to the Michigan Road, then rode through Augusta. Polly continued to ride lying down in her family's wagon.

The group completed their sojourn in Marion County that morning, managing two and one-half more miles to the county line. The wagons, with women and children, continued across the corner of Hamilton County for a mile and three quarters, while the men detoured, quickly checking on another property of Richard's. He had bought an eighty acre plot of land, about two miles to the East, across the road from a forty acre farm owned by Lavina's mother.

With some difficulty, Mary avoided speaking to Lavina during the morning, but the woman seemed not to notice how deeply she had hurt Mary's feelings. After several hours of riding, Mary allowed the antics of the children to distract her from Lavina's strangeness.

Once inside Boone County, the group stopped, all of them hungry. They had reached a point adjacent to the Michigan Road where Richard owned one hundred twenty acres. (This property was Southeast of the future Zionsville.) The men built a fire, and Mary and Lavina cooked cornmeal mush, ham, and some eggs purchased from a farm they had passed. Mary still felt uneasy about saying anything to Lavina. But Polly, who had done so well at the Wheatley's and at the Ball's was bleeding again, feeling quite ill. All the cramp bark given by Alice Wheatley had been used, and the women could think of nothing else to do for her.

After the mid-day stop, they traveled scarcely a mile before approaching Eagle Village. Gazing at the log buildings ahead, Mary spotted a symbol she recognized – a physician's caduceus (a winged staff entwined by two snakes). Mary kicked her horse to catch up with Hendricks, who at this point drove the wagon where Polly lay, and nodded toward the sign.

"Polly needs to see the doctor," she told him, "if you really want this baby."

Hendricks read the name on the sign: "H. G. Larimore, M.D." He turned his horses, tied them to the rail before the doctor's house, and ran to the door. "Go on!" he yelled to the other men, "We'll catch up later."

Mary bid Polly a tearful goodby, wishing her the best.

Hurrying along the Michigan Road, Mary and the others passed a brick house – the first they had seen since Indianapolis – owned by Austin Davenport. They forded Little Eagle Creek and entered Clarkstown (later called Hamilton), a thriving settlement. Various shops and a tavern lined the Michigan Road, and once again the women were able to purchase wheat bread. Just beyond Clarkstown, they stopped for the night.

As Bram sat on a log, eating his ham, boiled greens, roasted potato and bread, Mary approached him.

"I know that you have built a log house for us near Frankfort, but we *will* have a real house eventually, won't we?"

Bram grinned at her.

"Yep. There'll be a farmhouse built to your specifications Ma'am, within a few years. We just need to get the right location..."

Mary was less concerned with location than appearance.

"Well, I saw my house today. Do you want to hear about it?"

"Why not? I don't seem to be terribly busy at the moment..."

"It was back there, along the road...it had been built recently, in a style I never saw before, except it reminded me a little of my *grand-mère's* house in Denton. It was rectangular, two storys, with four tall windows and a door at the center across the front on each level. It seemed to be two rooms deep, and had a front porch with support columns, and a veranda on top of the porch roof. But the unique part was the front roof line...it had a triangular peak in the middle."

"I think I saw it," said Bram. "You must draw a picture, so that we both remember what it looked like, when the time comes."

Mary lost no time, but found a piece of charcoal and an exposed board inside their covered wagon. In the rapidly waning light, she sketched the front of the house, the porch with veranda, and the roof line, indicating the windows where she wanted them. This would be *her* house, and she was certain that the pirate's money she had inherited from Grandfather Gold would more than pay for it, especially after the sale of her house at Aurora.

By mid-morning on Wednesday, it occurred to Mary that they had entered a more civilized county than the one South of Indianapolis; they crossed Findly Creek before passing through Northfield, where there was another tavern, then forded Big Eagle Creek. Both fords were excellently maintained. But in the afternoon, one of the wagons broke down; it was necessary to stop at Slabtown (later called Waugh) while a wheel was repaired. A cold rain contributed to the general discomfort.

Hendricks and Polly rejoined the group as they all waited. Polly would be able to complete the trip; her baby was expected in November. By late Thursday, camped by the road, Mary felt as if she had spent her entire life in Boone County, and she wanted *out*.

"Tomorrow," Bram told Mary, sensing her agitation, "you'll be in your new home!" He hugged her gently and kissed her cheek. "I know this hasn't been easy for you, but you're strong. A real pioneer."

It had never been Mary's goal to be a pioneer; she wasn't sure how pleased she was to be labeled as one. The only positive aspect she had seen in this relocation was that she could keep Lavina's friendship; now she wasn't sure of that, either.

Friday crept by in agonizing anticipation. The surrounding landscape had become very flat. Mile after mile, the dark cover of thick woods alternated with open sky above innumerable swamps. As they passed a carved wood post, Richard told the group they had entered Clinton County. Soon after, Bram edged his horse next to Mary's, and nodded ahead.

"Look," he said with quiet satisfaction. "The Twelve-Mile Prairie!"

Slowly, the woods dropped away behind them, and the families entered a world of wide open grasslands.

At Kirk's Crossroads (later called Kirklin), they left the Michigan Road, angling to the Northwest toward what the men assured them was Frankfort, and beyond that, Lafayette. Not long after, the light faded, and the men lit torches so that the families could continue toward their new homes.

As if in a dream, Mary turned her horse away from the other families to follow Bram and their own wagon a short distance North of the main road as the other family members waved farewell. They drove behind a log house, leaving the wagon near the back door before taking the animals to the barn.

While Mary held a torch aloft, Bram and Raper unhitched the oxen, unsaddled the horses, shutting them and the cow in the barn with rations of hay and corn. After collecting the sleepy children from the wagon, the family approached the house together.

Mary wept in relief. No one had died on this journey, but it had been an emotional drain that would take some recovery time. She let Bram show her and the children the house. A glorified cabin, it featured one room with a flagstone and clay hearth occupying most of one wall. A rude table of planks had been set up, with upended logs positioned around the sides.

Recalling her days with the Silas Davis family, Mary could not help making comparisons. Bram had troubled to install real glass windows, but the bed was a rough wooden frame with corn-shuck mattress. A loft overhead would contain the four older children (Raper, Altha, Elizabeth, and Burr) at night; little Dailey would sleep on a pallet near his parents. The "kitchen" consisted of rough plank counters extending from the back wall, supported by angled wood braces with storage bins underneath; open plank shelves lined the walls above. A wooden trough on legs with a drainage bucket underneath served as a sink for washing. A well had been dug the previous fall, but had not yet been used this spring; it would require some pumping before clear water could be obtained.

In the morning, Bram and Raper started a fire in the hearth (using wood left from the cabin's construction, piled behind the house), and, after some effort with the well and the cow, fetched water and milk before staking the cow, horses, and oxen out to graze. While Altha kept an eye on Burr and Daily, Mary and Elizabeth found cooking pots, cloths, utensils and tableware in the wagon, bringing it all inside and setting up the new kitchen as they worked.

During and after breakfast, Bram discussed plans for spring planting with Raper, much as if the twelve year old were a grown man. Mary saw the boy maturing before her eyes as he ventured to give opinions on which chores to tackle first. She held back tears of pride as father and son left the house to look at the fields where corn would soon be planted, and a pen where young hogs would soon be installed to grow for the Norrises' winter food. Even though Bram had already hired several young men to work the farm, from this moment Raper would be at his father's side, learning the job every day.

On Sunday morning, Bram and Raper rode to church with the Methodists at Wabash and Main Streets in Frankfort; Mary and the other children remained at home. It was difficult to concentrate on prayer; so many ideas for the new household kept popping into Mary's mind. Finally, she gave up and began preparing dinner – ham again, with potatoes, greens, and corn bread. She even made a desert from dried apples with oats crumbled over the top.

Mary had brought seeds for a kitchen garden, and, after Bram had plowed a plot in the back yard, she put in lettuces, radishes, spinach, carrots, and beets. As the weather warmed, she added other vegetables as well, and soon set Altha and Elizabeth the chore of keeping the weeds at bay.

Mary did not see Lavina for two weeks. Even though their two cabins were only a mile apart, the women were overwhelmed by setting up new households without the servants they had depended upon at Aurora. When Mary stopped at Lavina and Richard's home, on her way to Frankfort with Bram, Lavina let Mary know that her own ways of doing things were by far the best, and that Mary would never be able to compete. When she did visit Bram and Mary's cabin for the first time, her comments were less than complimentary.

"This place needs a lot of work!" she said.

By this point, Mary was ready to write Lavina off as a friend.

At Frankfort, Mary was not surprised to find the usual feature of new county seats: A central courthouse, a one-and-a-half story temporary structure made of hewn logs. The county board had paid contractors Allen & Michael the sum of $20 to build it. The courthouse was surrounded by dirt streets and businesses, residences, and churches made of logs and stone. The Methodist church, built over three years previously at Wabash and Main streets, had become the head of the local Methodist circuit served by the Reverend Eli Rogers. The personnel serving Methodist circuits changed frequently, due in part to short life expectancies of the period. The circuits themselves fluctuated due to the rapid expansion of pioneer populations. In subsequent years, therefore, Mary was scarcely able to keep pace with the identity of the current minister–especially since she rarely heard any of them preach.

On June 15th of this year, Arkansas entered the Union as its 25th state.

Spring continued into summer, and Mary's pregnancy advanced. She was working harder, for more hours every day, than she had for many years. Even though she tried to pace herself, resting frequently, she remained exhausted. Without consulting her, Bram asked Lavina for help.

Lavina arrived on a Sunday afternoon near the end of July.

"Hell-o, my dear!" she sang as she breezed in. "Ooh, but you *do* look tired. Polly and I decided to help out, since your confinement's so near. She'll be here tomorrow, so you *must* take it easy!"

Mary opened her mouth to say that she did not *need* any help, then closed it again. Perhaps this was for the best.

"And guess what!" Lavina chattered on. "I'm expecting again!"

"Oh, then you shouldn't be coming over to help me..."

"Don't be silly. Richard hired one of the neighbor girls to help me out, and I'm bored to tears. Anyway, I'm not due until December, and still have lots of energy."

Lavina and Polly (who had recovered from her early pregnancy complications) faithfully assisted Mary up to, during, and after the birth of Mary's baby on July 11th. Before allowing Bram into the room, Lavina asked Polly to fetch more water from the kitchen. While Polly was gone, Lavina and Mary hastily baptized the new little one.

Bram, who had always deferred to Mary's wishes when naming the baby girls, asked, "What will you call her?"

"Lavina. Lavina Jane," whispered Mary. Somewhere, in the depths of her being, Mary would always worship the beautiful, confident (if not always considerate) Lavina.

In August, the Potawatomie Indians signed the Treaty of Yellow River. In exchange for their Indiana lands, the tribe was offered $1 per acre and each tribe member was granted a 320 acre parcel of land in Kansas. The tribe agreed to vacate their Indiana lands within two years.

The presidential Election of 1836 was hotly contested. The incumbent Vice President, Martin Van Buren, riding the coattails of President Andrew Jackson, topped the Democratic ticket. During the 1834 midterm elections, the Whig party (having absorbed the National Republican Party and the Anti-Masonic Party) emerged as the chief opposition to the Democratic Party.

Unable to identify a single candidate who could please all their constituents, the Whig Party ran several presidential candidates in different regions of the country, hoping that each would be popular enough to defeat Van Buren in their respective areas. The House of Representatives could then decide between the competing Whig candidates.

The Whigs started by presenting four presidential and vice-presidential tickets: William Henry Harrison (hero of the Battle of Tippecanoe) and Francis Granger in the North and the border states, and Hugh L. White and John Tyler in the middle and lower South. In Massachusetts, the ticket consisted of Daniel Webster and Francis Granger, but in South Carolina, it consisted of Willie P. Mangum and John Tyler.

By the middle of this year, Harrison ranked as the Whig nominee in all free states except Massachusetts, where Daniel Webster remained the choice. White was the favorite in the South.

Election Day during this period often involved over-the-top exuberant behavior: As an example, on this year's date, November 7th, the directors of the branch bank as well as members of the local temperance society at Fort Wayne, Indiana were carried home drunk. Martin Van Buren carried Clinton County by ninety-six votes, much to the Norris men's disgust. For the entire State of Indiana, the election resulted in a landslide for William Henry Harrison.

Nation wide, the Whig strategy failed. Harrison was the most effective of his opponents, but Van Buren's superior Democratic party organization carried the day, earning him a majority. Van Buren defeated Harrison by a 51% - 49% vote in the North, and he defeated White by a similar 51% - 49% margin in the South.

A few days before Advent, Lavina and Mary assisted Polly as she delivered her first daughter, Altha J. Norris. Mary fantasized that *Aaltje* smiled from heaven.

In late December, Lavina, attended by Mary and Polly, delivered baby James Luther. On Mary's way home, a sudden freezing wind blew in from the West. There had been melting snow on the ground previously, and this wind instantly solidified the slush, as well as the nearby creek. Mary was alarmed by this, and grateful to reach home safely.

1837

Michigan entered the Union as the 26th state on January 26th. In March, Dekalb and Lake Counties were formed by the Indiana Legislature, as well as Kirklin Township within Clinton County. Clinton County contracted with John Elder to construct its first brick courthouse at Frankfort; The structure cost $12,000 and was used for forty-five years.

Martin Van Buren was inaugurated on March 4th.

Inventions during this year included the John Deere plow for prairie sod; Colonel Samuel T.B. Morse gave the first demonstration of the telegraph.

Lavina and Mary met regularly to pray. When Lavina heard that a new Irish Catholic parish, named St. John the Evangelist, had formed at Indianapolis, she secured an ecclesiastical calendar from the priest there. This ensured that the women stayed on schedule for the holy days. The Lenten season began early, with Ash Wednesday on February 8th, and ended March 26th, Easter. The Norris women baptized and prayed over their infants, but longed for a real priest who could christen them properly.

The Panic of 1837 began in May. Caused by nation-wide inflation plus speculation, this first Great Depression in the United States was followed by disruptions in financial markets for about five years. It diverted national attention from many other issues.

Mary and Lavina heard the latest gossip from their former home. In late summer, the Presbyterian Church at Lawrenceburg, Indiana had received a new minister, Henry Ward Beecher (brother of Harriet Beecher Stowe).

Henry's new wife, Eunice, had invited a group of ladies from the church over for tea. Their primary purpose in visiting had been to find fault with her housekeeping skills. When they feigned amazement that Eunice would cover the tea table with a cloth, she assured them that her husband received ALL his meals at this table with a linen cover and napkins. That was all these ladies needed. Word spread all over town about Eunice' elitist attitudes, exemplified by her extravagant use of textiles. Thus, Eunice had supposedly proven herself unsuitable for life on the frontier. Mary and Lavina giggled. They *knew* better, and had used tablecloths regularly at Aurora. Someone was out to make Eunice feel uncomfortable in her new position as their minister's wife.

Before long, Beecher received his first national publicity, becoming involved in the break between "New School" and "Old School" Presbyterianism. At issue were the topics of original sin and slavery. Henry was an active colonizationalist, which means that he favored sending black people "back to Africa," regardless of their individual places of birth or upbringing. When Beecher refused to swear an oath of allegiance to Old School views, his official confirmation as minister in Lawrenceburg was blocked. His church rallied behind him, declaring its independence from the Synod in order to retain him as its pastor. The resulting controversy split the Western Presbyterian Church into rival synods. This would not be Beecher's last exposure to the national spotlight.

By October, sickness ran rampant through Frankfort; few escaped. Mary struggled to isolate baby Lavina from people who might infect her with the illnesses that plagued nearly everyone. This served as a convenient excuse for avoiding the Methodist church services. But when the other children in the family came down with fevers, it became impossible to protect little Lavina completely. Luckily, her children all recovered, and built resistance to the frontier illnesses as they grew.

Mary was more or less forced to entertain the new Methodist circuit rider, Thomas J. Brown, when he dropped by the cabin at supper time one evening during the summer. He made a special point of inviting her to services held in Frankfort. She was deeply embarrassed by the lack of the fine furnishings that she had used in Aurora. But the food was good, and she managed to give him the impression that she might possibly be Methodist.

In return, he made gestures and innuendos that indicated he would like to know Mary MUCH better, on a personal level. Having been in this situation before served Mary well, and she hoped she had discouraged him adequately.

"*I'm not a sweet young thing any longer,*" she thought. "*Why don't these men look elsewhere?*"

The gubernatorial race in Indiana was one-sided this year. The Whigs had thoroughly trounced the Democrats in the elections of 1835, and the Whig candidate, David Wallace, ran unopposed.

At one time, Governor Wallace had been an attractive man, with a well-proportioned body, black hair, dark eyes and a ruddy complexion. He was cultured and an accomplished orator. But in recent years he had become obese, and apparently had lost many of his other outstanding characteristics.

Having served as Lieutenant Governor under Noah Noble, Wallace had been deeply involved in the financial fiasco associated with Indiana's internal improvement initiatives. On December 6th, he opened the legislative session with a fanciful and meandering account of how Indiana could augment state capital in the bank.

The two Norris women prepared for Advent Season, which began on Sunday, December 3rd. Together they prayed, reflecting that neither one had ever worked so hard, with so little reward, as they had during this past year.

1838

Madison Township within Clinton County was formed as the county became more populous.

The history of the railroad in Indiana began in earnest this year, when the first steam train traveled from North Madison (near the Ohio River) to Graham's Ford, carrying Governor Wallace, legislators, and other dignitaries on an 8 miles-per-hour, 15-mile inspection trip.

The Lenten season began early, with Ash Wednesday on February 28th. Lavina and Mary had difficulty finding anything to give up, and finally decided to avoid the maple syrup that was being boiled down from that season's fresh sap. Two of Mary's children, Altha and Elizabeth, followed her example, but Raper, at 13 years, had decided that Methodism was a much less troublesome and much more entertaining form of worship, and accompanied his father to the services and camp meetings. Burr, Dailey, and Lavina Jane were, of course, too young to observe Lent.

Illness raced through Clinton County in the late winter and early spring, affecting every family. By late March, the Methodist Sabbath School in Frankfort closed because both teachers and many students had fallen ill.

Lavina and Mary had planned elaborate family meals for Palm Sunday on April 8th, and were going to spend the Saturday before together, baking enough pies to feed an army, or at least both their families. But early on Saturday, Lavina sent her seven year old step-daughter, Lucretia to Mary with a message: Papa is ill. Mama Lavina must stay home to care for him. And sister Mary Catherine (Lavina's first baby, then age 3) was also very sick.

Disappointed, Mary set to work with her daughters Altha and Elizabeth.

Together they turned out ten pies filled with various dried fruits and nuts from their larder, along with two cream pies, the cream obtained from their newly freshened cow. At mid-afternoon, Mary packed half the cooled desserts, loaded them into her light buggy (a Christmas gift from Bram), and drove the mile West to Richard and Lavina's place.

As had become common during this time of illness, she stacked the pies on the front porch, rapped loudly at the front door, and retreated to her buggy. When two of the children appeared at the entrance, she waved and drove quickly away.

Mary cooked a big breakfast on Sunday morning, saw Bram and Raper off to church, set a stuffed chicken in the oven to roast, then spent the remainder of the morning in prayer with her children gathered around. Altha, Elizabeth, and Burr knew the prayers by heart, and she had made rosaries for them out of acorns strung onto leather thongs, with hand-carved wooden crosses attached.

(The crosses had been given to Mary by Father Ferneding on her last Sunday at Lawrenceburg. She still found his misty-eyed farewell kiss disturbing to contemplate.)

Dailey and little Lavina Jane played quietly, only interrupting the others occasionally. Mary counted herself blessed indeed to have this time with them.

Two days later, on Tuesday, Bram arrived at noon with Raper, both of them looking quite upset.

"What's wrong, Papa?" asked Elizabeth.

He took the girl's hand, and sadly replied, "Your grandpa Norris is dead, gone to Heaven."

Mary turned, gasping in dismay. Her mind churned as she thought of things to say, then rejected most of them as too close to truth. Richard was *not* Elizabeth's grandfather, but her father; he certainly would not be admitted to Heaven if Mary were in charge of such things.

Finally, she moved close to Bram's side, murmuring, "I'm so sorry, sweetheart." She thought for another moment. "I should go over there…"

"No." Bram's voice was harsh. "We'll stay away. Whatever pestilence is attacking them must not come here."

"But…" Mary began to protest, wanting to say that no one knew where the illness came from – it was everywhere! But Bram cut her off.

"We do not know what caused this fever, but the more isolated families seem to stay healthier. We must not risk our little ones, nor ourselves." He fought back tears.

Mary thought back to the time she had spent with Bram and his mother, *Aaltje*, and how he had always protected the younger children. She thought of Lavina, surrounded by Richard's corpse and Richard's children, several of them ill.

"But they're *family*, Bram! They need our help."

He sighed. "Perhaps you're right. I must retrieve my father's papers, at any rate, to begin the probate process. Do you suppose the children can manage without us until supper time?"

Altha, Elizabeth, and Burr nodded solemnly, while Raper said, "I'll get your horse, Mama."

Mary found her shawl and straw bonnet, then joined Bram on the short ride to Lavina's house.

Living there at this time were Lavina, with Richard's sons by Catherine (Will, 27 and George, 15 years), his children by Clarinda (Lucretia, 7 and Thomas, 5 years), and Lavina's young children Mary and James Luther.

Once in the door, Mary was nearly overwhelmed by the odor of illness and death. She noted Lavina, bent over little Mary Catherine, vainly trying to get the child to swallow milk and/or water. Baby Luther sat alone in a corner, toys clenched in each fist, his arms rising and falling as he entertained himself. His diaper was in serious need of a change.

Bram said, "I'll do it," and lifted the child to the bench used to dress and clean the children.

Mary continued toward the bed in the corner where Richard lay. He was a mess. No one had ventured to wash or dress him; his stained and smelly night shift concealed all but the outline of his disease-ravaged form. But the expression on his face revealed the horror of a soul totally unprepared for death, shocked by the very notion that his life had ended.

"*Good*," thought Mary. "*He got what he deserved.*"

Cornering Will and George, she rapped out her orders: "Get some planks. Rip them off the barn if you must, but nail them together and make a box for your father. Then park him in the barn, because Bram says he's going to Aurora for burial."

She got water, soap, and a cloth, then stripped and washed Richard's wasted remains. When she was through, Bram helped her wrestle the body into a shirt, pants, and jacket suitable for Sunday church services. As soon as the box was ready, Richard's sons lifted him into it. Mary then retreated while the family members gathered beside the corpse for prayer. Oddly, none of the prayers for the dead came into Mary's heart and head as they had at the death of *Aaltje*; it was difficult to avoid thinking of the multiple sins of the flesh this body had committed.

Next morning, Bram and Richard's son Will rode to Frankfort to report Richard's death and to file a petition at the courthouse for legal distribution of Richard's estate. The legal proceedings would take a long time to be processed; the court would not begin to consider the petition until November.

At mid-afternoon, Reverend Brown conducted a Methodist funeral service for the Norris family at the church in Frankfort. On Thursday morning, Bram with his brothers Joseph and Hendricks, as well as his half-brothers Will and George Norris loaded their father's coffin onto a wagon and headed toward Aurora, where Richard was to be buried beside his previous wives *Aaltje*, Catherine, Margaret, and Clarinda.

During a rather intense conversation with Bram, Lavina had let it be known that she would *not* be traveling to Aurora for the burial, and that she herself must *never* be buried there with Richard and his "other women." Mary could see that Bram was wounded by this not-so-subtle denigration of his mother and other three step-mothers, but he let the moment pass without making an issue of it. Bram had told Mary that Lavina was well provided for in Richard's will, which made this display from Lavina seem particularly nasty.

Mary spent part of every day that week at Lavina's house, cooking, cleaning, and helping with the younger children so that Lavina could sleep. Despite their love and care, little Mary Catherine died on Easter Sunday morning as her mother prayed over her still form.

When Mary arrived at Lavina's, the two women chanted prayers for the dead as they washed and dressed the child for burial. Mary's son Raper and one of Richard's hired men made a small coffin and buried Mary Catherine in the orchard without benefit of clergy. Someday, Mary promised herself, she would have a priest bless the child's resting place. Later, she was able to have the remains moved to Old South Cemetery, where many of the other Norrises were buried.

Early planting season had come and gone, and the families enjoyed locally produced rhubarb, asparagus, lettuce, and chives. Limited quantities of new potatoes were available, Mary's hens had begun laying a plentiful supply of eggs, and the cow produced both a bull calf and plenty of milk.

By mid-May, Mary was sure that she was with child once again, and she took extra care to eat well and rest more often in order to grow a strong baby. On his return from Aurora, Bram had brought a destitute young woman, Agnes, who begged to be allowed to cook and clean for the Norrises in exchange for food and shelter. With his characteristic generosity, Bram offered to pay her in addition to providing what she asked. With this help, Mary felt more certain of getting through the long hot summer.

The legal division of Richard's estate began in November and would bring many changes. Lavina got the house farm of 400 acres, plus several other plots. Richard's children Bram, Neil, Joseph, Richard H., William L, George C., Lucretia, Thomas C., and James L. all inherited property as well. But the actual legal process would continue, and not be complete until February of the following year.

Because he had inherited multiple parcels of land from his father, Bram's income from rents and produce would increase significantly.

The Native American families of Indiana were experiencing relocation in a radically different way than the Norris families. Government plans for Indian removal had been in place for years; the pressure from impatient pioneers determined to settle Northern and central Indiana forced government action. This chapter in Pottawatomi history, from September 4 to November 4, 1838, has been titled the Trail of Death.

In 1832, the official deadline for the tribe to leave the state had been set for August 5, 1838. By then nearly the entire Pottawatomi Nation had migrated peacefully to Kansas. The exception was the Twin Lakes village of Chief Menominee, near present day Plymouth, Indiana. After the deadline passed and this last group refused to leave, Governor David Wallace ordered them, along with other stragglers found within state borders, to be removed forcibly. Their destination was present-day Osawatomie, Kansas, a distance of 660 miles away.

General John Tipton mobilized the state militia in support of **United States** Colonel A.C. Pepper. On August 30, one hundred soldiers surrounded Twin Lakes to round up the inhabitants. Finding that the tribe's priest, Father Benjamin Marie Petit, was away at South Bend, Indiana, the tribe's chapel was closed. Then their crops and homes were burned to discourage them from returning home in the future. Chief Menominee, Chief Black Wolf, and Chief Pepinawa were placed in a jail wagon.

A few days later, Father Petit returned and immediately began serving the needs of the sick and hearing confessions. On September 4th, the journey began. The number removed totaled about 859 Native Americans; their priest accompanied them and kept a journal of the experience.

In a letter to Bishop Brute dated November 13, 1838, Father Petit described the scene:

"The order of march was as follows: the United States flag, carried by a dragoon; (mounted soldier) then one of the principal officers, next the staff baggage carts, then the carriage, which during the whole trip was kept for the use of the Indian chiefs, then one or two chiefs on horseback led a line of 250 to 300 horses ridden by men, women, children in single file, after the manner of savages. On the flanks of the line at equal distance from each other were the dragoons and volunteers, hastening the stragglers, often with severe gestures and bitter words. After this cavalry came a file of forty baggage wagons filled with luggage and Indians. The sick were lying in them, rudely jolted, under a canvas which, far from protecting them from the dust and heat, only deprived them of air, for they were as if buried under this burning canopy - several died."

In the first day they traveled twenty-one miles and camped near Rochester, Indiana. Ironically, the route used to remove the Pottawatomi had become a road only because the Pottawatomi Nation had granted permission for Indiana to build it through their lands – present day State Road 25.

On the second day they reached Fulton County, Indiana and by the third day they reached Logansport, Indiana. Several of the sick and elderly were left at Logansport to recover, and several of the dead were buried there.

On September 10th, the march resumed from Logansport and the caravan moved along the Wabash River. After eleven more days of travel the caravan reached Perrysville, Indiana where several more members of the tribe were buried.

At Perrysville, Father Petit wrote:

"On Sunday, September 16, I came in sight of my Christians marching in a line guarded on both sides by soldiers.... Almost all with babes, exhausted by heat, were dead or dying. I baptized several newly born little ones who went from the land of exile to heaven."

The caravan continued overland to Danville, Illinois where they resupplied and rested.

On September 20th, General Tipton and all but fifteen of the Hoosier militia returned to Indiana and left the tribe under the control of Judge William Polke, the Indian Agent in Illinois. Polke led the tribe for the remainder of the journey. From Sandusky Point, Illinois they passed through Decatur, Springfield, Jacksonville, and Naples. On October 10th the tribe left Illinois and crossed into Missouri.

Marching through Missouri, the tribe passed through Quincy, Palmyra, Clinton, Paris, Huntsville and finally Keatsville, where they rested for about a week. On November 1st, they resumed their march and on November 4th reached the end of their journey. On arrival there were less than 700 Pottawatomie left out of the 859 that started the journey. Not all of the missing 159 died, as many straggled or escaped.

Father Petit died in St. Louis on February 10, 1839, as a result of the rigors of the journey. Chief Menominee died three years later, never returning to Indiana. Many of the exiles attempted to return to Indiana.

A statue of Chief Menominee was erected in 1909 near Twin Lakes on South Peach Road, five miles West of **United States Route** 31. A boulder with a metal plaque marks the site of the log chapel and village. Kansas named a county after the tribe and a reservation for the descendants of the tribe was still in existence in 2012.

The Strawtown Road, running from Cincinnati, Ohio through the center of Frankfort, Indiana to Lafayette brought multitudes of settlers, eager to replace the ousted Indian population. Frankfort itself "abounded in wickedness," in the view of those inclined to say such things, because the Temperance cause had been neglected there. Venturing into the town filled with drunken strangers had become an adventure, indeed.

On December 1ˢᵗ, "The Prophet" Joseph Smith and other Mormons were imprisoned in Liberty Jail at Liberty, Missouri.

Lavina had brought Mary the dates for Advent: The first Sunday would be December 2ⁿᵈ, followed by the Feast of the Immaculate Conception on December 8ᵗʰ, and the second Sunday of Advent on December 9ᵗʰ.

Mary dutifully celebrated these, along with her youngest children, Elizabeth, Burr, and Dailey. (Raper and Altha had defected to the Methodists, to Mary's sorrow.)

But on Saturday December 15ᵗʰ, during preparation for a Gaudette Sunday feast next day, Mary felt the familiar sensation of incipient labor. She went to her bed, and Bram rode to Lavina's house to get help for his wife. Late that night, Mary was delivered of a son upon whom his father bestowed the name Abraham Hendrickson. The two women carried out the infant baptism while Bram went out to the necessary house.

The rest of the season passed Mary in a blur, as she let the serving woman and her other children take over the chores; she concentrated on her tiny infant.

In Rome during this year, Pope Gregory XVI took the remarkable step of condemning the slave trade, but held back from renouncing the notion of slavery. After all, the finances of many Catholics in many places depended on slavery for sustenance.

1839

Blackford County, Indiana was established during this year by the Indiana State Legislature.

The Wabash & Erie Canal had been scheduled for completion during 1839. However, the ditch dug in Ohio was not the same width and depth as that in Indiana. Neither ditch had been completed in either state, and the original route had changed. The success of canals connecting the Great Lakes to the Ohio river continued to be a volatile political and economic issue.

Toward the end of January, Mary received a visit that wrenched her from the cozy environment she was constructing for herself and her family. Richard Norris and Catherine's two sons, Will and George, stopped by, their brows furrowed in concern.

"Have you seen Lavina lately?" Georgie wanted to know.

"N-no," Mary replied. "Is something amiss?"

Since the birth of baby Abe in December, the weather had been cold and wet, and visits between her and Lavina had dropped off.

"There's definitely something wrong," said Will. "Some days, she barely gets out of bed. The children and the house are filthy; there's never anything to eat unless we cook it."

"We've had it," said George. "We're ready to move out, but we can't leave the little ones...they couldn't manage on their own."

Mary had heard enough. "Just hold out for a short time longer," she told them. "Bram, Van, and I will go over there and take some kind of action."

Mary didn't take the trip to Lavina's, but when Bram and Van returned from her farm, they brought their youngest step-siblings with them: Lucretia, 8 years, Thomas, 6, and James, 2, looked as forlorn as any children Mary had ever seen, and her heart melted. Van took these children to the farmhouse he had built, where his housekeeper added them to Van's own brood of four from his marriage to Mary Early: William, 14 years, Richard, 7, Rachel, 4, and Abraham, 5 months.

"What of Lavina?" she asked Bram.

"She'll be escorted to her family tomorrow," he replied, brusquely. "She's beyond our help, now."

Mary never saw Lavina again, and hardly ever heard anything about her, although she often thought about her and some of the things she had said. At various points during her life, Mary would imagine Lavina's reaction to this or that, and wish that she could have another close Catholic friend, perhaps one with a kinder way of expressing her views.

On February 13th, Lavina was discharged by the Clinton County Court as guardian for the minor heirs of Richard Norris, including her own son, James. Lavina apparently recovered somewhat, because she married again in April of 1840, to John Pointer. After the birth of a daughter and Pointer's death, she married Amos Gaugh, but they divorced a short time afterward.

Bram had been serving as legal guardian of Will and Georgie (Richard and Catherine's sons), along with their inherited properties, and was discharged from responsibility on the same date.

After the loss of Lavina, Mary was reduced to calculating the holy days on her own; extrapolating them from those celebrated by the Methodists. She consulted the circuit riders, Joseph White and George Stafford. By taking their dates for Easter, then Christmas, she was able to count backwards and celebrate the proper number of fasts and feasts. Mary was never absolutely sure of the accuracy of her calculations, but it was the best she could do.

Contagious illness continued to plague Frankfort. During the year, forty families in the Frankfort area suffered from disease, and twenty of its citizens died.

On a perfectly beautiful Sunday afternoon in April, Bram took Mary for a carriage ride. They traveled slowly, Northeast over rutted dirt roads for about three miles toward Boylestown.

"Here," said Bram, halting the horses and nodding toward a cleared area North of the roadway.

"What?" Mary wanted to know.

"This is the location for your new house. You know, the one you wanted to build with the triangle roofline."

Mary's eyes grew round with amazement. She thought that Bram had forgotten about her longing for a house like the one she had seen on the Michigan Road.

"When?" she asked.

"Soon! I have a construction crew assembled, and they will start work tomorrow. We should be able to move in before July. But you need to meet with the foreman to finalize the plans."

Mary turned away, wiping tears of joy from her eyes. Finally, she would have a real house instead of the makeshift cabin! For the next two months she was obsessed with plans for the family's new home. Even in her sleep, she seemed to think about all the possibilities, and often woke with new ideas to make the place even more lovely, at least in her view.

Bram, on the other hand, was occupied with plans for their new property, plans that included planting wheat in late summer, along with a kitchen garden near the house, as well as the acquisition of chickens, hogs, a bull and a few beef cows to begin production of a new herd. In addition, he planned an orchard for family use, containing apple, peach, and cherry trees, as well as a row of grape vines.

By early June, Mary's new house was nearly complete, but lacked flooring in some of the rooms. This prevented the family from moving in, since it posed a hazard to the children. Mary's impatience consumed her, and she tried distracting herself with hard work, despite her pregnancy.

Mary's house was completed toward the end of June. On moving day, she cried tears of joy several times.

Upon approach from the front, which faced the Boylestown Road on the South, it would have been difficult for a visitor to recall that the place was a *farmhouse*. A set of wide, smooth limestone steps led to the center of a covered wooden porch running the full width of the home. The first view beyond the carved, dark walnut door was of a foyer containing a bench, brass coat hooks, and a landing for the broad, curved staircase (also of walnut with carved walnut rails) winding up to the second story. To the left, access to the parlor had deliberately been left open to provide a view of the limestone fireplace with carved walnut mantel and surround. Walnut mouldings accented each window and door, and also encased the room with carved strips at floor and ceiling level.

Bram had found a group of craftsmen who covered every moulding with intricate designs involving cherubs, leaves, vines, feathers, shells, and little birds. Mary often thought that she could have spent days following the designs around the parlor, always finding some new, previously undisclosed creature lurking in the carved surfaces. Sofas upholstered in deep green velvet had been ordered from Indianapolis, as well as matching velvet drapes for the two long windows facing Boylestown Road. Lace curtain panels already hung there, ready to provide contrast when the covering drapes arrived. At the back of the parlor, a door led to Bram and Mary's bedroom where their furnishings from Aurora were set up. Mary had insisted on an exit from her bedroom to the kitchen, which also meant that there was easy egress to the necessary house in the back yard.

To the right of the front foyer, a sliding wooden panel opened to the dining room. The table could be expanded and set for twenty people by the addition of matching, polished walnut boards (called "leaves"), but most of the time Mary had it set up for ten. In this way the family could be served meals together and accommodate guests as well. (At the log cabin, meals had become an ordeal involving logistics and intricate timing just to keep everyone fed; often, it developed that some family members ate standing up.) A sideboard containing napkins, silver and protective table pads occupied one wall; a corner china cabinet contained the best serving bowls, platters, and plates (some of which had not been unpacked since the trip from Aurora). Two windows flanked by extra chairs faced the Boylestown Road; more chairs and a fireplace claimed the side wall; this hearth shared a chimney with the hearth in the small traveler's bedroom at the back of the house. At the rear of the dining room, an exit led to the kitchen and to the traveler's bedroom, which contained a bed, lamp, and desk, and doubled as Bram's office.

At the top of the stairs were two enormous rooms, one for boys and one for girls. The girls' bedroom could also be used for sewing and craft work, while the boys' accommodated storage of their various pieces of equipment and books.

The kitchen had originally been planned as a space between the Norris' bedroom and the traveler's bedroom, but it had been expanded toward the back yard to allow for laundry, bathing, food preparation and storage. It had its own fireplace, with the necessary iron hooks, cranes, and large pots for heating water as well as for cooking. Two ovens had been built into the hearth, one on each side, and they could be adjusted to different temperatures by regulating the amount and kind of burning wood below each one. Mary considered ordering a cookstove; she went so far as to reserve space for it as well as for a stove pipe to carry smoke out the back wall. There were two sets of sinks–one for washing food and dishes, the other for laundry. A hand pump above a well had been installed in the kitchen itself; there would be no trips into the yard to fetch water. The kitchen also had indoor steps leading to the limestone-lined cellar, where jars, crocks, sacks, barrels, and bins of food were kept.

As the house neared completion, Bram ordered the construction of a log school house ("The Norris School") on a corner of their property one mile to the East along the Boylestown Road. "The children will have no excuse for missing school," he declared.

The Indiana State Legislature had in 1821 established the following qualifications for teachers in public schools: Each must be "of good moral character, well versed in reading, writing, arithmetic, English grammar, geography and surveying." School was generally in session only during the months least essential to agricultural activity because so many of the students doubled as farm hands. Pay for teachers had been set at $15 per month; most young men found more lucrative employment in almost any other lawful business.

The general public remained overwhelmingly apathetic toward education, but the Norris family retained a deep commitment to it. Abraham Hendrickson, nephew of *Aaltje*, would serve as the teacher at the Norris School, and all of the Norris children would become literate.

Once the school building was up, it doubled as a meeting place for the Morris Chapel Methodist Society. Bram became the Society's first Steward and original trustee; David Maish was the first class leader. The name "Morris" is said to be an amalgamation of Maish and Norris. Original members included David, Sr. and Hannah Maish, Hendrickson and Mary Norris, Bram and Van Norris and Daniel Brittain who was in the process of moving his family to the area from New Jersey. The building was dedicated in late August by Reverend Joseph White, the Methodist circuit rider assigned to Frankfort.

Because the church meeting place was so close, it became very difficult for Mary to excuse herself from services. And when Bram purchased a small piano for the building, she could hardly stay away. Bram soon convinced her to play hymns for congregational singing, and she almost felt like a Methodist, albeit a sinful one, for a time.

Contemplating the winter Holy Days restored Mary's senses. It was *sin* for Catholics to attend Protestant services. When it was discovered that one of the other women could serve as pianist, Mary reluctantly gave up the position, but continued to visit the building when it was otherwise unoccupied in order to practice the tunes she remembered from childhood. Eventually, she persuaded Bram to have her piano brought from storage in Aurora to the parlor of her new house.

In December, Governor Wallace described Indiana's acute financial crisis to the State Legislature. His popularity with the general public never recovered.

1840

Benton County, Indiana, was formed by the State Legislature during this year.

Improved transportation routes and methods brought life to Indianapolis, swelled the population, and dropped profits into merchants' pockets.

The population of Clinton County had increased to 7,508 by this year.

During this decade, a campaign began to create an effective statewide system of education. Out of a state population of 266,700 persons over twenty years old, one in seven was illiterate. Out of the twenty-eight states in the Union, Indiana ranked eighteenth in literacy. Despite this effort, no real progress in education was made until after the Civil War.

More than seventy Indiana news "sheets" were being published by this time. These contained little local information, but presented political news, passionate editorials, commentary, speeches, and letters from readers. Most papers identified themselves either with the Democrats or with the Whigs. In Indianapolis, the INDIANA SENTINEL presented Democratic truth, while the INDIANA JOURNAL offered the Whig gospel. Each featured vitriolic and often personal attacks on opposing party leaders. Each party blamed the other for Indiana's fiscal woes.

The Democrats, the "party of the common man" promoted private construction of transportation projects, separation of the state from banking, low taxes, and strict economy in government. They emphasized the primacy of individual liberty and limited government. Their most consistent strength lay among voters in Southern Indiana (not with the Norris family!).

The Whigs were less fearful of active government, and supported greater government efforts to secure economic growth and development. They pushed internal improvements, public education, and favored the regulation of alcohol. They opposed the expansion of slavery, and found more support among Hoosiers of central and Northern Indiana, including the Norris family.

In October, the Indiana State Treasurer reported an embarrassing fiscal insolvency for the state, as well as a patchwork of uncompleted public works including the National Road and railroads. Some of these public works were transferred to private companies, others to local public control. Construction continued, but more slowly than originally promised. The 140 mile Indiana portion of the Wabash & Erie canal, begun in 1832, was completed during this year, but the Ohio portion still lagged behind.

This year's state elections reflected the high tide of National Republican-Whig domination of state politics that had its beginning in the middle 1820s. Within the state, this year's bitterly personal and intense "log cabin and hard cider" presidential campaign stirred more excitement than any other of the pioneer era. The wealthy gentleman, William Henry Harrison, tried desperately to present himself as a common pioneer. Politics had become entertainment, sometimes informative, but more often merely a diversion.

One Saturday in early October, Bram convinced Mary to accompany him into Frankfort. Mary generally avoided such trips because they delayed her home work schedule, but the weather was beautiful and she really needed a day off.

Saturday was market day, and local produce including apples, squash, herbs, and hard cider were being sold from wagons parked around the town square. While sampling apple butter served on a small cube of bread, Mary became aware of a commotion in the street.

People were marching toward them, chanting and waving banners. Uncertain as to what might happen next, Mary seized Bram's arm and held on. Soon she could make out the words, "Tippecanoe and Tyler, too!" being shouted by dozens of voices. Swept up in the excitement, Bram and Mary joined the crowd headed for an elevated speaker's stand in front of the courthouse. Bram told Mary that the individual ascending the steps, written speech in hand, was Samuel Bigger, Whig candidate for governor of Indiana.

Bigger was a man "of fine form and presence," six feet two inches in height weighing 240 pounds. His hair was black, his eyes a blue hazel, and his complexion dark.

As Bigger launched into his oration, the crowd divided itself into supporters and non-supporters. All were vocal about their views, most had sampled the hard cider provided by the campaign, and Bigger was having a rough time making himself heard. It seemed to Mary that the opponents by far outnumbered Bigger's supporters.

After an hour of mostly senseless verbiage, Mary tugged at Bram's arm, pleading with her eyes for him to get them out of the crowd. He sighed, and made his way back to the edge of the square where their horses were tied.

"There's going to be a barbecue when he's through," said Bram.

"You go right ahead. I've got plenty of food for supper at home," she responded.

Bram took her home and stayed there with her; she rewarded him after supper with a sweet whipped cream and pumpkin concoction often served by her *grand-mère*. Closely in tune with her body, Mary later realized that she became pregnant that night, and ever after associated passionate politics with rather intense sexual activity.

In late October, Willie Norris, Bram's step-brother, married Rachel Lee, a Scots-Irish woman born in Pennsylvania. After the ceremony, Willie introduced Mary to his bride as "the lady who taught me manners." Mary smiled.

Over the years, several members of the Lee and Norris families of Clinton County, Indiana were married.

When the elections for seventh Governor of Indiana were held in November, Samuel Bigger was elected, defeating General Tilghman A. Howard.

William Henry Harrison (the Whig candidate supported by the Norrises) was elected President of the United States, defeating the Democrat Martin Van Buren. But in Clinton County, Van Buren got 698 votes while Harrison only received 582.

Born to a wealthy family on a Virginia plantation in February of 1793, William Henry Harrison was well-educated before joining the United States Army as an ensign at age eighteen. Serving as a lieutenant under Major General "Mad Anthony" Wayne, he participated in Wayne's decisive victory at the Battle of Fallen Timbers on August 20, 1794, which brought the Northwest Indian War to a close.

Harrison was a signatory of the Treaty of Greenville in 1795. Under the terms of the treaty, a coalition of Native Americans ceded a portion of their lands to the federal government that opened two-thirds of present-day Ohio to settlement by European Americans.

Harrison began his political career when he resigned from the military in 1798. He campaigned for and received a post in the Northwest Territorial Government. Harrison frequently served as acting Territorial Governor during the absences of Governor Arthur St. Clair.

Harrison became the Northwest Territory's first Congressional Delegate, and served in the Sixth United States Congress from March, 1799, to May, 1800.

Harrison became chairman of the Committee on Public Lands and successfully promoted passage of the Land Act of 1800, which made it easier to buy land in the Northwest Territory in smaller tracts at a low cost. The sale price for public lands was set at $2 per acre. This motivated rapid population growth of the Northwest Territory.

Harrison also served on the committee that decided how to divide the Northwest Territory into smaller sections. The Eastern section, which continued to be known as the Northwest Territory, comprised the present-day state of Ohio and Eastern Michigan; the Western section was named the Indiana Territory, and consisted of the present-day states of Indiana, Illinois, Wisconsin, a portion of Western Michigan, and the Eastern portion of Minnesota. The two new territories were formally established in 1800.   In May, 1800, President John Adams appointed Harrison as Governor of the newly established Indiana Territory, based on his ties to the West and seemingly neutral political stances. Harrison, caught unaware, was reluctant to accept the position until he received assurances from the Jeffersonians that he would not be removed from office after they gained power in the upcoming elections. After Harrison's Governorship was confirmed by the United States Senate, he resigned from Congress to become the first Indiana Territorial Governor in 1801. In 1805 Harrison built a plantation-style home near Vincennes that he named Grouseland, alluding to the birds on the property. The thirteen-room home was one of the first brick structures in the territory, and still stands. During his term as Territorial Governor, Harrison's home served as a center of social and political life in the territory.

On November 7, 1811, in what is now Battle Ground, Indiana, the Battle of Tippecanoe was fought between American forces led by Territorial Governor Harrison and Native American warriors associated with the Shawnee leader Tecumseh. Tecumseh and his brother Tenskwatawa (commonly known as "The Prophet") were leaders of Native Americans from various tribes that opposed United States expansion into their territory. As tensions and violence increased, Governor Harrison marched with an army of about 1,000 men to disperse the Native Americans' headquarters at Prophetstown, near the confluence of the Tippecanoe and Wabash rivers.

Tecumseh, not yet ready to oppose the United States by force, was away recruiting allies when Harrison's army arrived. Tenskwatawa, a spiritual leader but not a military man, was in charge. Harrison camped near Prophetstown on November 6th, and arranged to meet with Tenskwatawa the following day. Early the next morning, however, warriors from Prophetstown attacked Harrison's army. Although the outnumbered attackers took Harrison's army by surprise, Harrison and his men stood their ground for more than two hours. The Native Americans were ultimately repulsed when their ammunition ran low. After the battle, they abandoned Prophetstown and Harrison's men burned it to the ground, destroying the food supplies stored for the winter. The soldiers then returned to their homes. The defeat was a setback for Tecumseh's confederacy from which it never fully recovered.

Harrison, having accomplished his goal of destroying Prophetstown, proclaimed that he had won a decisive victory. He gained the nickname "Tippecanoe," which was popularized in the campaign song, "Tippecanoe and Tyler Too," during Harrison's presidential campaign.

In December, 1812, Harrison resigned his position as Territorial Governor to continue his military career. During the winter of 1812 – 13 Harrison constructed a defensive position along the Maumee River in Northwest Ohio. After receiving reinforcements in 1813, Harrison took the offensive and led the army North to battle the Shawnee and their British allies. Harrison won victories in the Indiana Territory and in Ohio and recaptured Detroit, before invading Upper Canada (present-day Ontario). Harrison's army defeated the British on October 5, 1813, at the Battle of the Thames, in which Tecumseh was killed. This pivotal battle is considered to be one of the great American victories in the War of 1812, second only to the Battle of New Orleans.

In May 1814, Harrison resigned from the army. After the war ended, Congress awarded Harrison a gold medal for his services during the War of 1812.

Following the defeat of the British and their Indian allies in Western Canada, Harrison and Lewis Cass, Governor of the Michigan Territory, were delegated the responsibility for negotiating a peace treaty with the Indians in 1814, known as the Treaty of Greenville. In this treaty, the Native Americans ceded a portion of their lands in the Northwest Territory to the white Americans.

In 1815, Harrison was appointed to serve as one of the commissioners responsible for negotiating a second postwar treaty with the Indians that became known as the Treaty of Spring Wells.

In 1816 Harrison was elected to complete the term of John McLean of Ohio in the United States House of Representatives, where Harrison represented the state from October 8, 1816, to March 3, 1819.

In 1817 Harrison declined to serve as Secretary of War under President Monroe. In 1819 he was elected to the Ohio State Senate and served until 1821, having lost the election for Ohio Governor in 1820. In 1822 he ran for a seat in the United States House, but lost by 500 votes. In 1824 Harrison was elected to the United States Senate, where he served until May of 1828. Fellow Westerners in Congress called Harrison a "Buckeye," a term of affection (indicating residence in Ohio) related to the native Ohio buckeye tree. He was an Ohio Presidential Elector in 1820 for James Monroe and for Henry Clay in 1824.

In 1828, Harrison resigned from Congress when he was appointed as Minister Plenipotentiary to Gran Colombia. Arriving in Bogota in late December, he found the condition of Columbia saddening. He reported to the Secretary of State that the country was on the brink of anarchy, and included his opinion that Simon Bolívar was about to become a military dictator.

While in Columbia, Harrison wrote a rebuke to Bolívar, stating that "the strongest of all governments is that which is most free." He encouraged Bolívar to develop a democracy.

In response, Bolívar wrote, "The United States...seem destined by Providence to plague America with torments in the name of freedom," a sentiment that achieved fame in Latin America.

When the new administration of President Andrew Jackson began in March 1829, Harrison was recalled so that the new president could make his own appointment to the position. Harrison returned to the United States in June. Harrison then settled on his farm in North Bend, Ohio, after nearly four decades of government service. Having accumulated no substantial wealth during his lifetime, he subsisted on his savings, a small pension, and the income produced by his farm. Harrison cultivated corn and established a distillery to produce whiskey.

After a brief time in the liquor business, he became disturbed by the effects of alcohol on its consumers, and closed the distillery. In a later address to the Hamilton County, Ohio Agricultural Board in 1831, Harrison said he had sinned in making whiskey, and hoped that others would learn from his mistake and stop the production of liquors. Harrison also earned money from his contributions to a biography written by James Hall, entitled <u>A Memoir of the Public Services of William Henry Harrison</u>, published in 1836.

In 1836, Harrison made an unsuccessful run for the presidency as a Whig candidate. Between 1836 and 1840, Harrison served as Clerk of Courts for Hamilton County, Ohio. He held that office until he was elected president in 1840. During the 1830s, Harrison met African-American abolitionist and Underground Railroad conductor George DeBaptiste who lived in nearby Madison. The two became friends, and DeBaptiste became his personal servant, staying with Harrison until his death.

By 1840, when Harrison campaigned for president a second time, over a dozen books had been published about his life. He was hailed by many as a national hero. Harrison was the Whig candidate and faced the incumbent Van Buren in the 1840 presidential election. He was chosen over more controversial members of the party, such as Clay and Webster, and based his campaign on his military record and on the weak United States economy, caused by the Panic of 1837. In a ploy to blame Van Buren for the depressed economy, the Whigs nicknamed the latter "Van Ruin."

The Democrats ridiculed Harrison by calling him "Granny Harrison, the Petticoat General," because he resigned from the army before the War of 1812 ended. When asking voters whether Harrison should be elected, the Democrats asked what Harrison's name spelled backwards would be: "No Sirrah." They also cast Harrison as a provincial, out-of-touch, old man who would rather "sit in his log cabin drinking hard cider" than attend to the administration of the country. This strategy backfired when Harrison and John Tyler, his Vice Presidential running mate, adopted the log cabin and hard cider as campaign symbols. Their campaign used the symbols on banners and posters, and created bottles of hard cider shaped like log cabins, all to connect the candidates to the "common man."

Although Harrison had come from a wealthy, slaveholding Virginia family, his campaign promoted him as a humble frontiersman in the style popularized by Andrew Jackson. In contrast, the Whigs presented Van Buren as a wealthy elitist.

A Whig chant in which people would spit tobacco juice as they chanted "wirt-wirt," also exhibited the difference between candidates from the time of the election:

> Old Tip he wore a homespun coat, he had no ruffled shirt: wirt-wirt,
> But Matt he has the golden plate, and he's a little squirt: wirt-wirt!

The Whigs boasted of Harrison's military record and his reputation as the hero of the Battle of Tippecanoe. The campaign slogan, "Tippecanoe and Tyler, Too," became one of the most famous in American politics. Harrison won a landslide victory in the Electoral College, 234 electoral votes to Van Buren's 60, although the popular vote was much closer. Harrison received 53 percent of the popular vote to Van Buren's 47 percent, with a margin of less than 150,000 votes.

1841

Due to the expanding population of Clinton County, two additional townships, Honey Creek and Sugar Creek, were formed.

The winter crept by, slowly, as Mary's pregnancy advanced. She huddled indoors as much as possible with her younger children, Lavina, 4 years old and Abe, 2. The older five, Raper, 17, Altha, 15, Elizabeth, 11, Burr, 9, and Dailey, 7, were up and off to school, out of the house for most of their waking hours. They had become adept at finishing their chores and school work quickly, then taking off for horseback rides through the neighborhood with their cousins and friends. Mary envied them their happy childhoods; she and Bram had carefully shielded them from many of the trials that they themselves had faced as youths.

Their father took the older children to weekly Sunday services held at the nearby schoolhouse. Mary remained at home with Lavina and Abe. She especially enjoyed the quiet of Sunday mornings, when she was able to pray, think, and prepare dinner, undisturbed.

On March 4th, William Henry Harrison was inaugurated President of the United States. He delivered his inaugural address in snow and freezing rain without adequate clothing, then went out dancing and drinking at multiple inaugural balls. During the celebration, he developed chills and fever that developed quickly into pneumonia. On April 4th, he died and John Tyler was sworn in as his successor.

Harrison became the first United States President to die in office. His last words were to his doctor, but they were assumed to be directed at Vice President Tyler: "Sir, I wish you to understand the true principles of the government. I wish them carried out. I ask nothing more." Harrison served the shortest term of any American president: March 4 – April 4, 1841, 30 days, 12 hours, and 30 minutes.

During this winter, John Quincy Adams (former President of the United States and at that time United States Representative from Massachusetts) and Roger Sherman Baldwin (a prominent attorney) represented the defendants in United States v. The Amistad Africans before the Supreme Court of the United States. It was an unusual "freedom suit," as it involved international issues and parties, as well as United States law. The widely publicized court case in the United States bolstered the abolitionist cause.

After the American Civil War, the Amistad Abolitionist Committee founded numerous schools and colleges for freedmen in the Southern United States.

On May 6th, Mary was delivered of her fifth son, named by his father William Harrison Norris. Bram called in the Methodist circuit rider, William Wilson, to pray over the infant. Mary surreptitiously baptized her son, following Father Fernidig's instructions: Pour common water on the head of the person to be baptized, and say while pouring it, "I baptize thee in the name of the Father, and of the Son, and of the Holy Ghost." She felt quite smug about being able to say this in Latin, which had been beyond Lavina's abilities when Lavina baptized two of Mary's previous infants, Lavina and Abraham.

During the late fall, the Ohio portion of the Wabash & Erie Canal neared completion. It was predicted to be "in perfect order" by August 1, 1843, but this did not happen for over one additional year.

In mid-December, Bram and Mary attended the wedding of George ("Georgie") Norris, Bram's step-brother, to Caroline Britton. Watching the young man that she remembered as a fractious toddler make solemn vows of matrimony made Mary feel old.

1842

Mary's life was settling into a comfortable rhythm, mostly in response to the predictably changing seasons. Most difficult, of course, was harvest, when she had to find ways to preserve and store food for winter. Drying continued to be effective for fruits and some vegetables, smoking, salting and pickling for meats. She liked the fact that Bram was at home most of the time; other than weekly, short trips into Frankfort, he left only three or four times a year for business purposes. Trips to Lawrenceburg by way of Indianapolis and to Lafayette were necessary to facilitate the purchase and sale of seeds, produce, livestock, and land. Sometimes, Mary was able to accompany him, but she mostly stayed at the homestead with the children. Mary much preferred to purchase (rather than manufacture) fabric for household use and for clothing, although she liked sewing – it gave her an excuse to work sitting down!

During this year son Raper did not attend school in the fall, as he had turned 19, but continued working full time with Bram. Altha, at 16, was a great help to her mother, doing much of the cooking and cleaning, as well as watching out for the younger children. Elizabeth, 13, did not see why she should have to exert herself, preferring to stay alone upstairs with a book. "Burr" turned 11 in May, and was sure that he already knew everything necessary for life – it was all his parents could do to convince him to continue attendance at the nearby schoolhouse that they had worked so hard to establish and maintain. Dailey, 8, tried to copy Burr, but his parents squelched both boys' attempts to avoid becoming educated. Lavina, who turned 6 in July, could not wait to begin school in the fall; she recognized this as a step toward being a grownup. Little Abe, at 3, was in the way of anything purposeful being done, and it was necessary for someone to supervise him constantly to prevent injury. Baby William Harrison turned a year old in

May, and garnered as much attention as he possibly could from the rest of his family members. Mary was surprised when Bram took over some of this responsibility, holding the little fellow and walking outside with him in good weather.

Mary found it nearly impossible to celebrate the holy days specified by the ecclesiastical calendar. She continued to extrapolate those dates that she could from those being celebrated by the local Methodists, and continued to observe the prayer, fasting, and other dietary restrictions learned in her youth. Her most fervent prayer continued to be that a priest would come to Frankfort.

1843

Clinton County, Indiana continued to increase population during this year, and the townships of Johnson and Owen were formed as a result.

George Norris' wife, Caroline, was safely delivered of a son, George Holcomb, or "Holk," in mid-January.

Mary had been ill during the previous fall, and her milk for nursing baby Harrison had dried up. She fed him goat's milk and he thrived, but her reproductive system swung into action earlier than it would have if she had continued to nurse the baby. By early March, she was fairly certain that she was again with child.

Her son, Raper, was exceedingly good-looking, and reminded Mary more every day of his grandfather, Richard, who shared his first name. Whenever he left the farm, whether going to school, to church, or to town, young ladies swarmed about him. In the spring, as the weather warmed, Mary noticed that he often stayed out all night, and then one early morning saw him near the barn, helping a disheveled girl onto a horse after kissing her passionately.

When he reached the house, Mary confronted him.

"Raper, who *was* that young lady?"

Grinning sheepishly, he replied, "That was Mary Grove. She couldn't ride home last night–it was raining!"

"And when are you planning to introduce Mary to your family? In particular, when am *I* going to meet her?"

He scratched his chin, which was in need of a shave, and muttered, "I hadn't thought..."

"Of *course*! You weren't *thinking*! That explains everything. Raper, where do babies come from?"

He stared at his mother as if she had gone mad.

"Babies," she continued, "arrive all the time. They don't *care* whether the parents are ready for them or not. It's the *parents'* jobs to make sure they are ready for children. Are you and Mary ready?"

"I-I don't know."

"Have you been doing things that might produce a baby?"

He did not reply.

"Raper, you are a man now. It's up to you to plan your life. Don't let things just happen, and then wonder why they turned out as they did. Think!"

Mary turned away, near tears. Raper put his arm around her shoulders, and hugged her gently.

"Mama, is it all right if I bring Mary to supper tonight?"

"Yes. Yes, of course it is."

It developed that Mary Grove was a seventeen year old serving girl of Frankfort, quiet and reserved. In mid-June, she and Raper were married by a Justice of the Peace, and set up housekeeping in the Norris cabin where the family had first lived in Clinton County. Soon after their marriage, Raper generously took in two of his grandfather Richard Norris' children, Lucretia, 13, and James Luther, 7.

In April, the Wabash & Erie Canal opened from the Wabash River to Lafayette, Indiana, eleven years after construction of the Indiana section began. On July 4th, there was a major celebration at Fort Wayne complete with barbecues, a German band in uniform, and speeches expressing the expansionist sentiments of "Manifest Destiny."

Mary felt ill during most of September, as her pregnancy drew to a close. She spent much of her time in bed, reflecting on those who had made differences in her life, and especially on those who had helped along the way. On October 4th, she was delivered of a healthy daughter, whom she named Phoebe Elvira, after the black lady to whom she owed her survival. Mary baptized her new daughter, feeling again the intense longing for a priest to come to Frankfort.

During that fall, James Whitcomb campaigned for the governorship of Indiana. He was a large man, strongly built, with a dark complexion and black hair. He followed this premise: "Give the people plenty of whiskey, and stir them up with a long pole, and their votes are certain." His opponent was incumbent Governor Samuel Bigger, whom he defeated by a majority of 2,013 votes.

Whitcomb was the first Democratic governor of Indiana, the first bachelor to hold that office, and the first New Englander. A quote from the Indiana State Sentinel, referring to the outcome of this election: "The sun of Whiggery is about to set."

Whigs were widely blamed for the State of Indiana's $13,000,000 debt. Taxes had risen within the state due to this debt. Democrats claimed to be the true heirs of the American Revolution and of Thomas Jefferson. The Norrises were not pleased.

1844

During this legislative session, Tipton County and Richardville County, Indiana were organized.

Richardville County was named for Joseph deRichardville (born about 1761, died 13 August 1841), also known as Jean Baptiste and as Peshewa ("Wildcat"). As last chief of the united Miami tribe, he was perhaps the most remarkable and effective of all the Indiana Native American chiefs in delaying the Anglo-American takeover of Indian property.

DeRichardville was born in the village of Kekionga, present-day Fort Wayne, Indiana, to a French merchant named Joseph Drouet deRicherville and Tacumwah, sister of the Miami chief Pacanne. He was well educated, and could speak Miami, Iroquois, French, and English, although he later refused to speak "white" languages or wear "white" clothing styles.

During the late 1700s, the main source of income for deRichardville's family had been the fur trade and control of a portage connecting the Maumee River to the Little Wabash River. The Miami lost control of the portage in the 1796 Treaty of Greenville. However, deRichardville acquired a trade license in 1815 which gave him a monopoly on carry-over services at the portage, and his family again prospered.

In 1818, deRichardville signed the Treaty of St. Mary's, in which the Americans took away most of central Indiana from the Miami Tribe. However, deRichardville negotiated land grants to individual Miami families, and offered his private lands as a refuge for other Miami. This allowed about half of the Miami people to remain in Indiana when the tribe was officially removed in 1846, five years after deRichardville's death.

After signing the Treaty of Mississinewa (also called the Wabash Treaty) in 1826, deRichardville constructed Richardville House, in Fort Wayne, Indiana.

The federal government paid $600 toward the building, which was a stipulation of the treaty. DeRichardville also used $2200 of his own funds towards the mansion, and in 1827 it became the first Greek Revival style house in Indiana. The historic mansion still exists.

DeRichardville is considered to have been the richest man in the state of Indiana at the time of his death in 1841. In 1991, his house was acquired by the Allen County-Fort Wayne Historical Society, which has worked toward its restoration.

Three Indiana locations were named for deRichardville: Wildcat Creek, Richardville County, and Richardville, Indiana. Unfortunately, the name Richardville County was soon changed to Howard County, and Richardville, Indiana was misspelled and eventually changed to Russiaville, Indiana.

In the spring, Mary and Bram's first grandchild was born to Raper and Mary Norris, a son named James. Unlike the other Norris sons, this one bore no middle name. When Mary asked Raper why, he grinned and said, "I couldn't think of a worse moniker than the one I got saddled with—we'll just call him Jimmy!"

During May and July of this year, The Philadelphia Nativist Riots, also known as the Philadelphia Prayer Riots, the Bible Riots and the Native American Riots, took place in Philadelphia, Pennsylvania, as well as in adjacent districts of Kensington and Southwark. The riots were a result of rising anti-Catholic sentiment due to the growing population of Irish Catholic immigrants.

In the months prior to the riots, nativist groups had been spreading a rumor that Catholics were trying to remove the Bible from public schools. A nativist rally in Kensington erupted in violence on May 6th and started a riot resulting in the destruction of two Catholic churches and many other buildings. Riots erupted again in July after it was discovered that St. Philip Neri's Catholic Church in Southwark had armed itself for protection. Fierce fighting broke out between the nativists and the soldiers sent to protect the church, resulting in numerous deaths and injuries.

On May 24th, the first telegraph message was sent from Washington to Baltimore by Samuel Morse, "What hath God wrought?"

On June 27th, "The Prophet" Joseph Smith and his brother Hyrum were slaughtered in the Carthage, Hancock County, Illinois jail. Largely due to public anti-Mormon sentiment, all men who were tried for these murders were acquitted. Ongoing persecution pushed the remaining Mormons West, where their president Brigham Young established their center at Salt Lake Valley, Utah, in 1847.

Annexation of Texas became a hot political issue. Congressman Caleb B. Smith, a Hoosier Whig, said that the United States Constitution made no provision for the annexation of Texas or of any foreign country, and that taking Texas from Mexico by force was a war of conquest. Congressman Robert Dale Owen, a Hoosier Democrat, said that Texas had won her independence from Mexico and become a foreign state, and annexation was for the United States and Texas to decide.

In November, Democrat James K. Polk was elected President of the United States. In Indiana, Henry Clay was the favorite candidate of Hoosier Whigs such as the Norrises. In Clinton County, Polk got 944 votes, while Clay got 645; James Birney of the Free Soil or Liberty party got 12.

The United States Democratic Party, appealing to expansionist sentiment, asserted that the United States had a valid claim to the entire Oregon Country up to Russian America at parallel 54°40' North. President Polk sought a compromise boundary along the 49th parallel, the same boundary proposed by previous United States administrations. Negotiations between the United States and England broke down, however, and tensions grew as American expansionists urged Polk to annex the entire Oregon Country to the parallel 54°40' North, as the Democrats had called for in the election. The turmoil added weight to slogans such as "Fifty-four Forty or Fight!" and to the catchphrase "Manifest Destiny."

Mary spent December preparing tor the holidays. She secretly prepared handmade gifts for each member of her household, plus a warm, knitted blanket for grandchild Jimmy. She had learned to couple her knitting stitches to repetitions of the Rosary, and felt very satisfied when the blanket was complete.

1845

This year is considered to be the beginning of the Irish potato famine, which lasted for six years. The famine killed over a million men, women and children in Ireland and caused another million to flee the country, many coming to the United States. Those who came to the United States faced poverty, prejudice and discrimination that often lasted for generations.

The first section of the Miami and Erie Canal from the Maumee River near Toledo, Ohio to Junction, Ohio was finally completed during this year. It was an effort to improve the transport of products to improve the economy. The ultimate goal was to link Lake Erie to the Ohio River.

In Mexico, Generalissimo Santa Anna was exiled to Cuba during January.

In February, Congress voted to annex Texas. On March 1st, lame duck President John Tyler signed the annexation bill.

On March 3rd, Florida entered the Union as the 27th state.

On March 4th, President James K. Polk announced in his inaugural address that he intended to "consummate the reannexation of Texas." As soon as the Mexican authorities heard this, they broke off diplomatic relations with the United States, vowing to take Texas back by force.

In Fort Wayne, a Whig newspaper editor wrote, "Mexicans are the filthiest race of modern times. The country swarms with fleas, ticks, bugs, and vermin of all kinds. The Mexicans have diseases wholly unknown in the United States, and their women pass most of their time drinking gin and picking the lice from each other's persons." This statement was typical of Americans with expansionist views, and the denigration of any group has continued to be used as a valid argument to push political agendas.

By mid-July, Mary realized that she was with child once again. "*I'm getting too old for this!*" she thought.

During that month, Texans voted in favor of joining the United States.

During June, July and August, President Polk sent a 3,500 member "army of observation" to Corpus Christi, at the mouth of the Nueces River, on the North edge of the "disputed territory" between Texas and Mexico.

In November, President Polk sent John Slidell to Mexico in a failed attempt to buy New Mexico and California for $30 million, with the Texas border being moved South from the Nueces River to the Rio Grande river.

Tension continued between the United States and England over possession of the Oregon Territory.

On November 15th, Indiana Division #1 of the Sons of Temperance was organized at Brookville, Franklin County in Southeastern Indiana.

As the year came to a close, Bram and Mary attended the funeral of Joseph Norris, Bram's younger brother. He had been killed while cutting trees for winter fuel. His wife had died previously in Dearborn County, and there were no children, so the funeral was simple and quiet. This left Bram with only two full siblings from his father's marriage to Aaltje: Van and Hendricks.

At the funeral, Mary noticed Van being comforted by his housekeeper, Nancy McCartney. The woman, although seventeen years younger than Van, had taken good care of the seven children (four of Van's and three of Richard and Lavina's) in Van's household. Mary couldn't resist wondering how long it would be before Nancy turned up pregnant by Van. She soon had her answer when they were married on February 1st, shortly before Nancy's condition began to "show."

On December 29th, Texas entered the Union as the 28th state.

1846

During this legislative session, the name of Richardville County, Indiana, was changed to Howard County - a last insult to the memory of deceased Miami chief Joseph deRichardville. The county was re-named for General Tilghman Howard, United States Representative from Indiana, who had died in 1844.

Still intent on his expansionist policies, President Polk was convinced that Mexico could be bullied into selling New Mexico and California to the United States. He therefore sent orders to General Zachary Taylor to advance South and West from Corpus Christi, Texas into disputed territory between the Nueces and the Rio Grande Rivers.

By mid-February, it seemed to Mary that she had been pregnant for her whole life, and she rejoiced when her son was born on February 26th, the day after Ash Wednesday. After a few snide comments from her about never getting to name the boy children, Bram let her call the child Silas Davis, on condition that he be permitted to name the next girl. Even though her love for Silas Davis, Jr. had been unrequited, it gave Mary satisfaction to recall those feelings and deal with them from this great distance. Silas Davis, Sr. had been kind to her, but Mary reflected that her life might have been much better had her mother remained with the Hobbs family, where at least she could have been protected from the likes of John Davis.

It took a day and a half before Mary could manage to be alone with her baby long enough to baptize him. She had warmed the water before pouring it onto his head, but Baby Silas cried anyway, startled by the sensation.

In late March, General Zachary Taylor built Fort Texas inside the disputed

Mexican-American territory overlooking Matamoros, which was located on the South side of the Rio Grande River. United States Commodore David Connor was ordered to Veracruz, prepared with ships to transport United States soldiers wherever needed along the Texan or Mexican coast, as well as to block the mouth of the Rio Grande River.

On April 25th, in the contested territory North of the Rio Grande River, a Mexican cavalry unit of 2,000 men ambushed a patrol of seventy United States soldiers under Captain Seth B. Thornton, killing eleven of them and taking fifty-two prisoners in what became known as the "Thornton Affair." General Taylor sent a letter to President Polk, stating that "hostilities have begun."

Part of the Mexican Army at this time consisted of the Legión de Extranjeros (Legion of Foreigners). These men would later make up the core of the Saint Patrick's battalion, or San Patricios, responsible for some of the fiercest resistance met in many battles by United States forces invading Mexico. Among the San Patricios were Catholics from many nations, as well as deserters from the United States Army and escaped slaves. Whenever United States forces captured any of the San Patricios, they treated them with exceptional cruelty, usually resulting in death. The San Patricios, anticipating the treatment they would receive from the American soldiers, always fought against them with more vigor and tenacity than the regular Mexican soldiers did.

On May 3rd through the 9th, United States forces withstood Mexican bombardments at Fort Texas, although their commander, Major Jacob Brown, was killed. The location was later named Brownsville, Texas. In this area of the contested territory, the first major battles of the Mexican-American War were fought.

Known as the Battles of Palo Alto (May 8th) and Resaca de la Palma (May 9th), between United States troops under General Taylor and Mexicans under General José Mariano Martín Buenaventura Ignacio Nepomuceno García de Arista Nuez, these conflicts resulted in United States victory. Part of the reason for the American success was its deployment of light weight cannon, called "Flying Artillery," that moved quickly from place to place on horse-drawn caissons.

As a result of these victories, General Taylor became a hero to the American people, known for his casual demeanor, strict discipline, and stubbornness in battle. Within weeks he received a brevet (honorary) promotion to Major General and a formal commendation from Congress. In 1848 he became a reluctant, but successful presidential candidate.

General Arista, on the other hand, suffered humiliation. He was recalled by the Mexican government, and removed from command.

*On May 11th, President Polk sent a message to Congress, stating that "Mexico has passed the boundary of the United States, has invaded our territory and shed American blood upon American soil." (Of course, the Mexicans considered that United States forces had invaded **their** territory, and the Mexicans were doing their best to resist.) Congress approved Polk's declaration of war on May 13th. The resulting war bill called for 50,000 volunteers from the states for an enlistment of twelve months.*

By May 18th, Taylor's United States troops had occupied Matamoros with no resistance. More than three hundred sick and wounded Mexicans had been captured in the hospitals. Taylor quickly developed a reputation among the Mexicans for fair and humane treatment of captives, which enraged many of the war-hungry Americans.

On May 21st, Elder Jesse C. Little of the Mormon Pioneers in Illinois arrived in Washington, D.C. to seek assistance from the federal government for the Mormon Pioneers who were being persecuted by anti-Mormon mobs in Illinois. Desperate for President Polk's approval and protection, Little offered "a few hundred" Mormon volunteer soldiers for the Mexican War effort. As a result, 500 Mormon volunteers became the only religiously based military unit in United States history, serving under Stephen Watts Kearny from July 1846 to July 1847.

At the outbreak of the Mexican War, the people of Indiana seemed totally unprepared for military involvement. This was mostly because there had been no official international hostilities involving American troops since the War of 1812, over thirty years previously, before Indiana was organized as a state. Whatever militia existed within Indiana was loosely organized, poorly trained, with no weapons nor equipment. Those who participated had come to be derided as the "cornstalk militia," because they drilled carrying cornstalks as if they were rifles and cornsilk tassels in their caps.

On May 22nd Indiana Governor James Whitcomb called for 2,790 cavalry, infantry, artillery, and riflemen. Fortunately, Indiana's Adjutant-General, David Reynolds, was an extremely capable man. He facilitated the collection of the state's quota of volunteer troops, which was completed within nineteen days.

Each volunteer under the rank of commissioned officer had to be a physically able man between the ages of eighteen and forty-five years. A company was comprised of eighty privates, one captain, one first and one second lieutenant, four sergeants, four corporals and two musicians, for a total of ninety-three in each company.

On May 26th, Governor James Whitcomb took a personal loan in the amount of $10,000 from the Bank of Indiana's Madison branch in order to purchase arms, equipment, uniform clothing and food for the state's recruits. On the same day, he sent letters to other branches of the bank requesting equivalent loans. Enough Indiana banks responded that he was able personally to fund the three regiments requested by the federal government. Once the Indiana General Assembly convened, they repaid Whitcomb and assumed responsibility for his debts to the banks.

In May, hearing of the congressional war bill, James Henry Lane, a lawyer of Lawrenceburg, Dearborn County, organized what became Company K of the 3rd Indiana Regiment, the "Dearborn Volunteers." On June 1st, Dearborn County became the first to report a complete enlisted company to the governor. Early in June this company, composed "chiefly of young farmers and mechanics of the best character," traveled down the Ohio River by steamboat to the designated rendezvous point near New Albany, Indiana.

The 3rd Indiana Regiment was composed of ten companies, each named for a letter of the alphabet. For some reason, the letter J was not used:

A - Monroe Guards, Monroe County, Captain John M. Sluss
B - Washington Guards, Jefferson County, Captain William Ford
C - Johnson Guards, Johnson County, Captain David Allen, succeeded by John Slater
D - Switzerland Riflemen, Switzerland County, Captain Scott Carter
E - Brown County Blues, Brown County, Captain James Taggart, succeeded by Reese Brummet
F - Bartholomew Volunteers, Bartholomew County, Captain Isaac S. Boardman
G - Madison Rifles, Jefferson County, Captain Thomas L. Sullivan
H - Shelby Riflemen, Shelby County, Captain Vorhees Conover
I - Clark Guards, Clark County, Captain Thomas W. Gibson
K - Dearborn Volunteers, Dearborn County, Captain James Henry Lane. Lane was elected Colonel of the entire 3rd Regiment, and George Dunn, of Lawrenceburg, succeeded Lane in the captaincy of the company.

At Indianapolis, Lew Wallace (future author of Ben Hur: A Tale of the Christ, and son of former Indiana Governor David Wallace) opened a store-front recruitment office, hired a fifer and a drummer, obtained flags and banners, and collected a company of volunteers in three days. They became part of the 1st Indiana Regiment.

In Clinton County, Indiana, there was no extant local militia. One company assembled under Captain Thomas Kinnan, 1st Lieutenant James F. Suit, and 2nd Lieutenant Thomas Dunn. These were called "The Clinton boys." This unit reported after the requisition was full, and were held in reserve "for future exigency." Most of them never served in the Mexican-American conflict.

Indiana Adjutant-General Reynolds issued General Order No. 1 on June 4th, directing the companies to assemble at old Fort Clark, on an island in the Ohio River below Jeffersonville and about one mile above New Albany, Indiana. The volunteers were told to arrive as soon as possible, by the shortest route, and at their own expense for transportation and subsistence.

At that time Indiana had only one railroad, running between Madison and Edinburg. There were few improved highways and no telegraphs. All long distance communication was by mail, mostly carried by men on horseback. There were no daily newspapers, but rather one or two small news organizations per county supplying weekly news sheets. Despite these handicaps, the war news traveled fast, and the volunteer troops gathered quickly.

The roads of Indiana were soon filled with marching men, helped on by patriotic farmers, who furnished wagons for transportation and whose kind-hearted wives fed the hungry volunteers. By the 10th of June, thirty companies had reported at old Fort Clark (renamed Camp Whitcomb), and had been mustered into service, while an overflow of twenty-two companies reported from their home counties clamoring for acceptance.

Mary overheard some of the above in bits and pieces as Bram, Burr, and Dailey discussed current events at meals during May and June. She dismissed most of it as insignificant until Raper rode by one afternoon in early June as she was outside walking baby Silas, rubbing his back, trying to soothe his colic. Raper's wife Mary had recently given birth to baby Luther, who was doing very well.

"Did you hear about Georgie?" Raper asked.

"Georgie" was Richard and Catherine's son. Mary always thought of him as the uncontrolled brat who she had smacked into submission at Aurora so long ago. He had retained his impulsive nature as an adult, his behavior always somewhat unpredictable.

"What about him?" she asked.

"He joined Jim Lane and the army at Lawrenceburg - he's off to fight the Mexicans!"

"Georgie?" It was impossible for Mary to imagine him marching, standing guard, or, especially, taking orders. And what about his wife and son?

"Yep. We may not see him again for quite a while."

Raper whipped out a folded paper from his pocket. "Here's what the New York papers are saying about the situation: *Mexico must be thoroughly chastised!*" he read. *"Let our arms now be carried...America knows how to crush, as well as how to expand!* - that's from Walt Whitman. People all over the country are rising to fight the Mexicans. The question is: Will we have to fight the British again, as well?"

"What do you mean?" Mary asked him.

"Haven't you heard the boys yelling, *'Fifty-four Forty or Fight!'*?"

Mary half-nodded. The children were always running, yelling nonsense they had picked up at church or at school.

"It's all part of the Democrat's expansionist agenda. First, they wanted to move the Oregon Territory's boundary with Canada North to the 49th parallel. Then, fools like our own Senator Hannegan, claiming 'Manifest Destiny,' as if they know the mind of God Almighty, started pushing to expand even farther North, to 54°40', which sent the Brits into a tizzy – they may declare war over it. Now, Polk has backed off, and wants to sign a treaty naming the 49th parallel as the permanent border. But if negotiations break down again..."

"It will be 1812 all over again," finished Mary.

"Yep," said Raper. "But they likely won't come through here. I guess I'd better get along home."

Mary thought about Raper's little wife, Polly, and her two young sons. Polly had recently, after a difficult pregnancy, given birth to baby Luther. As far as Mary could tell, Richard's daughter, Lucretia, 15, who lived with Raper and Polly, was helping Polly a great deal. Mary fervently hoped that Raper was keeping his hands off the young woman. But he was a Norris, after all...

"You want a beef stew pie to take home? They are cooling in the kitchen." Raper grinned and headed for the back door. "Yes! Thanks, Mamma!"

Pope Gregory XVI died on June 9th at Rome. Gregory had sent missionaries to Abyssinia, India, China, Polynesia, and to the North American Indians. He increased the number of bishops in the United States.

But the fear that the Papal States could not long outlast him proved well founded. The unyielding attitude of Gregory XVI and of his secretary of state, Cardinal Lambruschini, had brought the Papal States to the verge of a revolution.

Gregory's successor, Pope Pius IX, whose coronation took place June 21st, was in favor of political reform. His first political act was the granting of a general amnesty to political exiles and prisoners on July 16th. This act was hailed with enthusiasm by the people, but some extreme reactionaries denounced the Pope as being in league with the Freemasons and the Carbonari. It had not occurred to the kindly nature of Pius IX that many of the pardoned political offenders would use their liberty to further their revolutionary ideas. Pius IX became the longest-reigning elected Pope in the history of the Catholic Church, serving for over 31 years.

The Oregon Treaty, an agreement between the United States and England, was made official on June 15th, and the 49th parallel (not 54°40') remained the land boundary between the United States and Canada.

The 4th of July fell on a Saturday, and Mary and Bram decided to take the children into Frankfort for the parades, speeches, music and dancing that were part of the celebrations.

As usual in these situations, Mary carefully paired her children so that she did not have to watch them all every second. Altha, 20 years old, was put in charge of Phoebe, age 2½. Eliza, 17, would hold on to 5 year old Willie. Burr, at 15, would take Abe, age 7, with him wherever he went. Mary herself would carry baby Silas, passing him off to Bram whenever she needed a break.

Altha at this time was being courted by David Maish, Jr., a 23 year old local man who was working, building cisterns during this summer, being paid twelve dollars per month. Every time Mary saw them together at this event, David was holding little Phoebe, either balancing her on his shoulders or bending over, holding her hand as she toddled about.

"He'll make a good father!" Mary thought.

While at the celebration, Mary saw Caroline Norris, Georgie's wife, with their son Holk, then three years old. The child appeared well grown, and exhibited some of the impulsive nature that surely came from his father.

Greeting Caroline with a warm smile, Mary asked, "How are you doing Mrs. Norris?"

Caroline shrugged her shoulders. "We're getting by." She did not sound very confident.

"Have you heard anything from Georgie?"

Caroline pulled a folded paper from her sleeve and handed it to Mary.

"I got this letter - we could go sit under that tree and read it, if you like."

"You'll have to read it to me – I never learned," replied Mary, heading toward the shade, where she sat in the grass. Shifting baby Silas to one side, she gathered Holk onto her lap, and he snuggled against her.

Unfolding the letter, Caroline began to read:

Monday, June 15, 1846
Third Regiment, Company K
Camp Whitcomb
On the Ohio River

Dear Caroline,

Greetings from the fort on the river!

I hope brother Will told you that I won't be home for awhile - perhaps for a year. I signed up with Jim Lane (I'm sure you remember when we met him in Lawrenceburg - he was the lawyer we consulted about my father's land distributions) for the Dearborn Volunteers at the end of May. Cap' Lane says we must put the needs of our nation first, before all else. He says that whether we live or die, our souls will be blessed by the gratitude of our entire nation. We will be bathed in glory and honor.

My hope is that glory and honor smell much better than the river water in which we are currently compelled to bathe. Before enlistment, most of the men had shaved their faces daily, either partially or completely. Such are conditions here that virtually every one now sports a wealth of facial hair, with the result that he might not be recognized by his friends and family at home.

I figure that the war with Mexico will be over before our company even gets to Texas, and I'll be ahead the money (they are supposed to pay us $16 every two months), plus some clothing and the good will of our business contacts in Lawrenceburg. At the least, it should be a great adventure! Excitement has overwhelmed us all.

"I see," thought Mary. "He's mostly in it for the adventure!"

Our Dearborn Volunteers took a steamboat, the Pike No. 7, from Lawrenceburg to Camp Whitcomb, a beautiful island in the Ohio River, and we were put to work clearing brush so that all the volunteers who follow us can pitch their tents.

Our company is divided into groups of six men, each group called a mess. Each mess will eventually receive a tent, a coffee-pot, one camp kettle, and a short fry pan. Since we were among the first to arrive, the equipment has been lacking, and we have had to improvise. Each member of the mess takes it in turn to cook (Yes! I am now able to cook!). The basic method is to throw a collection of ingredients into the pot with water to cover, and boil it until everything dissolves into a mushy soup. The result is not often tasty, but goes down easily and warms the stomach. We have had to scavenge most of our own food - fish taste better than the wild game, or even stray hogs, at this time of year. The flour and corn meal issued to us for cooking is not the freshest ever seen - I suspect that these became damp at some point, and one is apt to find mould, and bugs crawling through. Pre-made bread from the nearby towns is not any better - by the time it gets to us, it is no longer tasty and has either become stiff and hard to chew, or else mouldy, with bugs. We have been ordered to drink the river water, which tastes horrible! I always thought that spring or well water was better, but the old river traders consider the river water most wholesome and say that we soldiers will soon get accustomed to its use and become fond of it.

We have been promised shirts, pantaloons, uniform coats and caps, as well as woolen socks with sturdy leather shoes for marching, or boots for cavalry, but so far we are wearing whatever we arrived in. The wait for expected clothing is a major hindrance to our departure for the South, and I am sure that uniforms will help our units identify each other in time of battle. Each man has a blanket, which is more used for padding the hard ground beneath us at night than for cover, as the weather has been quite warm. Mosquitoes are everywhere, day and night, and anyone remaining still for more than half a minute finds himself under attack from the cursed little beasts.

Some of our weapons have arrived, and we are being trained to use either a muzzle-loading rifle or a musket, although the muskets are quicker and easier to load. Their range and accuracy, however, leave something to be desired. I've been told that I may eventually be assigned to a light, or flying artillery unit with horses, but that part of my training will have to wait until arrival in the South. The sound of the drum is used to assemble troops - I'm guessing they can't find a horn, nor anyone who knows how to blow it properly.

More volunteers land on the island daily, and I heard that the expected total is 2,790 men. It's difficult to imagine that many people assembled here - I'm assuming that they will ship some of us South in order to make space for the later arrivals. The soldiers of each regiment must pass inspection here, and there have been a few rejections for deformities and disabilities.

We were astonished at what happened in Captain Walker's Evansville company. After the inspection, by an accidental, embarrassing circumstance, it was discovered that one of the inspected volunteers was a female. With tears in her eyes, she stated that she was poor and friendless, that her father was a soldier with General Taylor on the Rio Grande and that she knew of no other way of getting to her father than by joining the army which was going there. Her dramatics were rewarded by a financial contribution from the company and she left on a steamboat bound down river. The truth behind her story, as well as whether she will be allowed to proceed to the Rio Grande are both questionable!

Most of the Indiana troops appear to be in good spirits, anxious to begin their service to the country. There are some slight cases of sickness due to change of water, diet and mode of living. Those who have received their uniforms and equipment look neat, clean and comfortable. Rumor has it that we will depart during the first week of July aboard a steamboat that will transport us to Camp Jackson, below New Orleans.

My dear Brother Will has promised to take care of you and Little Holk. He will oversee the farm, and hire men to do the harvest, as well as next spring's planting. Should anything happen to me, you must rely on his good judgment and assistance in continuing as best you can the life we had planned together.

Your Husband,
George

Mary considered Georgie, at Camp Whitcomb, for a long time afterwards. *"Malaria!"* she thought. *"Yellow fever!"* Camping outdoors along the Ohio River seemed a sure way to sicken the soldiers before they ever saw battle. And poor Caroline seemed quite dejected, feeling as if she had been forever abandoned.

On July 7th, the United States Navy under Commodore John Sloat occupied Monterey, California, and two days later, after the Battle of Yerba Buena, they occupied what later became San Francisco, California.

In early July, Mexican General Tomas Requena had garrisoned Monterrey, Mexico with 1,800 men. The remnants of Arista's army, plus additional forces from Mexico City arrived by the end of August until the Mexican forces totaled 7,303 men.

During July, United States President Polk's emissary visited the former Mexican Generalissimo, Santa Anna, who had been exiled to Havana, Cuba. Santa Anna had previously written to the government in Mexico City, saying that he did not want the presidency, but would gladly lead soldiers to protect his homeland against foreign invasion of Mexico. But he pledged to Polk's emissary that, if he were returned to Mexico through the United States naval blockade, he would work to sell all contested Mexican territory to the United States at a reasonable price.

During the summer of 1846 the war in Northeastern Mexico entered a lull due to the logistics of United States troop replacement. Many of the first, unauthorized (by Congress) volunteer regiments had signed up for three or six month tours. Congress declared that no regiment raised for less than twelve months could be kept in federal service. By August, many of General Taylor's troops would be gone, although some re-enlisted for various reasons including loyalty to the cause. Frustrated by the Quartermaster's Department at New Orleans, Taylor was unable to move farther into Mexico for lack of personnel and supplies. Even though his troops had first taken possession of the next staging point, a small Mexican town called Camargo on July 14th, Taylor and the thousands under his command had to wait until the end of July before they could begin moving upriver.

Later in August, Mary was pleased that Raper's wife Polly stopped by for a visit, bringing with her Georgie's wife Caroline. These two women were of about the same age, and apparently had become friends. Caroline brought with her another letter from Georgie, which she read aloud:

Wednesday, July 15, 1846
Third Regiment, Company K
Camp Jackson
Mississippi Delta

Dearest Caroline,

    I miss you and Little Holk more every day. If only this war would end quickly, I could return home!
    Our company finally received uniforms at the very end of June – not dress or parade uniforms, but rather a gray-blue hunters coat and pantaloons without straps. My coat reaches halfway down my thigh, and has a double row of white military buttons, eagle stamped, the high neck made to close around my throat. Each man got two

cotton shirts and a cloth cap, as well as woolen socks and leather boots or shoes.

We had intended to spend the whole day celebrating July 4th at Camp Whitcomb, but it was announced that we would depart for Mexico next day. With the planned activities as our motivation, we rapidly got ready to break camp by noon on the 4th. We then enjoyed the holiday with music, marching, speeches and a feast of roasted fish, greens, and our reserved whiskey, as well as by firing the cannon. The day went off well, with the exception that one of the lieutenants of the Wabash Rangers was stabbed by a private in that company, a former blacksmith. The private was immediately taken into custody, to be tried later by court-martial.

On July 5th, we arose early in the morning, took down our tents and rolled them up – everything was soon ready. Just before we broke camp, two gentlemen showed up, handing out New Testaments. Many of our number appreciated this gesture, whether they were able to read or not. Book pages make great tinder when one is lighting a fire.

With flags flying, and Yankee Doodle playing on fife and drum, we boarded the steamboat James Hewitt. The wharf and river bank were filled with spectators who cheered wildly, waving white handkerchiefs as the cannon roared a farewell.

The nine-day trip between the river banks of the Ohio River, then the Mississippi was very beautiful and peaceful, the only disturbance being an incident when we reached Vicksburg. While at the landing there two days ago, one of the volunteers, Freeman H. Cross, fell between the boat and the wharf, and was drowned. Another man has died of the measles, and our sick list totals thirty.

We arrived at New Orleans yesterday, and were delivered to Camp Jackson, South of the city. Camp Jackson is the site of Andrew Jackson's glorious triumph over the British in 1815. This field where we are encamped is little better than a swamp. We have not a wisp of straw to soak up the moisture, and our blankets have turned into blubbery slime.

The only drinking water available is from the sandy, muddy river, and I hope you cannot imagine how terrible it feels going down *our throats. Our rations consisted of beans, coffee, sugar, pickled pork, salt, and flour. The only biscuit available is infested by brown bugs, which are the freshest meat in our diet. The pork was not entirely pickled, and is partly spoiled. We also have a kind of stuff called smoked meat that used to be sides of hog, now half liquid and half solid. Whenever a piece is picked up you can see something ooze out that resembles lard oil. It was taken on the boat at New Albany, and I cannot wait until it is all used up. I would rather starve than eat it.*

Many among us have begun to be ill, vomiting and running fevers from time to time. And the diarrhea!! Horrible.

Here we sit until such time as we get transport by clipper ship from the United States Navy across the Gulf of Mexico to Brazos Santiago Island.

Here Caroline paused. "What's a clipper ship?"

Mary briefly explained, and the two young women were duly impressed by her knowledge of ships and the shore, where they had never been.

Caroline continued to read:

In a few days begins our trial by fire in Mexico. Pray for me that I will be equal to this test of manhood.

Some of the men are receiving mail from home. We all anxiously await every arrival of the mail. Please write and let me know how you and Little Holk are faring. Our letters are to be directed to Dearborn Volunteers, 3rd Regiment, Indiana Brigade, in care of Colonel J.H. Lane, Port Isabel, Texas, from whence they will be sent to us. Could not some of our good friends send us a news sheet occasionally? The last news from home was July 5th.

You are in my thoughts,
George

While Taylor & Scott threatened Mexico South of the Rio Grande, President Polk sent Colonel Stephen Watts Kearny to secure the area that became New Mexico and California. Part of Kearny's strategy included securing the cooperation of Mexican settlers as well as Navajo Indians in New Mexico. At least temporarily, both of these groups agreed not to interfere in the war. In early August, Kearny defeated Mexican Governor Manuel Armijo on the way to Santa Fe, New Mexico.

On August 8th, General Taylor was finally able to establish the headquarters for his Army of Occupation in Camargo, Tamaulipas, Mexico. However, he still lacked the adequate supply lines necessary to move his entire army there.

Early in August, Mary was cooking in the kitchen, listening to her son, Burr, read from a news sheet. An election had been held for the United States Congress, and Burr was reading the list of winners. "Abraham Lincoln, from Illinois," he said.

"Who?" Mary asked.

"Abraham Lincoln, Mama."

"I once met an Abe Lincoln, but he lived in Indiana," she said.

"Could be the same one – it's not that common a name," Burr responded.

Mary wondered, but could think of no way to find out whether the new Congressman was indeed the Abe who helped her so long ago.

A month later, during harvest season in mid-September, Mary encountered Caroline on the road to Frankfort and was invited to listen to Georgie's latest letter.

Saturday, August 15, 1846
Third Regiment, Company K
Camp Belknap
Mexico

My Dearest Darling Caroline,

It has been a month since I wrote, but it has seemed an eternity. I am not as homesick as before, but have rather succumbed to a dull aching longing for you, our family, and our friends. The distance between us seems an insurmountable gulf, and this saddens me deeply.

We sat in the mud at Camp Jackson for three days. Finally, on

July 18th, we rinsed ourselves in the surf and boarded our clipper ship for what should have been a two or three day transit to Brazos Santiago Island, on the Western edge of the Gulf of Mexico, near the mouth of the Rio Grande River. Our destination turned out to be just one of a long, thin line of sand dune islands thrown up by the Gulf along the shores of Mexico and Texas. We sailed out of the Mississippi River delta in a few hours, entering the Gulf. Some of us felt a slight queasiness, never having experienced the rolling and heaving motion of a ship at sea before. This feeling did not dissipate for most of us, but rather intensified. At mealtimes, some men affected by nausea would spew whatever they had just eaten over the rest of us, heightening our feelings of disgust and discomfort.

Mary recalled her trip down the Chesapeake Bay to Petersburg, Virginia, and the feeling not unlike morning sickness that had resulted.

Despite my protesting gizzard, I was able to gaze about as we sailed. The natural beauty of the waves, the sky, and the seabirds thrilled my soul. In the distance, I could see dark banks of clouds, a dire threat.

The main issue with shipboard life was not food, but space, or rather the lack of it. Because the hold was full of equipment and supplies being delivered to General Taylor, there was scarcely any place for our own supplies, nor for our men to lie down. Most of us actually had to take turns with the available sleeping spots, while others became extremely creative, sleeping in places not conducive to repose (such as atop the curled anchor chain).

During the voyage, the value of serving as an officer became apparent to us low-ranking volunteers. Officers slept in a cabin. They were served chicken, beef, higher quality pork, potatoes, raisin pudding, and they indulged in other luxuries served from bottles purchased at New Orleans. I thought that appetizing food might have overcome my seasickness, but was not sure that spirited drink would have set well at all.

I should mention that some of our men had been ill with measles and diarrhea before we even left Camp Jackson. While we were at sea, several of these died. For lack of better arrangements, they were sewn into their blankets and, after brief prayers were said, cast into the waves. One had not been properly weighted, and we could see him bobbing up and down until we had sailed into the distance. A sailor remarked that the unfortunate men's corpses would make good food for the fish.

    I should not disparage the sailors, as their skill and efforts undoubtedly saved our lives during this transit. Several of them treated us with merciful goodness, helping the sick find more comfortable space, and providing food as well as drink from their own rations. They taught me that rum has a surprisingly beneficial effect on a mildly distressed stomach.

    The threatening clouds I had observed descended upon us, delivering storms with torrential rains for three days and nights. At about 4 o'clock of the morning on the 22nd, the violent wind and waves shoved our ship onto a low sand bank one mile from a barely visible shore. The captain declared that every man on board would go to the bottom in five minutes, and none doubted that he was right. However, the longboat was hauled from beneath our supplies, and after many trips through a dangerous surf, all our men landed safely. We did, unfortunately, lose some provisions and camp equipment. It turned out that, blown off course, we had located twelve miles from Brazos Santiago Island. We camped there for five days. As soon as the waves calmed somewhat, two sailors and an officer boarded the longboat, and followed the shoreline in search of rescue. They were able to commandeer another ship to haul us to our proper destination. Upon arrival at dusk off Brazos Santiago Island, the ship's cannon gave notice that we approached, and the sailors cast anchor as near as was possible. The Captain went ashore to procure a smaller vessel to transfer us to shore, but he did not return until the following day.

    In the morning light, I beheld two islands that flanked the inlet to a wide bay that constituted the mouth of the river. Each island sported a beach backed by low, shifting hills of sand. All that was visible on Padre Island to our right, on the North side, was one hut with a chimney of barrels, half buried in driftage, curtained by hides flapping in the wind. The island that stretched South from the inlet, Brazos Santiago, seemed completely bare. There was no town, no grass, not a tree. It appeared that once again we would be building a camp from the ground up. We could not see that some of the volunteer army already present had begun this process on the West side of the dunes, where we would eventually dock. Across the bay, several miles to the Northwest rose a snow white tower, the lighthouse of Point Isabel, General Taylor's base of operation in the area.

We were taken ashore by a steamboat. As the clipper ship was much higher, we had to climb down the outside of our ship on a rope ladder, and jump over to the steamboat. This boat took us through the inlet to the Western side of Brazos Santiago Island, where we debarked with great relief.

Waiting there were Taylor's three and six month volunteers who were being discharged and sent home via the ships that delivered our company. Many of us wondered whether we would look like them in a year. A few seemed hale and hearty, but many appeared sickly, exhausted, and not a little grateful to be rid of the sandy shoreline where they had waited. Even so, some said they would re-enlist as soon as they reached home.

When we got ashore, we were led past previously established camps containing many thousands of men to our own designated area. After attending to our sick as well as we could, we pitched tents and drew rations for four days. These included the usual pickled pork, coffee, beans, salt, sugar, cornmeal, and flour. Additional foods such as fruit, bacon, and simple baked goods were available from sutlers at exorbitant prices. On that first day, we cooked, ate and relaxed for the first time in more than a week. We were able to safely bathe and rinse our clothing in the surf. If not for the constantly blowing sand in our eyes and food, life would have been rather enjoyable, as this is one of the most beautiful places I have ever seen. The constant, cooling breeze is a blessing, as we would be too warm in the sun without it.

Our company remained on Brazos Santiago Island for about a week, during which time we received our rifles and ammunition, then drilled and marched, while our officers decided whether and when we would be fit for duty on the shore.

When the order came to move out, on August 3rd, all the volunteers began transport across the bay at the rate of about one regiment per day. When it was our turn, we formed a long line of marching men, embarked and then debarked the steamboat onto the mainland. Our column passed many shops with hucksters as well as gambling houses. The prices seemed outrageous: 12 cents for a glass of ice water, 30 cents per pound for ice, 5 cents per sheet for this foolscap paper that I am writing on, 10 cents per pound for slightly better flour than our current rations, $1.50 per pound for tobacco, 20 cents per pound for bacon, 25 cents for one tin cup. We proceeded up the Rio Grande to Camp Barita, soon renamed Camp Belknap for our Inspector-General, but located across the river from the miserable little town of Barita. Barita consists of some thirty huts formerly occupied by Mexicans. The huts resemble our one-story pig pens in Indiana, but are not half so substantial.

Along the way, an American soldier was observed floating down the Rio Grande, dead. He was brought to shore and a thimble was found in his pocket, but no papers or anything revealing his name. We said a fast prayer over him, and interred him beside the road.

Camp Belknap seemed a fairly decent location at first, in a thicket of thorny mesquite bushes, or chaparral, about one mile from the river. But no one had warned us about the Mexican ants. These critters are large, robust, with strong jaws ready for the attack. They seemed as hostile as the human Mexicans, and for the same reasons - we have invaded their territory. Before many days had passed, most of the ant nests had been shovelled out and destroyed. The human Mexican "greasers" can look forward to the same treatment from our troops.

We have no fuel for cooking except the chaparral. The volunteer army is encamped along the banks for ten miles, including regiments from Indiana, Ohio, Mississippi, Georgia, and other states. If they all remain here long, the bushes will all be cut down, leaving very few to shade us from the burning sun.

The rainy season here began in May, and should end in another month or so. There has been a rise in the Rio Grande and the plain between it and our encampment is overflowed, so that we can not obtain any water to drink without wading a muddy pond half a mile wide. There is still considerable sickness among the volunteers, and the dead march is heard nearly every day.

Our food is abominable; when I break a biscuit, I can see it move (if the critters are not dead from being toasted). The pork and bacon are disgusting. We would not mind this so much, if they would only supply us enough. If not for the wild beef we shoot, we should starve.

Our daily schedule consists of the morning company drill at 7 o'clock for two hours; at 5 o'clock is a regimental drill of two hours. Besides that, there is water to be carried, ground to be cleared and other tasks too tedious to mention.

It has developed that the 1st Indiana Regiment will, on orders from General Taylor, return to Brazos Santiago Island to guard our rear. Those boys are NOT happy. Rear guard duty presents precious little opportunity for the glorious heroics of war. Brazos' location makes it crucial to supplying and supporting General Zachary Taylor's troops, protecting us against attack from the rear. Our regiment, the 3rd Indiana, is supposed to remain here, at Camp Belknap, until the end of August. Then we should move to Camargo, our place of rendezvous with General Taylor. From there, we hope to join the march toward Monterrey.

I expect to begin training with the flying artillery while here. This will consist of driving a horse-drawn wagon bearing cannon around a battlefield area. Once the wagon is parked, two of us will manage the horses, while the rest load, aim and fire the cannon. Very exciting, under real conditions, as we would be at risk from enemy fire the whole time. The main advantage is that we would not have to march for miles, carrying thirty pounds of gear on our backs; we can throw our stuff onto the wagon during travel.

When I'm able, I will write again, but until then, I will anxiously await letters from you!

With Much Love,
Your Husband,
George

On August 18th, **United States** forces under Colonel Stephen Watts Kearny occupied Santa Fé, New Mexico. **Kearny was soon promoted to Brigadier General.**

Next day, **United States** troops under Zachary Taylor advanced from Camargo toward Cerralvo, Mexico.

The September heat faded into a cooler October, and Mary sought out Caroline on market day to hear Georgie's most recent letter:

Tuesday, September 15, 1846
Third Regiment, Company K
Camp Belknap, Mexico

Precious Caroline,

I live in hope that another of your letters will reach me; I am grateful that you receive my missives, albeit long after I have written them. Please exercise special care so that Little Hoke will survive all the common illnesses, for I long desperately to see him on my return.

I finally caught sight of General Taylor! He visited Camp Belknap about two weeks ago, assessing our readiness for battle. While here, "Old Rough and Ready" observed our training session with the artillery wagons and rode slowly past our column with our officers, seemingly deep in discussion with them. He is the least military in appearance of all the soldiers here. He had uniform pants and tall boots, but over his shirt wore a linen duster, a straw hat on his head. He reminds me of an old farmer from Clinton County, but we all trust that he knows a thing or two about battle.

Taylor has established his new headquarters for the Army of Occupation at Cerralvo, about halfway between Camargo and Monterrey. It seems that the Indiana regiments are his back-up troops, for use as a last resort. If he attacks Monterrey, it would take us more than a week to get there, so we would have plenty of warning.

We received news today that has spread like wildfire through the troops – only time will tell whether there is truth to the story. It seems that the Mexican expatriate general, Santa Anna, has arrived at Veracruz, through the United States naval blockade. It remains to be seen whether he will work with or against us. All are rather anxious at the thought of doing battle against the famous Mexican general.

It has just been announced that letters for home are being collected, so I must sign off in haste--

With Undying Love,
George

*The former Mexican general, Santa Anna, proved to be the sort of person who would promise anything to anyone in order to get what he wanted. After returning from exile in Cuba to Mexico with United States assistance, he arrived in Mexico City, offering his services to the Mexican government. Then, after being appointed commanding general, he seized the presidency and marched against the United States at the head of the Mexican army. Essentially, he broke the promises he had made to the **United States** (to sell Northern Mexican lands at a reasonable price), as well as to his own country (that he had no interest in political power there).*

*El Presidente Generalissimo Santa Anna sent orders to General Pedro de Ampudia to retreat from Monterrey, Mexico to the city of Saltillo, in order to establish a defensive line against the **United States** troops. Ampudia disobeyed, sensing glory if he could stop Taylor's advance. Ampudia's forces at Monterrey included over 3,000 reinforcements sent from Mexico City, and totaled about 10,000 men.*

***United States** Army General Zachary Taylor departed from his camp at Marin on September 18th, headed for Monterrey. The Indiana troops remained behind – the 1st Regiment at Brazos Santiago, the 2nd and 3rd at Camp Belknap.*

Throughout the late summer and early fall, the officers of Indiana's troops had tried to get their volunteers moved to the forefront of the action, with no success. Many of them, especially those of the 1st Regiment, came to believe that their service was deemed unnecessary by their superior officers.

What most Indiana soldiers did not realize was that their officers were very busy playing political games, wrangling for power. Whether a particular commander's troops were called into battle was often determined by whom he knew, rather than by what he knew.

September 22-30 saw the Siege of Los Angeles, led by General José María Flores, where Californeros and Mexicans retook Los Angeles, California from United States occupation.

The city of Monterrey, well-fortified and well-supplied, had been considered "impregnable." Because the city was defended by Mexican troops concentrated and "dug in" at various points, Taylor used a variety of tactics to surround them, tunnel through adobe walls, and force their surrender in three days, between September 20th and 24th.

The resulting armistice signed between Generals Taylor and Ampudia had major effects upon the outcome of the war. Taylor was lambasted by some in the federal government, where President Polk insisted that army personnel had no authority to negotiate truces, only to "kill the enemy." In addition, Taylor's terms of armistice, which allowed Ampudia's forces to retreat with battle honors and all of their weapons, were seen as foolish and short-sighted by some **United States** observers, since those men and weapons would undoubtedly be used again to fight the **United States** invasion. The result for Taylor was that President Polk resolved to shift management of the war from him to General Winfield Scott.

The planet Neptune had been mathematically predicted by Urbain Le Verrier before it was directly observed. On the night of September 23rd, working from Le Verrier's calculations, astronomer Johann Gottfried Galle (assisted by Heinrich Louis d'Arrest) discovered Neptune by telescopic observation at the Berlin Observatory. It turned out that Neptune had been observed many times before, but not recognized as a planet. The discovery of Neptune led to the discovery of its moon Triton by William Lassell seventeen days later.

Altercations between Mexican and United States citizens continued throughout California. On September 26th – 27th, at the Battle of Chino, the Californeros defeated and captured twenty-four Americans, led by Benjamin D. Wilson, who were hiding in an adobe house in Rancho Santa Ana del Chino, near present-day Chino, California.

On October 7th, the Californeros, led by José Antonio Carrillo, defeated 203 **United States** Marines led by **United States** Navy Captain William Mervine at the Battle of Dominguez Rancho.

Miami Indians had in 1840 promised to leave Indiana by 1845, but removal had been delayed. Over 600 of them remained on their ancestral lands. As canal construction through North and central Indiana progressed, Indiana government officials decided that the Miami presented an obstacle to development of the area.

Joseph deRichardville had previously negotiated land grants to individual Miami families, and also had offered his private property as a refuge for other Miami. This allowed about half of the 600 Miami people to legally remain.

However, on October 6th, over 100 other members of the tribe with their baggage were loaded onto three canal boats at Peru, and proceeded to Ft. Wayne via the Wabash & Erie Canal.   At Ft. Wayne, additional Miami and baggage were added, plus more boats, and the expedition proceeded by canal into Ohio, then by canal to Cincinnati. From there, they were transported by steamboat to Kansas City, then to Kansas, arriving at their reservation on Nov 9th.

329 Miami began the trip, and there were six deaths before arrival. This represented less hardship than the Potawatomi removal in 1838, but Indiana's treatment of Native Americans remains an ugly stain on the state's history.

On October 24th-26th, **United States** *Commodore Matthew C. Perry occupied Tabasco, on the Mexican coast. He then withdrew his troops, resulting in an inconclusive victory.*

In early November, Indiana Governor Whitcomb was re-elected, beating Joseph G. Marshall, the Whig Candidate, by 3,958 votes.

During that same month, the **United States** *Congress issued an additional call for volunteers. In all, 26,922 regulars and 73,260 volunteers served at some point during the Mexican War. The regulars were largely immigrants, the poor, and those who had few other options for employment in the private sector. The volunteers, due to their lack of training, discipline, and of fighting experience, were denigrated by regulars. Soldiers in camp sought various means by which to reduce their boredom. Some attended Mexican fandangos where they sought the company of young women. Some found solace in drink, and this often led to* violations of military rules. Soldiers committing offenses faced court martial proceedings, but the Articles of War gave the courts considerable leeway in assessing penalties.

Officers during the Mexican war consisted of older, experienced men as well as younger, well-trained West Point graduates. Of 523 West Point graduates who served in the Mexican-American war, 432 received battlefield promotions or awards for bravery.

On November 14th, the **United States** Navy occupied Tampico, Tamaulipas located on the Eastern Mexican coast, in preparation for the eventual invasion of Mexico City.

It was a cold November day when Caroline with Little Holk stopped at Mary and Bram's house for a visit, bearing what turned out to be Georgie's final letter from Mexico:

Thursday, October 15, 1846
Third Regiment, Company K
Camp Belknap, Mexico

Dearest Darling Caroline,

As you can see from the above, we are still stationed near Barita. We were not called to assist General Taylor with his conquest of Monterrey. He seems to be doing just fine without the help of Indiana regiments.
Two weeks ago, our troops were sent on maneuvers to Matamoros, and two of our companies to Reynosa, then to Palo Alto, but we all have returned here. Perhaps the intent was to make the Mexicans think that we are more numerous and more mobile than is actually the case. Some of the locations were much drier than here, and the health of our men started to improve. Now that we have returned, we have been assigned to build more permanent bunks for the sick, in order to get them off the muddy ground. This had the effect of helping many of them recover somewhat, and I think that if our stock of medicines was replenished, even more would regain their health.

We have buried at least 100 Indiana men here, and for what? We would very likely not have lost more in battle, and at least those lost would have counted for something.

Most of our days are filled with incredible boredom. Perhaps I am just discouraged, but I fail to understand how sitting in the mud and dying of disease is gaining our country more than a few additional acres of barren wasteland.

When I contemplate the remaining months of my enlistment, I cannot help but wish there were some way to return home sooner. If there is a way, I will find it!

*Yours forever,
George*

November 16th saw the Battle of Natividad in the Salinas Valley of Northern California, an American victory.

On the same day, the **United States** Army under General Taylor occupied Saltillo, Coahuila, Mexico.

By December 5th, the 3rd Indiana Regiment embarked by steamboat for Camargo. Once there, they broke "wild mules" to harness, then proceeded to Monterrey and Saltillo by land, arriving by the end of this month. They were soon followed by the 2nd and 1st Indiana Regiments, but differing orders from various commanding officers threatened to send them back to Brazos Santiago Island. Frustrated and disgusted by long inaction, the Indiana troops ignored orders and proceeded into the Mexican interior.

On December 6th, the Californeros and Presidial Lancers of Mexico defeated Brigadier General Stephen Watts Kearny at the Battle of San Pasqual (near present-day San Diego, California), inflicting heavy casualties.

Mid-December brought a major storm to the Ohio Valley, affecting Indiana residents as far North as Clinton County. Up to twelve inches of snow and ice fell across the region. As it melted, the area was awash in inches of liquid during the week before Christmas. During the holiday week itself, three to five inches of rain interfered with most holiday plans.

Everyone had retired for the evening at Norris House on Christmas night except for Mary. She had remained behind the rest of the family, straightening the rooms and putting away utensils from the large dinner she had served. Hearing a faint knock at the front door, she opened it, and was astonished when Georgie Norris stumbled across the threshold.

"I'm home!" he gasped. "Tell Caroline..."

Mary caught his arm, then supported him toward a sofa, where she helped him lie down. Then she ran to the bedroom, rousting Bram.

Assessing the situation, Bram made an executive decision: "You'll stay here tonight," he told Georgie. "We'll get you home in the morning!"

Georgie appeared too weak to argue with his step-brother, although Mary could tell that he desperately wanted to get home immediately. She and Bram cared for Georgie, replacing his wet clothing and warming him by the fire, feeding him bread, turkey broth, and a judicious amount of whiskey.

Even though exhausted, Georgie wanted to talk. His story poured forth, interrupted only by painful coughs soothed by additional sips of whiskey.

"I've left the best friends I ever knew," he said. "We went through Hell together. There is no place like the army to show what a man really is – all the best and worst of his soul."

Perhaps fearing that Georgie had deserted, Bram asked, "How did you get home?"

"I was discharged December 10th on a surgeon's certificate," his step-brother responded. "I had the bloody flux. I was at Camargo, and embarked on a steamboat bound for the mouth of the Rio Grande. From Brazos Santiago, I took passage on a sailing vessel for New Orleans, arriving there a few days later. I then reembarked on a steamboat that took me to Lawrenceburg. I got part way home by canal boat, the rest of the way by wagon; I walked here from the Michigan Road. The closer I got to home, the better I felt, until the walking part. I'm beat..."

"Just rest," said Bram. "You'll see your family soon!"

Next morning, after a breakfast of hot cornmeal mush cooked with chunks of apples, Georgie felt well enough to ride home on horseback escorted by Bram and Burr.

On December 16th, the Mormon Battalion captured Tuscon, Sonora (later Arizona). The Mormons soon continued their nearly 2,000 mile march from

Council Bluffs, Iowa to San Diego, thus establishing the first Southern wagon route to California.

On Christmas Day, Colonel Alexander William Doniphan's 1st Mounted Missouri volunteer regiment of 500 men was en route to rendezvous with General John E. Wool inside Mexico at Chihuahua. Doniphan had halted his unit at 1 o'clock in the afternoon at El Brazito on the Rio Grande, when his men spotted a dust cloud caused by a Mexican scouting party to the South.

Before long, 1,200 Mexicans under the command of Major Antonio Ponce de Leon arrived, consisting of the Chihuahua infantry on the left, the El Paso militia with a howizer in the center, and the Veracruz lancers on the right.

In parley, Ponce de Leon demanded American surrender.

"Charge and be damned!" responded Doniphan.

His men had used the parley delay to fully form their battle line. Then the Mexicans attacked. Doniphan ordered his troops to hold their fire until the Mexicans came within easy range. At 50 yards, the Americans opened fire with rifles and muskets; the Mexicans fled. Mexican lancers next attacked Doniphan's wagon train, but were driven off by the teamsters. The Mexican force retreated after Ponce de Leon was wounded, abandoning their howitzer, which Leiutenant Nicholas B. Wright's company recovered. As the Mexican forces fell back, they were harassed by Apache natives who had been watching the battle.

The Mexicans lost forty-three killed and one hundred and fifty wounded; the Americans lost seven wounded, who all recovered.

Doniphan's men reached El Paso on December 27th, where they seized from the Mexicans five tons of powder, 500 arms, 400 lances and four artillery pieces.

On December 28th, Iowa became the 29th state.

1847

As far as the United States was concerned, the Mexican-American war continued to be the most important and newsworthy topic of this year. Battles continued in California, in what is now New Mexico, as well as within the borders of current day Mexico.

Early in January, **United States** General Winfield Scott (known to his men as "Old Fuss and Feathers," due to his extreme attention to his appearance) took charge of General Zachary Taylor's best (most experienced) 8,000 troops. He would use Taylor's troops to besiege Veracruz on the Mexican coast, then to invade Mexico, marching West to attack Mexico City. Taylor assumed that removing his men was a political move ordered by officials in Washington, D.C., done in order to "mortify" him.

Mexican Generalissio Santa Anna discovered, through an intercepted letter from Scott, that Taylor had lost more than half of his troops, and resolved to take advantage of the situation. Taylor's remaining 6,000 men included only a few hundred experienced regular army soldiers; the rest had never seen battle. When Taylor did not retreat toward the Texas-Mexico border, but continued Southwest into Mexico from Saltillo, Santa Anna prepared an attack.

There was a smaller Miami Indian removal from Indiana during this year, but fewer than one-half of the Miami tribe stayed in the West because many returned to live with relatives who never immigrated. As a result, those remaining in Indiana constituted a majority of the tribe.

However, those Miami who remained in Oklahoma gained **United States** federal recognition as an independent nation, while the Eastern Miami of Indiana have been repeatedly denied that legal designation, along with any potential resulting benefits.

For Indiana, transportation continued as a primary political and economic issue during this year. The Central Canal at Indianapolis, as projected in the internal improvements act of 1836, was to connect with the Wabash and Erie Canal at Peru, go up the Mississinewa Valley to Marion, to the valley of the West Fork of White River, through Anderson and Indianapolis and finally to Evansville. Work had begun on various portions of this project, but only twenty miles between Broad Ripple, Indianapolis and Waverly were ever completed. Several years of state operation of this section had brought no profit, only an ongoing battle between the government and the lessees.

The Central Canal project ended during this year with a disastrous flood which swept away the Fall Creek aqueduct. In 1881, an eight mile section of the canal between Broad Ripple and Indianapolis was acquired by the Indianapolis Water Company. The Central Canal then became an important part of the city's water system.

Later, part of the Central Canal was repurposed as a park with accompanying Canal Walk, stretching several miles through the heart of Indianapolis, designed for kayaks, pedal boats, and pedestrians.

Growth of railroads during and after this year was rapid, due to the beginning of private company financing. The Chicago, Indianapolis & Louisville Railway, known commonly as the Monon, remained entirely a Hoosier entity. It was chartered during this year as the New Albany & Salem Railroad and in 1859 became the Louisville, New Albany & Chicago. It was the first to connect the Ohio River and Lake Michigan, carrying Northbound coal and other commodities until its acquisition and closing in 1971.

Indiana volunteers were finally allowed to see action in Mexico. Georgie was especially pleased to read that his former regiment, the 3rd Indiana, was brought to the front lines during the Battle of Buena Vista on February 23rd. This fight, one of the largest of the Mexican-American war, between General Taylor's 6,000 troops and 20,000 men under Santa Anna was held South of Saltillo, Mexico. It was the only battle in which the Iniana volunteers of 1846 got to participate. Santa Anna seemed to be winning until he received word of a civil uprising in Mexico City; he suddenly abandoned the field. Both Generals claimed victory, but at the end of the day, Taylor remained in position, with far fewer dead and wounded than Santa Anna. Santa Anna claimed to have halted the **United States** army's advance.

Unfortunately, General Taylor made a mis-informed and mis-interpreted charge of cowardice against the 2nd Indiana regiment. He apparently saw some Indiana regimental colors left behind on the battlefield. During the battle, part of that regiment was given an order to retreat. When another portion of the regiment saw them leaving the field, they followed, assuming that they could not have heard the order. Quite naturally this controversy attracted a great deal of attention in the state. The controversy over the conduct of the Second regiment was long and bitter. Buena Vista was fought over time and again in the newspapers of Indiana, and Taylor's charge of cowardice against the Second was made the paramount issue in the presidential campaign of 1848.

The Indiana troops were so defiant of Taylor's opinion, and so proud of their role in this battle, that they adopted a motto/battle cry, "Indiana Forever!" Of course, Indiana officers developed their own political squabbles, a result of the differing reports from this battle.

It seemed as if Clinton County avoided the main Indiana issues of this year, for the most part. No canals were ever planned or constructed through it. The Clinton Boys did not join the war effort until October. No Miami Indians resided in the county. And railroads had not yet reached the county.

But to Mary, the most important event of the year was the wedding of her daughter, Altha, to David Maish on Thursday, February 4th. Altha had requested that only close family attend, and a Justice of the Peace came to the house for a brief ceremony, followed by a wedding supper. David had worked hard at various jobs to earn enough money to buy his own 160 acre farm, where he had constructed a log cabin, later replaced by a farmhouse. The couple moved in, facing the winter cold together. Altha became pregnant within a few days of the wedding.

Georgie, however, remained ill with bloody diarrhea and occasional vomiting. His health would improve temporarily, then regress into intense discomfort. To make matters worse, his wife Caroline seemed to be coming down with the same condition, and the two were quite miserable. Little Holk went to live with Georgie's brother Will, in the hope that Holk would be spared the seemingly contagious condition, as well as to give his mother a break from caring for him.

On February 28th, Colonel Alexander William Doniphan's regiment defeated a larger Mexican force at the Sacramento River Pass on his way to invade Chihuahua.

Beginning on March 9th with Marine landings, **United States** forces under General Winfield Scott besieged and gradually encircled Mexican marines and their coast guard in a vicious twenty-day attack on the port city of Veracruz in order to invade Mexico. Veracruz was at that time one of the strongest fortifications in the Western Hemisphere. After three days and nights of shelling by American cannon, as a result of receiving no support from Santa Anna, Veracruz surrendered on March 27th.

On March 21[st,] Santa Anna resumed the presidency of Mexico.

During this spring, an anti-war movement in the United States gained strength, as Whigs increasingly questioned Polk's motivation for and conduct of the war. The Mexican War became a hot political issue for the coming presidential election of 1848. Abe Lincoln called Polk "Young Hickory," and defied him to show the spot on the map where Mexicans shed American blood on American soil. Lincoln's opposition to the Mexican War aroused public sentiment against him, and helped to limit his congressional service to one term.

Mary again heard Lincoln's name mentioned, and wondered whether she would ever be able to verify that he was the child who helped her so long ago.

Mid-April saw the Battle of Cerro Gordo Pass in Mexico. Dubbed the "Thermopylae of the West," this battle has since been used as an example of a patriotic army defending its native soil.

El Presidente Generalissimo Santa Anna chose the location, fifty miles inland from Veracruz, East of Xalapa, to defend Mexico City against General Winfield Scott's advancing army. The terrain seemed to be in Santa Anna's favor: Three high hills controlled by 12,000 Mexicans with cannon guarded the most direct path to Mexico City.

But Lieutenant Pierre G.T. Beauregard and Captain Robert E. Lee of the **United States** Army Corps of Engineers determined that possession of the higher, unguarded Atalaya Hill could enable the Mexican position to be turned. After five nights of constructing pathways and hoisting cannon to the heights under cover of darkness, the Americans took the hill which had been considered to be impregnable by Santa Anna. In the meantime, Colonel Bennet C. Riley made his way to the rear of the Mexican forces with the 2nd **United States** Infantry.

At 7 A.M. on April 18th, the Americans opened fire. Mexican General Vasquez was killed, and **United States** Captain John B. Magruder turned the captured Mexican cannon on the retreating Mexicans. Simultaneously, James Shields' brigade attacked the Mexican camp and took possession of the Xalapa road. Once they realized they were surrounded, the Mexican commanders on the three hills surrendered and the remaining Mexican forces fled by 10:00 A.M.

Generalissimo Santa Anna, caught off guard by the 4th Illinois Volunteer Infantry while he was lunching on roast chicken, was compelled to flee without the carriage that contained his artificial leg. The American sergeant who grabbed the cork leg from the carriage later exhibited it at county fairs for a dime a peek. Since 1922 the leg has been the property of the Illinois National Guard and has been displayed at the Illinois State Military Museum in Springfield, Illinois. Santa Anna had a replacement leg made which resides at the Museo Nacional de Historia in Mexico City.

Santa Anna's real leg had been amputated near Veracruz after he was hit by cannon fire while fighting the invading French in 1838. In 1842, he ordered the shriveled leg to be interred in a Mexico City monument with full military honors including cannon salvos, poetry and lofty orations. But in 1844, an angry crowd tore down Santa Anna's statues and dug up his leg. They tied the severed appendage to a rope and dragged it through the streets of Mexico City while shouting, "Death to the cripple!"

On April 21st, the Sons of Temperance Chapter, Clinton Division #73 was founded at Frankfort. The Grand Division also decided on this date not to issue charters to colored persons or to initiate colored persons into existing charters.

Mary's family always had alcoholic drinks in the house, and of course, wine was used as part of holy sacraments. In addition, whiskey was quite useful when anyone was sick or injured. She understood that many people destroyed their lives by over-consumption, but she considered prohibiting its sale to be stupid, a waste of energy. She and Bram agreed that what they drank within their own house was no one else's affair, and Bram was able to easily access spirits whenever he traveled to Lawrenceburg or Indianapolis.

The Clinton Boys did not as a unit answer the call for duty in Mexico on Apr 24th, when an additional ten companies of infantry were called to create the 4th Indiana Volunteer Regiment. A handful of Clinton County men served by enlisting in the companies formed in other counties, as Georgie had done.

Dearborn County, on the other hand, sent two companies. Company C became known as the Dearborn County Guards, while Company K was called the Hoosier Boys of Dearborn.

Mary heard news tinged with gossip from Bram, who had just returned from Indianapolis in early June. Henry Ward Beecher had moved in 1839 from pastoring the 1st Presbyterian Church at Lawrenceburg to the 2nd Presbyterian Church at Indianapolis. Bram had heard rumors that Beecher was quite the ladies' man. He and Mary speculated whether the man's relocation was motivated by increase in pay or by fear of retribution for his extramarital affairs, or both.

Beecher had served as chairman of a committee planning the Indiana State Common School Convention, held May 26th-28th at Indianapolis. At that time, there was no law requiring Indiana parents to send their children to school. Reports published after the convention revealed that fewer than one-half of youths between the ages of five and twenty-one years attended school for as much as three months per year. Bram and the other Norrises were dismayed by this information, and resolved to improve school attendance in their local area.

In June, the term of enlistment of the 3rd Indiana Regiment expired. The men with their officers, including Colonel James Henry Lane, returned to Indiana.

On June 16th, **United States** *Commodore Perry, in the second Battle of Tabasco, captured Villahermosa, the last unconquered port city on the Mexican Gulf coast.*

On July 26, in West Africa, Liberia proclaimed its independence from the American Colonization Society.

August 10th saw the Battle of Churubusco, where regular Mexican troops and the San Patricio's Battalion under Manuel Rincón held a fortified monastery against General Winfield Scott's forces. Over half of the San Patricios were killed or captured (then either branded on their faces with a "D" for deserter, or else executed by hanging); the rest retreated with the remaining the Mexican forces in the area.

On August 27th, Indiana Governor Whitcomb issued a proclamation for Colonel James Henry Lane to raise a 5th Indiana Volunteer Infantry regiment. David Reynolds, as Adjutant General of the Indiana Militia, gave an order specifying in great detail the terms of service, no doubt based on experience gained during the previous year after he had issued a similar order with much looser terminology. Certain preferences were given to soldiers who chose to re-up after serving during the 1846-47 enlistment period. The process again took about nineteen days, less than three weeks to complete enlistments.

Colonel Lane, by the authority of the president, then organized from all parts of the State the 5th Regiment Indiana Volunteers. Company G of this regiment, from Dearborn County, became known as the "Grabbers."

The place of rendezvous was Madison, Indiana where Lane was again elected Colonel. The men were at once ordered to the front and soon joined the main army of General Scott at the City of Mexico. This regiment, together with the 4th, remained in the service until peace was declared.

The Clinton Boys did not as a group answer the call on Aug 31st for the 5th Indiana Volunteer Infantry.

September 12th-13th saw the Battle for Mexico City, or "Battle of Chapultepec." Etched into Mexico's history is the tale of Los Niños Héroes, six teenage military cadets who refused to flee the American force, and died defending their posts. One is believed to have wrapped himself in the Mexican flag before jumping from the top of Chapultepec Castle to his death. Some captured San Patricios were executed by **United States** soldiers during this battle.

On September 15th, the US Army occupied Mexico City. On the 16th, El Presidente Generalissimo Santa Anna fled, escaping Mexico to Guatemala, then sailing to exile in Kingston, Jamaica.

The 5th Indiana Regiment, while yet in Mexico, held a meeting of its officers and men and voted to obtain for their Colonel, James Henry Lane, a sword to cost $1,000. The funds were placed in the hands of a committee, which purchased the sword and presented it to Lane on his return from the war.

On October 1st, at 3:00 P.M., the first steam locomotive train arrived in Indianapolis from Madison, Indiana – eighty-six miles away. A crowd gathered to see the train, and Governor Whitcomb gave a speech. Henry Ward Beecher, leaving Indianapolis after eight years as minister of the 2nd Presbyterian Church, took the return trip to Madison. The train car consisted of a wood box with wooden seats; people sometimes brought their horses along.

On October 9th, Colonel James Henry Lane gave an hour-long speech to the citizens of Greenfield, Indiana, advocating the "justice" of the Mexican American War, urging its speedy and successful completion. He claimed there were many men in the United States enjoying the blessings of liberty who were "Mexicans at heart," who were opposing the war for political gain. He described the hardships of a soldier s life, but stated that one year of camp life was worth five of inactive civil life. He contradicted the "unfounded statement" that the climate in Mexico was detrimental to health. He claimed that Mexico had the most pleasant and congenial climate in the world and that all reports to the contrary were circulated by persons opposed to the war.   When Bram read excerpts of this speech to Mary from a news sheet, she decided that Col. Lane's mind must have been affected by the Mexican climate. Rumor had it that Lane suffered from a similar ailment to Georgie's. Lane later moved to Kansas, and was a partisan during the Bleeding Kansas period that immediately preceded the Civil War. Lane became known in Kansas as "the Grim Chieftain," as well as "Bloody Jim." During the Civil War itself, Lane served as a United States Senator and as a general for the Union Army. Although reelected as a Senator during 1865, Lane committed suicide the next year.

A small number of Clinton County men (including Bram's cousin Joseph Norris in Company C) volunteered with Company I of the 5th Indiana Regiment, and on October 31st left "Camp Reynolds" at Madison, Indiana for New Orleans, then Veracruz, Mexico. Most fighting had ended by this time, and the regiment performed garrison duty until the end of the Mexican-American War four months later.

On November 8th, Mary was awakened before dawn by pounding at the front door, and by a man's voice calling. Bram wakened instantly, and ran to admit his desperate son-in-law, David Maish. Hastily pulling on a robe, Mary heard David's voice, "Please, Altha needs her mother – she is ready to have our child!"

Bram hastened to fetch and saddle Mary's horse, while Mary got dressed. Having given birth so many times, and having assisted other mothers in their deliveries, she felt able to help Altha with this delivery. Within a few hours, Altha had a new baby boy, William, who appeared strong and healthy.

During the fall, the Indiana Legislature passed a local option bill allowing voters in a argued that temperance legislation was a dangerous union of church and state, a meddlesome threat to individual liberty. Presbyterians advocated crusades against alcohol, which eventually attracted a large majority of Hoosiers.

Also during this fall, the Ohio River Valley weather combined heavy rain and rapidly melting snow to create flooding on a large scale. Brookville, Indiana was nearly wiped away, while Dayton, Ohio sustained major damage. On December 17th, the Ohio River at Louisville crested at 68.8', the 10th highest stage on record.

1848

In January, former slave Frederick Douglass wrote: "Mexico seems a doomed victim to Anglo Saxon...love of dominion...The determination of our slaveholding President to prosecute the war, and the probability of his success...is made evident...by the puny opposition arrayed against him."

Mid January weather brought another two to three inches of rain to the Ohio River Valley, raising fears of another catastrophic flood, but the remainder of the winter remained drier than normal.

On January 24, gold nuggets were found by James W. Marshall at Sutter's Mill in Coloma, California. Although Marshall tried to keep the discovery secret, word got out. Within the next few years, the lure of gold brought about 300,000 people to the state.

Wooden plank road construction began this year in Indiana, continuing through1855, when the effort was replaced by railroad construction. The Wabash & Erie Canal was complete to Lafayette, Delphi, and Thorndon. When the canal boat came to town, the mariners blew horns to summon the populace.

During this year, the Independent Order of Odd Fellows purchased and opened a cemetery in Frankfort. Because this charitable organization existed partly to provide burial arrangements for widows, orphans and the poor, this facility allowed the group to carry out that portion of their mission.

On February 2nd, **United States** negotiators led by Executive Agent Nicholas Trist signed the Treaty of Guadalupe Hidalgo, the official end to the Mexican-American War. The treaty was rushed to Washington, where President Polk, furious over the lenient terms of the agreement, signed it. Polk then fired Trist for insubordination, and refused to pay Trist any wages after October, 1847, when Polk had attempted to recall Trist, wanting to force a more aggressive diplomatic agenda.

In Italy, on February 8th, a street riot extorted the promise of a lay ministry from the Pope and on March 14th he saw himself obliged to grant a constitution. Riot followed riot. The Pope was denounced as a traitor to his country. His prime minister Rossi was stabbed to death while ascending the steps of the Cancelleria, where he had gone to open the parliament. On the following day the Pope himself was besieged in the Quirinal. Palma, a papal prelate, who was standing at a window, was shot, and the Pope was forced to promise a democratic ministry. With the assistance of the Bavarian ambassador, Count Spaur, and the French ambassador, Duc d'Harcourt, Pius IX escaped from the Quirinal in disguise on November 24th. He fled to Gaëta where he was joined by many of the cardinals. Meanwhile, Rome was ruled by "traitors and adventurers."

On February 21, Joseph Norris was discharged after four months' service in the Army. In early spring, his family held a "Welcome Home" party, and Mary attended with Bram. She was shocked at the change in this formerly robust and cheerful young man, who was now pale and serious in demeanor. He had only been gone for a few months, but she feared that he would never be the same, as was true of many former soldiers she had seen.

Two days later, on February 23rd, President Polk sent the Treaty of Guadalupe Hidalgo to Congress.

On March 6th, a truce officially ended formal hostilities between Mexico and the United States, awaiting the ratification of the Treaty of Guadalupe Hidalgo. However, due to the lack of reliable communications over the region, cessation of hostilities was spotty until August. Mexican partisans continued to resist the **United States** Army of Occupation. Attacks, skirmishes, and other action continued until everyone had heard about the agreements, and the Mexican guerrilla units were eventually crushed by the Mexican Army under terms of the truce.

On March 10th, the treaty was ratified by the **United States** Senate.

The spring season had proceeded beautifully in Clinton County. In early May, a new church bell was installed at the Methodist Church, and was used for the first time on Sunday, May 7th. Mary considered the bell to be a vast improvement over the tin horn that had previously called worshipers to church. It was rung joyously on Thursday, May 18th, when Bram's step-sister, Lucretia married a Scots-German, William Finley Lee, who had been born in Pennsylvania.

On May 25th, the Treaty of Guadalupe Hidalgo was ratified by the Mexican Congress.

On May 29th, Wisconsin became the 30th state.

On Jun 12th, **United States** *troops left Mexico City*

On July 4th, the ratified treaty arrived in Washington, D.C.

On July 19 – 20, at Seneca Falls, New York, the first Women's Rights Convention was held, to discuss the social, civil, and religious conditions and rights of women. A heated debate sprang up regarding women's right to vote, with many urging the removal of this concept, but Frederick Douglass argued eloquently for its inclusion, and the suffrage resolution was retained. Exactly 100 of approximately 300 attendees signed the document, mostly women. Indiana, however, continued to deny women equal rights (such as equal job opportunities) with men in many categories until well into the 20th century, with some equal rights (especially reproductive control over their own bodies and equal pay for equal work) not granted as of the 21st century.

On July 28th, the 5th Indiana Regiment arrived at Madison, Indiana from Mexico, and mustered out.

During the Mexican-American War, the participation of a large number of graduates from the United States Military Academy had worked in favor of the **United States** Army. These officers, mostly lieutenants and captains, formed a tight knit corps whose leadership ability and training helped offset the initial shortage of manpower. These men included George G. Meade, Ulysses S. Grant, George B. McClellan, P.G.T. Beauregard, Braxton Bragg, Joseph E. Johnston, and Robert E. Lee, who served as prominent officers during the Civil War.

Since 1848, Native Americans and Mexican Americans have struggled to achieve political and social equality within the United States, often citing the Treaty of Guadalupe Hidalgo as a document that promised civil and property rights. Although the treaty promised **United States** citizenship to former Mexican citizens, the Native Americans in the ceded territories, who in fact had been Mexican citizens, were not given full **United States** citizenship until the 1930s. Former Mexican citizens were almost universally considered foreigners by **United States** settlers who moved into the new territories. In the first fifty years after ratification of the Treaty of Guadalupe Hidalgo, hundreds of state, territorial, and federal legal bodies produced a complex tapestry of conflicting opinions and decisions concerning the meaning of the treaty. The property rights guaranteed in Articles VIII and IX of the treaty (and in the Protocol of Queretaro) were not all they seemed. In **United States** courts, the property rights of former Mexican citizens in California, New Mexico, and Texas proved to be fragile. Within a generation Mexican-Americans became a disenfranchised, poverty-stricken minority.

In November, four political parties vied for their nominees to become **United States** President. These were Zachary Taylor, Whig; Lewis Cass, Democratic; Martin Van Buren, Free Soil; and Gerrit Smith, of the Liberty party. With 47.3% of the popular vote, Taylor triumphed, becoming the last Whig President to take office.

Before his second term as Indiana Governor ended, James Whitcomb was elected to the **United States** Senate, and resigned as Governor December 26th. By skillfully guiding the state through its bankruptcy as well as through the Mexican-American War, Whitcomb is usually credited as being one of the most successful of Indiana's governors. He also convinced most Hoosiers of the importance of establishing common schools and providing a fund for their maintenance.

Paris C. Dunning, of Guilford County, North Carolina, who had served the Indiana government for years and who had been elected Lieutenant Governor, succeeded Whitcomb as Governor, serving the remainder of the term.

The Norris family settled in for the winter, grateful that the country and their state had reached a condition of calm, no matter how temporary it might be.

1849

By 1849 the population of Clinton County had risen to about 11,000 people. The county seat, Frankfort, had eight stores, five lawyers, five physicians, and five churches. The churches included Old School Presbyterian, Episcopal, Methodist, Christian, and Associate Reformed. Of course, more doctors, as well as school houses and churches were scattered throughout the county. Four merchant mills, eleven water and two steam sawmills, and two carding machines also served local customers. The Sons of Temperance organized three more divisions in Clinton County, at Michigantown, Rossville, and at Jefferson. The annual value of agricultural products exported from the county was estimated at $200,000.

Telegraph lines had reached Indiana by this year.

In January, Bram was named one of the "incorporators" of the Frankfort Branch Railroad Company, with railroad tracks to be built in Clinton County to connect Lafayette and Thorntown. But the actual railroad was not constructed for many years, finally running into Frankfort in 1870.

The traitors and adventurers who had driven Pius IX from Rome abolished the temporal power of the Pope on February 9th, 1849, and under the name of a democratic republic terrorized the people and committed untold outrages. The Pope appealed to France, Austria, Spain, and Naples. On June 29th, French troops under General Oudinot restored order in his territory. On April 12th, 1850, Pius IX returned to Rome, no longer a political liberalist.

Mary considered her life to have become more stabilized with each passing year. She followed the seasons and the weather to regulate daily activities. Even though she had married off two of her offspring, ten remained at home including Elizabeth Altha, 20, Burr, 18, Dailey, 16, Lavina, 13, Abe,

11, William, 8, Phoebe, 6, and Silas, 3. The girls had been well trained to assist her with household chores and with care of the smallest children, while the boys were quickly drafted to help their father manage the farm. But she realized that she would never reach the same level of what she considered to be civilization as her parents and grandparents, who had used slave labor for most of their needs. Her household "help" at Aurora had given her a temporary feeling of being totally in charge of her life. She supposed that when all her girls had left home, she would be able to hire local young ladies to do chores, but such arrangements were fleeting and not always acceptable. Mary still longed for regular access to a priest to meet her spiritual needs, but she had accepted that she must wait, likely for a long time. Mary did not know whether there were any Catholics in Clinton County, and did not dare to enquire among the local populace, for fear of raising negative reaction against her family.

Mary's relationship with Bram continued to be satisfying. Mary managed to keep lascivious other men at bay without having to disguise her seemingly ageless beauty. At age 43, she had mostly retreated from the outside world, only venturing into town when accompanied by Bram or when surrounded by several of her children. Van had matured somewhat, much more than his father Richard ever had. Even though he lived just across the road to the South, Van no longer attempted to bed Mary, largely because opportunities for such behavior were very limited due to the large number of people in Mary's house.

Bram's affection continued unabated, and in mid-March, Mary became pregnant for what turned out to be the last time.

On April 5th, Mary attended the birth of daughter Altha's second child, a son named George O. Maish.

On November 7th, Mary was called to assist Raper's wife Mary at the birth of Raper's third son, Henry Clay Norris. Not having attended the births of the previous two boys, she always felt closer to Henry as a result.

On December 5th, Joseph A. Wright became the second Democratic Governor of Indiana, and held that office for seven years. Born 1810 in Washington, Pennsylvania, Joseph became an important factor in shaping legislation and moulding public opinion. He was popular with Hoosiers, but not respected by political leaders. Governor Wright was tall and raw boned. He had a large head and an unusually high forehead. His hair was light and thin, his eyes blue, and his nose and mouth large and prominent. He was an effective speaker, mainly on account of his earnestness and simplicity.

Just over a week later, on December 13th, daughter Mary Eliza was born, and Mary surreptitiously baptized her child as she had all the others. Even in an era of large families, bearing a total of eleven strong, healthy children was an accomplishment, and Mary glowed with pride.

During this year, the second section of the Wabash & Erie Canal opened, allowing shipments of goods from Toledo, Ohio to Terre Haute, Indiana in 1 - 2 days. Clinton County farmers including the Norrises began sending goods by wagon to markets at Lafayette and Delphi, Indiana for shipment.

1850

On September 9th, California entered the Union as the 31st state.

Ex-Generalissimo and El Presidente Santa Anna still longed to parade upon the world stage. During this year, he moved to Turbaco, Colombia.

According to the 1850 census, over 70,000 Hoosiers over age 21 were unable to read or write.

Largely due to the advent of the railroad, the population of Indianapolis, the hub of seven railroads, passed that of all other Indiana cities. The Indianapolis Union Railway provided links to other carriers. The railroad became the central impetus of Indiana's development. New construction during the 1850s was in East-West orientation, providing connections for Western travel.

On July 9th, President Zachary Taylor died just 16 months into his term. The cause of his death is not well understood. On July 4, 1850, Taylor consumed a snack of milk and cherries at an Independence Day celebration. Upon his death five days later, the cause was listed as gastroenteritis, but some of his symptoms indicated possible heat stroke. He was buried in Louisville, Kentucky, at what is now the Zachary Taylor National Cemetery.

Millard Fillmore, thirteenth President of the United States, from 1850 until 1853, became the last member of the Whig Party to hold that office. He was the second Vice President to assume the Presidency upon the death of a sitting President. Despite his best efforts, Fillmore was never elected President. After serving out Taylor's term, he failed to gain the nomination for the Presidency by the Whigs in 1852. Four years later, in 1856, he again failed to win election as the Know Nothing Party and Whig candidate.

As President Fillmore appointed his own cabinet, he caused an abrupt political shift in the administration of government. Taylor, himself, had been about to replace his entire scandal-ridden cabinet at the time of his death. But Fillmore, beginning with the appointment of Daniel Webster as Secretary of State, caused his cabinet to be dominated by individuals who, with the exception of Treasury Secretary Thomas Corwin, favored what would come to be called the Compromise of 1850.

Fillmore dealt with increasing party divisions within the Whig party; party harmony became one of his primary objectives. He tried to unite the party by pointing out the differences between the Whigs and the Democrats; he proposed tariff reforms that negatively reflected on the Democratic Party. Another primary objective of Fillmore was to preserve the Union from the intensifying slavery debate.

Henry Clay's proposed bill to admit California to the Union aroused all the arguments for and against the extension of slavery without any progress toward settling the major issues. The South continued to threaten secession. Fillmore recognized that Clay's plan was the best way to end the sectional crisis. Clay, exhausted, left Washington to recuperate, passing leadership to Senator Stephen A. Douglas of Illinois. At this critical juncture, President Fillmore announced his support of the Compromise of 1850.

On August 6, 1850, Fillmore sent a message to Congress recommending that Texas be paid to abandon its claims to part of New Mexico. This, combined with his mobilization of 750 Federal troops to New Mexico, helped shift a critical number of Northern Whigs in Congress away from their insistence upon the Wilmot Proviso — the stipulation that all land gained by the Mexican War must be closed to slavery.

Douglas' effective strategy in Congress, combined with Fillmore's pressure gave impetus to the Compromise movement. Breaking up Clay's single legislative package, Douglas presented five separate bills to the Senate:

- Admit California as a free state.
- Settle the Texas boundary and compensate the state for lost lands.
- Grant territorial status to New Mexico.
- Place federal officers at the disposal of slaveholders seeking escapees — the Fugitive Slave Act.
- Abolish the slave trade in the District of Columbia.

Each measure obtained a majority, and, by September 20, President Fillmore had signed them into law. Webster wrote, "I can now sleep of nights." Whigs on both sides refused to accept the finality of Fillmore's law (which led to more party division, and a loss of numerous elections), which caused Northern Whigs to say "God Save us from Whig Vice Presidents."

Fillmore's greatest difficulty with the Fugitive Slave Act was how to enforce it without seeming to favor Southern Whigs. His solution was to appease both Northern and Southern Whigs by calling for the enforcement of the Fugitive Slave Act in the North, and enforcing in the South a law forbidding involvement in Cuba for the sole purpose of adding it as a slave state.

Another issue that presented itself during Fillmore's presidency was the arrival of Lajos Kossuth (exiled leader of a failed Hungarian revolution). Kossuth wanted the United States to abandon its non-intervention policies when it came to European affairs and recognize Hungary's independence. The problem came with the enormous support Kossuth received from German-American immigrants to the United States (who were essential in the re-election of both Whigs and Democrats). Fillmore refused to change American policy, and decided to remain neutral despite the political implications of neutrality.

Fillmore appointed Brigham Young as the first governor of the Utah Territory in 1850. Utah now contains a city and county named after Millard Fillmore.

Fillmore's administration sent Commodore Matthew C. Perry to open Japan to Western trade, though Perry did not reach Japan until Franklin Pierce had replaced Fillmore as president.

Fillmore, a bookworm, found the White House devoid of books and initiated the White House library.

Late in this year, Raper Norris' wife Mary gave birth a fourth time, producing a baby girl called Mary.

The third section of the Wabash & Erie Canal, the Cross Cut Canal from Terre Haute, Indiana to Worthington, Indiana was completed during this year. Canals competed with railroads as a transportation method, but ultimately failed.

1851

The New Indiana Constitution prohibited black people from voting, and forbade black people from immigrating to the state. 11,262 black and mulatto people lived in state at this time; the majority of delegates to the Constitutional Convention voted to persuade them to leave Indiana. "Unless we protect ourselves, Indiana will be the great refuge of all the worthless, the halt, the maimed, and the blind negroes that are to be found in the Southern States."

The state constitution included a measure protecting the property rights of married women. Robert Dale Owen was the chief architect of this provision and the women of Indiana honored him with a silver pitcher.

The 1816 Constitution had been shorter and more general; the new one was more detailed, with emphasis on economic protection for the state budget.

By March 19th, the Indiana Sentinel reported that there were two hundred and forty-five miles of railroad in Indiana; it was expected that five hundred miles would be in operation by the end of the year. The first railroad, the Lafayette & Indianapolis, passed across the Southwest corner of Clinton County during this year, through Perry Township, through a village named Midway for its position between the two cities connected by the rail line. Midway later became Colfax, Indiana.

Mary was called to assist daughter Altha on Apr 7th, when she gave birth to baby Elizabeth Maish.

The Independent Order of Odd Fellows became the first national fraternity to include both men and women when it adopted the Beautiful Rebekah Degree on September 20th. This degree was written by I.O.O.F. member Schuyler Colfax, who had moved to New Carlisle, St. Joseph County, Indiana in 1836. Colfax was a newspaper editor, an anti-slavery national political candidate who served both as Speaker of the House of Representatives and as Vice President of the United States from 1868-1873. The Odd Fellows and Rebekahs became the first fraternal organization to establish homes for senior members and for orphaned children.

1852

During this year, the first plank road was constructed from Delphi to Frankfort, Indiana. In addition, the first train track was constructed through Boone County, Indiana, to the South of Clinton County. Both of these facilitated the transport of produce and of passengers.

The Independent Order of Odd Fellows organized a Lodge in Frankfort, Clinton County. The group operated as a "secret society," with initiations held by men in white robes or black suits, with V-shaped neck ribbons and an apron pouch. Their pledge ceremony required initiates to contemplate their own mortality while facing a human skeleton. Their key ideals, featured on their logo in overlapping oval rings, are "Friendship" "Love" and "Truth." Noting its noble purposes as a charitable organization and also its availability as a social club, several of the Norris men joined up. Most of them, with their wives, ended up being buried in the I.O.O.F. cemetery in Frankfort. Bram and Mary are buried there, as well as nine of their eleven children.

Fire destroyed the mill where Mary's son-in-law David Maish worked. Afterwards, he rented the Spring Mill property in Washington Township for one year, then continued farming his own land, where he and Altha reared their children.

Franklin Pierce, a Democrat, was elected **United States** President in the fall, with zero support from the Norris family. Pierce and his running mate, William R. King won by a landslide, defeating the Whig Party ticket of Winfield Scott and William A. Graham.

In early November, Mary's 24 year old daughter Elizabeth Altha woke her mother late on a Sunday night. When the two reached the kitchen, Eliza collapsed into a chair, sobbing. Alarmed, Mary asked, "What is wrong, sweetheart?"

Unable to speak for some minutes, Eliza sadly replied, "I must marry, and very soon."

"And why is that?"

"Francis has been after me for months, and tonight – he took advantage of me!"

Mary thought about the local Methodist minister, Francis Cox, who had been calling on Eliza during the summer and fall. He had seemed harmless enough, but apparently was not the same person in private as he had seemed in groups of people.

"Are you remembering what I have tried to teach you?" asked Mary. "You could make a personal act of contrition, and look for a better man who would suit your needs..."

"But I'm getting OLD," replied Eliza. "This is the first man who has even been interested in me...I don't want to die an old maid!"

Mary sighed. She had not won her struggle with Methodism over her own desperately held Catholic beliefs.

"This is your life, Eliza. Do what you must, but remember that there is always recourse, should you decide to take it!"

Eliza and the Rev. Francis Cox were married on November 23rd, but Eliza insisted on a civil ceremony, which caused some gossip among the local Methodists.

Lavina and Richard Norris, Sr.'s son, James Luther, 16 years old, married Mary Jane Eldridge on December 1st.

William L. Norris, Bram's step-brother (who Mary would always remember as the fractious child, "Willie" died on December 12th. Willie's wife Rachel (Lee) had died in April. The couple had four young children, along with their ward George, orphaned son of Georgie. All of these now needed care, and were divided among family members as was the Norris family's custom. This meant that all three of Catherine and Richard Norris, Sr.'s children were dead.

1853

Thomas Bartlett was the Methodist circuit rider during this year. On February 20th, a new brick Methodist church was dedicated in Frankfort, with Rev. J.M. Stallard & Rev. Luther Taylor officiating.

On March 4th, Franklin Pierce began service as the fourteenth President of the United States. Pierce was a Democrat and a "doughface" (a Northerner with Southern sympathies) who had served in the **United States** House of Representatives and Senate. Pierce had taken part in the Mexican-American War and become a brigadier general. His private law practice in his home state, New Hampshire, was so successful that he was offered several important positions, which he turned down. Pierce was sometimes referred to as "Baby" Pierce, an apparent reference to Pierce's youth relative to previous presidents.

Pierce's good looks and inoffensive personality caused him to make many friends, but he suffered from alcoholism. As President, he made decisions which were widely criticized and divisive in their effects, thus giving him the reputation as one of the worst presidents in **United States** history. Pierce's popularity in the North declined sharply after he came out in favor of the Kansas-Nebraska Act, repealing the Missouri Compromise and reopening the question of the expansion of slavery in the West. Pierce's credibility was further damaged when several of his diplomats issued the Ostend Manifesto (a rationale for the **United States** to purchase Cuba from Spain as a repository for slaves). These views discredited "Manifest Destiny" and popular sovereignty.

In April 1853, Santa Anna was invited back to Mexico by rebellious conservatives with whom he succeeded in re-taking the government. This administration was no more successful than his earlier ones. He funneled government funds to his own pockets, sold more territory to the **United States** *in the Gadsden Purchase (which became Arizona and New Mexico) and declared himself dictator-for-life with the title "Most Serene Highness."*

Mary attended the birth of daughter Altha's fourth child, Hannah Maish, during this year.

On September 28th, the first Union Station in the country opened at Indianapolis. This innovation allowed passengers and freight to transfer in one facility, rather than transferring via wagon to other locations in the city, a typical practice in other major cities.

In October, the first agricultural fair in Clinton County was held at Frankfort, on the farm of Isaac Armstrong, on the West side of Main Street and Main Avenue. James Gaster won, in the Farming Utensils category: Best Buggy, Best Buggy Harness, Best Saddle, Best Span of Matched Horses. Abraham Hollcraft exhibited a 35# pumpkin.

Also in October, the Crimean War began in Eastern Europe between the Russian Empire and an alliance of the Ottoman Empire, France, Britain, and Sardinia. The immediate cause involved the rights of Christian minorities in the "Holy Land," which was a part of the Ottoman Empire. The French promoted the rights of Roman Catholics, while Russia promoted those of the Eastern Orthodox Church. The longer-term causes involved the decline of the Ottoman Empire, and the unwillingness of Britain and France to allow Russia to gain territory and power at Ottoman expense. It has been noted that the causes, in one case involving an argument over a key, have never revealed a "greater confusion of purpose," yet led to a war noted for its "notoriously incompetent international butchery." While the churches eventually worked out their differences and came to an agreement, Nicholas I of Russia and French Emperor Napoleon III refused to back down.

On November 3rd, Mary's son John Burroughs Norris married Clarissa Fudge. Bram's comment: "Four down, seven to go!" Mary did not even smile. She was not anxious to be rid of her remaining children.

Colonel James Henry Lane (who led Indiana soldiers during the Mexican War) became a Congressman from Indiana during this year, serving until 1855.

1854

In January, the Sons of Temperance met at Indianapolis. Beforehand, meeting at the Methodist Church in Frankfort, the local group chose delegates to attend.

Strong resolutions were adopted:

Resolved, That no prohibitory law will satisfy the temperance sentiment of this state which does not contain the principles of seizure, confiscation and destruction of liquors kept for illegal sale.

Resolved, That the principles for which we contend are and have been recognized by all civilized governments, as well as by the divine government, as fundamental to the existence and well being of society.

Resolved, That attached as we are to our respective political parties, we have no disposition to interfere with their organization; but, we distinctly declare that we will not vote for any candidate for the legislature, of any party, who is not fully committed in favor of the principles avowed in the two preceding resolutions.

The above resolutions "set the state on fire" with hot debate on the temperance issue. Clinton County citizens joined the fight promptly. There was dissension concerning the question of "search, seizure and confiscation," as an invasion of personal rights.

The Wabash & Erie Canal, at over 460 miles, was the longest canal ever built in North America. The last section of it, the Central Canal, was completed this year from Worthington, Indiana to Evansville on the Ohio River. This last section of the canal allowed water transport from New

York City (across Lake Erie), across Ohio and Indiana, to the Ohio River. Travel along the canal was accomplished by freight and passenger "packets," floating rafts pulled by horses or oxen who trod a path along the canal bank. A passenger packet consisted of a series of rooms built along the length of the raft. Towards the front was the main saloon, where meals were eaten, and where the men slept at night. The ladies' saloon was towards the back of the boat, and the women slept there. Canal boat travel was not particularly comfortable nor pleasant, due to weather, mosquitoes, and crowded conditions. The canal was abandoned by 1873, due to difficulties with maintenance of the waterway and to competition from the more effective and efficient transportation by railroad.

AND, a new line of railroad opened from Lafayette to Indianapolis through Frankfort. This was a significant improvement in transportation for all citizens of Clinton County, and the Norrises rejoiced.

The Kansas-Nebraska Act passed in the **United States** government this year, allowing individual states to decide about slavery within their borders. The Missouri Compromise was repealed by this Act bringing the United States one step closer to Civil War.

It was still cold weather when Mary's son Raper dropped by to talk to his mother.

"My wife, Mary is very ill," he said.

Mary leaned forward in her chair, unsure how to respond.

"The doctor does not think she has long to live," he continued, bending and covering his face with his hands.

Mary put on her warm coat, made Raper saddle her horse, and rode with him to his house. The place was a mess, and the children (aged 10, 8, 5 and 3) were in need of tender loving care. Mary sent Raper to fetch a neighbor woman who specialized in nursing care to help out with Mary. She bundled up the children, and took them home where she could clean and feed them. Despite all efforts, Raper's wife died on March 3rd, and he descended into emotional instability that lasted for several years.

Mary's son Burr's wife, Clarissa, delivered baby Altha Anna Norris this year.

In Mexico, on April 1st, the Plan of Ayutla removed Santa Anna from power.

On Wednesday, April 26th, a neighbor passing by Mary's house expressed sympathy to her on the death of her daughter, Elizabeth Altha Cox, the day before. Mary stared at the man, not knowing how to respond – she had heard nothing about it. She stammered a thank you to the man, then ran to the barn to find Bram. He saddled their horses, and together they rode, as quickly as possible, the miles to Eliza and Francis' house. There they found a group of neighbors conducting an impromptu farewell service for their daughter, praying and singing. In their midst was Francis, appearing somber but not overly distraught as one might expect. He rushed forward to greet Bram and Mary, as if he had expected them to show up. Mary later mentally excused Francis for not notifying them of their daughter's sudden death – Elizabeth Altha had been expecting her first child, but went into early labor. She and the child both died.

Mary grieved for a long time. What distressed her the most was that she could not be alone with Eliza and the infant's bodies to recite the Last Rites that she considered so important. She had to wait until after the burial, and came back alone to do this, hoping that her effort would be efficacious. Surely God would understand!

The Morris Chapel Methodist Society constructed a new church building this year. The Norris and Maish families had been worshiping in the schoolhouse previously. The new facility featured pews of black walnut; five graves were already in the church yard prior to construction. George W. Stafford, the Methodist circuit rider, came to dedicate the new building.

The second Clinton County Agricultural Fair was held from Thursday, October 2nd through Saturday October 4th. Mary's son Abe won a prize for the "best lot of onions," and as a result endured teasing from his siblings for years afterward.

1855

During this session, the Indiana State Legislature passed a "Sabbath Law," imposing fines on "persons found rioting, quarreling, hunting, fishing, or engaging at common labor or their usual vocation on Sunday, works of charity and necessity only excepted." Mary grinned when she heard this – no one considered women's work – cooking and cleaning up afterward – as actual labor. Those who did avoid cooking on the Sabbath, eating leftovers – undoubtedly deserved the sub-standard meals that resulted, and the mess that remained until Monday for cleanup!

During this year, Bram acquired an iron plow to assist with preparing and planting the wheat and corn crops. This enabled him, and his sons, as they cleared more land, to increase the number of acres they cultivated, and to sell more produce every year.

On June 12th, a law went into effect in Clinton County authorizing agents of the county to sell "pure and unadulterated spiritous and vinous and intoxicating liquors" for "medicinal, chemical, and mechanical uses only, and pure wine for sacramental use." Sale by others than the agents was prohibited and purchase from others than the agents was a penal offense. Again, Mary's reaction was to think her way past the law, making sure that Bram could get whatever alcoholic beverages they wanted brought in from elsewhere.

The Frankfort <u>Crescent</u>: "We have not seen a man in town the least 'fuddled' since the new law took effect; and firmly believe it will accomplish the great end for which it was designed–the suppression of drunkenness."

Despite his generous payoffs to the military for loyalty, by this year even conservative allies had seen enough of Santa Anna. On August 9th, a group of liberals led by Benito Juarez and Ignacio Comonfort overthrew Santa Anna, who again fled to Cuba. As the extent of his corruption became known, he was tried in absentia for treason; all his estates were confiscated by the government.

On December 20th, Indiana's prohibition laws were declared unconstitutional by the United States Supreme Court; counties ceased liquor control, except as licensers. The Sons of Temperance rallied quickly, and moved for a constitutional amendment for prohibition, but other national issues overshadowed this one for many years.

The Wabash Cannonball Trail ran on the two lines originally established by the Wabash Railroad. The Southwestern leg was built in 1855, making it one of the oldest rail lines in Northwest Ohio. The Cannonballs were known as the super trains of their time. They were equipped with smokers, parlor coaches, and Pullman Palace Sleeping Cars.

James Henry Lane, who had left Indiana, moving to Kansas, organized the defense of Lawrence during the "Wakarusa War" in December. This became a turning point in his career. Until this time, Lane had been fairly conservative, but as the strife of the Kansas-Missouri Border War increased, he became more and more controversial, due to his speeches, ruthlessness, and tactics.

1856

In this year, Indianapolis railways were connected to St. Louis.

The steady progress of railroads seemed like Providence to many young men in Indiana. They sought employment in jobs that fed their imagination with the "romance of the rails." Although railroad companies soon standardized operating rules, this era saw a major struggle for fair labor practices, punctuated by strikes. The 'romance,' however, stood up in the harsh face of reality, and many continued a lifetime of work for the railroads.

This year's presidential election saw the abandonment of Franklin Pierce by his (Democratic) party in favor of James Buchanan, who was elected. (Of course, the Norrises did not approve.) After losing the Democratic nomination, Pierce continued his lifelong struggle with alcoholism as his marriage to Jane Means Appleton Pierce fell apart. His reputation was destroyed during the American Civil War when he declared support for the Confederacy, and personal correspondence between Pierce and Confederate President Jefferson Davis was leaked to the press. He died in 1869 from cirrhosis.

James Buchanan, like his predecessor, was a "doughface" (a Northerner with Southern sympathies) who battled Stephen A. Douglas for control of the Democratic Party. As Southern states declared their secession in the lead-up to the American Civil War, he held that secession was illegal but that going to war to stop it was also illegal. His inability to avert the Civil War has subsequently been assessed as the worst single failure by any President of the United States. Buchanan has been consistently ranked by scholars as one of the worst Presidents.

Ashbel Parsons Willard, from Vernon, New York was elected governor of Indiana this year after an exciting political contest. Governor Willard was very prepossessing; his head and face were "cast in finest moulds;" his eyes were blue, his hair auburn and his complexion florid. A more magnetic and attractive man could nowhere be found, and "had he lived to the allotted age of mankind he must have reached still higher honors."

1857

This year saw passage of the infamous Dred Scott decision by the **United States** Supreme Court. The upshot of the ruling was that black people could not be **United States** citizens.

Dred Scott (who lived from about 1799 through September 17, 1858) was an enslaved African American who sued for his freedom and that of his wife and their two daughters. Scott claimed that he and his family should be granted their freedom because they had lived in Illinois and the Wisconsin Territory for four years, where slavery was illegal.

After the Supreme Court had heard arguments in the case but before it had issued a ruling, President-elect James Buchanan wrote to his friend, **United States** Supreme Court Associate Justice John Catron, asking whether the case could be decided by the court before Buchanan's inauguration in March. Buchanan hoped the decision would quell unrest in the country over the slavery issue by issuing a ruling that put the future of slavery beyond the realm of political debate.

The court decided 7–2 against Scott, finding that neither he nor any other person of African ancestry could claim American citizenship, and therefore could not bring suit in federal court. Moreover, Scott's temporary residence outside Missouri did not bring about his emancipation under the Missouri Compromise, which the court ruled unconstitutional as it would "improperly deprive Scott's owner of his legal property."

The Dred Scott Decision immediately spurred vehement dissent from anti-slavery elements in the North. The decision was hailed in Southern slave-holding society as a proper interpretation of the **United States** Constitution. According to Jefferson Davis, then a United States Senator from Mississippi, and later President of the Confederate States of America, the Dred Scott case was merely a question of "whether Cuffee should be kept in his normal condition or not." ("Cuffee" was a term commonly used to describe a black person.) The Dred Scott Decision became an indirect catalyst for the American Civil War.

Perhaps the most immediate business consequence of the Dred Scott Decision was to help trigger the Panic of 1857. Uncertainty about whether the entire West would suddenly become either slave territory or engulfed in combat like "Bleeding Kansas" immediately gripped Northern markets. Financial support for the East–West railroads collapsed immediately (although North–South running lines were unaffected), causing, in turn, the near-collapse of several large banks and the runs that ensued.

On March 4th, James Buchanan was inaugurated as President.

On May 26th, Dred Scott's current owner filed papers of manumission for the Scott family at St. Louis, Missouri. Afterwards, Scott worked as a porter in a local hotel, while his wife took in laundry.

In June, a Grand Excursion from Baltimore to St. Louis celebrated the railway that linked the two cities via the American Central Route.

At about this time, Mary's son Burr's wife Clarissa delivered baby Emma Jane Norris.

But for Mary, the most upsetting event of the year was when Raper dropped by for an announcement: "I'm off for the Gold Rush, Mama! And John and Luther will go with me…"

Raper had never regained his reasonable nature after the illness and death of his wife Mary, three years previously. But his mother was totally unprepared for this.

Mary, shocked, asked, "You're going WHERE?"

"California, Mama! And don't worry, I'll write you. When I return, I'll have so much money that we'll ALL be rich!"

"But what about little Henry? And Mary?"

"Oh. I never thought. Could you take them in?"

Mary gulped. Adding two children, ages eight and six, had not been on her agenda.

"Of course. But let me know when to expect them…"

"What about tomorrow morning?"

"Um, all right, I guess. But you need to tell your father about this, yourself!"

Mary retreated to the house to digest this information, while Raper went in search of Bram.

1858

The spring of this year brought unusually heavy rains and severe weather from Missouri to Pennsylvania in April, May, and June. The Ohio, White, and Wabash Rivers were all in major flood. The National Road Bridge over the Wabash was demolished by raging waters, and had to be reconstructed

On May 11, Minnesota entered the Union as the 32nd state.

When Pope Pius IX visited his provinces in the summer of 1857, he had received everywhere a warm and loyal reception. But the doom of his temporal power was sealed, when a year later Cavour and Napoleon III met at Plombières, concerting plans for a combined war against Austria and the subsequent territorial extension of the Sardinian Kingdom. They sent their agents into various cities of the Papal States to propagate the idea of a politically united Italy.

The loss of his temporal power was only one of the many trials that filled the long pontificate of Pius IX. There was scarcely a country, Catholic or Protestant, where the rights of the Church were not infringed upon. In Russia, Italian Catholic clergy and their parishoners were persecuted and cast out, replaced by what became the Russian Orthodox Church.

Pius IX's greatest achievements were of a purely ecclesiastical and religious character. The healthy and extensive growth of the Church during his pontificate was chiefly due to his unselfishness. He appointed to important ecclesiastical positions only such men as were famous both for piety and learning.

On September 29th, 1850, he re-established the Catholic hierarchy in England by erecting the Archdiocese of Westminster with the twelve suffragan Sees. The widespread commotion which this act caused among English fanatics, and which was fomented by Prime Minister Russell and the London Times, temporarily threatened to result in an open persecution of Catholics.

In the United States of America he erected the Dioceses of Albany, Buffalo,

Cleveland, and Galveston in 1847; Monterey, Savannah, St. Paul, Wheeling, Santa Fe, and Nesqually (Seattle) in 1850; Burlington, Covington, Erie, Natchitoches, Brooklyn, Newark, and Quincy (Alton) in 1853; Portland, Maine in 1855; Fort Wayne and Sault Sainte Marie (Marquette) in 1857; Columbus, Grass Valley (Sacramento), Green Bay, Harrisburg, La Crosse, Rochester, Scranton, St. Joseph, and Wilmington in 1868; Springfield and St. Augustine in 1870; Providence and Ogdensburg in 1872; San Antonio in 1874; Peoria in 1875; Leavenworth in 1877; the Vicariates Apostolic of the Indian Territory and Nebraska in 1851; Northern Michigan in 1853; Florida in 1857; North Carolina, Idaho, and Colorado in 1868; Arizona in 1869; Brownsville, Texas and Northern Minnesota in 1874. Pius IX established at Rome the College of the United States of America, at his own private expense, in 1859.

His was the longest pontificate in the history of the papacy. In 1877 he celebrated his golden episcopal jubilee. His tomb is in the church of San Lorenzo fuori le mura. The process of his beatification was begun on 11 February, 1907, and Pope Pius IX was beatified on September 3, 2000.

On June 16th, Abraham Lincoln, upon accepting the Illinois Republican Party's nomination as that state's United States Senator, gave his famous House Divided speech in Springfield, Illinois. The speech created a lasting image of the danger of disunion because of slavery, and it rallied Republicans across the North.

From August to October of this year, a series of seven debates was held in Illinois between Abraham Lincoln and Stephen A. Douglas (incumbent Illinois Senator). Even though Illinois was a free state, the main topic of the debates was slavery in the United States, and the speeches given were published and widely distributed.

The words of Abraham Lincoln were read to Mary by her husband and children. As she listened, Mary began thinking more deeply than before about the institution of slavery, and what it meant to the daily lives of those directly involved. But she remained unconvinced that slavery should or ever could be eliminated completely.

Although Lincoln provided active support to the winner of this year's presidential campaign, Zachary Taylor, Abe lost his own senatorial contest and was not appointed to any position by Taylor.

On November 7th, Dred Scott died of tuberculosis only 18 months after attaining his freedom.

1859

In January 1859, after Abraham Lincoln lost his **United States** Senate campaign to Stephen A. Douglas, financial necessity forced him to pay more attention to his legal career. Practicing law, however, had lost some of its luster after the political "high" of the national attention surrounding the previous year's campaign. As the foremost Republican in Illinois, Lincoln felt an obligation to lead the fractious Illinois Republican political alliance and craft a vision for party success in 1860. Lincoln was particularly concerned about Douglas' attempts to position himself as a centrist presidential candidate who could siphon off some of the fledgling Republican Party's conservative-to-moderate internal factions.

On February 14th, Oregon entered the Union as the 33rd state.

The citizens of Honey Creek Township in Northeast Clinton County had petitioned the commissioners of Clinton County to join Howard County. Their request was granted in March of this year. This explains the missing Northeast corner of Clinton County as seen on maps.

On April 6th, Mary's son Dailey married Amanda Jane Fudge.

At the wedding, Mary overheard several people discussing a Catholic mission being set up in Kokomo, Howard County, Indiana. Fifty people would be served there, by traveling priests. Then she heard very exciting news: Father Edward O'Flaherty of Crawfordsville was scheduled to visit Frankfort. In addition, Father Hamilton of Crawfordsville and Father A.B. Oechterling of Delphi occasionally would serve Frankfort's Catholic occupants. They would baptize those in need, hear confessions, and console the dying.

By this time, all of Mary's children were attending the Methodist services, thoroughly inculcated with Protestantism. She dared not stir up the Morris Chapel by trying to change her children at this point. Besides, she HAD baptized them; there was not much that a priest could do for Protestants unwilling to make confession or to be confirmed in the church.

But Mary found out where and when the priest would be next (at a nearby farmhouse), and arranged to ride her horse there on the appointed day. She noticed familiar faces at the event, and saw that they were surprised, if not shocked, to find out that she was of the Catholic faith. Mary made confession, was granted absolution, and prepared to leave. But from then on, she knew who contact about the holy dates, as well as about future visits from the priests. She became more emotionally content about what she believed to be her spiritual condition than she had been for many years.

Mary's family was somewhat surprised when she began serving feasts at unexpected times, and when her routine of prayer and fasting increased.

In late September, Mary's son Abe was reading to her from the Indianapolis Atlas dated September 20th.

"Your pal, Abe Lincoln gave a speech last night at the Indianapolis Masonic Hall, Mama!"

Mary began to protest, "But I don't KNOW if this is the same man..."

"Mama, Listen! 'Away back in the fall of 1816, when he was in his eighth year, his father brought him over from the neighboring State of Kentucky, and settled in the State of Indiana, and he grew up to his present enormous height on our own good soil of Indiana. The scenes he passed through to-day are wonderfully different from the first scenes he witnessed in the State of Indiana, where he was raised, in Spencer county, on the Ohio river. There was an unbroken wilderness there then, and an axe was put in his hand; and with the trees and logs and grubs he fought until he reached his twentieth year.'"

Mary sank into a nearby chair, stunned by the confirmation of what she had only half-believed to be true.

"Son, if that man ever comes near here, I shall go to visit him! I really want to see him one more time!"

Newton County, in Northwest Indiana had been formed in 1835. It was abolished and combined into Jasper County in 1839. On December 8th of this year, Newton was recreated, its borders redrawn.

1860

On January 17th, Dailey and Amanda had their first child, William Smith Norris. By this time, Dailey was working as a carpenter, and lived close enough that Mary could attend the birth, and also help the new mother afterwards.

In May, Burr's wife Clarissa delivered her third daughter, Florence May Norris. Their home was very close, to the East along the Boylston Road, and Mary visited often. She considered grandmotherhood to be one of the most satisfying roles of her life.

During the summer, Indiana Governor Ashbel Parsons Willard's health gave way, and he went to Minnesota in quest of a more beneficial atmosphere. He died there on October 4th, the first Governor of Indiana to die in office.

Lieutenant Governor Abram Adams Hammond succeeded to the governorship on the death of A.P. Willard. He was a native of Brattleboro, Vermont, born 1814, who came to Indiana at six years of age, and was raised near Brookville. He served as Governor until the inauguration of Governor Henry Smith Lane in January 1861.

Mary was advised by one of her Catholic friends that Father George A. Hamilton of Lafayette would be visiting the area to baptize, hear confession, and console the dying. She joined the group on the appointed day, made confession, and received a list of the upcoming holy days and dates (which Bram or her children could read for her). This information became an ongoing blessing, making her feel that she still belonged to the Church, her soul safe from the fires of Hell.

Mary's son Abe came to her in September, bringing the young lady with whom he had been keeping company, Sarah Maria Fudge. They told her that they wanted to be married, and had set the date for October 23rd. Mary warmly agreed that they should marry, later earnestly praying that their union should be blessed.

Members of the Fudge family had come to Clinton County, Indiana from Springboro, Warren County, Ohio in 1828 and 1829; they were among the first residents of what became Frankfort, the county seat. Included in this group were Henry Christian Fudge with his brothers Peter and Moses, and their sister Sarah who had married William Pence, one of the founders of Frankfort. Their brother David Fudge, who became a Methodist minister, came to Clinton County in 1834. At least five Norrises eventually married Fudge family members.

The presidential campaign of this year was memorable. The Norrises supported the Republican candidate, Abraham Lincoln, who was elected. In Clinton County, Lincoln got 1454 votes, while Douglas (the Democrat candidate) got 1437. Breckinridge got 61 votes, Bell 6.

For Indiana Governor, Thomas A. Hendricks got 1437 votes, but Henry Smith Lane got 1385. During the 1860s, most of Clinton County voted for Republican candidates except that during non-presidential years on state and local tickets, the Democrats fared better.

On November 9th, the South Carolina General Assembly passed a "Resolution to Call the Election of Abraham Lincoln as **United States** President a Hostile Act," and stated its intention to declare secession from the United States. South Carolinian religious leader James Henley Thornwell stated that slavery was justified under the Christian religion, and thus, those who viewed slavery as being immoral were opposed to Christianity. He called those who opposed slavery "atheists, socialists, communists, red republicans, Jacobins." Thornwell's statements reflected the views of many South Carolinians (46% of residents of the state owned at least one slave). South Carolina seceded from the Union on December 20th.

Overhearing the discussions of slavery, Mary kept her mouth shut. She thought the whole issue had been blown out of proportion, despite the abuses she had experienced and witnessed at the John Davis household. The Hobbs family had treated their slaves well. Perhaps what the country needed was better oversight of slave owners, better laws controlling violence against slaves. How could plantations like those the Hobbs Family owned succeed without slave labor? And negroes – were they really people? Despite her relationships with her mammy in Maryland, and with Phoebe Elvira, some of them had seemed to her like high-functioning animals! To go to war over such a question seemed, well, silly!

1861

On January 9th, Mississippi seceded from the Union; Florida on January 10th, Alabama January 11th, Georgia January 19th, Louisiana January 26th.

On January 29th, Kansas entered the Union as the 34th state.

On February 1st, Texas seceded from the Union. On February 4th, the seven seceded states held a convention in Montgomery, Alabama, where they elected Jefferson Davis as their President.

In early February, Bram came into the kitchen, waving a news sheet at Mary.

"Guess what! Our new President will be traveling from Springfield, Illinois to Washington, D.C. by train. He's going to stop at Lafayette, and perhaps speak to the public!"

Mary's heart fluttered. Perhaps she would finally get to see Abe Lincoln again.

"Can we go?" she asked.

Bram shrugged, "I don't see why not, barring a blizzard..."

Mary hugged her husband, making him curious about her eagerness to meet Lincoln. "Should we take the train, or ride our horses?" she asked.

"We can control our own schedule if we ride horseback," he responded, "as well as save a few dollars. Again, depending on weather..."

"I like to ride my horse," she answered.

"Just WHY is it that you think you know 'Honest Abe,' as some call him?" he asked.

Mary thought that she had told Bram about meeting Lincoln so many years before, but recounted the tale briefly, and said, "He helped me at a time when I desperately needed assistance. If not for him, it is possible that I might not have arrived at Louisville, at least not in time to have met you. Bless him!"

Mary began making plans. At this point, she had seven children living at home: Lavina, 24 years, Harrison, 19, Phoebe, 17, Silas, who would soon turn 15, Mary Eliza who had just turned 11, as well as Raper's two children, Henry Clay, 10, and Mary, 8. She gave them all explicit instructions about what to do and not do while their parents were gone, and felt confident that they would manage quite well on their own. She had trained them well, knowing that they would some day have to function as adults.

Mary laid out the clothing she intended to wear when she met Abe Lincoln – a fancy ruffled gown, delicate shoes, a warm cloak, gloves, a matching hat decorated with a curled feather. Then she began to think about what she should say to the president-elect.

For his part, Bram sent a message to the owner of a rooming house in Lafayette where he and his sons had often stayed while delivering produce to the markets there. He requested a room where he and Mary could spend two nights before returning home.

The distance from Bram and Mary's house to Lafayette was just over twenty-three miles. Bram had of course traveled the route frequently. Since the weather remained mild, they decided to ride their horses.

The two of them left before dawn on Saturday, February 9th, warmly dressed, and rode as quickly as possible, arriving in late afternoon at their destination. Even though it was getting dark, Mary could see the advantage of staying there – the place was within sight of the Lafayette railroad station.

The proprietor greeted Bram with a smile, and led the couple to a private, simply furnished bedroom where they placed their belongings. While Mary unpacked, Bram made sure that their horses were well attended at the stable. Then the Norrises ventured into the dining hall, where dinner had been set out for patrons already seated at a long table.

Mary had rarely eaten in public facilities, but Bram had reassured her that the food would be quite good. Because it was still winter, the fare consisted of produce that stored easily. Ham, potatoes, cornbread, and a baked apple dessert made the rounds on heavily laden platters; there was plenty for the twenty-some people who gathered.

The Norrises had no sooner sat down, Bram giving a brief grace thanking

God for the food and Mary surreptitiously crossing herself after repeating a silent blessing, when a young man sitting nearby glanced at them oddly.

"You really think that there is a deity expecting your thanks at every meal?" he asked.

"Nice to meet you, too," responded Bram, a hint of sarcasm in his voice. "I'm Abraham Norris, and this is my wife, Mary. Why are you questioning our dining habits?"

"I'm Putnam Jenners," he said. "I'm just sharing my conviction that religion is a massive lie, used by the powerful to manipulate people in order to steal their money."

"No matter your beliefs, nor lack of them, I assure you that we will make no additional attempts to manipulate you, nor to take your money," replied Bram. "And I hope that you will restrain yourself from further commentary while we try to enjoy our food!"

Mary and Bram quickly finished eating, excused themselves, and went to pay for their meal.

Mary asked the owner of the facility, "What ails that Putnam Jenners who accosted us at the table?"

"Oh, so sorry, Ma'am," replied the woman. "He is a painter, sometimes a carriage-maker here in town. Putnam was born here, and it seems that this town will never be rid of him. He is rude and crude – no doubt about that!"

Bram helped Mary into her warm cloak for the short walk to their room, and commented, "One never knows what kind of detritus will turn up at these rooming-houses. It's entertainment, but not worth being overly concerned about."

"But what do you call people like that Putnam?" she asked. "I never heard anyone speak about religion like that before!"

Bram answered, "There are a variety of schools of thought, with different approaches to understanding religion. Groups that come to mind are atheists, freethinkers, even atheistic feminists who think that men are using the concept of god to control women.

I know that you have your own strong religious views, Mary," he said. "And I hope that I have done nothing to make you think I disapprove. My own observation is that religion helps us most when we are able to join a group of those who share our beliefs. You have your Catholic friends, I have my Methodists..."

"Yes, Bram. You are right that we each gain strength from our religious friends. And I thank you so much for your tolerance and patience – I have tried to return your respectful attitude!"

The brick Church of Sts. Mary and Martha stood at the intersection of Fifth and Brown Streets in Lafayette. Mary knew that the church existed, and wanted to attend mass on Sunday morning. The proprietor of their boarding house gave her directions, as well as finding out the times for confession and for mass. On Sunday, after breakfasting with Bram at the dining hall, Mary found her way to the house of worship, and made confession. The priest seemed puzzled, as she was not one of his established parishioners, but he granted her absolution anyway, and she was able to partake of the sacraments at the mass afterwards. She made her way back to the rooming-house, feeling more at peace than she had for many years.

On Monday morning, the Norrises rose early, breakfasted at the dining hall, and returned to their room to wait for Lincoln's arrival. Bram pulled out a book he had been reading. Mary fidgeted, arranging and re-arranging her hair, hat, and her skirt. She finally collapsed into a chair, glad that she had brought an embroidery project (a pillow case) along. She seldom had time at home for such things, given all the work needed to maintain the farmhouse while keeping her family fed and dressed. On this morning, she was able to make significant progress on the decoration for this piece, and for years afterward the events of this morning were recalled whenever she looked at it.

Noticing that people were gathering at the train station, Bram suggested that they join the crowd. Wrapped in her warm cloak, Mary clung to his arm to maintain her balance on the uneven ground.

Before long, they felt rather than heard the approach of the steam engine pulling several cars to the station. The train's whistle blew, a sound which carried through the town, and dozens of people came running. Bram had positioned himself and Mary so that when the engine pulled past the deck surrounding the ticket office, the Norrises were in the front row of people facing the last car. This train car featured a small platform at the rear, surrounded by a wrought iron railing.

Several soldiers came out of the train car, looking around. They ducked back inside, and a tall bearded man dressed in a white linen shirt with a dark tie looped at his throat, black pants, a black overcoat and a tall stove-top hat bowed his way out the door. As he straightened, the crowd burst into cheers of greeting.

The president-elect launched into a short "whistle-stop" speech which turned out to be a warm-up for the longer one he would give at Indianapolis that evening:

"While I do not expect, upon this occasion, or on any occasion, till after I get to Washington, to attempt any lengthy speech, I will only say that to the salvation of this Union there needs but one single thing - the hearts of a people like yours. When the people rise in masses in behalf of the Union and the liberties of their country, truly may it be said, 'The gates of hell shall not prevail against them.' I, as already intimated, am but an accidental instrument, temporary, and to serve but for a limited time, but I appeal to you again to constantly bear in mind that with you, and not with politicians, not with Presidents, not with office-seekers, but with you, is the question, 'Shall the Union and shall the liberties of this country be preserved to the latest generation?'"

Lincoln half-bowed as he turned toward the train door, the crowd again erupting into cheers. His gaze swept across the front row of admirers, and he stopped, transfixed by Mary's face. Lincoln grasped the arm of one soldier-guard, spoke to the man, and gestured toward the Norrises. Then he re-entered the train car.   The soldier extended his hand toward Bram and Mary, beckoning for them to step up onto the train platform, and to follow him inside the car. Mary felt Bram close behind her, supporting her arms as she climbed up. She took a deep breath of the cold air, then walked through the train entrance. She had heard that Lincoln had a phenomenal memory for people's faces from his past, and apparently the reports were true!
Inside, Lincoln sat at a table, sipping from a steaming cup of coffee. He had removed his heavy coat, his tall hat, and loosened his tie. To his right sat a short, stout ordinary looking woman with a very round face and hair tightly bound to the back of her head, where it was arranged into curls. Mary would not have described her as happy, but rather as smug and self-satisfied. Her eyes dared Mary or anyone else to disagree with her in any way.   Mary curtsied to the Lincolns, while Bram bowed. The Norrises waited for Lincoln to speak.   "Looks as if you found your way," he said to Mary. "Did the Sheriff ever catch you?"   Mary swallowed, hard, shook her head, then responded, "I've done very well, thanks to your help!

This is my husband, Abraham Norris. My name is Mary, and we have had eleven children, and thirteen grandchildren."

Lincoln laughed, and said, "So here we have TWO Abrahams married to TWO Marys! This is my wife." He nodded in Mary Todd Lincoln's direction, and the woman grimaced at the Norrises, who bowed and nodded in acknowledgement of the introduction.

Mary looked at the floor, then back into Lincoln's eyes.

"Slavery," she said. "I know you think it's morally wrong. But can you stop it?"

"Maybe," he replied. "We may have to watch it die a long, slow death. Would it matter to you? After all, here you are in the Hoosier State..."

"Some of the best people I ever knew were slaves," she said. "And I was treated as if a slave just before I met you. But, back in Maryland, my family depended on slave labor in order to survive!" "Yes," he said. "We must think of the whole country, not just our own situations. Getting everyone to agree with *that* will be nearly impossible." "You must take one step at a time," said Mary. "It will be your job to continue what the founding fathers began – to make sure that the country is governed by and for ALL the people. We, ourselves, may not live to see the outcome..."

"True," mused Lincoln, as if deep in thought. "And I depend on people such as yourselves to back me up. Thanks for your support!"

Mary responded, "And thanks again for your assistance, so long ago. Without that, I think I would not be in my present comfortable position."

Lincoln stepped forward, shook Bram's hand, then bent to embrace Mary as his own wife scowled in disapproval.

"Bless you," Mary whispered as he released her. Then she and Bram turned, leaving the train car.

Lincoln's train continued to Indianapolis, where Governor Oliver Hazard Perry Throck Morton and 20,000 cheering supporters welcomed him with a thirty-four gun salute. He addressed the crowd from the train platform before he disembarked to his hotel room at Bates House, on the Northwest corner of Illinois and Washington Streets, where he and his entourage spent the night. Lincoln adherents called upon the president-elect later that evening, and he delivered an ad hoc speech from a balcony of the hotel.

Next morning, on February 12th, Lincoln's fifty-second birthday, Lincoln ate breakfast at the governor's mansion on the Northwest corner of Illinois and Market Streets, after which Lincoln and Governor Morton walked to the statehouse at the Northwest corner of Washington and Capitol where Lincoln met with members of the legislature.

At 11:00 A.M. the Lincoln family boarded the train and continued their journey. Lincoln greeted well-wishers and delivered short speeches at Shelbyville, Greensburg, Morris, and Lawrenceburg as his train proceeded to Cincinnati and eventually (after Lincoln assumed a disguise at Baltimore to thwart possible assassins) to Washington, D.C.

The Norrises spent Monday night at the rooming house, then made their way back to their home East of Frankfort the following day.

Henry Smith Lane, Governor of Indiana for two days, was born 1811, in Montgomery County, Kentucky. After being admitted to the bar in Mt. Sterling, Kentucky, he moved to Crawfordsville, Indiana in about 1835.

In 1846, when the Mexican War began, Henry Smith Lane (NOT the same man as Col. James Henry Lane from Lawrenceburg, commander of the Third and later the Fifth Indiana Regiment who later went to Kansas) at once organized a company, was chosen Captain, and later became Lieutenant Colonel of the First Indiana Regiment Infantry. This regiment spent most of the war in Mexico, guarding supply lines and military posts, and saw little action. When the First Indiana Regiment was mustered out of service, Henry Smith Lane helped to organize the Fifth Indiana Regiment Infantry, and served in Mexico with them until the war ended in 1848.

On February 27, 1860, Henry Smith Lane was nominated by acclamation for Governor of Indiana, with Oliver Hazard Perry Throck Morton as Lieutenant Governor. The two men shared the understanding that Morton would succeed to the position of Governor if Lane won the **United States** Senate race being held that year. The men canvassed throughout the entire state of Indiana.

After a major speech in Evansville, Lane in mid-May attended the second Republican National Convention at Chicago, Illinois, and was influential in helping Abraham Lincoln win the presidential nomination. Lane and Lincoln had a friendly relationship and Lincoln once said of Lane, "Here comes an uglier man than I am."

Lane was elected Governor over Honorable Thomas A. Hendricks by a majority of about 1,000 votes. On January 16th, two days after beginning his term as Governor, Lane received the news that he had won election to the Untied States Senate. Having anticipated this development, he at once resigned the governorship, the shortest term of office on record in Indiana.

When Lane's senatorial term expired, he returned to his home in Crawfordsville. He never sought public office again, but was later appointed Indiana Commissioner by President Grant.

In person, Henry Smith Lane was tall, slender and somewhat stoop shouldered. His face was thin and wore a kindly expression. In his later days, the long beard he wore was white as snow. He moved quickly, and his bearing was that of a cultured man.

Oliver Hazard Perry Throck Morton, Indiana's Civil War Governor and United States Senator, was born in Saulsbury, Wayne County, Indiana, 1823. The family name was originally Throckmorton, and Bram was Governor Morton's second cousin, once removed.

When a boy, Morton attended the academy of Professor Hoshour, at Centerville, but owing to the poverty of his family, he was taken from school, and at the age of fifteen, with an older brother, began learning the hatter's trade. After working as a hatter for a few years, he decided to pursue the legal profession, and entered Miami University in 1843 where he studied for two years.

Up to his thirty-first year, Morton was a Democrat. He was opposed to the extension of slavery, however, and upon the organization of the Republican Party he entered the movement, and in 1856 was one of three delegates from Indiana to the Pittsburgh convention.

His prominence was such that in 1856 he was unanimously nominated by the new party for Governor of Indiana, against Ashbel P. Willard. Willard was an able and brilliant speaker, the superior of Morton as an orator, but inferior as a logician and debater. The two men canvassed the state together, and drew immense crowds. Willard's speeches were florid, eloquent and spirit stirring, while Morton's style was earnest, convincing and forcible. Morton never appealed to men's passions, but always to their intellect and reason. Although beaten at the polls, Morton came out of the contest with his popularity increased, and with the reputation of being one of the ablest public men in the state.

In 1860 he was nominated for Lieutenant Governor on the ticket with Honorable Henry Smith Lane, with the understanding that, if successful, Lane should go to the Senate, and Morton become Governor. Morton made a vigorous canvas, and the result of the election was a Republican success, which placed Lane in the Senate and Morton in the gubernatorial chair.

From the day of his inauguration, Morton gave evidence of possessing extraordinary executive ability. It was while filling this term as Governor that he did his best public work and created for himself a lasting fame. The Civil War was beginning when Morton became Governor, and few so well anticipated what would be its magnitude as he. Perceiving the danger, he visited Washington soon after the inauguration of President Lincoln, to advise vigorous action and to give assurance of Indiana's support to such a policy.

Father A.B. Oechtering of Delphi visited Frankfort this year, and Mary joined the other Catholics in pleading with God to stop the war looming on the horizon. God did not listen.

On March 4th, Abraham Lincoln was inaugurated as President, and the Norris family rejoiced.

Following declarations of secession by the Confederate States of America, South Carolina demanded that the **United States** Army abandon its facilities at Fort Sumter in Charleston Harbor. On Friday, April 12th at 4:30 A.M., Confederate troops under Brigadier General P.G.T. Beauregard fired on the fort. The Union garrison under Major Robert Anderson formally surrendered the fort to Confederate personnel at 2:30 P.M. on April 13th. No one from either side was killed during the 34-hour bombardment. Following the capture of Fort Sumter, the states of Virginia, North Carolina, Arkansas and Tennessee joined the Confederacy.

Missouri and Virginia were divided on the issue of fighting for or against the rebellion; division led to the creation of a new state, West Virginia. Both Missouri and West Virginia continued to allow slavery; Missouri eventually sent twenty-two military units to fight for the Union and seventeen for the Confederacy; about 17,000 soldiers from West Virginia joined Confederate military units, while about 32,000 fought for the Union.

Three days after the Fort Sumter attack, on April 15th, President Lincoln called for 75,000 men to enlist for ninety days to put down the rebellion.

Three months' service time reflects the naivete of most people at the beginning of the Civil War. Little did they know that the resulting armed conflict would continue for four years in over 10,000 locations across the American continent, involving as many as three million warriors and killing over 600,000 of them, killing over 50,000 civilians, wounding and maiming many more. These figures vary according to who is doing the arithmetic, since the records kept at the time were not accurate. But no one disputes that the national scars from that war remain, and will likely never completely heal.

Indiana became the first Northern state to mobilize for the Civil War. Its geographical location, large population (fifth largest among Northern states), its railroad network with access to the Ohio River and Great Lakes for transport of troops and supplies, and its agricultural production of grain and livestock made the state's wartime support critical to the Union's success.

Lincoln requested 4,683 Indiana men, to be divided into six regiments for three months' service.

Indiana's Governor Morton sent Lincoln the following telegram:

Indianapolis, April 15, 1861.
To Abraham Lincoln, President of the United States: On behalf of the state of Indiana, I tender to the authority of the government, 10,000 men.
Oliver P. Morton,
Governor of Indiana

Orders were issued on April 16th to form the state's first regiments and for the men to gather at Indianapolis.

On April 18th, Robert E. Lee, the most promising officer of the regular United States Army, was called to Washington, D.C., and met with Francis Preston Blair, Sr. Empowered by Lincoln to "ascertain Lee's intentions and feelings," Blair asked Lee to assume command of the Union army being raised to put down the rebellion. Lee declined the offer and proceeded immediately to General Winfield Scott's office, where he recounted his conversation with Blair and reiterated that he would not accept the proffered command. Tradition has it that Scott, a fellow Virginian, replied, "Lee, you have made the greatest mistake of your life; but I feared it would be so." Word of Virginia's secession, voted by the state's convention on April 17th, appeared in local newspapers on the 19th. In the early morning hours of April 20th, Lee composed a one-sentence letter of resignation from the United States Army to Secretary of War Simon Cameron. Later that day he wrote a much longer letter to Scott that announced his decision and included one of the most frequently quoted sentences Lee ever penned or spoke: "Save in the defense of my native State, I never desire again to draw my sword."

The War Department took five days to process Lee's resignation, which became official on April 25th.

On April 21st, the governor of Virginia, John Letcher, appointed Lee to command the state militia. Lee traveled to Richmond on April 22nd, talked with Letcher and accepted his native state's call. On the morning of April 23rd, a four-man delegation from the secession convention accompanied Lee to the capitol. Shortly after noon, the five men entered the building, where delegates were in private session. Robert E. Lee accepted command of Virginia's forces. By so doing, Lee transferred his stated loyalty from the United States of America to Virginia, and to the Confederate States of America. It is impossible to assign blame for the horrific conflict known as the American Civil War to any one person, but at this moment in history, Robert E. Lee chose to become responsible for ensuring that armed conflict would begin. He proceeded to carry out warfare against his own countrymen, building and lengthening the fight perhaps more than anyone else could have done. Lee thereby became complicit in historic damage to the United States of America. His actions helped spread and strengthen an horrific national mind-set that to this day questions the equality of all humankind and proclaims the glory of war.

At that time, Frankfort, Indiana had no telegraph communication with the outside world, and waited until news was brought in from Lafayette, the nearest telegraph office. From there a message was sent to Governor Morton:

Lafayette, April 20, 1861

A letter just received from Judge Blake requests me to telegraph you that he has a company organized in Clinton County, which will be ready to move by Monday (April 22nd) or Tuesday, and that you must be sure to accept it. Of course you will.

John S. Williams

By April 25th, over 12,000 Indiana volunteers assembled at Indianapolis. They stayed at the former State Fair Grounds, which was renamed Camp Morton. Later during the war, the property also was used as a prison for captured Confederate soldiers; by 1868 it was restored, repaired, and returned to use as the State Fair Grounds.

Morton was instrumental in planning the overwhelming response of Indiana men, and from that time forth was known throughout the nation as "The Great War Governor."

On April 25th the new 11th Regiment, the Indiana Zouaves, gathered to receive their banners from their commander, Lew Wallace, who had been serving as Indiana's Adjutant General. He made them kneel and swear that they would never desert their regimental colors, and that they would avenge the disgrace cast upon Indiana soldiers after the Battle of Buena Vista by General Taylor.

The Clinton County company assembled promptly, and mustered in April 25th as Company C of the 10th Indiana Regiment, commanded by Colonel Joseph J. Reynolds.

Bram, however, had quickly called a meeting of his sons (except for Raper who was in California) and one son-in-law. Present were David Maish, Burr, Dailey, Abe, Harrison, and Davis (who had just turned 15). Many of their acquaintances and friends had rushed to sign on as soldiers, and they all were feeling pressure to do likewise.

"Do you think this war is important? Does it concern us?" Bram asked them. "And is it worth dying for?"

Harrison replied, eagerly, "Of course it's important! I want to go – God will protect me!"

Dailey said, "Preserving the Union for ourselves and our children is vital. How could we survive in a country where states keep breaking away, with no unifying national control over the economy?"

Abe chimed in, "And slavery. I have heard tales of the daily torture endured by black people in the South, and the horrific depravity of the white people who claim to own them. How can one person own another? If some of us must die to stop these conditions, at least we will have made the country a better place!"

Burr added, "But, the war is bound to be short anyway. It seems as if the boys who already signed up will be able to wrap things up quickly!"

David said, "And they will need food and supplies – which we are producing here at home."

Bram concluded the discussion. "The volunteer regiments are full. Our help is needed most to maintain a stable home front. If things change, we can re-evaluate and make more decisions. Whatever we do, we should do it together, as a family!"

Before hearing this, Mary had been quite anxious about the effect of the coming conflict upon her family. Bram was able to calm her somewhat, assuring her that the war was likely to be brief with a positive outcome.

The 6th Indiana Volunteer Infantry Regiment was raised in different parts of the state and organized at Indianapolis between April 22nd and April 27th. The 7th Indiana Volunteer Infantry had been organized at Indianapolis between April 21st and April 27th. These two regiments were sent to Grafton (now West Virginia) on May 30th. On June 3rd, they participated in the Battle of Philippi, one of the first land battles of the Civil War, a Union victory. They became the first Indiana troops to fight in the war.

In the counties along the Ohio River, men volunteered in May for the Indiana Legion, a state militia formed to stabilize the home front and protect against invasion from Confederate troops.

The 10th Indiana regiment (which included Clinton County soldiers) performed duty near Evansville, Indiana, until June 7th. It was then ordered to Western Virginia and attached to Brigadier General William Starke Rosecrans' Brigade, McClellan's Army of Western Virginia, where it occupied Buckhannon on June 30th.

Rosecrans' victories at Rich Mountain and Corrick's Ford in July of this year were among the very first Union victories of the war.

The 10th Indiana Infantry remained on duty at Beverly until July 24th, where there was an engagement on July 12th. Victorious Union troops captured 553 Confederate prisoners. The 10th Indiana men were mustered out of service on August 2nd. During three months of service, the regiment lost a total of six men: four killed or mortally wounded and two from disease. Many of the surviving men re-enlisted, joining other regiments.

During the entire period of the war Governor Morton performed intensive service, counseling the president, encouraging the people, organizing regiments, hurrying troops to the field, forwarding supplies, and inspiring all with the enthusiasm of his own earnestness. His labors for the relief of the soldiers and their dependent and needy families were held up as matters of emulation by the governors of other states, and the result of his efforts seconded by the people was that during the war over $600,000 of money and supplies were collected and conveyed to Indiana soldiers in camp, field, hospital and prison. He displayed extraordinary industry and ability, and his efforts earned him the title "Soldiers' Friend."

On July 17th, Dailey and Amanda's second child, Mary Indiana Norris was born, with Mary in attendance.

Ever since the attack at Fort Sumter in April, the Northern public had been clamoring for a march against the Confederate capital of Richmond, Virginia, which was expected to bring an early end to the rebellion. Yielding to political pressure, on July 21st, Abraham Lincoln sent Union forces under Brigadier General Irvin McDowell from Washington, D.C. toward Manassas Junction about 25 miles to the Southwest. The goal was to cut a railroad connection at Manassas, and then to attack Richmond, Virginia some 85 miles farther to the South. They crossed Bull Run toward Confederate troops under General P.G.T. Beauregard in Prince William County, Virginia. The Union troops were attempting a surprise attack, but were so slow at positioning themselves that Rebel reinforcements under Brigadier General Joseph E. Johnston had time to reinforce Beauregard's position. This action, the first major battle of the Civil War, was called the First Battle of Bull Run/Manassas. Each side had about 18,000 poorly trained, inexperienced and poorly led troops. As the Union troops withdrew under fire, many panicked and their retreat turned into a rout. This resulted in a Confederate victory, and it is considered to be the largest and bloodiest battle in United States history up to that point.

The Northern public was shocked at the unexpected defeat of their army when an easy victory had been widely anticipated. Both sides began to realize that the war would be longer and more brutal than they had imagined.

On July 26th, Mary was called to assist Sarah Maria with the birth of Abe's first child, Emma Luella Norris. As she usually did, Mary surreptitiously baptized the infant at her first opportunity. Because Abe and Sarah lived just across the road (N County Road 250 E), closest of all Mary's children, Mary was able to bond well with Sarah, and to help with baby Emma's care.

James Henry Lane (from Lawrenceburg, Indiana) was elected as one of Kansas' first United States Senators during this year, and was appointed Brigadier General of volunteers in December during this year. As such, he raised the "Frontier Guard" as well as commanding what was referred to as "Lane's Brigade" or the "Kansas Brigade," comprised of the Third, Fourth, Fifth, Sixth and Seventh Kansas Volunteers. He was also responsible for forming the First Kansas Colored Volunteers, the first regiment of African American troops to see action on the side of the Union during the Civil War.

After the Battle of Wilson's Creek, Missouri on August 10th, the Union army retreated, leaving the Kansas border exposed to attack from Rebel troops. To combat this, Lane organized his men and led them into action against Confederate General Sterling Price, in the Battle of Dry Wood Creek on September 2nd.
Even though his troops lost that battle, Lane continued on, fighting in a skirmish at Paninsville, Missouri on September 5th. Lane continued his cause, fighting through the towns of Butler, Harrisonville, and Clinton, Missouri, before he ended his campaign at Osceola, Missouri on September 23rd. Lane had heard that hidden caches of Confederate supplies and money were being held in Osceola. He therefore determined to wipe the town from the map. He and his men first stripped the buildings of all valuable goods, which were loaded into wagons taken from the townspeople. Though Lane's men found no hidden Confederate supplies nor money, nine citizens were given a farcical trial and shot. Finally, Lane's men brought their frenzy of pillaging and murder to a close by burning the entire town. The settlement suffered more than $1,000,000 worth of damage including belongings of pro-Union citizens. Lane's Brigade then celebrated by getting drunk, so much so, that according to reports, many of the men were unable to march when it came time to leave, and had to ride in wagons and carriages. With them, they took their plunder including Lane's personal share, which included a piano and a quantity of silk dresses. The troops then proceeded to Kansas City, Missouri.

From the end of July onward, many Clinton County as well as other

Indiana soldiers who had mustered out rejoined the Union army; new regiments and companies were formed, while old ones re-formed.

On July 29th, the 19th Indiana Infantry Regiment organized at Indianapolis. It was combined at Washington, D.C. into a brigade including regiments from Wisconsin and, eventually, Michigan, and was first activated on October 1st, fighting entirely in the Eastern Theater of the war. This brigade was noted for several things, including strong discipline, unique uniform appearance (hence the nickname, "Black Hats"), and tenacious fighting ability (engendering the nickname "Iron Brigade"). There were several other units known as Iron Brigade during the Civil War, but this particular one (known as "of the West") suffered the highest percentage of casualties of any in the war.

On August 22nd, the 3rd Regiment, Indiana Cavalry, Company E, with many men from Clinton County, organized at Madison, Indiana. They mustered out August 7, 1865 at Louisville, Kentucky.

The 3rd Battery, Indiana Light Artillery had many men from Clinton County. They organized at Connersville, Indiana, and mustered in at Indianapolis on August 24th. They mustered out August 21, 1865 at Indianapolis.

In September, the 14th and 15th Indiana regiments served during the Cheat Mountain campaign in Western Virginia.

The 10th Regiment, Indiana Infantry, Company C, and Reorganized Company C formed at Indianapolis, Indiana, September 18th with many men from Clinton County. The Veterans and Recruits transferred to the 58th Indiana Infantry on September 8, 1864. The old members mustered out September 19, 1864.

The 30th Regiment, Indiana Infantry, Reorganized Company D with many men from Clinton County formed at Fort Wayne, Indiana and mustered in September 24th. They performed duty in Texas during July, and duty at various other points till November 25th, 1865 when they mustered out.

The 51st Regiment, Indiana Infantry, Company B with many Clinton County men, organized at Indianapolis, Indiana, and mustered in December 14, 1861. It had duty at Green Lake and San Antonio till December 13th, 1865 when they mustered out.

The 40th Regiment, Indiana Infantry, Companies C, and E, with many men from Clinton County organized at Lafayette and Indianapolis, Indiana, and mustered in December 30th. It saw duty at Green Lake and San Antonio, Texas, and at Port Lavacca till they mustered out December 21, 1865.

That fall, Indiana Governor Morton went to Washington, D.C. to secure overcoats for Indiana troops.

By this time, railroads had definitely triumphed over canals in Indiana.

1862

After the South seceded and their delegates left Congress, the Republicans and other supporters from the upper South were finally able to pass the **United States Homestead Act.** *This act allowed independent farmers free access to new lands West of the Mississippi River. Southern legislators had feared that immigrants and poor Southern whites would take over the West, rather than wealthy planters who would develop it with the use of slaves, forcing "yeomen farmers" onto marginal lands. Selling the best land only to wealthy Southern planters would, of course, have extended slavery into the Western territories/states.*

The 12th Battery, Indiana Light Artillery had many men from Clinton County. They organized at Jeffersonville and Indianapolis, Indiana, and mustered in January 25th. The non-Veterans mustered out December 23, 1864. The remaining troops of the Battery mustered out July 7, 1865.

On March 8th and 9th, the Battle of Hampton Roads, also known as the Battle of the Ironclads, was fought in Virginia where the Elizabeth and Nansemond rivers meet the James River just before it enters Chesapeake Bay adjacent to Norfolk. This most noted naval battle of the American Civil War was part of the effort of the Rebels to break the Union blockade, which had cut off Virginia's largest cities, Norfolk and Richmond, from international trade.

The result of the battle was inconclusive, but this use of ironclads received worldwide attention. It had immediate effects on navies around the world. The preeminent naval powers, Great Britain and France, halted further construction of wooden-hulled ships in favor of metal. The new ships had guns mounted so that they could be fired in all directions, as well as rams installed in the hulls. The navies of other countries followed suit.

The Indiana Legislature was not in accord with the political views of Governor Morton. It refused to receive his message, and in other ways treated him with "want of consideration and respect." The Legislature was close to taking from Morton the command of the militia, when the Republican members withdrew, leaving both houses without a quorum. In order to carry on the state government and pay the state bonds, Morton obtained advances from banks and the county boards, and appointed the Bureau of Finance, which for two years made all disbursements of the state. During this period, he refused to summon the Legislature, and the Supreme Court condemned his arbitrary course, but the people subsequently applauded his action. By assuming great responsibilities, he kept the machinery of the state in motion and preserved its financial credit by securing advances through an Eastern banking house to pay the interest on the public debt.

The Battle of Shiloh, also known as the Battle of Pittsburg Landing, was fought on April 6th and 7th, in Southwestern Tennessee. Union troops under Major General Ulysses S. Grant faced Confederates under General Albert Sidney Johnston (who was mortally wounded during the fighting). Johnston's second-in-command, Brigadier General P.G.T. Beauregard, took over but decided against pressing an attack late in the evening. Overnight, Grant was reinforced by one of his own divisions stationed further North and was joined by three divisions under Major General Don Carlos Buell. This allowed Grant to launch an unexpected counterattack the next morning which completely reversed the Confederate gains of the previous day. Confederate forces were forced to retreat from the area, ending their hopes of blocking the Union advance into Northern Mississippi.

Fourteen Indiana regiments fought at Shiloh, which was the bloodiest battle in American history up to that time. The Union suffered 1,754 killed, 8,408 wounded, and 2,885 missing, while Confederates lost 1,728 killed, 8,012 wounded, and 959 missing or captured. About one-tenth of Union casualties were Indiana soldiers.

On April 8th, Indiana Governor Morton chartered river steamers to bring wounded soldiers home to Indiana. He sent 60 surgeons and 300 nurses to Tennessee.

Because Lew Wallace had failed to bring his Indiana troops into the battle quickly enough, he was not allowed battlefield command for some time afterward. He spent the remainder of his life trying to resolve the accusations and change public opinion about his role in the battle. In his autobiography, he lamented, "Shiloh and its slanders! Will the world ever acquit me of them? If I were guilty I would not feel them as keenly."

Slaves in the District of Columbia were freed on April 16th, and their owners were compensated.

The capture of New Orleans by the Union Army took about seven days, from April 25th to May 1st. This capture of the largest Confederate city and port was of international importance, affecting trade routes.

On June 19th, Congress prohibited slavery in all current and future United States territories (not in actual states), and President Lincoln quickly signed the legislation.

In July, during the "dark days of summer" of this year, Congress passed and Lincoln signed the Confiscation Act, containing provisions for court proceedings to liberate slaves held by convicted "Rebels" or of slaves that had escaped from the Confederacy to Union lines.

On July 18th, Confederate officer Adam Johnson invaded Indiana at Newburgh with a force of about thirty-five Kentucky guerrilla recruits. He convinced the town's Union garrison that he had cannon on the surrounding hills, although these were actually camouflaged stovepipes, charred logs and wagon wheels. Without a shot being fired, the Confederate commander confiscated supplies and ammunition; he also acquired the lasting nickname of Adam "Stovepipe" Johnson. Newburgh became the first town in a Northern state to be captured during the war, although it was held by the Confederates only briefly. The raid convinced the United States government of the need to supply Indiana with a permanent force of regular Union Army soldiers to counter future raids.

The Seven Days Battles were fought from June 25th to July 1st, near Richmond, Virginia. Confederate General Robert E. Lee drove the invading Union Army of the Potomac under Major General George B. McClellan away from Richmond and into a retreat down the Virginia Peninsula. Union forces lost over 15,000 men to casualties, while Confederates lost over 20,000. Regardless of these losses, the series of battles viewed together were considered a Confederate victory.

The 4th Regiment, *Indiana Cavalry, Company I had many men from Clinton County. This Unit was organized at Indianapolis, Indiana, and mustered in August 22nd. They had duty at Macon, Georgia until May and at Nashville and Edgefield, Tennessee, until June. They mustered out June 29th, 1865.*

The 72nd Indiana Infantry, Company K was organized at Lafayette, Indiana, and had many men from Clinton County. They mustered in for a three-year enlistment at Indianapolis on August 16th under the command of Colonel Abram O. Miller. The regiment was attached to nine other Union units during the three years: To the 40th Brigade, 12th Division, Army of the Ohio through November 1862; then to the 2nd Brigade, 5th Division, Center, XIV Corps, Army of the Cumberland, through January 1863; then to the 2nd Brigade, 5th Division, XIV Corps, through June 1863, with whom they took part in the Capture of Macon, Georgia April 20th and the pursuit of Jefferson Davis from May 6th - 10th; then to the 1st Brigade, 4th Division, XIV Corps, through October 1863; then to Wilder's Mounted Infantry Brigade, Cavalry Corps, Army of the Cumberland, through December 1863; then to the 3rd Brigade, 2nd Cavalry Division, Army of the Cumberland, through January 1864; then to the 3rd Brigade, Grierson's Cavalry Division, XVI Corps, Army of the Tennessee through March 1864; then to the 3rd Brigade, 2nd Cavalry Division, Army of the Cumberland, through October 1864; then to the 1st Brigade, 2nd Division, Wilson's Cavalry Corps, Military Division Mississippi, through June 1865. The 72nd Indiana Infantry moved to Nashville, Tennessee, May 23rd – June 15th 1865 where they mustered out of service on June 26th.

On August 28th - 30th, Major General John Pope led Union troops against Confederates under General Robert E. Lee at the Second Battle of Bull Run/Manassas in Prince William County Virginia. It was a battle of much larger scale and numbers than the First Battle of Bull Run/Manassas fought on July 21st, 1861 on the same ground. Lee led about 50,000 troops to victory against about 62,000 soldiers under Pope. This was a significant tactical victory for the Confederates, who would proceed to the North afterwards, and it was another blow to Union morale. The Union's Iron Brigade of the West covered Pope's retreat.

The 85th Regiment, Indiana Infantry, Companies G and H had many men from Clinton County, and mustered in September 4th at Lafayette, Indiana. They had operations in East Tennessee between March 15th and April 22nd and at Nashville till June. They mustered out June 6, 1865.

The 100th Regiment, Indiana Infantry, Company I organized at Fort Wayne, Indiana, and mustered in September 10th. Partly comprised of men from Clinton County, it marched to Washington, D.C., via Richmond, Virginia, April 29th - May 20th, and participated in the Grand Review May 24th. They mustered out July 8, 1865.

The Battle of Harpers Ferry, (now West Virginia) was fought on September 12th – 15th. At the confluence of the Potomac and Shenandoah Rivers, the ferry was the site of an historic Federal arsenal founded by President George Washington in 1799. In 1859, Harpers Ferry was the site of abolitionist John Brown's attack. The Rebels needed to control Harpers Ferry in order to secure their supply lines into Virginia, as well as to seize its supplies of rifles and ammunition. During this September, as General Robert E. Lee's Confederate army invaded Maryland, a portion of his army under Major General Thomas J. "Stonewall" Jackson surrounded, bombarded, and captured 12,419 men of the Union garrison at the arsenal, a major victory at the relatively minor cost of 286 Rebels killed or wounded.

On September 17th, the Battle of Antietam was fought near Sharpsburg, Maryland. It was the bloodiest single-day battle in American history, with a combined tally of 22,717 dead, wounded, or missing. Confederate General Robert E. Lee's army had invaded Maryland, but after this battle against Union troops under Major General George B. McClellan, the Rebels were forced to withdraw across the Potomac into Virginia. But the result of the actual fight was deemed inconclusive because McClellan, despite having superiority of numbers, failed to destroy Lee's army. McClellan's refusal to pursue Lee's army into Virginia led to his removal from command by President Lincoln in November.

The 14th Indiana Infantry regiment was nicknamed the "Gibraltar Brigade" for maintaining its position at the Battle of Antietam, while the 27th Indiana Infantry regiment earned the nickname "Giants in the Cornfield" at the same engagement.

Lincoln had been waiting for a Union victory in order to issue an Emancipation Proclamation. This was a political decision, designed not only to please Abolitionists, but the timing was also intended to reinforce the idea for non-abolitionists that the purpose of freeing slaves owned by Confederates was to preserve the Union.

On September 22nd, five days after the Battle of Antietam, Lincoln called his Cabinet into session and issued the Preliminary Emancipation Proclamation. Lincoln told Cabinet Members that he had made a covenant with God, that if the Union drove the Confederacy out of Maryland, he would issue this Proclamation. The Proclamation was "Preliminary," because it would not take effect for 100 days. It therefore functioned as a warning to states in rebellion, a threat as to what would happen if they continued to resist the Union.

Near the end of this year, James Henry Lane recruited the all African American 1st Kansas Volunteer Infantry (Colored) regiment, which skirmished with Confederates in October, becoming the first African-American Union unit to see combat during the Civil War.

The Battle of Fredericksburg, Virginia was fought on December 11th–15th between Confederates under General Robert E. Lee and the Union Army of the Potomac commanded by Major General Ambrose Burnside. Fredericksburg was a key transportation link between Richmond and Washington, D.C. The Union Army's futile frontal attacks on December 13th against entrenched Confederate defenders on Marie's Heights behind the city are remembered as one of the most one-sided battles of the war, with Union casualties more than three times as heavy as those suffered by the Confederates. A visitor to the battlefield described the battle to President Lincoln as a "butchery." Union forces suffered 12,653 casualties; Confederates lost 4,201 killed, wounded, captured or missing.

The Battle of Stones River or Second Battle of Murfreesboro was fought from December 31st - January 2nd in Middle Tennessee. Although the battle itself was inconclusive, the Union repulse of two Confederate attacks and the subsequent Confederate withdrawal were a much-needed boost to Union morale after the defeat at the Battle of Fredericksburg, and it dashed Confederate aspirations for control of Middle Tennessee. Of the major battles of the Civil War, Stones River had the highest percentage of casualties on both sides: Over 10,000 Union and 13,000 Confederate troops.

1863

On January 1st, the Emancipation Proclamation was issued by President Lincoln. It never became a law, and was never voted upon in Congress. Instead, the Proclamation was classified as part of the president's "war powers," what today might be called an Executive Order.

Under this proclamation, only the slaves within the ten states that had seceded were freed, and these freed slaves were authorized to enlist as units of Northern troops. The reaction among Northerners, especially Democrats, was not all favorable, and anti-war movements gained strength. Secret anti-war societies were formed, such as the Knights of the Golden Circle, (reorganized as the Order of American Knights, then as the Order of the Sons of Liberty), their leaders dubbed "Copperheads." The name came from heads of "Liberty" snipped from copper pennies and worn on clothing of the movement's adherents.

As the war dragged on, the Northern anti-war societies gained strength from their view that it was impossible to defeat the Confederacy, and that an armistice was the best solution to the war. Their opinions were strengthened by economic issues such as increased taxes to fund the war, and also by negrophobia whether conscious or subliminal.

On March 3rd the Enrollment Act, passed by the United States Congress was signed into law by President Lincoln. The purpose was to provide fresh manpower for Union military forces. A form of conscription, it required the enrollment of every male citizen between ages twenty and forty-five and also immigrants of the same age group who had filed for citizenship. This included each of Mary's sons except for Silas Davis, who had just turned seventeen. Luckily, the quota for soldiers from Clinton County had already been filled, and none of her sons was required to do more than enroll.

Bram had not been feeling well all winter, and Mary worried about him. He had no energy, no appetite, and had lost interest in many things (such as news of the war) that formerly had fascinated him. Mary and her daughters cooked his favorite foods, while his sons kept him updated on current events that they hoped would stimulate him to talk.

By early April, Bram had taken to his bed. His doctor could find nothing obvious wrong except for an irregular heartbeat, and he prescribed stimulants for Bram.

On April 12th, Mary awoke to find that Bram had died in his sleep. Her shriek of dismay and loud exclamations, followed by sobs, brought the children running. Mary of course washed Bram's body, dressing it in his best suit. When she could be alone, Mary prayed over his body, having baptized it with blessed water, pleading with God to admit Bram to eternal bliss. She covered all the mirrors in the house

As an important previous member of the Morris Chapel, Bram's body was taken to the church for a funeral. Mary claimed to be too distraught to attend. He was then interred at the relatively new (established 1848) I.O.O.F. (Independent Order of Odd Fellows) cemetery in Frankfort. As the Odd Fellows were a non-denominational group, Mary agreed with her children that she herself should be buried there when the time came. The family eventually erected a marker over Bram and Mary's remains, a tall metal pillar with pointed top and the Norris names and dates on rectangular plates around the base.

Mary's children gathered around her in support, but it took many months before she was able to function normally again. She reflected that meeting Bram had been the most wonderful event of her life, changing a mostly horrific past into a beautiful future.

Mary requested that a message be sent to California to notify Raper of his father's passing, and her son returned home in late June. She hardly recognized him, as he had gained a confident air as well as a deep tan from years of fortune-seeking in the California sun. Two of his sons, James and Luther, remained in California, but Henry Clay and Mary, who had been only seven and six years old when their father and brothers left, had trouble connecting with Raper after six years of separation.

The Vicksburg Campaign, from March 29th- July 4th, was a series of

maneuvers and battles directed against Vicksburg, Mississippi, a fortress city that dominated the last Confederate-controlled section of the Mississippi River. The Union Army of the Tennessee under Major General Ulysses S. Grant gained control of the river by capturing this stronghold and defeating Lieutenant General John C. Pemberton's forces stationed there. Losses at Vicksburg between May 18th and July 4th totaled Confederate 32,697 (29,495 surrendered), Union 4,835.

The Battle of Chancellorsville was fought from April 30th – May 6th in Spotsylvania County, Virginia. It was part of a campaign that pitted Major General Joseph Hooker's Army of the Potomac against General Robert E. Lee's Confederate Army of Northern Virginia. Chancellorsville is known as Lee's "perfect battle" because his risky decision to divide his army in the presence of a much larger enemy force resulted in a significant Confederate victory. The Confederates lost 13,460 troops, while the Union lost 17,304.

The victory, a product of Lee's audacity and Hooker's timid decision making, was tempered by heavy casualties, including Lieutenant General Thomas J. "Stonewall" Jackson. Jackson was hit by friendly fire, requiring his left arm to be amputated. He died of pneumonia on May 10th, a loss that Lee likened to losing his own right arm.

On May 10th, Amanda Norris bore Dailey his 3rd child, Laura Belle Norris. Mary reflected that the Norris-Fudge marriage unions seemed to be working out well.

In late May, General Robert E. Lee headed North with a total of 65,000 men: Three corps under Lieutenant General James Longstreet, Lieutenant General Richard S. Ewell and Lieutenant General A.P. Hill on June 16th crossed into Maryland, raiding for supplies along the way. Also under Lee was a cavalry division commanded by Major General J.E.B. Stuart, but this division was on its own, galloping through the countryside, around Union troops, and eventually into Pennsylvania. Stuart's cavalry did not join Lee until he reached Gettysburg, Pennsylvania in July.

West Virginia entered the Union on June 20th as the 35th state.

June 11th through July 26th saw Brigadier General John Hunt Morgan's raid, in which his 2,000 horsemen proceeded from Sparta, Tennessee;

North across Kentucky; across the Ohio River at Brandenburg; East across Southern Indiana through Corydon, Salem, Vienna, and North Vernon, into Ohio; East across Ohio, then North to Salineville.

The raid was meant to draw Union troops away from the major campaigns and also to frighten Northern civilians into demanding that their troops be recalled to defend them.

On June 17th, one of Morgan's officers, Captain Thomas Hines and approximately 80 men crossed the Ohio River to search for horses and support from Hoosiers in Southern Indiana. During this minor incursion, "Hines' Raid," local citizens and members of Indiana's home guard pursued the Confederates and captured most of them without a fight. Hines and a few of his men escaped across the river into Kentucky.

On July 8th, General Morgan crossed the Ohio River, landing at Mauckport, Indiana with 2,400 troopers. Their arrival was initially contested by a small party from the Indiana Legion, who withdrew after Morgan's men began firing artillery from the river's Southern shore. The state militia quickly retreated towards Corydon, Indiana where a larger body was gathering to block Morgan's advance. The Confederates advanced rapidly on the town and engaged in the Battle of Corydon on July 9th. This was the only pitched battle of the Civil War that occurred in Indiana. After a brief but fierce fight, Morgan took command of high ground South of town, and Corydon's local militia and citizens promptly surrendered after Morgan's artillery fired two warning shots. Corydon was sacked, but little damage was done to its buildings. Morgan continued his raid North and burned most of the town of Salem.

When Morgan appeared to be headed toward Indianapolis, panic spread through the capital city. Governor Morton had called up the state militia as soon as Morgan's intention to cross into the state was known, and more than 60,000 men of all ages volunteered to protect Indiana against Morgan's men. Morgan considered attacking Camp Morton to free more than 5,000 Confederate prisoners of war imprisoned there, but decided against it. Instead, his raiders turned abruptly East and began moving towards Ohio. With Indiana's militia in pursuit, Morgan's men continued to raid and pillage their way toward the Indiana-Ohio border, crossing into Ohio on July 13th. By the time Morgan left Indiana, his raid had become a desperate attempt to escape across the Ohio River to the South. He was captured on July 26th in

Northeastern Ohio near the Pennsylvania border, and forced to surrender what remained of his command. Morgan and other senior officers were kept in the Ohio state penitentiary, but they tunneled their way out and casually took a train to Cincinnati, where they crossed the Ohio River to safety.

General Robert E. Lee had led his Confederate troops North into Pennsylvania by late June. His objective was to engage the Union army on its own territory, and destroy it, thus ending the conflict.

On July 1st, Lee's troops headed towards Gettysburg, Pennsylvania in search of shoes. General John Buford's Union cavalry met them on low ridges Northwest of the town, and was joined by two corps of Union infantry including the 19th Indiana regiment. Two large Confederate Corps assaulted them, collapsing the hastily developed Union lines, sending them through the streets of the town to the hills to the South.

The 19th Indiana pushed part of James J. Archer's Confederate brigade off McPherson's Ridge, and then defended the heights later in the day. When the I Corps retreated to Cemetery Hill, the Iron Brigade of the West (including the 19th Indiana regiment) was sent to nearby Culp's Hill, where they entrenched with Buford's troops, who were rallied on Culps Hill and Cemetery Ridge by Union Major General Winfield Scott. The 19th Indiana Regiment lost 123 men on that day.

By July 2nd, most of both armies had assembled for battle. The Union line was laid out in a defensive formation resembling a fishhook. In the late afternoon, Lee launched a heavy assault on the Union left flank, and fierce fighting raged at Little Round Top, the Wheatfield, Devil's Den, and the Peach Orchard. On the Union right, Confederate troops made full-scale assaults on Culp's Hill and Cemetery Hill. Despite significant losses, the Union defenders held their lines.

On July 3rd, fighting resumed on Culp's Hill, and cavalry battles raged to the East and South. The main event of that day was Pickett's Charge, a dramatic infantry assault by 12,500 Confederates against the center of the Union line on Cemetery Ridge. The charge was repulsed by Union rifle and artillery fire, at great loss to the Confederate army.

Between 46,000 and 51,000 soldiers from both armies were casualties in the three-day Battle of Gettysburg, the most costly in US history.

Indiana regiments that suffered heavily at Gettysburg included the 7th, 14th, 19th and 20th.

Lee led his army on a torturous retreat towards Virginia.

On August 21st in Kansas, James Henry Lane was the main target of what became known as "Quantrill's Raid" and "The Lawrence Massacre." Confederate partisan leader William Quantrill attacked pro-Union Lawrence, Kansas, killing an estimated 200 people. Senator Lane escaped the massacre by spending the night hiding in a cornfield.

On September 19th - 20th, the Battle of Chickamauga was fought in Georgia. William Rosecrans' Army of the Potomac met Braxton Bragg's Army of Tennessee. This was the first major battle of the war fought in Georgia, the most significant Union defeat in the Western Theater, and involved the second-highest number of casualties after the Battle of Gettysburg. From Indiana, 28 regiments of infantry, 2 regiments plus one battalion of cavalry, and 8 batteries of artillery participated. Eli Lilly commanded the 18th artillery that fired the first shell on Bragg's advancing troops. For Indiana, this was the costliest battle of the war, with over 3,000 casualties.

On October 1st, the 7th Regiment, Indiana Cavalry, Company K, with many men from Clinton County, was organized at Indianapolis, Indiana, and mustered in. They mustered out at Austin, Texas, February 18, 1866.

On October 3rd, President Abraham Lincoln announced a national day of Thanksgiving, to be observed on the last Thursday of November. His proclamation read, in part: "In the midst of a civil war of unequaled magnitude and severity … peace has been preserved with all nations, order has been maintained, the laws have been respected and obeyed, and harmony has prevailed everywhere, except in the theater of military conflict."

It took another year before very many people actually celebrated this as a holiday. But Mary served a special dinner in early afternoon, complete with ham, fresh breads and pies. She considered any proclamation from Lincoln to be of utmost import, worthy of her attention and effort. Besides, it distracted her from the lingering sadness brought on by Bram's death.

The 11th Regiment, Indiana Cavalry, Company M had many men from Clinton County. They organized at Lafayette, Kokomo and Indianapolis between November 10th, 1863 and April 2nd, 1864. They were attached to the District of Northern Alabama, Department of the Cumberland, through November 1864; then to the 1st Brigade, 5th Division, Cavalry Corps, Military Division of Mississippi through May 1865; then to the District of Kansas, Department of Missouri through September 1865. They mustered out at Fort Leavenworth, Kansas, on September 19, 1865.

On November 19, President Lincoln used the dedication ceremony for the Gettysburg National Cemetery to honor the fallen Union soldiers and redefine the purpose of the war in his historic Gettysburg Address.

1864

On January 12th, the War Department notified Indiana Governor Morton that a new Indiana regiment (recruitment had begun in December 1863) would be called the "28th Regiment of **United States** Colored Troops." Additional recruits for these Colored Troops, with many men from Clinton County, mustered in on April 20th. On April 25th, six companies of the 28th left Indianapolis for Washington, D.C., where they were attached to the capital's defenses.

On July 30th, the 28th sustained heavy casualties at the Battle of the Crater at the Seige of Petersburg, Virginia, when nearly half of its soldiers were killed or wounded. Following the Battle of the Crater, the depleted ranks of the 28th were filled with four more companies of recruits from Indiana, sent to make the command a full regiment. The commander, Lieutenant Colonel Russell, was reappointed as the regimental commander with the rank of Colonel on August 23rd. Russell was also brevetted Brigadier General on July 30th in recognition of the 28th's performance at The Crater.

After the Confederate surrender at Appomattox in 1865, the 28th was moved to the Mexican border in Texas as part of the American response to the French intervention in Mexico.

The 28th was formally mustered out in Corpus Christi, Texas on November 8, 1865. It returned to Indianapolis January 6, 1866, to a reception in its honor. The regiment suffered a total of 212 fatalities: Two officers and 45 enlistees killed and mortally wounded in combat and one officer and 164 enlistees who died of disease.

During 1864, the first County Farm in Clinton County, Indiana, was established on 303 acres. This was a home maintained at county taxpayer expense for the poor, handicapped and elderly who had no other means of support. Those residents able to do so maintained the property, growing crops and livestock to assist in feeding the others.

During this year, Oliver Hazard Perry Throck Morton was again nominated for Indiana Governor against the Honorable Joseph E. McDonald. These two distinguished men made a joint canvas of the state, and passed through it with the utmost good feeling.

On February 27th, Santa Anna returned to Veracruz after promising General Achille Bazaine not to be politically active. Santa Anna nevertheless continued to seek power. Since he had violated the terms of his re-entry, Bazaine deported Santa Anna from Veracruz on March 12th.

In March, Ulysses S. Grant was summoned from the Western Theater of the Civil War, promoted to Lieutenant General, and given command of all Union armies. This left Major General William Tecumseh Sherman in charge of the Western portion of the Union Army.

General Grant, President Lincoln, and Secretary of War Edwin Stanton devised a coordinated strategy to strike at the heart of the Confederacy from multiple directions, including attacks against Lee near Richmond, Virginia, as well as against Confederates in the Shenandoah Valley, West Virginia, Georgia, and in Mobile, Alabama. This was the first time the Union armies had a coordinated offensive strategy across a number of theaters.

May 5th - 7th saw the Battle of the Wilderness in Virginia, where Indiana troops suffered heavy losses. This was followed by the Battle of Spotsylvania Courthouse from May 8th - 21st, with more heavy losses for Indiana troops. These battles were an attempt by Union Generals Grant and Meade to wear down Lee's Confederate forces. The Union lost 17,666 men, while the South lost 11,033.

On May 7th, Major General Sherman's troops, including large numbers of Indiana soldiers, began a march from Chattanooga to Atlanta. This movement became a continuous running battle. After the fall of Atlanta, one half of the Indiana regiments under Thomas pursued Hood toward Nashville, helping to defeat him there. The other half of the Indiana regiments accompanied Sherman to Savannah, then North into the Carolinas.

The 135th Regiment, Indiana Infantry, Companies B, C, F, and H with many men from Clinton County organized at Indianapolis, Indiana, and mustered in May 23rd. It served as the Railroad Guard in Tennessee and Alabama, Department of the Cumberland, until September. The survivors were mustered out September 29th.

May 31st – June 12th saw the Battle of Cold Harbor, with the most significant fighting occurring on June 3rd. It is remembered as one of American history's bloodiest, most lopsided battles. Thousands of Union soldiers under Generals Grant and Meade were killed or wounded in a hopeless frontal assault against the fortified positions of General Robert E. Lee's Rebel army. Indiana troops suffered heavy losses. Grant said of the battle in his memoirs, "I have always regretted that the last assault at Cold Harbor was ever made. No advantage whatever was gained to compensate for the heavy loss we sustained."

The 139th Regiment, Indiana Infantry, Companies B, C, F, and H with many Clinton County men, organized at Indianapolis, Indiana, and mustered in June 5th. They mustered out September 29th, 1865.

June 9th of this year - March 5th of 1865 saw the Siege of Petersburg, Virginia. The 19th Indiana Regiment served there with the Iron Brigade of the West. The campaign consisted of nine months' warfare in which Union forces commanded by Lieutenant General Ulysses S. Grant assaulted Petersburg unsuccessfully, constructing trench lines that eventually extended over 30 miles from the Eastern outskirts of Richmond, Virginia, around the Eastern and Southern outskirts of Petersburg. Petersburg was crucial to the supply of Confederate General Robert E. Lee's army as well as to the Confederate capital of Richmond. Numerous raids were conducted and battles fought in attempts to cut off the Richmond and Petersburg Railroad. The effectiveness of this siege led to Lee's surrender at Appomattox Court House in April 1865.

In July, Lew Wallace marched Indiana troops out of Baltimore to slow Jubal Early's Rebels at the Battle of Monocacy, possibly saving Washington, D.C. from capture.

On July 21st, Abe and Sarah Norris had their second child, George Lincoln Norris. Mary of course assisted with the delivery of her grandson, as well as caring for three year old Emma during Sarah's recovery from childbed.

Proclamation 118 - Thanksgiving Day
By the President of the United States of America

It has pleased Almighty God to prolong our national life another year, defending us with His guardian care against unfriendly designs from abroad and vouchsafing to us in His mercy many and signal victories over the enemy, who is of our own household. It has also pleased our Heavenly Father to favor as well our citizens in their homes as our soldiers in their camps and our sailors on the rivers and seas with unusual health. He has largely augmented our free population by emancipation and by immigration, while He has opened to us new sources of wealth and has crowned the labor of our workingmen in every department of industry with abundant rewards. Moreover, He has been pleased to animate and inspire our minds and hearts with fortitude, courage, and resolution sufficient for the great trial of civil war into which we have been brought by our adherence as a nation to the cause of freedom and humanity, and to afford to us reasonable hopes of an ultimate and happy deliverance from all our dangers and afflictions:

Now, therefore, I, Abraham Lincoln, President of the United States, do hereby appoint and set apart the last Thursday in November next as a day which I desire to be observed by all my fellow-citizens, wherever they may then be, as a day of thanksgiving and praise to Almighty God, the beneficent Creator and Ruler of the Universe. And I do further recommend to my fellow-citizens aforesaid that on that occasion they do reverently humble themselves in the dust and from thence offer up penitent and fervent prayers and supplications to the Great Disposer of Events for a return of the inestimable blessings of peace, union, and harmony throughout the land which it has pleased Him to assign as a dwelling place for ourselves and for our posterity throughout all generations.

In testimony whereof I have hereunto set my hand and caused the seal of the United States to be affixed.

Done at the city of Washington, this 20th day of October, A.D. 1864, and of the Independence of the United States the eighty-ninth.

ABRAHAM LINCOLN

On October 19th, Mary and her children went to the Common Pleas Court in Frankfort to complete the division of Bram's property. Since Bram had owned plots of land in various locations, the written descriptions were rather complicated. The upshot was that Mary received 1/3 of Bram's land, including their house. She left the meeting saddened, but grateful that the process was completed.

On October 31st, Nevada entered the Union as the 36th state.

In November, Abraham Lincoln was re-elected President with a new Vice-President, Andrew Johnson. In Clinton County, Indiana, Lincoln got 1,413 votes while his opponent, George B. McClellan got 1,501.

For Governor, Clinton County gave Joseph E. McDonald 1,513 votes; Oliver Hazard Perry Throck Morton got 1,473. But after all votes in the state were tallied, Morton won re-election for Governor by an overwhelming majority.

On Thursday, November 24th, the Norris family gathered at Mary's house to celebrate their second Thanksgiving Day dinner. In anticipation of the event, Mary had in the spring induced her children to rear several turkeys, of which the largest was chosen for the feast.

After dinner, the family gathered to sing. Mary accompanied them, playing her new harmonium, or pump organ. *Shall We Gather At The River* was a popular hymn at this time, and the Norris family sang it with gusto.

On November 30th the United States Department of War authorized Governor Morton to raise one regiment of infantry composed of African Americans. On December 3rd, the state's Adjutant General issued orders to begin accepting enlistments on December 24th.

1865

Prior to the Civil War, two lines of the Underground Railroad passed near Clinton County, but not through it. One went from Indianapolis to Westfield, through Russiaville to Logansport; the other from Terre Haute through Crawfordsville and Darlington to Lafayette. During the war, many black refugees came to Indiana, many settling near Thorntown, from where they gradually spread to neighboring territory including Frankfort. Towards the end of the war, there was a scandal at Frankfort involving a negro and a white woman, and a crowd collected to "clean out the niggers." For a while there was danger of a riot and/or a lynching. But cooler heads prevailed, and it was agreed to pack the black people up and take them back to Thorntown "where they belonged." Farmers near the town gave assistance, loading the colored colony into wagons, hauling them to Thorntown, and dumping them there.

Governor Morton suffered a partial paralytic stroke, affecting the lower part of the body, so that he never walked afterward without the use of canes. His mind, however, was in no wise affected by the shock, but continued to grow stronger while he lived.

Santa Anna attempted to return and offer his services during the French Invasion of Mexico, posing once again as Mexico's defender and savior, only to be refused by Benito Juarez, who was well aware of Santa Anna's character.

The Indiana Legislature banned the sale of intoxicants on Sundays. This remained in effect for the next 153 years!

The 150th Regiment, Indiana Infantry, Companies D, F, I, and K, with many men from Clinton County organized at Indianapolis, Indiana, and mustered in on March 9th. They mustered out on August 5th in Virginia.

In early April, Mary was visited by four of her sons: Raper the 41 year-old widower with two teenage children; Daily, 31, who had married Amanda Jane Fudge and had three children; Abe, 24, who lived across the road with his wife Sarah and their two young children; and William, 23, who was not married. The men had brought along a cousin, Thomas Norris.

"The war is winding down, Mama," said Raper. "We're going to join up and help finish it off!"

Mary sank into a chair, in shock. She had heard that the war was likely to end soon, but remembered well that this notion had been presented as fact for *years*, and had turned out to be wrong. She, at 59 years old, had been depending on the fact that her sons were all nearby, able and willing to care for her during the remaining years of her widowhood.

"But what about your farms, your families? Who will care for them while you are gone?" she asked.

"Don't worry, Mama," said Abe. "We'll be back before you know it. And we each get a $400 bounty to enlist!"

"And you still have Altha and Burr with their families, and of course Lavina, Phoebe and Eliza, plus Raper's kids Henry and Mary here at your house," added Daily.

The Norris men left Frankfort for Indianapolis a few days later, where they mustered into Company F of the 154th Indiana Infantry on April 10th. The thirty-five Clinton County men in this group each received a $400 bounty to enlist. This was the end of war bounties, and none of these men saw actual battle. The complete 154th Indiana Infantry, totaling 1,380 men was organized at Indianapolis on April 20th. All these were one year enlistments, but the men were discharged early because the war had ended.

On April 9th, Confederate General Robert E. Lee surrendered at Appomattox. But the battles, raids, and other conflict continued throughout North America as the war slowly ground to a halt.

The men of the 154th Indiana Infantry left Indianapolis by train for Parkersburg, West Virginia on April 28th, arriving there on April 30th. They were moved to Stevenson's Station in the Shenandoah Valley, Virginia between May 2nd and 4th, where they remained until June 27th, doing guard duty. They proceeded to Opequam Creek, doing guard duty at Winchester, Virginia until mustered out at Opequam Creek on August 4th.

Early on the morning of April 15th, Mary's son Burr arrived at her house. The expression on his face frightened her, and the words from his mouth upset her horribly.

"President Lincoln has been shot," he said. "He died last night, but they haven't caught the assassin yet."

Mary began to cry. Grief overwhelmed her, and she mourned for many days. It did not help that four of her sons had left to join the army. She felt as if the chaos of the war was descending upon her.

In mid-April, Andrew Johnson took charge of Presidential Reconstruction, the first phase of Reconstruction which lasted until the Radical Republicans gained control of Congress in the 1866 elections. His conciliatory policies towards the South, his hurry to reincorporate the former Confederates back into the union, and his vetoes of civil rights bills embroiled him in a bitter dispute with some Republicans.

Abraham Lincoln's nine-car funeral train arrived at Indianapolis at 7 AM on Sunday, April 30th. The coffin was carried to the Indiana State House in a hearse topped by a silver-gilt eagle. 100,000 people had gathered there to view his bier. Although rain had been almost an everyday occurrence on the journey, it was so heavy at Indianapolis that the giant procession was canceled and the entire day devoted to the viewing inside the State House. Because of the rain, Governor Oliver Hazard Perry Throck Morton declined to give his oration. Streetcars in Indianapolis bore slogans of mourning: Car #10 said, "Sorrow for the Dead; Justice for the Living; Punishment for Traitors." Car #13 said, "Fear Not, Abraham; I Am Thy Shield; Thy Reward Shall Be Exceedingly Great." Car #20 said, "Thou Art Gone and Friend and Foe Alike Appreciate Thee Now."

Late in the evening the Lincoln Special departed Indianapolis destined for Chicago, a journey of 210 miles. The train was scheduled to pass through Whitestown, Lebanon, Thorntown, Colfax, Clarksville, Lafayette, and other towns.

Burr had let Mary know about the route as well as the schedule for the funeral train, and she prevailed on him to take her on horseback to Thorntown, where they stayed in a boarding house on Sunday night. In the early hours of the morning, before dawn, Burr and Mary rose from their cots and joined the crowd at the railroad station. A bonfire burned brightly, and a minister led the crowd in hymns and prayers.

As the funeral train passed by, many people, including Mary, cried and called upon God to bless the soul of Abraham Lincoln.

The first group calling itself the Ku Klux Klan was founded in Southern states, and existed until the early 1870s when Federal laws limited their activities. In subsequent years, at least two additional incarnations of the Ku Klux Klan formed in different parts of the United States, and the organization continues as a curse upon the American political landscape to this very day.

On May 12th and 13th the Battle of Palmito Ranch or Battle of Palmito Hill, was fought on the banks of the Rio Grande East of Brownsville, Texas as part of the Union Invasion of Texas. The 34th Indiana Veteran Volunteer Infantry Regiment, nicknamed *The Morton Rifles*, participated in this action. One of their number became the last soldier killed during the war, Private John J. Williams (born in Jay County, Indiana) of Company B.

On August 7th, the 154th Indiana Infantry, including Mary's sons and nephew, arrived at Indianapolis. On August 8th, they attended a reception for returning regiments on the capitol grounds, and soon after 32 officers and 734 men were discharged from service. The regiment lost one enlisted man killed, and forty died from disease.

When her sons returned home a few days later, Mary cried tears of relief.

During the Civil War, Indiana furnished one hundred twenty-nine infantry regiments to the Union Army. In addition, the state furnished thirteen cavalry regiments plus three companies of cavalry, one heavy artillery regiment, and twenty-six light artillery batteries. Another 1,078 Indiana men served as sailors and marines. Altogether, Indiana men fought in at least 308 military engagements in seventeen states.

The total number of men serving from Indiana was about 196,363. It is estimated that 7,243 of these died of battle wounds; 17,785 died of other causes such as disease; and 10,000 deserted during their service.

General Robert E. Lee completed his time on the stage of 19th-century **United States** history without a dominant national identity. Intense private grievances and political scar tissue from the war guaranteed that his renewed loyalty to the United States, compelled by defeat on the battlefield, never could equal what it had been before the secession crisis. His postwar letters and statements abound with evidence that he thought of himself most often as a Virginian and a white Southerner, the antebellum loyalties that had taken him away from the United States and into the Confederacy.

Members of the Whig and Republican parties blamed the Civil War (as well as the Mexican War) on the Democrats.

On September 7th, Mary's son Dailey and his wife Amanda' fourth child, a daughter, was born, but she died on December 17th.

After returning from Civil War service, Mary's son Raper married a widow, Rachel (Lee) whose husband Albert P. Hendrickson had died.

The Civil War forever altered Indiana's economy. Despite hardships during the war, Indiana's economic situation improved. Farmers received higher prices for their agricultural products. Railroads and commercial businesses thrived in the state's cities and towns, and manpower shortages gave laborers more bargaining power.

The war also helped establish a national banking system to replace state-chartered banking institutions; by 1862 there were thirty-one national banks in the state. Prosperity was particularly evident in Indianapolis, whose population had more than doubled during the war, reaching 45,000 by the end of 1864.

Increased wartime manufacturing and industrial growth in Hoosier cities and towns ushered in a new era of economic prosperity. By the end of the war, Indiana had become less rural that it previously had been. The state's Southern counties experienced growth after the war at a slower rate than its other counties, as the state's population shifted to central and Northern Indiana, where new industries and cities began to develop around the Great Lakes and the railroad depots erected during the war.   In 1876, Colonel Eli Lilly opened a new pharmaceutical laboratory in Indianapolis, founding what later became Eli Lilly and Company. Indianapolis was also the wartime home of Richard Gatling, inventor of the Gatling Gun, one of the world's first machine guns. Although his invention was used in some Civil War-era campaigns, it was not fully adapted for use by the **United States** Army until 1866. Charles Gerard Conn, another war veteran, founded C.G. Conn, Ltd. in Elkhart, Indiana, where the manufacturing of musical instruments became a new industry for the town.   Post-war development was different in Southern Indiana. The state's commerce along the Ohio River was reduced during the war, especially after the closure of the Mississippi River to commercial trade with the South and increased competition from the state's expanding railroad network. Some of Indiana's river towns, such as Evansville, recovered by providing transport to Union troops across the Ohio River, but others did not. Before the war, New Albany was the largest city in the state, primarily due to its commerce with the South, but its trade dwindled during the war. After the war much of Indiana viewed New Albany as too friendly to the South. New Albany's formerly robust steamboat-building industry ended in 1870; the last steamboat built in New Albany was named the Robert E. Lee. New Albany never regained its pre-war stature; its population leveled off at 40,000, and only the antebellum, early-Victorian Mansion Row district remains from its boom period.

Based on an average family size of four persons, more than half of Indiana's households contributed a family member to fight in the war, making the effects of the conflict widely felt throughout the state. More Hoosiers died in the Civil War than in any other conflict. Although twice as many Hoosiers served in World War II, almost twice as many died in the Civil War. After the war, veterans programs were initiated to help wounded soldiers with housing, food, and other basic needs. In addition, orphanages and asylums were established to assist women and children. After the war, some women who had been especially active in supporting the war on the home front turned their organizational skills to other concerns, especially prohibition and women's suffrage. In 1874, for example, Zerelda Wallace, the wife of former Indiana Governor David Wallace and stepmother of General Lew Wallace, became a founder of the Indiana chapter of the Women's Christian Temperance Union and served as its first president.

1866

On April 11th, Mary's nephew who had served in the Civil War with her sons, Thomas C. Norris, died. It is suspected that he caught one of the common diseases of the era while in the military. He left a family of young children, and the family gathered to help his widow.

In the fall, Burr's wife Clarissa delivered a baby boy, John Wilford Norris.

The years following the Civil War saw Indiana's railroads providing increased service for passenger transportation, plus delivery of fuel and raw materials to support Indiana's growing manufacturing businesses. Improvements during this period included standardization of track and compatible wheels, couplers and brakes, which permitted interchange of cars instead of unloading and reloading freight.

On July 1st, Senator James Henry Lane, 52 years old, originally from Lawrenceburg, Indiana, shot himself in the head as he jumped from his carriage in Leavenworth, Kansas. He was allegedly deranged, depressed, had been charged with abandoning his fellow Radical Republicans and had been accused of financial irregularities. He died ten days after the self-inflicted gunshot.

1867

In January, Governor Morton of Indiana was elected to the United States Senate, and immediately thereafter resigned the governorship to Conrad Baker, who served the remainder of the gubernatorial term.

Conrad Baker, Governor of Indiana from 1867 to 1873, was born in Franklin County, Pennsylvania in 1817. He was educated at the Pennsylvania College, Gettysburg, read law at the office of Stevens & Smyser, and was admitted to the bar in the spring of 1839, at Gettysburg, where he had a lucrative practice for two years.

He came to Indiana in 1841, and settled at Evansville, where he practiced his profession until after the commencement of the rebellion.

He was elected to the lower house of the General Assembly of Indiana in 1845, and served one session. In 1852, he was elected Judge of the district composed of the counties of Vanderburg and Warrick, in which capacity he served about one year, and then resigned. In 1856, he was nominated for Lieutenant Governor by the Republican Party without his knowledge, on the ticket with Oliver Hazard Perry Throck Morton. They were defeated by Willard and Hammond. In 1861, Mr. Baker was commissioned Colonel of the 1st Cavalry Regiment of Indiana Volunteers, which he organized, and with which he served until September 1864, when he was elected Lieutenant Governor.

In 1865, Governor Morton convened the General Assembly in special session, and immediately after delivering his message, started for Europe in quest of health, leaving Colonel Baker in charge of the Executive Department of the state government. Governor Morton was absent five months, during which time the duties of the Executive office were performed by Lieutenant Governor Baker.

In February 1867, Governor Morton was elected to the Senate of the

United States, in consequence of which the duties of Governor devolved upon Mr. Baker. He was unanimously nominated by the Republican convention of 1868, for Governor, and was elected over Thomas A. Hendricks, by a majority of 961 votes. He served as Governor with ability and dignity, until the inauguration of Mr. Hendricks in 1873, after which he engaged in the practice of law in Indianapolis, being a member of one of the strongest and most widely known law firms in the state.

Mary's daughter Lavina Jane married Edward C. Ewbank on January 9th. Edward's parents, Robert born in Kilburn, Yorkshire, England and Jane (Milburn) born in Indiana Ewbank, had married in Dearborn County, Indiana in 1832 and moved to Clinton County, Indiana where they became founding members of the Michigantown Methodist Episcopal Church in Spring of 1837.

On March 1st, Nebraska entered the Union as the 37th state.

On March 30th, the United States reached an agreement to purchase Alaska from Russia for a price of $7.2 million. The Treaty with Russia was negotiated and signed by Secretary of State William Seward and Russian Minister to the United States Edouard de Stoeckl.

On June 3rd, Santa Anna returned to Veracruz, claiming **United States** endorsement for ruling Mexico. On June 4th, with help from **United States** troops, he was removed to Sisal, Yucatán, and imprisoned on July 30th. But on November 2nd, he sailed to Havana, Cuba, and then to the Bahamas.

1868

On January 25th, Mary's son Dailey and his wife Amanda had their 5th child, Charles E. Norris.

The Radicals in the House of Representatives impeached President Andrew Johnson during this year while charging him with violating the Tenure of Office Act, a law enacted by Congress in March 1867 over Johnson's veto. He was acquitted by a single vote in the Senate.

During the presidential election of this year, in Clinton County, General Ulysses S. Grant, the Republican nominee, got 1,794 votes while New York Governor Horatio Seymour, the Democrat, got 1,764. Grant was elected President, and became the first President to serve for two full terms since Andrew Jackson forty years before. He led Radical Reconstruction and built a powerful patronage-based Republican party in the South, with the adroit use of the army. He took a hard line that reduced violence by groups such as the Ku Klux Klan.

Schuyler Colfax, born 1823, had moved with his mother, step-father, and siblings from New York to New Carlisle, Indiana in 1836. Between 1855 and 1869, he served as a member of the House of Representatives and Speaker of the House. In 1868, he was the successful Indiana Republican nominee for Vice President. His son later served as Mayor of South Bend, Indiana.

Presidential experts typically rank Ulysses S. Grant in the lowest quartile of **United States** Presidents, primarily for his tolerance of corruption. In recent years, however, his reputation as President has improved somewhat among scholars impressed by his support for civil rights for African Americans. Unsuccessful in winning the nomination for a third term in 1880, bankrupted by bad investments, and terminally ill with throat cancer, Grant wrote his memoirs, which were enormously successful among veterans, the public, and the critics.

1869

During this year, the trans-continental railroad was completed. Construction for the first railroad line through Frankfort, Indiana, began, connecting Terre Haute and Logansport.

On March 4th, Ulysses S. Grant was inaugurated President of the United States.

Mary's son Burr's wife Clarissa delivered their fifth child, a son, Clinton Clay Norris during this year.

74-year-old Santa Anna, who was living in exile on Staten Island, New York, was trying to raise money for an army to return to and take over Mexico City.

1870

On January 23rd, Mary's son Dailey's nearly two year old son, Charles E. Norris, died. Dailey's wife Amanda, already pregnant with their next child, delivered Clinton M. Norris on August 15th.

During the Vatican Council's fourth solemn session, on July 18th, Papal Infallibility was made a dogma of the Church.

On July 19th, France declared war on Prussia, igniting the Franco-Prussian War. Some German allies of Prussia also joined the conflict. This war was provoked by Otto Von Bismarck, the Prussian Chancellor, who wanted to unite Germans by making them fight together against a common enemy. Bismarck did this by irritating the Emperor of France, Napoleon III, or Louis-Napoleon Bonapart. The war ended on May 10th of 1871, with Prussia claiming victory.

President Grant offered Indiana Senator Oliver Hazard Perry Throck Morton the English mission, which was declined.

In the 1870 census, Mary Gold Hobbs Norris is listed as living with her sons William, Silas, and daughters Phebe and Mary Eliza.

The same census lists Mary's brother in law Cornelius (Van) Norris with his family living across the road; her son Abe, his wife Sarah, and their family were listed across the road on their own farm.

The census also lists Bram's nephew, Thomas C. Norris' widow, Alice (Van Clift) with her children living about five farms down the road. About ten farms away lived the Lees, Thomas and Isabelle with their son James Gaster who would later marry Abe and Sarah's daughter Emma Luella.

During this year, the first grain mill in Clinton County was opened.

On October 14th, the first train of cars ran into Frankfort, Indiana on the newly constructed rail line. At that time, the Frankfort population was 1300.

By 1886, possibly due to the railroad connection, the population increased to nearly 5000.

Mary's daughter Mary Eliza married Edward Bruce Wilson of Michigantown on December 31st.

1871

During this year, the Great Fire destroyed much of Chicago.
　The brick Methodist Church at Frankfort was enlarged.
　On November 9th, Mary's daughter Phoebe Elvira married William E. Ewbank, brother of her sister Lavina's husband Edward.

1872

In the presidential election of this year, Ulysses S. Grant, running as a Republican, got 1993 votes in Clinton County, while Horace Greeley of the Liberal Party got 1847; Charles O'Connor, the Democrat, got 20. Grant won the Presidency.

Thomas A. Hendricks was elected Governor of Indiana.

1873

The years 1873 – 78 saw an economic depression, during which many banks failed.

In January, Thomas A. Hendricks, born 1819 in Muskingum, Ohio, became Governor of Indiana and served through January of 1877. Thomas was the nephew of William Hendricks, Indiana's second Governor who served from 1822 – 1825. In January 1863, Thomas had been elected to the United States Senate, which position he held for six years. Mr. Hendricks went before the people as a temperance proponent, opposed to prohibition, but willing to sign any constitutional legislation looking toward the amelioration of crime and the advancement of temperance. He was elected and kept his pledges to the letter.

Mary reminded her children that both Governors Hendricks were distant cousins on their paternal grandmother (Aaltje's) side.

In 1880, Indiana's representatives placed the name of Thomas A. Hendricks in nomination for the presidency at Cincinnati, where his nomination was strongly urged in the convention. In 1884, he was a delegate to the Chicago Democratic convention, and as chairman of the Indiana delegation presented in fitting terms and masterly manner the name of Joseph E. McDonald for the presidency. After the latter had positively refused to accept the second place on the ticket, Mr. Hendricks was unanimously chosen, and the successful ticket for 1884 became Grover Cleveland and Thomas A. Hendricks.

But Vice President Hendricks died of heart disease on November 25, 1885, at his home in Indianapolis.

Oliver Hazard Perry Throck Morton was re-elected to the United States Senate and continued as a leading member of that body while he lived. In the Senate he ranked among the ablest members, was Chairman of the

Committee on Privileges and Elections, was the acknowledged leader of the Republicans, and for several years exercised a determining influence over the course of the party. He labored zealously to secure the passage of the Fifteenth Amendment, was active in the impeachment proceedings against Andrew Johnson and was the trusted adviser of the Republicans of the South.

On June 7th, Abe and Sarah Norris had their third child, Oris Bruce.

1874

March of this year saw the Draypin Riot at Frankfort, Indiana. The people of the town were aroused in favor of the new temperance movement. Pressure against saloons was very heavy. Three new permits for saloons had just been approved by county commissioners. A stock of liquor arrived for one saloon, on the West side of the Frankfort town square. At the same time, a meeting of indignation was being held at the Presbyterian church. The temperance proponents prevented all but the first barrel of whiskey from being unloaded. A major disturbance was averted by the liquor being hauled back to the train depot.

However, Miss Mattie Shortle, a teacher in the Frankfort schools, found herself alone in the saloon with the barrel of whiskey and a hatchet. In some way the bung was knocked from the barrel, and the whiskey went after it. A judgment for damages was brought against several men on the temperance side (Miss Mattie being above suspicion or reproach), and the women of the town took up a collection to pay the judgment.

April 15: PROCLAMATION - *No person will be permitted to sell intoxicating liquors, by the glass, pint, quart, gallon or barrel, in the town of Frankfort. We are organized, armed and equipped. "Forewarned is to be forearmed."* - By the order of the vigilance committee, Frankfort, Indiana.

A few saloon keepers went out of business on account of the crusade, but most resumed business after the women had "worn themselves out."

On July 4th, the first trains began running from Frankfort to Kokomo, Indiana.

Reverend Father Francis Lordemann of Kokomo visited Frankfort. After this, he conducted Catholic services every three weeks for eight years.

Santa Anna took advantage of a general amnesty and returned to Mexico. Crippled and almost blind from cataracts, he was ignored during this year by the president of the Mexican government, Lerdo de Tejada, at the celebration of the anniversary of the Battle of Churubusco.

1875

A Catholic mission of St. Mary was established at Frankfort, ministered to by priests from Lafayette as well as Father Francis Lordemann of Kokomo. Forty-two families attended monthly services there and supported the mission. A quote from one of the Catholics: "If we be not active, the children will fall into the claws of the Methodists and Baptists." Mary grinned when she heard this.

The first high school in Frankfort opened during this year.

Mary's son Burr built a new house. It was large, with two storys, square with a cupola, but had no porches or basement.

1876

This year marked the Centennial of the signing of the United States Declaration of Independence. To celebrate, the first World's Fair was held at Philadelphia, Pennsylvania from May 10th to November 10th. The number of first day attendees was 186,272 people, 110,000 of whom entered with free passes. Officially named the International Exhibition of Arts, Manufactures and Products of the Soil and Mine, it was held in Fairmount Park along the Schuylkill River on fairgrounds designed by Herman J. Schwarzmann. Nearly 10 million visitors attended the exhibition and thirty-seven countries participated in it. Inventions displayed at the exhibition included the typewriter, sewing machine, and telephone.

At the national Republican convention in June, Governor Oliver Hazard Perry Throck Morton of Indiana received next to the highest number of ballots for the presidential nomination. He was defeated by the eventual winner of the most fiercely disputed presidential election in American history, Rutherford B. Hayes. Thomas A. Hendricks of Indiana ran for Vice President with Hays.

On June 20th, Santa Anna died in poverty at his home in Mexico City at age 82. He was buried in Panteón del Tepeyac Cemetery.

When news of the June 25th - 26th Battle of Little Big Horn in Montana became available in Frankfort, there was widespread shock. The event caused massive debate throughout the East. War hawks demanded an immediate increase in federal military spending and swift judgment for the non-compliant Sioux. A systematic plan to end all native resistance was approved, and the Indians of the West would never see another victory like the Little Big Horn.

On June 27th, Mary's children gathered to let her know that her daughter Altha, 52 years old, wife of David Maish, had died. Mother of ten children, Altha had been ailing for several months, and had suddenly taken a turn for the worse. The Norrises and Maishes grieved together.

On August 1st, Colorado entered the Union as the 38th state.

August 3rd was a Thursday, and Mary was hard at work cleaning the front parlor when she glanced out the front window. Across the road, she noticed a number of horse-drawn wagons and carriages pulled up to Van's house. She could think of no special occasion that should have drawn a crowd. She was about to ask Emma, her fourteen-year-old granddaughter who had walked across the road to help Mary clean house, to find out what was going on, when two of Van's adult daughters, Melissa and Sarah, arrived at the front door.

Rushing into the parlor, they immediately sank onto the settee, covered their faces with handkerchiefs, and burst into sobs.

"What's wrong? What's happened?" asked Mary.

Melissa lifted her head, blurted, "Daddy – he's dead!" and again dissolved into tears.

Mary sat across from them, stunned by the news. She had to be careful – no one really knew about her previous relationship with Van, and his current wife, Nancy, was no fool. She had never made an attempt to befriend Mary, and Mary wanted to maintain the current arms-length relationship without seeming uncaring.

After comforting the nieces, Mary sent them back to Van's house, retreated to her kitchen, and began baking pies, with Emma's help. Later that afternoon, they delivered the pies, expressed sympathy to the family, and returned home.

Once Emma had left, Mary collapsed. She had not known that Van's illness was a final one, and nor did she realize how much Van still meant to her. Being loved by Van had bolstered her feelings of self-worth, of being wanted and needed. Her relationship with Bram, while satisfying and long-term, had never reached the level of passion, of naked desire that Van inspired in her.

For days, Mary mourned deeply whenever alone, but maintained a solemn but calm demeanor throughout the week of funereal proceedings and interment at the I.O.O.F. Cemetery in Frankfort.

And it is certain that grief over Van's death initiated a decline in Mary's health that ultimately took her life.

In the November Presidential election in Clinton County, Indiana, Rutherford B. Hays got 2236 votes; the Democrat, Samuel J. Tilden got 2556; Peter Cooper, of the Greenback or National party got 149.

Christmas of this year was marked by Mary's son William Harrison's wedding to Sarah Jane Fudge on December 25th.

1877

On January 2nd, Dailey and Amanda's six year old son, Clinton M. Norris, died. Mary attended the funeral, and allowed some of the private grief caused by Van's death to surface, which seemed normal to everyone around her.

On January 9th, James D. Williams was inaugurated as Governor of Indiana. Born January 16, 1808, he was nicknamed "Blue Jeans Bill" and became the only farmer ever elected Governor of Indiana. He held public office in the Indiana General Assembly for many years and was well known for his frugality and advocacy of agricultural development. He served as Governor until his death from kidney failure on November 20, 1880.

On March 4th, Rutherford B. Hayes was inaugurated as President of the United States.

Born in Ohio in 1822, President Hayes was educated at Kenyon College and Harvard Law School. After five years of law practice in Lower Sandusky, he moved to Cincinnati, where he flourished as a young Whig lawyer.

Hays fought in the Civil War, was wounded in action, and rose to the rank of Brevet Major General. While he was still in the Army, Cincinnati Republicans nominated him for the House of Representatives. He accepted the nomination, but would not campaign, explaining, "an officer fit for duty who at this crisis would abandon his post to electioneer...ought to be scalped."

Safe liberalism, party loyalty, and a good war record made Hayes an acceptable Republican candidate in 1876. He opposed Governor Samuel J. Tilden of New York.

Hays brought to the executive mansion dignity, honesty, and moderate reform. To the delight of the Woman's Christian Temperance Union, his wife

Lucy Webb Hayes carried out his orders to banish wines and liquors from the White House.

One Thursday in late May, Mary's granddaughter, Emma showed up to help with house cleaning as she usually did. Mary had noticed that Emma seemed to be putting on a little weight, but had not thought much nor commented about it. On this day, Emma turned to Mary and begged, "Grandma, help me!"

"What's wrong, sweetheart?" asked Mary.

"I've not been well, and finally went to see a doctor in town. He said that I'm in a family way!"

"What! How can that be??" Mary asked.

Emma began to cry. "I've been keeping company with one of Thomas Lee's sons, James Gaster Lee. I thought I knew all about breeding, from watching the farm animals, but what he had me do with him wasn't like that. At any rate, I think – that is, I know I'm expecting his child!"

On June 12th, Emma and the twenty-one year old James Gaster Lee were united in a civil ceremony.

James Gaster Lee was of course reared on his father, Thomas Lee's farm, and learned the tasks required of a farmer early in life. While still young, he found work in Frankfort at the railroad station, and, taking interest in mechanics, eventually became a "stationary engineer," which meant that he did not travel aboard the trains, but rather worked at the Frankfort roundhouse as a machinist.

For Emma, this was the longest summer she would ever know. On August 14th, she gave birth to baby Fred Carlton Lee. Fred would grow up in Clinton County, marry Clara Belle Hopper in 1900 at West Middleton, Indiana (near Kokomo), and move to South Bend, Indiana in 1910, where he found work as a machinist at Sibley Machine Tool Company. He and Clara produced and reared five children who grew up in the South Bend area.

Former Indiana Governor Oliver Hazard Perry Throck Morton was a member of the electoral commission. After visiting Oregon in the spring of this year, as chairman of a committee to investigate the election of Senator Grover, of that state, he suffered another stroke of paralysis, which terminated in his death on November 1st.

On December 4th, Mary's son Dailey's wife Amanda delivered their seventh and last child, Daisy Temple Norris.

1878

Mary was not feeling well on Sunday, January 27th when her son Dailey's daughter, Mary Indiana Norris was scheduled to marry Abraham Alonzo Hendryx. Since the ceremony was held at the Methodist church, Mary only attended the reception at Dailey's home, leaving early. At home, she went directly to bed, and as it turned out, she never got up again.

Mary's children sent an urgent message to Father Lordemann, who came to give Mary Last Rites.

Early in the morning on February 1st, Mary awoke to find herself alone in her bedroom. She was at a loss to understand the sensation that gripped her chest. She fingered the cross and rosary that lay beside her on the pillow. After an initial panic, the grey silk veil of death descended, and she found eternal peace.

The family gathered, and Father Lordemann performed the usual ceremonies. Afterwards, Mary was interred at the I.O.O.F. cemetery in Frankfort, next to Bram.

On February 7th, Pope Pius IX (GIOVANNI MARIA MASTAI-FERRETTI) died at Rome. Born at Sinigaglia 13 May, 1792, he had served as Pope since 1846.